BOOK THREE

THE

SERPENT'S SHADOW

D0028073

BOOK THREE

THE

SERPENT'S
SHADOW

RICK RIORDAN

Disney • Hyperion
Los Angeles New York

The Serpent's Shadow copyright © 2012 by Rick Riordan

"The Son of Sobek" copyright © 2013 by Rick Riordan

All rights reserved. Published by Disney · Hyperion, an imprint of Disney Book Group. No part of this book may be reproduced or transmitted in any form or by any means, electronic or mechanical, including photocopying, recording, or by any information storage and retrieval system, without written permission from the publisher. For information address Disney · Hyperion, 125 West End Avenue, New York, N.Y. 10023.

First Disney · Hyperion US Hardcover Edition, May 2012
First Disney · Hyperion US Paperback Edition, May 2013

10 9

FAC-025438-18051

Printed in the United States of America

This book is set in Goudy Old Style

Hieroglyph art by Michelle Gengaro-Kokmen

Library of Congress Control Number for Hardcover Edition: 2012454979

ISBN 978-1-4231-4202-7

Visit www.DisneyBooks.com

To three great editors who shaped my writing career:
Kate Miciak, Jennifer Besser, and Stephanie Lurie—
the magicians who have brought my words to life

Contents

CONTENTS

WARNING

This is a transcript of an audio recording. Twice before, Carter and Sadie Kane have sent me such recordings, which I transcribed as The Red Pyramid *and* The Throne of Fire. *While I'm honored by the Kanes' continued trust, I must advise you that this third account is their most troubling yet. The tape arrived at my home in a charred box perforated with claw and teeth marks that my local zoologist could not identify. Had it not been for the protective hieroglyphs on the exterior, I doubt the box would have survived its journey. Read on, and you will understand why.*

1. We Crash and Burn a Party

S
A
D
I
E

SADIE KANE HERE.

If you're listening to this, congratulations! You survived Doomsday.

I'd like to apologize straightaway for any inconvenience the end of the world may have caused you. The earthquakes, rebellions, riots, tornadoes, floods, tsunamis, and of course the giant snake who swallowed the sun—I'm afraid most of that was our fault. Carter and I decided we should at least explain how it happened.

This will probably be our last recording. By the time you've heard our story, the reason for that will be obvious.

Our problems started in Dallas, when the fire-breathing sheep destroyed the King Tut exhibit.

That night the Texas magicians were hosting a party in the sculpture garden across the street from the Dallas Museum of

1

Art. The men wore tuxedos and cowboy boots. The women wore evening dresses and hairdos like explosions of candy floss.

(Carter says it's called cotton candy in America. I don't care. I was raised in London, so you'll just have to keep up and learn the proper way of saying things.)

A band played old-timey country music on the pavilion. Strings of fairy lights glimmered in the trees. Magicians did occasionally pop out of secret doors in the sculptures or summon sparks of fire to burn away pesky mosquitoes, but otherwise it seemed like quite a normal party.

The leader of the Fifty-first Nome, JD Grissom, was chatting with his guests and enjoying a plate of beef tacos when we pulled him away for an emergency meeting. I felt bad about that, but there wasn't much choice, considering the danger he was in.

"An attack?" He frowned. "The Tut exhibit has been open for a month now. If Apophis was going to strike, wouldn't he have done it already?"

JD was tall and stout, with a rugged, weathered face, feathery red hair, and hands as rough as bark. He looked about forty, but it's hard to tell with magicians. He might have been four hundred. He wore a black suit with a bolo tie and a large silver Lone Star belt buckle, like a Wild West marshal.

"Let's talk on the way," Carter said. He started leading us toward the opposite side of the garden.

I must admit my brother acted remarkably confident.

He was still a monumental dork, of course. His nappy brown hair had a chunk missing on the left side where his griffin had given him a "love bite," and you could tell from the nicks on his face that he hadn't quite mastered the art of shaving. But since his fifteenth birthday he'd shot up in height and put on muscle from hours of combat training. He looked poised and mature in his black linen clothes, especially with that *khopesh* sword at his side. I could almost imagine him as a leader of men without laughing hysterically.

[Why are you glaring at me, Carter? That was quite a generous description.]

Carter maneuvered around the buffet table, grabbing a handful of tortilla chips. "Apophis has a pattern," he told JD. "The other attacks all happened on the night of the new moon, when darkness is greatest. Believe me, he'll hit your museum tonight. And he'll hit it hard."

JD Grissom squeezed around a cluster of magicians drinking champagne. "These other attacks . . ." he said. "You mean Chicago and Mexico City?"

"And Toronto," Carter said. "And . . . a few others."

I knew he didn't want to say more. The attacks we'd witnessed over the summer had left us both with nightmares.

True, full-out Armageddon hadn't come yet. It had been six months since the Chaos snake Apophis had escaped from his Underworld prison, but he still hadn't launched a large-scale invasion of the mortal world as we'd expected. For some reason, the serpent was biding his time, settling for smaller attacks on nomes that seemed secure and happy.

Like this one, I thought.

As we passed the pavilion, the band finished their song. A

pretty blond woman with a fiddle waved her bow at JD.

"Come on, sweetie!" she called. "We need you on steel guitar!"

He forced a smile. "Soon, hon. I'll be back."

We walked on. JD turned to us. "My wife, Anne."

"Is she also a magician?" I asked.

He nodded, his expression turning dark. "These attacks. Why are you so sure Apophis will strike *here*?"

Carter's mouth was full of tortilla chips, so his response was, "Mhm-hmm."

"He's after a certain artifact," I translated. "He's already destroyed five copies of it. The last one in existence happens to be in your Tut exhibit."

"Which artifact?" JD asked.

I hesitated. Before coming to Dallas, we'd cast all sorts of shielding spells and loaded up on protective amulets to prevent magical eavesdropping, but I was still nervous about speaking our plans aloud.

"Better we show you." I stepped around a fountain, where two young magicians were tracing glowing *I Love You* messages on the paving stones with their wands. "We've brought our own crack team to help. They're waiting at the museum. If you'll let us examine the artifact, possibly take it with us for safekeeping—"

"Take it *with* you?" JD scowled. "The exhibit is heavily guarded. I have my best magicians surrounding it night and day. You think you can do better at Brooklyn House?"

We stopped at the edge of the garden. Across the street,

a two-story-tall King Tut banner hung from the side of the museum.

Carter took out his mobile phone. He showed JD Grissom an image on the screen—a burned-out mansion that had once been the headquarters for the One Hundredth Nome in Toronto.

"I'm sure your guards are good," Carter said. "But we'd rather not make your nome a target for Apophis. In the other attacks like this one . . . the serpent's minions didn't leave any survivors."

JD stared at the phone's screen, then glanced back at his wife, Anne, who was fiddling her way through a two-step.

"Fine," JD said. "I hope your team is top-notch."

"They're amazing," I promised. "Come on, we'll introduce you."

Our crack squad of magicians was busy raiding the gift shop.

Felix had summoned three penguins, which were waddling around wearing paper King Tut masks. Our baboon friend, Khufu, sat atop a bookshelf reading *The History of the Pharaohs*, which would've been quite impressive except he was holding the book upside down. Walt—oh, dear Walt, *why?*— had opened the jewelry cabinet and was examining charm bracelets and necklaces as if they might be magical. Alyssa levitated clay pots with her earth elemental magic, juggling twenty or thirty at a time in a figure eight.

Carter cleared his throat.

Walt froze, his hands full of gold jewelry. Khufu scrambled

down the bookshelf, knocking off most of the books. Alyssa's pottery crashed to the floor. Felix tried to shoo his penguins behind the till. (He does have rather strong feelings about the usefulness of penguins. I'm afraid I can't explain it.)

JD Grissom drummed his fingers against his Lone Star belt buckle. "This is your amazing team?"

"Yes!" I tried for a winning smile. "Sorry about the mess. I'll just, um . . ."

I pulled my wand from my belt and spoke a word of power: *"Hi-nehm!"*

I'd got better at such spells. Most of the time, I could now channel power from my patron goddess Isis without passing out. And I hadn't exploded once.

The hieroglyph for *Join together* glowed briefly in the air:

Broken bits of pottery flew back together and mended themselves. Books returned to the shelf. The King Tut masks flew off the penguins, revealing them to be—gasp—penguins.

Our friends looked rather embarrassed.

"Sorry," Walt mumbled, putting the jewelry back in the case. "We got bored."

I couldn't stay mad at Walt. He was tall and athletic, built like a basketball player, in workout pants and sleeveless tee that showed off his sculpted arms. His skin was the color of hot cocoa, his face every bit as regal and handsome as the statues of his pharaoh ancestors.

Did I fancy him? Well, it's complicated. More on that later.

JD Grissom looked over our team.

"Nice to meet you all." He managed to contain his enthusiasm. "Come with me."

The museum's main foyer was a vast white room with empty café tables, a stage, and a ceiling high enough for a pet giraffe. On one side, stairs led up to a balcony with a row of offices. On the other side, glass walls looked out at the nighttime skyline of Dallas.

JD pointed up at the balcony, where two men in black linen robes were patrolling. "You see? Guards are everywhere."

The men had their staffs and wands ready. They glanced down at us, and I noticed their eyes were glowing. Hieroglyphs were painted on their cheekbones like war paint.

Alyssa whispered to me: "What's up with their eyes?"

"Surveillance magic," I guessed. "The symbols allow the guards to see into the Duat."

Alyssa bit her lip. Since her patron was the earth god Geb, she liked solid things, such as stone and clay. She didn't like heights or deep water. She definitely didn't like the idea of the Duat—the magical realm that coexisted with ours.

Once, when I'd described the Duat as an ocean under our feet with layers and layers of magical dimensions going down forever, I thought Alyssa was going to get seasick.

Ten-year-old Felix, on the other hand, had no such qualms. "Cool!" he said. "I want glowing eyes."

He traced his finger across his cheeks, leaving shiny purple blobs in the shape of Antarctica.

Alyssa laughed. "Can you see into the Duat now?"

"No," he admitted. "But I can see my penguins much better."

"We should hurry," Carter reminded us. "Apophis usually strikes when the moon is at the top of its transit. Which is—"

"*Agh!*" Khufu held up all ten fingers. Leave it to a baboon to have perfect astronomical sense.

"In ten minutes," I said. "Just brilliant."

We approached the entrance of the King Tut exhibit, which was rather hard to miss because of the giant golden sign that read KING TUT EXHIBIT. Two magicians stood guard with full-grown leopards on leashes.

Carter looked at JD in astonishment. "How did you get complete access to the museum?"

The Texan shrugged. "My wife, Anne, is president of the board. Now, which artifact did you want to see?"

"I studied your exhibit maps," Carter said. "Come on. I'll show you."

The leopards seemed quite interested in Felix's penguins, but the guards held them back and let us pass.

Inside, the exhibit was extensive, but I doubt you care about the details. A labyrinth of rooms with sarcophagi, statues, furniture, bits of gold jewelry—blah, blah, blah. I would have passed it all by. I've seen enough Egyptian collections to last several lifetimes, thank you very much.

Besides, everywhere I looked, I saw reminders of bad experiences.

We passed cases of *shabti* figurines, no doubt enchanted to come to life when called upon. I'd killed my share of those. We passed statues of glowering monsters and gods whom I'd fought in person—the vulture Nekhbet, who'd once possessed my Gran (long story); the crocodile Sobek, who'd tried to kill my cat (longer story); and the lion goddess Sekhmet, whom we'd once vanquished with hot sauce (don't even ask).

Most upsetting of all: a small alabaster statue of our friend Bes, the dwarf god. The carving was eons old, but I recognized that pug nose, the bushy sideburns, the potbelly, and the endearingly ugly face that looked as if it had been hit repeatedly with a frying pan. We'd only known Bes for a few days, but he'd literally sacrificed his soul to help us. Now, each time I saw him I was reminded of a debt I could never repay.

I must have lingered at his statue longer than I realized. The rest of the group had passed me and were turning into the next room, about twenty meters ahead, when a voice next to me said, "Psst!"

I looked around. I thought the statue of Bes might have spoken. Then the voice called again: "Hey, doll. Listen up. Not much time."

In the middle of the wall, eye-level with me, a man's face bulged from the white, textured paint as if trying to break through. He had a beak of a nose, cruel thin lips, and a high forehead. Though he was the same color as the wall, he seemed very much alive. His blank eyes managed to convey a look of impatience.

"You won't save the scroll, doll," he warned. "Even if you did, you'd never understand it. You need my help."

I'd experienced many strange things since I'd begun practicing magic, so I wasn't particularly startled. Still, I knew better than to trust any old white-spackled apparition who spoke to me, especially one who called me *doll*. He reminded me of a character from those silly Mafia movies the boys at Brooklyn House liked to watch in their spare time—someone's Uncle Vinnie, perhaps.

"Who are you?" I demanded.

The man snorted. "Like you don't know. Like there's *anybody* who doesn't know. You've got two days until they put me down. You want to defeat Apophis, you'd better pull some strings and get me out of here."

"I have no idea what you're talking about," I said.

The man didn't sound like Set the god of evil, or the serpent Apophis, or any of the other villains I'd dealt with before, but one could never be sure. There was this thing called *magic*, after all.

The man jutted out his chin. "Okay, I get it. You want a show of faith. You'll never save the scroll, but go for the golden box. That'll give you a clue about what you need, if you're smart enough to understand it. Day after tomorrow at sunset, doll. Then my offer expires, 'cause that's when *I* get permanently—"

He choked. His eyes widened. He strained as if a noose were tightening around his neck. He slowly melted back into the wall.

"Sadie?" Walt called from the end of the corridor. "You okay?"

I looked over. "Did you see that?"

"See what?" he asked.

Of course not, I thought. What fun would it be if other people saw my vision of Uncle Vinnie? Then I couldn't wonder if I were going stark raving mad.

"Nothing," I said, and I ran to catch up.

The entrance to the next room was flanked by two giant obsidian sphinxes with the bodies of lions and the heads of rams. Carter says that particular type of sphinx is called a *criosphinx*. [Thanks, Carter. We were all dying to know that bit of useless information.]

"*Agh!*" Khufu warned, holding up five fingers.

"Five minutes left," Carter translated.

"Give me a moment," JD said. "This room has the heaviest protective spells. I'll need to modify them to let you through."

"Uh," I said nervously, "but the spells will still keep out enemies, like giant Chaos snakes, I hope?"

JD gave me an exasperated look, which I tend to get a lot.

"I *do* know a thing or two about protective magic," he promised. "Trust me." He raised his wand and began to chant.

Carter pulled me aside. "You okay?"

I must have looked shaken from my encounter with Uncle Vinnie. "I'm fine," I said. "Saw something back there. Probably just one of Apophis's tricks, but . . ."

My eyes drifted to the other end of the corridor. Walt was staring at a golden throne in a glass case. He leaned forward with one hand on the glass as if he might be sick.

"Hold that thought," I told Carter.

I moved to Walt's side. Light from the exhibit bathed his face, turning his features reddish brown like the hills of Egypt.

"What's wrong?" I asked.

"Tutankhamen died in that chair," he said.

I read the display card. It didn't say anything about Tut dying in the chair, but Walt sounded very sure. Perhaps he could sense the family curse. King Tut was Walt's great-times-a-billion granduncle, and the same genetic poison that killed Tut at nineteen was now coursing through Walt's bloodstream, getting stronger the more he practiced magic. Yet Walt refused to slow down. Looking at the throne of his ancestor, he must have felt as if he were reading his own obituary.

"We'll find a cure," I promised. "As soon as we deal with Apophis . . ."

He looked at me, and my voice faltered. We both knew our chances of defeating Apophis were slim. Even if we succeeded, there was no guarantee Walt would live long enough to enjoy the victory. Today was one of Walt's *good* days, and still I could see the pain in his eyes.

"Guys," Carter called. "We're ready."

The room beyond the criosphinxes was a "greatest hits" collection from the Egyptian afterlife. A life-sized wooden Anubis stared down from his pedestal. Atop a replica of the scales of justice sat a golden baboon, which Khufu immediately started flirting with. There were masks of pharaohs, maps of the Underworld, and loads of canopic jars that had once been filled with mummy organs.

Carter passed all that by. He gathered us around a long papyrus scroll in a glass case on the back wall.

"This is what you're after?" JD frowned. "The Book of Overcoming Apophis? You do realize that even the best spells against Apophis aren't very effective."

Carter reached in his pocket and produced a bit of burned papyrus. "This is all we could salvage from Toronto. It was another copy of the same scroll."

JD took the papyrus scrap. It was no bigger than a post-card and too charred to let us make out more than a few hieroglyphs.

"'Overcoming Apophis . . .'" he read. "But this is one of the most common magic scrolls. Hundreds of copies have survived from ancient times."

"No." I fought the urge to look over my shoulder, in case any giant serpents were listening in. "Apophis is after only one particular version, written by this chap."

I tapped the information plaque next to the display. "'Attributed to Prince Khaemwaset,'" I read, "'better known as Setne.'"

JD scowled. "That's an evil name . . . one of most villainous magicians who ever lived."

"So we've heard," I said, "and Apophis is destroying only Setne's version of the scroll. As far as we can tell, only six copies existed. Apophis has already burned five. This is the last one."

JD studied the burned papyrus scrap doubtfully. "If Apophis has truly risen from the Duat with all his power, why would he care about a few scrolls? No spell could possibly stop him. Why hasn't he already destroyed the world?"

We'd been asking ourselves the same question for months.

"Apophis is afraid of this scroll," I said, hoping I was right. "Something in it must hold the secret to defeating him. He wants to make sure all copies are destroyed before he invades the world."

"Sadie, we need to hurry," Carter said. "The attack could come any minute."

I stepped closer to the scroll. It was roughly two meters long and a half-meter tall, with dense lines of hieroglyphs and colorful illustrations. I'd seen loads of scrolls like this describing ways to defeat Chaos, with chants designed to keep the serpent Apophis from devouring the sun god Ra on his nightly journey through the Duat. Ancient Egyptians had been quite obsessed with this subject. Cheery bunch, those Egyptians.

I could read the hieroglyphs—one of my many amazing talents—but the scroll was a lot to take in. At first glance, nothing struck me as particularly helpful. There were the usual descriptions of the River of Night, down which Ra's sun boat traveled. Been there, thanks. There were tips on how to handle the various demons of the Duat. Met them. Killed them. Got the T-shirt.

"Sadie?" Carter asked. "Anything?"

"Don't know yet," I grumbled. "Give me a moment."

I found it annoying that my bookish brother was the combat magician, while *I* was expected to be the great reader of magic. I barely had the patience for magazines, much less musty scrolls.

You'd never understand it, the face in the wall had warned. *You need my help.*

"We'll have to take it with us," I decided. "I'm sure I can figure it out with a little more—"

The building shook. Khufu shrieked and leaped into the arms of the golden baboon. Felix's penguins waddled around frantically.

"That sounded like—" JD Grissom blanched. "An explosion outside. The party!"

"It's a diversion," Carter warned. "Apophis is trying to draw our defenses away from the scroll."

"They're attacking my friends," JD said in a strangled voice. "My wife."

"Go!" I said. I glared at my brother. "We can handle the scroll. JD's *wife* is in danger!"

JD clasped my hands. "Take the scroll. Good luck."

He ran from the room.

I turned back to the display. "Walt, can you open the case? We need to get this out of here as fast—"

Evil laughter filled the room. A dry, heavy voice, deep as a nuclear blast, echoed all around us: *"I don't think so, Sadie Kane."*

My skin felt as if it were turning to brittle papyrus. I remembered that voice. I remembered how it felt being so close to Chaos, as if my blood were turning to fire, and the strands of my DNA were unraveling.

"*I think I'll destroy you with the guardians of Ma'at,*" Apophis said. "*Yes, that will be amusing.*"

At the entrance to the room, the two obsidian criosphinxes turned. They blocked the exit, standing shoulder to shoulder. Flames curled from their nostrils.

In the voice of Apophis, they spoke in unison: "No one leaves this place alive. Good-bye, Sadie Kane."

2. I Have a Word with Chaos

WOULD YOU BE SURPRISED TO LEARN that things went badly from there?

I didn't think so.

Our first casualties were Felix's penguins. The criosphinxes blew fire at the unfortunate birds, and they melted into puddles of water.

"No!" Felix cried.

The room rumbled, much stronger this time.

Khufu screamed and jumped on Carter's head, knocking him to the floor. Under different circumstances that would've been funny, but I realized Khufu had just saved my brother's life.

Where Carter had been standing, the floor dissolved, marble tiles crumbling as if broken apart by an invisible jackhammer. The area of disruption snaked across the room, destroying everything in its path, sucking artifacts into the

17

ground and chewing them to bits. Yes . . . *snaked* was the right word. The destruction slithered exactly like a serpent, heading straight for the back wall and the Book of Overcoming Apophis.

"Scroll!" I shouted.

No one seemed to hear. Carter was still on the floor, trying to pry Khufu off his head. Felix knelt in shock at the puddles of his penguins, while Walt and Alyssa tried to pull him away from the fiery criosphinxes.

I slipped my wand from my belt and shouted the first word of power that came to mind: *"Drowah!"*

Golden hieroglyphs—the command for *Boundary*—blazed in the air. A wall of light flashed between the display case and the advancing line of destruction:

I'd often used this spell to separate quarreling initiates or to protect the snack cupboard from late-night nom-nom raids, but I'd never tried it for something so important.

As soon as the invisible jackhammer reached my shield, the spell began to fall apart. The disturbance spread up the wall of light, shaking it to pieces. I tried to concentrate, but a much more powerful force—Chaos itself—was working against me, invading my mind and scattering my magic.

In a panic, I realized I couldn't let go. I was locked in a battle I couldn't win. Apophis was shredding my thoughts as easily as he'd shredded the floor.

Walt knocked the wand out of my hands.

Darkness washed over me. I slumped into Walt's arms. When my vision cleared, my hands were burned and steaming. I was too shocked to feel the pain. The Book of Overcoming Apophis was gone. Nothing remained except a pile of rubble and a massive hole in the wall, as if a tank had smashed through.

Despair threatened to close up my throat, but my friends gathered around me. Walt held me steady. Carter drew his sword. Khufu showed his fangs and barked at the criosphinxes. Alyssa wrapped her arms around Felix, who was sobbing into her sleeve. He had quickly lost his courage when his penguins were taken away.

"So that's it?" I shouted at the criosphinxes. "Burn up the scroll and run away as usual? Are you so afraid to show yourself in person?"

More laughter rolled through the room. The criosphinxes stood unmoving in the doorway, but figurines and jewelry rattled in the display cases. With a painful creaking sound, the golden baboon statue that Khufu had been chatting up suddenly turned its head.

"*But I am everywhere.*" The serpent spoke through the statue's mouth. "I can destroy anything you value . . . and anyone you value."

Khufu wailed in outrage. He launched himself at the baboon and knocked it over. It melted into a steaming pool of gold.

A different statue came to life—a gilded wooden pharaoh

with a hunting spear. Its eyes turned the color of blood. Its carved mouth twisted into a smile. "Your magic is weak, Sadie Kane. Human civilization has grown as old and rotten. I will swallow the sun god and plunge your world into darkness. The Sea of Chaos will consume you all."

As if the energy were too much for it to contain, the pharaoh statue burst. Its pedestal disintegrated, and another line of evil jackhammer magic snaked across the room, churning up the floor tiles. It headed for a display against the east wall—a small golden cabinet.

Save it, said a voice inside me—possibly my subconscious, or possibly the voice of Isis, my patron goddess. We'd shared thoughts so many times, it was hard to be sure.

I remembered what the face in the wall had told me . . . *Go for the golden box. That'll give a clue about what you need.*

"The box!" I yelped. "Stop him!"

My friends stared at me. From somewhere outside, another explosion shook the building. Chunks of plaster rained from the ceiling.

"Are these children the best you could send against me?" Apophis spoke from an ivory *shabti* in the nearest case—a miniature sailor on a toy boat. "Walt Stone . . . you are the luckiest. Even if you survive tonight, your sickness will kill you before my great victory. You won't have to watch your world destroyed."

Walt staggered. Suddenly I was supporting him. My burned hands hurt so badly, I had to fight down a surge of nausea.

The line of destruction trundled across the floor, still

heading for the golden cabinet. Alyssa thrust out her staff and barked a command.

For a moment, the floor stabilized, smoothing into a solid sheet of gray stone. Then new cracks appeared, and the force of Chaos blasted its way through.

"Brave Alyssa," the serpent said, "the earth you love will dissolve into Chaos. You will have no place to stand!"

Alyssa's staff burst into flames. She screamed and threw it aside.

"Stop it!" Felix yelled. He smashed the glass case with his staff and demolished the miniature sailor along with a dozen other *shabti*.

Apophis's voice simply moved to a jade amulet of Isis on a nearby manikin. "Ah, little Felix, I find you amusing. Perhaps I'll keep you as a pet, like those ridiculous birds you love. I wonder how long you'll last before your sanity crumbles."

Felix threw his wand and knocked over the manikin.

The crumbling trail of Chaos was now halfway to the golden cabinet.

"He's after that box!" I managed to say. "Save the box!"

Granted, it wasn't the most inspiring call to battle, but Carter seemed to understand. He jumped in front of the advancing Chaos, stabbing his sword into the floor. His blade cut through the marble tile like ice cream. A blue line of magic extended to either side—Carter's own version of a force field. The line of disruption slammed against the barrier and stalled.

"*Poor Carter Kane.*" The serpent's voice was all around us now—jumping from artifact to artifact, each one bursting from the power of Chaos. *"Your leadership is doomed. Everything you tried to build will crumble. You will lose the ones you love the most."*

Carter's blue defensive line began to flicker. If I didn't help him quickly . . .

"Apophis!" I yelled. "Why wait to destroy me? Do it now, you overgrown rat snake!"

A hiss echoed through the room. Perhaps I should mention that one of my many talents is making people angry. Apparently it worked on snakes, too.

The floor settled. Carter released his shielding spell and almost collapsed. Khufu, bless his baboon wits, leaped to the golden cabinet, picked it up, and bounded off with it.

When Apophis spoke again, his voice hardened with anger. *"Very well, Sadie Kane. It's time to die."*

The two ram-headed sphinxes stirred, their mouths glowing with flames. Then they lunged straight at me.

Fortunately one of them slipped in a puddle of penguin water and skidded off to the left. The other would've ripped my throat out had it not been tackled by a timely camel.

Yes, an actual full-sized camel. If you find that confusing, just think how the criosphinx must have felt.

Where did the camel come from, you ask? I may have mentioned Walt's collection of amulets. Two of them summoned disgusting camels. I'd met them before, so I was less than excited when a ton of dromedary flesh flew across my line of sight, plowed into the sphinx, and collapsed on top of it. The sphinx growled in outrage as it tried to free itself. The camel grunted and farted.

"Hindenburg," I said. Only one camel could possibly fart that badly. "Walt, why in the world—?"

"Sorry!" he yelled. "Wrong amulet!"

The technique worked, at any rate. The camel wasn't much of a fighter, but it was quite heavy and clumsy. The criosphinx snarled and clawed at the floor, trying unsuccessfully to push the camel off; but Hindenburg just splayed his legs, made alarmed honking sounds, and let loose gas.

I moved to Walt's side and tried to get my bearings.

The room was quite literally in chaos. Tendrils of red lightning arced between exhibits. The floor was crumbling. The walls cracked. Artifacts were coming to life and attacking my friends.

Carter fended off the other criosphinx, stabbing it with his *khopesh*, but the monster parried his strikes with its horns and breathed fire.

Felix was surrounded by a tornado of canopic jars that pummeled him from every direction as he swatted them with his staff. An army of tiny *shabti* had surrounded Alyssa, who was chanting desperately, using her earth magic to keep the room in one piece. The statue of Anubis chased Khufu around the room, smashing things with its fists as our brave baboon cradled the golden cabinet.

All around us, the power of Chaos grew. I felt it in my ears like a coming storm. The presence of Apophis was shaking apart the entire museum.

How could I help all my friends at once, protect that gold cabinet, *and* keep the museum from collapsing on top of us?

"Sadie," Walt prompted. "What's the plan?"

The first criosphinx finally pushed Hindenburg off its back. It turned and blew fire at the camel, which let loose one final fart and shrank back into a harmless gold amulet. Then the criosphinx turned toward me. It did not look pleased.

"Walt," I said, "guard me."

"Sure." He eyed the criosphinx uncertainly. "While you do what?"

Good question, I thought.

"We have to protect that cabinet," I said. "It's some sort of clue. We have to restore Ma'at, or this building will implode and we'll all die."

"How do we restore Ma'at?"

Instead of answering, I concentrated. I lowered my vision into the Duat.

It's hard to describe what it's like to experience the world on many levels at once—it's a bit like looking through 3D glasses and seeing hazy colorful auras around things, except the auras don't always match the objects, and the images are constantly shifting. Magicians have to be careful when they look into the Duat. Best-case scenario, you'll get mildly nauseous. Worst-case scenario, your brain will explode.

In the Duat, the room was filled with the writhing coils of a giant red snake—the magic of Apophis slowly expanding and encircling my friends. I almost lost my concentration along with my dinner.

Isis, I called. *A little help?*

The goddess's strength surged through me. I stretched out my senses and saw my brother battling the criosphinx. Standing in Carter's place was the warrior god Horus, his sword blazing with light.

Swirling around Felix, the canopic jars were the hearts of evil spirits—shadowy figures that clawed and snapped at our young friend, though Felix had a surprisingly powerful aura in the Duat. His vivid purple glow seemed to keep the spirits at bay.

Alyssa was surrounded by a dust storm in the shape of a giant man. As she chanted, Geb the earth god lifted his arms and held up the ceiling. The *shabti* army surrounding her blazed like a wildfire.

Khufu looked no different in the Duat, but as he leaped around the room evading the Anubis statue, the golden cabinet he was carrying flapped open. Inside was pure darkness—as if it were full of octopus ink.

I wasn't sure what that meant, but then I looked at Walt and gasped.

In the Duat, he was shrouded in flickering gray linen—mummy cloth. His flesh was transparent. His bones were luminous, as if he were a living X-ray.

His curse, I thought. *He's marked for death.*

Even worse: the criosphinx facing him was the center of the Chaos storm. Tendrils of red lightning arced from its body. Its ram face changed into the head of Apophis, with yellow serpentine eyes and dripping fangs.

It lunged at Walt, but before it could strike, Walt threw an amulet. Golden chains exploded in the monster's face, wrapping around its snout. The criosphinx stumbled and thrashed like a dog in a muzzle.

"Sadie, it's all right." Walt's voice sounded deeper and more confident, as if he were older in the Duat. "Speak your spell. Hurry."

The criosphinx flexed its jaws. The gold chains groaned. The other criosphinx had backed Carter against a wall. Felix was on his knees, his purple aura failing in a swirl of dark spirits. Alyssa was losing her battle against the crumbling room as chunks of the ceiling fell around her. The Anubis statue grabbed Khufu's tail and held him upside down while the baboon howled and wrapped his arms around the gold cabinet.

Now or never: I had to restore order.

I channeled the power of Isis, drawing so deeply on my own magic reserves, I could feel my soul start to burn. I forced myself to focus, and I spoke the most powerful of all divine words: "Ma'at."

The hieroglyph burned in front of me—small and bright like a miniature sun:

"Good!" Walt said. "Keep at it!" Somehow he'd managed to pull in the chains and grab the sphinx's snout. While the creature bore down on him with all its force, Walt's strange gray aura was spreading across the monster's body like an infection.

The criosphinx hissed and writhed. I caught a whiff of decay like the air from a tomb—so strong that I almost lost my concentration.

"Sadie," Walt urged, "maintain the spell!"

I focused on the hieroglyph. I channeled all my energy into that symbol for order and creation. The word shone brighter. The coils of the serpent burned away like fog in sunlight. The two criosphinxes crumbled to dust. The canopic jars fell and shattered. The Anubis statue dropped Khufu on his head. The army of *shabti* froze around Alyssa, and her earth magic spread through the room, sealing cracks and shoring up walls.

I felt Apophis retreating deeper into the Duat, hissing in anger.

Then I promptly collapsed.

"I told you she could do it," said a kindly voice.

My mother's voice . . . but of course that was impossible. She was dead, which meant I spoke with her only occasionally, and only in the Underworld.

My vision returned, hazy and dim. Two women hovered over me. One was my mum—her blond hair clipped back, her deep blue eyes sparkling with pride. She was transparent, as ghosts tend to be; but her voice was warm and very much alive. "It isn't the end yet, Sadie. You must carry on."

Next to her stood Isis in her white silky gown, her wings of rainbow light flickering behind her. Her hair was glossy black, woven with strands of diamonds. Her face was as beautiful as my mum's, but more queenly, less warm.

Don't misunderstand. I knew from sharing Isis's thoughts that she cared for me in her own way, but gods are not human. They have trouble thinking of us as more than useful tools or cute pets. To gods, a human life span doesn't seem much longer than that of the average gerbil.

"I would not have believed it," Isis said. "The last magician to summon Ma'at was Hatshepsut herself, and even she could only do it while wearing a fake beard."

I had no idea what that meant. I decided I didn't want to know.

I tried to move but couldn't. I felt as if I were floating at the bottom of a bathtub, suspended in warm water, the two women's faces rippling at me from just above the surface.

"Sadie, listen carefully," my mother said. "Don't blame yourself for the deaths. When you make your plan, your father will object. You must convince him. Tell him it's the only way to save the souls of the dead. Tell him . . ." Her expression turned grim. "Tell him it's the only way he'll see *me* again. You *must* succeed, my sweet."

I wanted to ask what she meant, but I couldn't seem to speak.

Isis touched my forehead. Her fingers were as cold as snow. "We must not tax her any further. Farewell for now, Sadie. The time rapidly approaches when we must join together again. You are strong. Even stronger than your mother. Together we will rule the world."

"You mean, *Together we will defeat Apophis*," my mother corrected.

"Of course," Isis said. "That's what I meant."

Their faces blurred together. They spoke in a single voice: "I love you."

A blizzard swept across my eyes. My surroundings changed, and I was standing in a dark graveyard with Anubis. Not the musty old jackal-headed god as he appeared in Egyptian tomb art, but Anubis as I usually saw him—a teenaged boy with warm brown eyes, tousled black hair, and a face that was ridiculously, annoyingly gorgeous. I mean, *please*—being a god, he had an unfair advantage. He could look like anything he wanted. Why did he always have to appear in *this* form that twisted my insides to pretzels?

"Wonderful," I managed to say. "If you're here, I must be dead."

Anubis smiled. "Not dead, though you came close. That was a risky move."

A burning sensation started in my face and worked its way down my neck. I wasn't sure if it was embarrassment, anger, or delight at seeing him.

"Where have you been?" I demanded. "Six months, not a word."

His smile melted. "They wouldn't let me see you."

"Who wouldn't let you?"

"There are rules," he said. "Even now they're watching; but you're close enough to death that I can manage a few moments. I need to tell you: you have the right idea. Look at what *isn't* there. It's the only way you might survive."

"Right," I grumbled. "Thanks for not speaking in riddles."

The warm sensation reached my heart. It began to beat, and suddenly I realized I'd been *without* a heartbeat since I'd passed out. That probably wasn't good.

"Sadie, there's something else." Anubis's voice became watery. His image began to fade. "I need to tell you—"

"Tell me in person," I said. "None of this 'death vision' nonsense."

"I can't. They won't let me."

"You still sound like a little boy. You're a god, aren't you? You can bloody well do what you like."

Anger smoldered in his eyes. Then, to my surprise, he laughed. "I'd forgotten how irritating you are. I'll try to visit . . . *briefly*. We have something to discuss." He reached out and brushed the side of my face. "You're waking now. Good-bye, Sadie."

"Don't leave." I grasped his hand and held it against my cheek.

The warmth spread throughout my body. Anubis faded away.

My eyes flew open. "Don't leave!"

My burned hands were bandaged, and I was gripping a hairy baboon paw. Khufu looked down at me, rather confused. "*Agh?*"

Oh, fab. I was flirting with a monkey.

I sat up groggily. Carter and our friends gathered around me. The room hadn't collapsed, but the entire King Tut exhibit was in ruins. I had a feeling we would not be invited to join the Friends of the Dallas Museum anytime soon.

"Wh-what happened?" I stammered. "How long—?"

"You were dead for two minutes," Carter said, his voice shaky. "I mean, *no heartbeat*, Sadie. I thought . . . I was afraid . . ."

He choked up. Poor boy. He really would have been lost without me.

[Ouch, Carter! Don't pinch.]

"You summoned Ma'at," Alyssa said in amazement. "That's like . . . impossible."

I suppose it was rather impressive. Using divine words to create an object like an animal or a chair or a sword—that's hard enough. Summoning an element like fire or water is even trickier. But summoning a concept, like Order—that's just not done. At the moment, however, I was in too much pain to appreciate my own amazingness. I felt as if I'd just summoned an anvil and dropped it on my head.

"Lucky try," I said. "What about the golden cabinet?"

"*Agh!*" Khufu gestured proudly to the gilded box, which sat nearby, safe and sound.

"Good baboon," I said. "Extra Cheerios for you tonight."

Walt frowned. "But the Book of Overcoming Apophis was destroyed. How will a cabinet help us? You said it was some kind of clue . . . ?"

I found it hard to look at Walt without feeling guilty. My heart had been torn between him and Anubis for months now, and it just wasn't fair of Anubis to pop into my dreams, looking all hot and immortal, when poor Walt was risking his life to protect me and getting weaker by the day. I remembered how he had looked in the Duat, in his ghostly gray mummy linen. . . .

No. I couldn't think about that. I forced myself to concentrate on the golden cabinet.

Look at what isn't there, Anubis had said. Bloody gods and their bloody riddles.

The face in the wall—Uncle Vinnie—had told me the box would give us a hint about how to defeat Apophis, *if* I was smart enough to understand it.

"I'm not sure what it means yet," I admitted. "If the Texans let us take it back to Brooklyn House . . ."

A horrible realization settled over me. There were no more sounds of explosions outside. Just eerie silence.

"The Texans!" I yelped. "What's happened to them?"

Felix and Alyssa bolted for the exit. Carter and Walt helped me to my feet, and we ran after them.

The guards had all disappeared from their stations. We reached the museum foyer, and I saw columns of white smoke outside the glass walls, rising from the sculpture garden.

"No," I murmured. "No, no."

We tore across the street. The well-kept lawn was now a crater as big as an Olympic pool. The bottom was littered with melted metal sculptures and chunks of stone. Tunnels that had once led into the Fifty-first Nome's headquarters had collapsed like a giant anthill some bully had stepped on. Around the rim of the crater were bits of smoking evening wear, smashed plates of tacos, broken champagne glasses, and the shattered staffs of magicians.

Don't blame yourself for the deaths, my mother had said.

I moved in a daze to the remains of the patio. Half the

concrete slab had cracked and slid into the crater. A charred fiddle lay in the mud next to a gleaming bit of silver.

Carter stood next to me. "We—we should search," he said. "There might be survivors."

I swallowed back a sob. I wasn't sure how, but I sensed the truth with absolute certainty. "There aren't any."

The Texas magicians had welcomed us and supported us. JD Grissom had shaken my hand and wished me luck before running off to save his wife. But we'd seen the work of Apophis in other nomes. Carter had warned JD: *The serpent's minions don't leave any survivors.*

I knelt down and picked up the gleaming piece of silver—a half-melted Lone Star belt buckle.

"They're dead," I said. "All of them."

3. We Win a Box
Full of Nothing

ON THAT HAPPY NOTE, Sadie hands me the microphone. [Thanks a lot, sis.]

I wish I could tell you that Sadie was wrong about the Fifty-first Nome. I'd love to say we found all the Texas magicians safe and sound. We didn't. We found nothing except the remnants of a battle: burned ivory wands, a few shattered *shabti*, scraps of smoldering linen and papyrus. Just like in the attacks on Toronto, Chicago, and Mexico City, the magicians had simply vanished. They'd been vaporized, devoured, or destroyed in some equally horrible way.

At the edge of the crater, one hieroglyph burned in the grass: *Isfet*, the symbol for Chaos. I had a feeling Apophis had left it there as a calling card.

We were all in shock, but we didn't have time to mourn our comrades. The mortal authorities would be arriving soon to check out the scene. We had to repair the damage as best we could and remove all traces of magic.

There wasn't much we could do about the crater. The locals would just have to assume there'd been a gas explosion. (We tended to cause a lot of those.)

We tried to fix the museum and restore the King Tut collection, but it wasn't as easy as cleaning up the gift shop. Magic can only go so far. So if you go to a King Tut exhibit someday and notice cracks or burn marks on the artifacts, or maybe a statue with its head glued on backward—well, sorry. That was probably our fault.

As police blocked the streets and cordoned off the blast zone, our team gathered on the museum roof. In better times we might have used an artifact to open a portal to take us back home; but over the last few months, as Apophis had gotten stronger, portals had become too risky to use.

Instead I whistled for our ride. Freak the griffin glided over from the top of the nearby Fairmont Hotel.

It's not easy finding a place to stash a griffin, especially when he's pulling a boat. You can't just parallel-park something like that and put a few coins in the meter. Besides, Freak tends to get nervous around strangers and swallow them, so I'd settled him on top of the Fairmont with a crate of frozen turkeys to keep him occupied. They have to be frozen. Otherwise he eats them too fast and gets hiccups.

(Sadie is telling me to hurry up with the story. She says you don't care about the feeding habits of griffins. Well, excuse me.)

Anyway, Freak came in for a landing on the museum roof. He was a beautiful monster, if you like psychotic falcon-headed lions. His fur was the color of rust, and as he flew, his giant hummingbird wings sounded like a cross between chain saws and kazoos.

"FREEAAAK!" Freak cawed.

"Yeah, buddy," I agreed. "Let's get out of here."

The boat trailing behind him was an Ancient Egyptian model—shaped like a big canoe made from bundles of papyrus reeds, enchanted by Walt so that it stayed airborne no matter how much weight it carried.

The first time we'd flown Air Freak, we'd strung the boat underneath Freak's belly, which hadn't been very stable. And you couldn't simply ride on his back, because those high-powered wings would chop you to shreds. So the sleigh-boat was our new solution. It worked great, except when Felix yelled down at the mortals, "Ho, ho, ho, Merry Christmas!"

Of course, most mortals can't see magic clearly, so I'm not sure what they *thought* they saw as we passed overhead. No doubt it caused many of them to adjust their medication.

We soared into the night sky—the six of us and a small cabinet. I still didn't understand Sadie's interest in the golden box, but I trusted her enough to believe it was important.

I glanced down at the wreckage of the sculpture garden. The smoking crater looked like a ragged mouth, screaming. Fire trucks and police cars had surrounded it with a perimeter of red and white lights. I wondered how many magicians had died in that explosion.

Freak picked up speed. My eyes stung, but it wasn't from the wind. I turned so my friends couldn't see.

Your leadership is doomed.

Apophis would say anything to throw us into confusion and make us doubt our cause. Still, his words hit me hard.

I didn't like being a leader. I always had to appear confident for the sake of the others, even when I wasn't.

I missed having my dad to rely on. I missed Uncle Amos, who'd gone off to Cairo to run the House of Life. As for Sadie, my bossy sister, she always supported me, but she'd made it clear she didn't want to be an authority figure. Officially, *I* was in charge of Brooklyn House. Officially, I called the shots. In my mind, that meant if we made mistakes, like getting an entire nome wiped off the face of the earth, then the fault was mine.

Okay, Sadie would never actually blame me for something like that, but that's how I felt.

Everything you tried to build will crumble. . . .

It seemed incredible that not even a year had passed since Sadie and I first arrived at Brooklyn House, completely clueless about our heritage and our powers. Now we were running the place—training an army of young magicians to fight Apophis using the path of the gods, a kind of magic that hadn't been practiced in thousands of years. We'd made so much progress— but judging from how our fight against Apophis had gone tonight, our efforts hadn't been enough.

You will lose the ones you love the most. . . .

I'd already lost so many people. My mom had died when I was seven. My dad had sacrificed himself to become the host of Osiris last year. Over the summer, many of our allies had fallen to Apophis, or been ambushed and "disappeared" thanks to the rebel magicians who didn't accept my Uncle Amos as the new Chief Lector.

Who else could I lose . . . Sadie?

No, I'm not being sarcastic. Even though we'd grown up separately for most of our lives—me traveling around with Dad, Sadie living in London with Gran and Gramps—she was still my sister. We'd grown close over the last year. As annoying as she was, I needed her.

Wow, that's depressing.

(And there's the punch in the arm I was expecting. Ow.)

Or maybe Apophis meant someone else, like Zia Rashid . . .

Our boat rose above the glittering suburbs of Dallas. With a defiant squawk, Freak pulled us into the Duat. Fog swallowed the boat. The temperature dropped to freezing. I felt a familiar tingle in my stomach, as if we were plunging from the top of a roller coaster. Ghostly voices whispered in the mist.

Just when I started to think we were lost, my dizziness passed. The fog cleared. We were back on the East Coast, sailing over New York Harbor toward the nighttime lights of the Brooklyn waterfront and home.

The headquarters of the Twenty-first Nome perched on the shoreline near the Williamsburg Bridge. Regular mortals wouldn't see anything but a huge dilapidated warehouse in the middle of an industrial yard, but to magicians, Brooklyn House was as obvious as a lighthouse—a five-story mansion of limestone blocks and steel-framed glass rising from the top of the warehouse, glowing with yellow and green lights.

Freak landed on the roof, where the cat goddess Bast was waiting for us.

"My kittens are alive!" She took my arms and looked me over for wounds, then did the same to Sadie. She tutted disapprovingly as she examined Sadie's bandaged hands.

Bast's luminous feline eyes were a little unsettling. Her long black hair was tied back in a braid, and her acrobatic bodysuit changed patterns as she moved—by turns tiger stripes, leopard spots, or calico. As much as I loved and trusted her, she made me a little nervous when she did her "mother cat" inspections. She kept knives up her sleeves—deadly iron blades that could slip into her hands with the flick of her wrists—and I was always afraid she might make a mistake, pat me on the cheek, and end up decapitating me. At least she didn't try to pick us up by the scruffs of our necks or give us a bath.

"What happened?" she asked. "Everyone is safe?"

Sadie took a shaky breath. "Well . . ."

We told her about the destruction of the Texas nome.

Bast growled deep in her throat. Her hair poofed out, but the braid held it down so her scalp looked like a heated pan of Jiffy-Pop popcorn. "I should've been there," she said. "I could have helped!"

"You couldn't," I said. "The museum was too well protected."

Gods are almost never able to enter magicians' territory in their physical forms. Magicians have spent millennia developing enchanted wards to keep them out. We'd had enough trouble reworking the wards on Brooklyn House to give Bast access without opening ourselves up to attacks by less friendly gods.

Taking Bast to the Dallas Museum would've been like trying to get a bazooka through airport security—if not totally impossible, then at least pretty darn slow and difficult. Besides, Bast was our last line of defense for Brooklyn House. We needed her to protect our home base and our initiates. Twice before, our enemies had almost destroyed the mansion. We didn't want there to be a third time.

Bast's bodysuit turned pure black, as it tended to do when she was moody. "Still, I'd never forgive myself if you . . ." She glanced at our tired, frightened crew. "Well, at least you're back safe. What's the next step?"

Walt stumbled. Alyssa and Felix caught him.

"I'm fine," he insisted, though he clearly wasn't. "Carter, I can get everyone together if you want. A meeting on the terrace?"

He looked like he was about to pass out. Walt would never admit it, but our main healer, Jaz, had told me that his level of pain was almost unbearable all the time now. He was only able to stay on his feet because she kept tattooing pain-relief hieroglyphs on his chest and giving him potions. In spite of that, I'd asked him to come to Dallas with us—another decision that weighed on my heart.

The rest of our crew needed sleep too. Felix's eyes were puffy from crying. Alyssa looked like she was going into shock.

If we met now, I wouldn't know what to say. I had no plan. I couldn't stand in front of the whole nome without breaking down. Not after having caused so many deaths in Dallas.

I glanced at Sadie. We came to a silent agreement.

"We'll meet tomorrow," I told the others. "You guys get some sleep. What happened with the Texans . . ." My voice caught. "Look, I know how you feel. I feel the same way. But it wasn't your fault."

I'm not sure they bought it. Felix wiped a tear from his cheek. Alyssa put her arm around him and led him toward the stairwell. Walt gave Sadie a glance I couldn't interpret—maybe wistfulness or regret—then followed Alyssa downstairs.

"*Agh?*" Khufu patted the golden cabinet.

"Yeah," I said. "Could you take it to the library?"

That was the most secure room in the mansion. I didn't want to take any chances after all we'd sacrificed to save the box. Khufu waddled away with it.

Freak was so tired, he didn't even make it to his covered roost. He just curled up where he was and started snoring, still attached to the boat. Traveling through the Duat takes a lot out of him.

I undid his harness and scratched his feathery head. "Thanks, buddy. Dream of big fat turkeys."

He cooed in his sleep.

I turned to Sadie and Bast. "We need to talk."

It was almost midnight, but the Great Room was still buzzing with activity. Julian, Paul, and a few of the other guys were crashed on the couches, watching the sports channel. The ankle-biters (our three youngest trainees) were coloring pictures on the floor. Chip bags and soda cans littered the coffee table. Shoes were tossed randomly across the snakeskin rug. In the middle of the room, the two-story-tall statue of Thoth, the ibis-headed god of knowledge, loomed over our initiates with his scroll and quill. Somebody had put one of Amos's old porkpie hats on the statue's head, so he looked like a bookie taking bets on the football game. One of the ankle-biters had colored the god's obsidian toes pink and purple with crayons. We're big on respect here at Brooklyn House.

As Sadie and I came down the stairs, the guys on the couch got to their feet.

"How did it go?" Julian asked. "Walt just came through, but he wouldn't say—"

"Our team is safe," I said. "The Fifty-first Nome . . . not so lucky."

Julian winced. He knew better than to ask for details in front of the little kids. "Did you find anything helpful?"

"We're not sure yet," I admitted.

I wanted to leave it at that, but our youngest ankle-biter, Shelby, toddled over to show me her crayon masterpiece. "I kill a snake," she announced. "Kill, kill, kill. Bad snake!"

She'd drawn a serpent with a bunch of knives sticking out of its back and X's in its eyes. If Shelby had made that picture at school, it probably would've earned her a trip to the guidance counselor; but here even the littlest ones understood something serious was happening.

She gave me a toothy grin, shaking her crayon like a spear. I stepped back. Shelby might've been a kindergartner, but she was already an excellent magician. Her crayons sometimes morphed into weapons, and the things she drew tended to peel off the page—like the red, white, and blue unicorn she had summoned for the Fourth of July.

"Awesome picture, Shelby." I felt like my heart was being wrapped tight in mummy linen. Like all the littlest kids, Shelby was here with her parents' consent. The parents understood that the fate of the world was at stake. They knew Brooklyn House was the best and safest place for Shelby to master her powers. Still, what kind of childhood was this for her, channeling magic that would destroy most adults, learning about monsters that would give anybody nightmares?

Julian ruffled Shelby's hair. "Come on, sweetie. Draw me another picture, okay?"

Shelby said, "Kill?"

Julian steered her away. Sadie, Bast, and I headed to the library.

The heavy oaken doors opened to a staircase that descended into a huge cylindrical room like a well. Painted on the domed ceiling was Nut, the sky goddess, with silver constellations glittering on her dark blue body. The floor was a mosaic of her husband, Geb, the earth god, his body covered with rivers, hills, and deserts.

Even though it was late, our self-appointed librarian, Cleo, still had her four *shabti* statues at work. The clay men rushed around, dusting shelves, rearranging scrolls, and sorting books in the honeycombed compartments along the walls. Cleo herself sat at the worktable, jotting notes on a papyrus scroll while she talked to Khufu, who squatted on the table in front of her, patting our new antique cabinet and grunting in Baboon, like: *Hey, Cleo, wanna buy a gold box?*

Cleo wasn't much in the bravery department, but she

had an incredible memory. She could speak six languages, including English, her native Portuguese (she was Brazilian), Ancient Egyptian, and a few words of Baboon. She'd taken it upon herself to create a master index to all our scrolls, and had been gathering more scrolls from all over the world to help us find information on Apophis. It was Cleo who'd found the connection between the serpent's recent attacks and the scrolls written by the legendary magician Setne.

She was a great help, though sometimes she got exasperated when she had to make room in *her* library for our school texts, Internet stations, large artifacts, and Bast's back issues of *Cat Fancy* magazine.

When Cleo saw us coming down the stairs, she jumped to her feet. "You're alive!"

"Don't sound so surprised," Sadie muttered.

Cleo chewed her lip. "Sorry, I just . . . I'm glad. Khufu came in alone, so I was worried. He was trying to tell me something about this gold box, but it's empty. Did you find the Book of Overcoming Apophis?"

"The scroll burned," I said. "We couldn't save it."

Cleo looked like she might scream. "But that was the last copy! How could Apophis destroy something so valuable?"

I wanted to remind Cleo that Apophis was out to destroy the entire world, but I knew she didn't like to think about that. It made her sick from fear.

Getting outraged about the scroll was more manageable for her. The idea that anybody could destroy a book of any kind made Cleo want to punch Apophis in the face.

One of the *shabti* jumped onto the table. He tried to stick a scanner label on the golden cabinet, but Cleo shooed the clay man away.

"All of you, back to your places!" She clapped her hands, and the four *shabti* returned to their pedestals. They reverted to solid clay, though one was still wearing rubber gloves and holding a feather duster, which looked a little odd.

Cleo leaned in and studied the gold box. "There's nothing inside. Why did you bring it?"

"That's what Sadie, Bast, and I need to discuss," I said. "If you don't mind, Cleo."

"I don't mind." Cleo kept examining the cabinet. Then she realized we were all staring at her. "Oh . . . you mean privately. Of course."

She looked a little upset about getting kicked out, but she took Khufu's hand. "Come on, *babuinozinho*. We'll get you a snack."

"*Agh!*" Khufu said happily. He adored Cleo, possibly because of her name. For reasons none of us quite understood, Khufu loved things that ended in -O, like avocados, Oreos, and armadillos.

Once Cleo and Khufu were gone, Sadie, Bast, and I gathered around our new acquisition.

The cabinet was shaped like a miniature school locker. The exterior was gold, but it must've been a thin layer of foil covering wood, because the whole thing wasn't very heavy. The sides and top were engraved with hieroglyphs and pictures of the pharaoh and his wife. The front was fitted with latched double doors, which opened to reveal . . . well, not much of anything. There was a tiny pedestal marked by gold footprints, as if an Ancient Egyptian Barbie doll had once stood there.

Sadie studied the hieroglyphs along the sides of the box. "It's all about Tut and his queen, wishing them a happy afterlife, blah, blah. There's a picture of him hunting ducks. Honestly? That was his idea of paradise?"

"I like ducks," Bast said.

I moved the little doors back and forth on their hinges. "Somehow I don't think the ducks are important. Whatever was inside here, it's gone now. Maybe grave robbers took it, or—"

Bast chuckled. "Grave robbers took it. Sure."

I frowned at her. "What's so funny?"

She grinned at me, then Sadie, before apparently realizing we didn't get the joke. "Oh . . . I see. You actually don't know what this is. I suppose that makes sense. Not many have survived."

"Not many what?" I asked.

"Shadow boxes."

Sadie wrinkled her nose. "Isn't that a sort of school project? Did one for English once. Deadly boring."

"I wouldn't know about school projects," Bast said haughtily. "That sounds suspiciously like *work*. But this is an *actual* shadow box—a box to hold a shadow."

Bast didn't sound like she was kidding, but it's hard to tell with cats.

"It's in there right now," she insisted. "Can't you see it? A little shadowy bit of Tut. Hello, shadow Tut!" She wriggled her fingers at the empty box. "That's why I laughed when you said grave robbers might have stolen it. Ha! That would be a trick."

I tried to wrap my mind around this idea. "But . . . I've heard Dad lecture on, like, every possible Egyptian artifact. I never once heard him mention a shadow box."

"As I told you," Bast said, "not many have survived. Usually the shadow box was buried far away from the rest of the soul. Tut was quite silly to have it placed in his tomb. Perhaps one of the priests put it there against his orders, out of spite."

I was totally lost now. To my surprise, Sadie was nodding enthusiastically.

"That must've been what Anubis meant," she said. "*Pay attention to what's not there.* When I looked into the Duat, I saw darkness inside the box. And Uncle Vinnie said it was a clue to defeating Apophis."

I made a "Time out" T with my hands. "Back up. Sadie, where did you see Anubis? And since when do we have an uncle named Vinnie?"

She looked a little embarrassed, but she described her encounter with the face in the wall, then the visions she'd had of our mom and Isis and her godly almost-boyfriend Anubis. I knew my sister's attention wandered a lot, but even *I* was impressed by how many mystical side trips she'd managed, just walking through a museum.

"The face in the wall could've been a trick," I said.

"Possibly . . . but I don't think so. The face said we would need his help, and we had only two days until something happened to him. He told me this box would show us what we needed. Anubis hinted I was on the right track, saving this cabinet. And Mum . . ." Sadie faltered. "Mum said this was the only way we'd ever see her again. Something is happening to the spirits of the dead."

Suddenly I felt like I was back in the Duat, wrapped in freezing fog. I stared at the box, but I still didn't see anything. "How do shadows tie in to Apophis and spirits of the dead?"

I looked at Bast. She dug her fingernails into the table, using it like a scratching post, the way she does when she's tense. We go through a lot of tables.

"Bast?" Sadie asked gently.

"Apophis and shadows," Bast mused. "I'd never considered . . ." She shook her head. "These are really questions you should ask Thoth. He's much more knowledgeable than I."

A memory surfaced. My dad had given a lecture at a university somewhere . . . Munich, maybe? The students had asked him about the Egyptian concept of the soul, which had multiple parts, and my dad mentioned something about shadows.

Like one hand with five fingers, he'd said. *One soul with five parts.*

I held up my own fingers, trying to remember. "Five parts of the soul . . . what are they?"

Bast stayed silent. She looked pretty uncomfortable.

"Carter?" Sadie asked. "What does that have to do—?"

"Just humor me," I said. "The first part is the *ba*, right? Our personality."

"Chicken form," Sadie said.

Trust Sadie to nickname part of your soul after poultry, but

I knew what she meant. The *ba* could leave the body when we dreamed, or it could come back to the earth as a ghost after we died. When it did, it appeared as a large glowing bird with a human head.

"Yeah," I said. "Chicken form. Then there's the *ka*, the life force that leaves the body when it dies. Then there's the *ib*, the heart—"

"The record of good and bad deeds," Sadie agreed. "That's the bit they weigh on the scales of justice in the afterlife."

"And fourth . . ." I hesitated.

"The *ren*," Sadie supplied. "Your secret name."

I was too embarrassed to look at her. Last spring she'd saved my life by speaking my secret name, which had basically given her access to my most private thoughts and darkest emotions. Since then she'd been pretty cool about it, but still . . . that's not the kind of leverage you want to give your little sister.

The *ren* was also the part of the soul that our friend Bes had given up for us in our gambling match six months ago with the moon god Khonsu. Now Bes was a hollow shell of a god, sitting in a wheelchair in the Underworld's divine nursing home.

"Right," I said. "But the fifth part . . ." I looked at Bast. "It's the shadow, isn't it?"

Sadie frowned. "The shadow? How can a shadow be part of your soul? It's just a silhouette, isn't it? A trick of the light."

Bast held her hand over the table. Her fingers cast a vague shadow over the wood. "You can never be free of your shadow—your *sheut*. All living beings have them."

"So do rocks, pencils, and shoes," Sadie said. "Does that mean *they* have souls?"

"You know better," Bast chided. "Living beings are different from rocks . . . well, *most* are, anyway. The *sheut* is not just a physical shadow. It's a magical projection—the silhouette of the soul."

"So this box . . ." I said. "When you say it holds King Tut's shadow—"

"I mean it holds one fifth of his soul," Bast confirmed. "It houses the pharaoh's *sheut* so it will not be lost in the afterlife."

My brain felt like it was about to explode. I knew this stuff about shadows must be important, but I didn't see how. It was like I'd been handed a puzzle piece, but it was for the wrong puzzle.

We'd failed to save the *right* piece—an irreplaceable scroll that might've helped us beat Apophis—and we'd failed to save an entire nome full of friendly magicians. All we had to show from our trip was an empty cabinet decorated with pictures of ducks. I wanted to knock King Tut's shadow box across the room.

"Lost shadows," I muttered. "This sounds like that *Peter Pan* story."

Bast's eyes glowed like paper lanterns. "What do you think *inspired* the story of Peter Pan's lost shadow? There have been folktales about shadows for centuries, Carter—all handed down since the days of Egypt."

"But how does that *help* us?" I demanded. "The Book of Overcoming Apophis would've helped us. Now it's gone!"

Okay, I sounded angry. I *was* angry.

Remembering my dad's lectures made me want to be a kid again, traveling the world with him. We'd been through some weird stuff together, but I'd always felt safe and protected. He'd always known what to do. Now all I had left from those days was my suitcase, gathering dust in my closet upstairs.

It wasn't fair. But I knew what my dad would say about that: *Fair means everyone gets what they need. And the only way to get what you need is to make that happen yourself.*

Great, Dad. I'm facing an impossible enemy, and what I *need* in order to defeat him just got destroyed.

Sadie must've read my expression. "Carter, we'll figure it out," she promised. "Bast, you were about to say something earlier about Apophis and shadows."

"No, I wasn't," Bast murmured.

"Why are you so nervous about this?" I asked. "Do gods *have* shadows? Does Apophis? If so, how do they work?"

Bast gouged some hieroglyphs in the table with her finger-nails. I was pretty sure the message read: DANGER.

"Honestly, children . . . this is a question for Thoth. Yes, gods have shadows. Of course we do. But—but it's not something we're supposed to talk about."

I'd rarely seen Bast look so agitated. I wasn't sure why. This was a goddess who'd fought Apophis face-to-face, claw to fang, in a magical prison for thousands of years. Why was she scared of shadows?

"Bast," I said, "if we can't figure out a better solution, we'll have to go with Plan B."

The goddess winced. Sadie stared dejectedly at the table. Plan B was something only Sadie, Bast, Walt, and I had discussed. Our other initiates didn't know about it. We hadn't even told our Uncle Amos. It was *that* scary.

"I—I would hate that," Bast said. "But, Carter, I really don't know the answers. And if you start asking about shadows, you'll be delving into very dangerous—"

There was a knock on the library doors. Cleo and Khufu appeared at the top of the stairs.

"Sorry to disturb," Cleo said. "Carter, Khufu just came down from your room. He seems anxious to talk with you."

"*Agh!*" Khufu insisted.

Bast translated from baboon-speak. "He says there's a call for you on the scrying bowl, Carter. A *private* call."

As if I weren't stressed enough already. Only one person would be sending me a scrying vision, and if she was contacting me so late at night, it had to be bad news.

"Meeting adjourned," I told the others. "See you in the morning."

4. I Consult the Pigeon of War

I WAS IN LOVE WITH A BIRDBATH.

Most guys checked their phone for texts, or obsessed over what girls were saying about them online. Me, I couldn't stay away from the scrying bowl.

It was just a bronze saucer on a stone pedestal, sitting on the balcony outside my bedroom. But whenever I was in my room, I found myself stealing glances at it, resisting the urge to rush outside and check for a glimpse of Zia.

The weird thing was—I couldn't even call her my girl-friend. What do you call somebody when you fall in love with her replica *shabti*, then rescue the real person only to find she doesn't share your feelings? And Sadie thinks *her* relationships are complicated.

Over the past six months, since Zia had gone to help my uncle at the First Nome, the bowl had been our only contact. I'd spent so many hours staring into it, talking with Zia, I could hardly remember what she looked like without enchanted oil rippling across her face.

By the time I reached the balcony, I was out of breath. From the surface of the oil, Zia stared up at me. Her arms were crossed; her eyes so angry, they looked like they might ignite. (The first scrying bowl Walt had made actually *did* ignite, but that's another story.)

"Carter," she said, "I'm going to strangle you."

She was beautiful when she threatened to kill me. Over the summer she'd let her hair grow out so that it swept over her shoulders in a glossy black wave. She wasn't the *shabti* I'd first fallen for, but her face still had a sculpted beauty—delicate nose, full red lips, dazzling amber eyes. Her skin glowed like terra-cotta warm from the kiln.

"You heard about Dallas," I guessed. "Zia, I'm sorry—"

"Carter, *everyone* has heard about Dallas. Other nomes have been sending Amos *ba* messengers for the past hour, demanding answers. Magicians as far away as Cuba felt ripples in the Duat. Some claimed you blew up half of Texas. Some said the entire Fifty-first Nome was destroyed. Some said— some said you were dead."

The concern in her voice lifted my spirits a little, but it also made me feel guiltier.

"I wanted to tell you in advance," I said. "But by the time we realized Apophis's target was Dallas, we had to move immediately."

I told her what had happened at the King Tut exhibit, including our mistakes and casualties.

I tried to read Zia's expression. Even after so many months, it was hard to guess what she was thinking. Just *seeing* her tended to short-circuit my brain. Half the time I could barely remember how to speak in complete sentences.

Finally she muttered something in Arabic—probably a curse.

"I'm glad you survived—but the Fifty-first destroyed . . . ?" She shook her head in disbelief. "I knew Anne Grissom. She taught me healing magic when I was young."

I remembered the pretty blond lady who had played with the band, and the ruined fiddle at the edge of the explosion.

"They were good people," I said.

"Some of our last allies," Zia said. "The rebels are already blaming you for their deaths. If any more nomes desert Amos . . ."

She didn't have to finish that thought. Last spring, the worst villains in the House of Life had formed a hit squad to destroy Brooklyn House. We'd defeated them. Amos had even given them amnesty when he became the new Chief Lector. But some refused to follow him. The rebels were still out there—gathering strength, turning other magicians against us. As if we needed more enemies.

"They're blaming me?" I asked. "Did they contact you?"

"Worse. They broadcasted a message to you."

The oil rippled. I saw a different face—Sarah Jacobi, leader of the rebels. She had milky skin, spiky black hair, and dark, permanently startled eyes lined with too much kohl. In her pure white robes she looked like a Halloween ghoul.

She stood in a room lined with marble columns. Behind her glowered half a dozen magicians—Jacobi's elite killers. I recognized the blue robes and shaven head of Kwai, who'd been exiled from the North Korean nome for murdering a fellow magician. Next to him stood Petrovich, a scar-faced Ukrainian who'd once worked as an assassin for our old enemy Vlad Menshikov.

The others I couldn't identify, but I doubted that any of them was as bad as Sarah Jacobi herself. Until Menshikov had released her, she'd been exiled in Antarctica for causing an Indian Ocean tsunami that killed more than a quarter of a million people.

"Carter Kane!" she shouted.

Because this was a broadcast, I knew it was just a magical recording, but her voice made me jump.

"The House of Life demands your surrender," she said. "Your crimes are unforgivable. You must pay with your life."

My stomach barely had time to drop before a series of violent images flashed across the oil. I saw the Rosetta Stone exploding in the British Museum—the incident that had unleashed Set and killed my father last Christmas. How had Jacobi gotten a visual of that? I saw the fight at Brooklyn House last spring, when Sadie and I had arrived in Ra's sun boat to drive out Jacobi's hit squad. The images she showed made it look like *we* were the aggressors—a bunch of hooligans with godly powers beating up on poor Jacobi and her friends.

"You released Set and his brethren," Jacobi narrated. "You broke the most sacred rule of magic and cooperated with the gods. In doing so, you unbalanced Ma'at, causing the rise of Apophis."

"That's a lie!" I said. "Apophis was rising anyway!"

Then I remembered I was yelling at a video.

The scenes kept shifting. I saw a high-rise building on fire in the Shibuya district of Tokyo, headquarters of the 234th Nome. A flying demon with the head of a samurai sword crashed through a window and carried off a screaming magician.

I saw the home of the old Chief Lector, Michel Desjardins— a beautiful Paris townhouse on the rue des Pyramides—now in ruins. The roof had collapsed. The windows were broken. Ripped scrolls and soggy books littered the dead garden, and the hieroglyph for Chaos smoldered on the front door like a cattle brand.

"All this you have caused," Jacobi said. "You have given the Chief Lector's mantle to a servant of evil. You have corrupted young magicians by teaching the path of the gods. You've weakened the House of Life and left us at the mercy of Apophis. We will not stand for this. Any who follow you will be punished."

The vision changed to Sphinx House in London, headquarters for the British nome. Sadie and I had visited there over the summer and managed to make peace with them after hours of negotiations. I saw Kwai storming through the library, smashing statues of the gods and raking books off the shelves. A dozen British magicians stood in chains before their conqueror, Sarah Jacobi, who held a gleaming black knife. The leader of the nome, a harmless old guy named Sir Leicester, was forced to his knees. Sarah Jacobi raised her knife. The blade fell, and the scene shifted.

Jacobi's ghoulish face stared up at me from the surface of the oil. Her eyes were as dark as the sockets of a skull.

"The Kanes are a plague," she said. "You must be destroyed. Surrender yourself and your family for execution. We will spare your other followers as long as they renounce the path of the gods. I do not seek the office of Chief Lector, but I must take it for the good of Egypt. When the Kanes are dead, we will be strong and united again. We will undo the damage you've caused and send the gods and Apophis back to the Duat. Justice comes swiftly, Carter Kane. This will be your only warning."

Sarah Jacobi's image dissolved in the oil, and I was alone again with Zia's reflection.

"Yeah," I said shakily. "For a mass murderer, she's pretty convincing."

Zia nodded. "Jacobi has already turned or defeated most of our allies in Europe and Asia. A lot of the recent attacks—against Paris, Tokyo, Madrid—those were Jacobi's work, but she's blaming them on Apophis—or Brooklyn House."

"That's ridiculous."

"You and I know that," she agreed. "But the magicians are scared. Jacobi is telling them that if the Kanes are destroyed, Apophis will go back to the Duat and things will return to normal. They *want* to believe it. She's telling them that following you is a death sentence. After the destruction of Dallas—"

"I get it," I snapped.

It wasn't fair for me to get mad at Zia, but I felt so helpless. Everything we did seemed to turn out wrong. I imagined Apophis laughing in the Underworld. Maybe that's why he hadn't attacked the House of Life in full force yet. He was having too much fun watching us tear each other apart.

"Why didn't Jacobi direct her message at Amos?" I asked. "He's the Chief Lector."

Zia glanced away as if checking on something. I couldn't see much of her surroundings, but she didn't seem to be in her dorm room at the First Nome, or in the Hall of Ages. "Like Jacobi said, they consider Amos a servant of evil. They won't talk to him."

"Because he was possessed by Set," I guessed. "That wasn't *his* fault. He's been healed. He's fine."

Zia winced.

"What?" I asked. "He *is* fine, isn't he?"

"Carter, it's—it's complicated. Look, the main problem is Jacobi. She's taken over Menshikov's old base in St. Petersburg. It's almost as much of a fortress as the First Nome. We don't know what she's up to or how many magicians she has. We don't know when she'll strike or where. But she's going to attack soon."

Justice comes swiftly. This will be your only warning.

Something told me Jacobi wouldn't attack Brooklyn House again, not after she'd been humiliated last time. But if she wanted to take over the House of Life and destroy the Kanes, what else could her target be?

I locked eyes with Zia, and I realized what she was thinking.

"No," I said. "They'd never attack the First Nome. That would be suicide. It's survived for five thousand years."

"Carter . . . we're weaker than you realize. We were never fully staffed. Now many of our best magicians have disappeared, possibly gone over to the other side. We've got some old men and a few scared children left, plus Amos and me." She spread her arms in exasperation. "And half the time *I'm* stuck here—"

"Wait," I said. "Where are you?"

Somewhere to Zia's left, a man's voice warbled, "Hell-ooooo!"

Zia sighed. "Great. He's up from his nap."

An old man stuck his face in the scrying bowl. He grinned, showing exactly two teeth. His bald wrinkly head made him look like a geriatric baby. "Zebras are here!"

He opened his mouth and tried to suck the oil out of the bowl, making the whole scene ripple.

"My lord, no!" Zia pulled him back. "You can't drink the enchanted oil. We've talked about this. Here, have a cookie."

"Cookies!" he squealed. "Wheee!" The old man danced off with a tasty treat in his hands.

Zia's senile grandfather? Nope. That was Ra, god of the sun, first divine pharaoh of Egypt and archenemy of Apophis. Last spring we'd gone on a quest to find him and revive him from his twilight sleep, trusting he would rise in all his glory and fight the Chaos snake for us.

Instead, Ra woke up senile and demented. He was excellent at gumming biscuits, drooling, and singing nonsense songs. Fighting Apophis? Not so much.

"You're babysitting *again*?" I asked.

Zia shrugged. "It's after sunrise here. Horus and Isis watch him most nights on the sun boat. But during the day . . . well, Ra gets upset if I don't come to visit, and none of the other gods want to watch him. Honestly, Carter . . ." She lowered her voice. "I'm afraid of what they'd do if I left Ra alone with them. They're getting tired of him."

"Wheee!" Ra said in the background.

My heart sank. Yet another thing to feel guilty about: I'd saddled Zia with nanny duty for a sun god. Stuck in the throne room of the gods every day, helping Amos run the First Nome every night, Zia barely had time to sleep, much less go on a date—even if I could get up the courage to ask her.

Of course, that wouldn't matter if Apophis destroyed the world, or if Sarah Jacobi and her magical killers got to me. For a moment I wondered if Jacobi was right—if the world *had* gone sideways because of the Kane family, and if it would be better off without us.

I felt so helpless, I briefly considered calling on the power of Horus. I could've used some of the war god's courage and confidence. But I suspected that joining my thoughts with Horus's wouldn't be a good idea. My emotions were jumbled enough without another voice in my head, egging me on.

"I know that expression," Zia chided. "You can't blame yourself, Carter. If it weren't for you and Sadie, Apophis would have already destroyed the world. There's still hope."

Plan B, I thought. Unless we could figure out this mystery about shadows and how they could be used to fight Apophis, we'd be stuck with Plan B, which meant certain death for Sadie and me even if it worked. But I wasn't going to tell Zia that. She didn't need any more depressing news.

"You're right," I said. "We'll figure out something."

"I'll be back at the First Nome tonight. Call me then, okay? We should talk about—"

Something rumbled behind her, like a stone slab grinding across the floor.

"Sobek's here," she whispered. "I hate that guy. Talk later."

"Wait, Zia," I said. "Talk about what?"

But the oil turned dark, and Zia was gone.

I needed to sleep. Instead, I paced my room.

The dorm rooms at Brooklyn House were amazing—comfortable beds, HD TVs, high-speed wireless Internet, and magically restocking mini-fridges. An army of enchanted brooms, mops, and dusters kept everything tidy. The closets were always full of clean, perfectly fitting clothes.

Still, my room felt like a cage. Maybe that's because I had a baboon for a roommate. Khufu wasn't here much (usually downstairs with Cleo or letting the ankle-biters groom his fur), but there was a baboon-shaped depression on his bed, a box of Cheerios on the nightstand, and a tire swing installed in the corner of the room. Sadie had done that last part as a joke, but Khufu loved it so much, I couldn't take it down. The thing was, I'd gotten used to his being around. Now that he spent most of his time with the kindergartners, I missed him. He'd grown on me in an endearing, annoying way, kind of like my sister.

[Yeah, Sadie. You saw that one coming.]

Screensaver pictures floated across my laptop monitor.

There was my dad at a dig site in Egypt, looking relaxed and in charge in his khaki fatigues, his sleeves rolled up on his dark muscular arms as he showed off the broken stone head of some pharaoh's statue. Dad's bald scalp and goatee made him look slightly devilish when he smiled.

Another picture showed Uncle Amos onstage at a jazz club, playing his saxophone. He wore round dark glasses, a blue porkpie hat, and a matching silk suit, impeccably tailored as always. His cornrows were braided with sapphires. I'd never actually seen Amos play onstage, but I liked this photo because he looked so energetic and happy—not like he did these days, with the weight of leadership on his shoulders. Unfortunately the photo also reminded me of Anne Grissom, the Texas magician with her fiddle, having so much fun earlier this evening just before she died.

The screensaver changed. I saw my mom bouncing me on her knee when I was a baby. I had this ridiculous 'fro back then, which Sadie always teases me about. In the photo, I'm wearing a blue onesie stained with pureed yams. I'm holding my mom's thumbs, looking startled as she bounces me up and down, like I'm thinking, *Get me off of this ride!* My mom is as beautiful as always, even in an old T-shirt and jeans, her hair tied back in a bandana. She smiles down at me like I'm the most wonderful thing in her life.

That photo hurt to look at, but I kept looking at it.

I remembered what Sadie had told me—that something was affecting the spirits of the dead, and we might not see our mom again unless we figured it out.

I took a deep breath. My dad, my uncle, my mom—all of

them powerful magicians. All had sacrificed so much to restore the House of Life.

They were older, wiser, and stronger than me. They'd had decades to practice magic. Sadie and I had had nine months. Yet we needed to do something no magician had ever managed—defeat Apophis himself.

I went to my closet and took down my old traveling case. It was just a black leather carry-on bag, like a million others you might see in an airport. For years I'd lugged it around the world as I traveled with my dad. He'd trained me to live with only the possessions I could carry.

I opened the suitcase. It was empty now except for one thing: a statuette of a coiled serpent carved in red granite, engraved with hieroglyphs. The name—*Apophis*—was crossed out and overwritten with powerful binding spells, but still this statuette was the most dangerous object in the whole house—a representation of the enemy.

Sadie, Walt, and I had made this thing in secret (over Bast's strong objections). We'd only trusted Walt because we needed his charm-making skills. Not even Amos would have approved such a dangerous experiment. One mistake, one mis-cast spell, and this statue could turn from a weapon against Apophis into a gateway allowing him free access to Brooklyn House. But we'd had to take the risk. Unless we found some other means of defeating the serpent, Sadie and I would have to use this statue for Plan B.

"Foolish idea," said a voice from the balcony.

A pigeon was perched on the railing. There was something

very un-pigeonlike about its stare. It looked fearless, almost dangerous; and I recognized that voice, which was more manly and warlike than you'd normally expect from a member of the dove family.

"Horus?" I asked.

The pigeon bobbed its head. "May I come in?"

I knew he wasn't just asking out of courtesy. The house was heavily enchanted to keep out unwanted pests like rodents, termites, and Egyptian gods.

"I give you permission to enter," I said formally. "Horus, in the form of a . . . uh . . . pigeon."

"Thank you." The pigeon hopped off the railing and waddled inside.

"Why?" I asked.

Horus ruffled his feathers. "Well, I looked for a falcon, but they're a little scarce in New York. I wanted something with wings, so a pigeon seemed the best choice. They've adapted well to cities, aren't scared of people. They're noble birds, don't you think?"

"Noble," I agreed. "That's the first word that comes to mind when I think of pigeons."

"Indeed," Horus said.

Apparently sarcasm didn't exist in Ancient Egypt, because Horus never seemed to get it. He fluttered onto my bed and pecked at a few Cheerios left over from Khufu's lunch.

"Hey," I warned, "if you poop on my blankets—"

"Please. War gods do not poop on blankets. Well, except for that one time—"

"Forget I said anything."

Horus hopped to the edge of my suitcase. He peered down at the statuette of Apophis. "Dangerous," he said. "Much too dangerous, Carter."

I hadn't told him about Plan B, but I wasn't surprised that he knew. Horus and I had shared minds too many times. The better I got at channeling his powers, the better we understood each other. The downside of godly magic was that I couldn't always shut off that connection.

"It's our emergency backup," I said. "We're trying to find another way."

"By looking for that scroll," he recalled. "The last copy of which burned up tonight in Dallas."

I resisted the urge to spike the pigeon. "Yes. But Sadie found this shadow box. She thinks it's some sort of clue. You wouldn't know anything about using shadows against Apophis, would you?"

The pigeon turned its head sideways. "Not really. My understanding of magic is fairly straightforward. Hit enemies with a sword until they're dead. If they rise again, hit them again. Repeat as necessary. It worked against Set."

"After how many years of fighting?"

The pigeon glared at me. "What's your point?"

I decided to avoid an argument. Horus was a war god. He loved to fight, but it had taken him years to defeat Set, the god of evil. And Set was small stuff next to Apophis—the primordial force of Chaos. Whacking Apophis with a sword wasn't going to work.

I thought about something Bast had said earlier, in the library.

"Would Thoth know more about shadows?" I asked.

"Probably," Horus grumbled. "Thoth isn't good for much except studying his musty old scrolls." He regarded the serpent figurine. "Funny . . . I just remembered something. Back in the old days, the Egyptians used the same word for *statue* and *shadow*, because they're both smaller copies of an object. They were both called a *sheut*."

"What are you trying to tell me?"

The pigeon ruffled its feathers. "Nothing. It just occurred to me, looking at that statue while you were talking about shadows."

An icy feeling spread between my shoulder blades.

Shadows . . . statues.

Last spring Sadie and I had watched as the old Chief Lector Desjardins cast an execration spell on Apophis. Even against minor demons, execration spells were dangerous. You're supposed to destroy a small statue of the target and, in doing so, utterly destroy the target itself, erasing it from the world. Make a mistake, and things start exploding—including the magician who cast it.

Down in the Underworld, Desjardins had used a makeshift figurine against Apophis. The Chief Lector had died casting the execration, and had only managed to push Apophis a little deeper into the Duat.

Sadie and I hoped that with a more powerful magic statue, both of us working together might be able to execrate Apophis completely, or at least throw him so deep into the Duat that he'd never return.

That was Plan B. But we knew such a powerful spell would tap so much energy, it would cost us our lives. Unless we found another way.

Statues as shadows, shadows as statues.

Plan C began forming in my mind—an idea so crazy, I didn't want to put it into words.

"Horus," I said carefully, "does Apophis have a shadow?"

The pigeon blinked its red eyes. "What a question! Why would you . . . ?" He glanced down at the red statue. "Oh . . . Oh. That's clever, actually. Certifiably insane, but clever. You think Setne's version of the Book of Overcoming Apophis, the one Apophis was so anxious to destroy . . . you think it contained a secret spell for—"

"I don't know," I said. "It's worth asking Thoth. Maybe he knows something."

"Maybe," Horus said grudgingly. "But I still think a frontal assault is the way to go."

"Of course you do."

The pigeon bobbed its head. "We are strong enough, you and I. We should combine forces, Carter. Let me share your form as I once did. We could lead the armies of gods and men and defeat the serpent. Together, we'll rule the world."

The idea might have been more tempting if I hadn't been looking at a plump bird with Cheerio dust on its plumage. Letting the pigeon rule the world sounded like a bad idea.

"I'll get back to you on that," I said. "First, I should talk to Thoth."

"Bah." Horus flapped his wings. "He's still in Memphis, at that ridiculous sports stadium of his. But if you plan on seeing him, I wouldn't wait too long."

"Why not?"

"That's what I came to tell you," Horus said. "Matters are getting complicated among the gods. Apophis is dividing us, attacking us one by one, just as he's doing with you magicians. Thoth was the first to suffer."

"Suffer . . . how?"

The pigeon puffed up. A wisp of smoke curled from its beak. "Oh, dear. My host is self-destructing. It can't hold my spirit for much longer. Just hurry, Carter. I'm having trouble keeping the gods together, and that old man Ra isn't helping our morale. If you and I don't lead our armies soon, we may not have any armies left to lead."

"But—"

The pigeon hiccupped another wisp of smoke. "Gotta go. Good luck."

Horus flew out the window, leaving me alone with the statuette of Apophis and a few gray feathers.

I slept like a mummy. That was the good part. The bad part was that Bast let me sleep until the afternoon.

"Why didn't you wake me up?" I demanded. "I've got things to do!"

Bast spread her hands. "Sadie insisted. You had a rough

night last night. She said you needed your rest. Besides, I'm a cat. I respect the sanctity of sleep."

I was still mad, but part of me knew Sadie was right. I'd expended a lot of magical energy the previous night and had gone to sleep really late. Maybe—just maybe—Sadie had my best interests at heart.

(I just caught her making faces at me, so maybe not.)

I showered and dressed. By the time the other kids got back from school, I was feeling almost human again.

Yes, I said *school*, as in normal old school. We'd spent last spring tutoring all the initiates at Brooklyn House, but with the start of the fall semester, Bast had decided that the kids could use a dose of regular mortal life. Now they went to a nearby academy in Brooklyn during the day and learned magic in the afternoons and on weekends.

I was the only one who stayed behind. I'd *always* been homeschooled. The idea of dealing with lockers, schedules, textbooks, and cafeteria food on top of running the Twenty-first Nome was just too much for me.

You'd think the other kids would have complained, especially Sadie. But, in fact, attending school was working out okay for them. The girls were happy to have more friends (and less dorky boys to flirt with, they claimed). The guys could play sports with actual teams rather than one-on-one with Khufu using Egyptian statues for hoops. As for Bast, she was happy to have a quiet house so she could stretch out on the floor and snooze in the sunlight.

At any rate, by the time the others got home, I'd done a lot of thinking about my conversations with Zia and Horus. The plan I'd formulated last night still seemed crazy, but I decided that it might be our best shot. After briefing Sadie and Bast, who (disturbingly) agreed with me, we decided it was time to tell the rest of our friends.

We gathered for dinner on the main terrace. It's a nice place to eat, with invisible barriers that keep out the wind, and a great view of the East River and Manhattan. The food magically appeared, and it was always tasty. Still, I dreaded eating on the terrace. For nine months we'd had all our important meetings there. I'd come to associate sit-down dinners with disasters.

We filled up our plates from the buffet as our guardian albino crocodile Philip of Macedonia splashed happily in his swimming pool. Eating next to a twenty-foot-long crocodile took some getting used to, but Philip was well trained. He only ate bacon, stray waterfowl, and the occasional invading monster.

Bast sat at the head of the table with a can of Purina Fancy Feast. Sadie and I sat together at the opposite end. Khufu was off babysitting the ankle-biters, and some of our newer recruits were inside doing their homework or catching up on spell crafting, but most of our main people were present—a dozen senior initiates.

Considering how badly last night had turned out, everyone seemed in strangely good spirits. I was kind of glad they didn't yet know about Sarah Jacobi's video death threat. Julian kept bouncing in his chair and grinning for no particular reason.

Cleo and Jaz were whispering together and giggling. Even Felix seemed to have recovered from his shock in Dallas. He was sculpting tiny *shabti* penguins out of his mashed potatoes and bringing them to life.

Only Walt looked glum. The big guy had nothing on his dinner plate except three carrots and a wedge of Jell-O. (Khufu insisted Jell-O had major healing properties.) Judging from the tightness around Walt's eyes and the stiffness of his movements, I guessed his pain was even worse than last night.

I turned to Sadie. "What's going on? Everybody seems . . . distracted."

She stared at me. "I keep forgetting you don't go to school. Carter, it's the first dance tonight! Three other schools will be there. We *can* hurry up the meeting, can't we?"

"You're kidding," I said. "I'm thinking about plans for Doomsday, and you're worried about being late to a dance?"

"I've mentioned it to you a dozen times," she insisted. "Besides, we need something to boost our spirits. Now, tell everyone your plan. Some of us still have to decide what to wear."

I wanted to argue, but the others were looking at me expectantly.

I cleared my throat. "Okay. I know there's a dance, but—"

"At seven," Jaz said. "You *are* coming, right?"

She smiled at me. Was she . . . flirting?

(Sadie just called me dense. Hey, I had other things on my mind.)

"Uh . . . so anyway," I stammered. "We need to talk about

what happened in Dallas, and what happens next."

That killed the mood. The smiles faded. My friends listened as I reviewed our mission to the Fifty-first Nome, the destruction of the Book of Overcoming Apophis, and the retrieval of the shadow box. I told them about Sarah Jacobi's demand for my surrender, and the turmoil among the gods that Horus had mentioned.

Sadie stepped in. She explained her weird encounter with the face in the wall, two gods, and our ghost mother. She shared her gut feeling that our best chance to defeat Apophis had something to do with shadows.

Cleo raised her hand. "So . . . the rebel magicians have a death warrant out for you. The gods can't help us. Apophis could arise at any time, and the last scroll that might've helped us to defeat him has been destroyed. But we shouldn't worry, because we have an empty box and a vague hunch about shadows."

"Why, Cleo," Bast said with admiration. "You have a catty side!"

I pressed my hands against the surface of the table. It would've taken very little effort to summon the strength of Horus and smash it to kindling. But I doubted that would help my reputation as a calm, collected leader.

"This is more than a vague hunch," I said. "Look, you've all learned about execration spells, right?"

Our crocodile, Philip, grunted. He slapped the pool with his tail and made it rain on our dinner. Magical creatures are a little sensitive about the word *execration*.

Julian dabbed the water off his grilled cheese sandwich.

"Dude, you can't execrate Apophis. He's *massive*. Desjardins tried it and got killed."

"I know," I said. "With a standard execration, you destroy a statue that represents the enemy. But what if you could crank up the spell by destroying a more powerful representation—something more connected to Apophis?"

Walt sat forward, suddenly interested. "His shadow?"

Felix was so startled he dropped his spoon, crushing one of his mashed-potato penguins. "Wait, what?"

"I got the idea from Horus," I said. "He told me statues were called shadows in ancient times."

"But that was just, like, symbolic," Alyssa said. "Wasn't it?"

Bast set down her empty Fancy Feast can. She still looked nervous about the whole topic of shadows, but when I'd explained to her that it was either this or Sadie and me dying, she'd agreed to support us.

"Maybe not," the cat goddess said. "I'm no expert on execration, mind you. Nasty business. But it's possible that a statue used for execration was originally meant to represent the target's shadow, which is an important part of the soul."

"So," Sadie said, "we could cast an execration spell on Apophis, but instead of destroying a statue, we could destroy his actual shadow. Brilliant, eh?"

"That's nuts," Julian said. "How do you destroy a shadow?"

Walt shooed a mashed-potato penguin away from his Jell-O. "It's not nuts. Sympathetic magic is all about using a small copy to manipulate the actual target. It's possible the whole tradition of making little statues to represent people and gods—maybe at one time those statues actually *contained* the target's *sheut*. There are lots of stories about the souls of the gods inhabiting statues. If a shadow was trapped in a statue, you might be able to destroy it."

"Could you make a statue like that?" Alyssa asked. "Something that could bind the shadow of . . . of Apophis himself?"

"Maybe." Walt glanced at me. Most of the folks at the table didn't know we'd already made a statue of Apophis that might work for that purpose. "Even if I could, we'd need to find the shadow. Then we'd need some pretty advanced magic to capture it and destroy it."

"Find a shadow?" Felix smiled nervously, like he hoped we were joking. "Wouldn't it be right *under* him? And how do you capture it? Step on it? Shine a light on it?"

"It'll be more complicated than that," I said. "This ancient magician Setne, the guy who wrote his own version of the Book of Overcoming Apophis, I think he must have created a spell to catch and destroy shadows. That's why Apophis was so anxious to burn the evidence. That's his secret weakness."

"But the scroll is gone," Cleo said.

"There's still someone we can ask," Walt said. "Thoth. If anyone knows the answers, he will."

The tension around the table seemed to ease. At least we'd given our initiates something to hope for, even if it was a long shot. I was grateful we had Walt on our side. His charm-making ability might be our only hope of binding a shadow to the statue, and his vote of confidence carried weight with the other kids.

"We need to visit Thoth right away," I said. "Tonight."

"Yes," Sadie agreed. "Right after the dance."

I glared at her. "You aren't serious."

"Oh, yes, brother dear." She smiled mischievously, and for a second I was afraid she might invoke my secret name and force me to obey. "We're attending the dance tonight. And you're coming with us."

5. A Dance with Death

CHEERS, CARTER. At least you have the sense to hand me the microphone for *important* things.

Honestly, he drones on and on about his plans for the Apocalypse, but he makes no plans at all for the school dance. My brother's priorities are severely skewed.

I don't think I was being selfish wanting to go to the dance. Of *course* we had serious business to deal with. That's exactly why I insisted on partying first. Our initiates needed a morale boost. They needed a chance to be normal kids, to have friends and lives outside Brooklyn House—something worth fighting for. Even armies in the field fight better when they take breaks for entertainment. I'm sure some general somewhere has said that.

By sunset, I was ready to lead my troops into battle. I'd picked out quite a nice black strapless dress and put black lowlights in my blond hair, with just a touch of dark makeup for

77

that risen-from-the-grave look. I wore simple flats for dancing (despite what Carter says, I do not wear combat boots all the time; just ninety percent of the time), the silver *tyet* amulet from my mother's jewelry box, and the pendant Walt had given me for my last birthday with the Egyptian symbol of eternity, *shen*.

Walt had an identical amulet among his own collection of talismans, which provided us a magic line of communication, and even the ability to summon the other person to our side in emergencies.

Unfortunately, the *shen* amulets didn't mean we were dating exclusively. Or even dating at all. If Walt had *asked* me, I think I would've been fine with it. Walt was so kind and gorgeous—perfect, really, in his own way. Perhaps if he'd asserted himself a bit more, I would've fallen for him and been able to let go of that *other* boy, the godly one.

But Walt was dying. He had this silly idea that it would be unfair to me if we started a relationship under those circumstances. As if that would stop me. So we were stuck in this maddening limbo—flirting, talking for hours, a few times even sharing a kiss when we let our guard down—but eventually Walt would always pull away and shut me out.

Why couldn't things be simple?

I bring this up because I literally ran into Walt as I was coming down the stairs.

"Oh!" I said. Then I noticed he was still wearing his old muscle shirt, jeans, and no shoes. "You're not ready yet?"

"I'm not going," he announced.

My mouth fell open. "What? Why?"

"Sadie . . . you and Carter will need me when you visit Thoth. If I'm going to make it, I have to rest."

"But . . ." I forced myself to stop. It wasn't right for me to pressure him. I didn't need magic to see that he really was in great pain.

Centuries of magical healing knowledge at our disposal, yet nothing we tried seemed to help Walt. I ask you: What's the point of being a magician if you can't wave your wand and make the people you care about feel better?

"Right," I said. "I—I was just hoping . . ."

Anything I said would've sounded bratty. I wanted to dance with him. Gods of Egypt, I'd *dressed up* for him. The mortal boys at school were all right, I suppose, but they seemed quite shallow compared to Walt (or, yes, fine—compared to Anubis). As for the other boys of Brooklyn House—dancing with them would have made me feel a bit odd, like I was dancing with my cousins.

"I could stay," I offered, but I suppose I didn't sound very convincing.

Walt managed a faint smile. "No, go, Sadie. Really. I'm sure I'll be feeling better when you get back. Have a good time."

He brushed past me and climbed the steps.

I took several deep breaths. Part of me did want to stay and look after him. Going without him didn't seem right.

Then I glanced down into the Great Room. The older kids were joking and talking, ready to leave. If *I* didn't go, they might feel obliged to stay too.

Something like wet cement settled in my stomach. All the joy and excitement suddenly went out of the evening for me. For months I'd been struggling to adjust to life in New York after so many years in London. I'd been forced to balance life as a young magician with the challenges of being an ordinary schoolgirl. Now, just when this dance had seemed to offer me a chance to combine both worlds and have a lovely night out, my hopes were dashed. I'd still have to go and pretend to have fun. But I'd only be doing it out of duty, to make the others feel better.

I wondered if this was what being a grown-up felt like. Horrible.

The only thing that cheered me up was Carter. He emerged from his room dressed like a junior professor, in a coat and tie, button-down shirt, and trousers. Poor boy—of course he'd never been to a dance any more than he'd been to school. He had no clue whatsoever.

"You look . . . wonderful." I tried to keep a straight face. "You do realize it's not a funeral?"

"Shut up," he grumbled. "Let's get this over with."

The school the kids and I attended was Brooklyn Academy for the Gifted. Everyone called it BAG. We had no end of jokes about this. The students were Baggies. The glamour girls with nose jobs and Botox lips were Plastic Bags. Our alumni were Old Bags. And, naturally, our headmistress, Mrs. Laird, was the Bag Lady.

Despite the name, the school was quite nice. All the

students were gifted in some sort of art, music, or drama. Our schedules were flexible, with lots of independent study time, which worked perfectly for us magicians. We could pop off to battle monsters as needed; and, as magicians, it wasn't difficult for us to pass ourselves off as gifted. Alyssa used her earth magic to make sculptures. Walt specialized in jewelry. Cleo was an amazing writer, since she could retell stories that had been forgot since the days of Ancient Egypt. As for me, I needed no magic. I was a natural at drama.

[Stop laughing, Carter.]

You might not expect this in the middle of Brooklyn, but our campus was like a park, with acres of green lawns, well-tended trees and hedges, even a small lake with ducks and swans.

The dance was held in the pavilion in front of the administration building. A band played in the gazebo. Lights were strung in the trees. Teacher chaperones walked the perimeter on "bush patrol," making sure none of the older students sneaked off into the shrubbery.

I tried not to think about it, but the music and crowd reminded me of Dallas the night before—a very different sort of party, which had ended badly. I remembered JD Grissom clasping my hand, wishing me luck before he ran off to save his wife.

Horrible guilt welled inside me. I forced it down. It wouldn't do the Grissoms any good for me to start crying in the middle of the dance. It certainly wouldn't help my friends enjoy themselves.

As our group dispersed into the crowd, I turned to Carter, who was fiddling with his tie.

"Right," I said. "You need to dance."

Carter looked at me in horror. "What?"

I called over one of my mortal friends, a lovely girl named Lacy. She was a year younger than I, so she looked up to me greatly. (I know, it's hard not to.) She had cute blond pigtails, a mouthful of braces, and was possibly the only person at the dance *more* nervous than my brother. She'd seen pictures of Carter before, however, and seemed to find him *hot*. I didn't hold that against her. In most ways, she had excellent taste.

"Lacy—Carter," I introduced them.

"You look like your pictures!" Lacy grinned. The bands of her braces were alternating pink and white to match her dress.

Carter said, "Uh—"

"He doesn't know how to dance," I told Lacy. "I'd be ever so grateful if you'd teach him."

"Sure!" she squealed. She grabbed my brother's hand and swept him away.

I started to feel better. Perhaps I could have fun tonight, after all.

Then I turned and found myself face-to-face with one of my *not*-so-favorite mortals—Drew Tanaka, head of the popular girl clique, with her supermodel goon squad in tow.

"Sadie!" Drew threw her arm around me. Her perfume was a mixture of roses and tear gas. "So glad you're here, sweetie. If I'd known you were coming, you could've ridden in the limo with us!"

Her friends made sympathetic "Aww" sounds and grinned to show they were not at all sincere. They were dressed more or less the same, in the latest silky designer bits their parents had no doubt commissioned for them during the last Fashion Week. Drew was the tallest and most glamorous (I use the word as an insult) with awful pink eyeliner and frizzy black curls that were apparently Drew's own personal crusade to bring back the 1980s perm. She wore a pendant—a glittering platinum and diamond *D*—possibly her initial, or her grade average.

I gave her a tight smile. "A limo, wow. Thanks for that. But between you, your friends, and your egos, I doubt there would've been extra room."

Drew pouted. "That's not nice, hon! Where is Walt? Is the poor baby still sick?"

Behind her, some of the girls coughed into their fists, mimicking Walt.

I wanted to pull my staff from the Duat and turn them all into worms for the ducks. I was pretty sure I could manage that, and I doubted anyone would miss them, but I kept my temper.

Lacy had warned me about Drew the first day of school. Apparently the two of them had gone to some summer camp together—blah, blah, I didn't really listen to the details—and Drew had been just as much of a tyrant there.

That did not, however, mean she could be a tyrant with *me*.

"Walt's at home," I said. "I *did* tell him you'd be here. Funny, that didn't seem to motivate him much."

"What a shame," Drew sighed. "You know, maybe he's not really sick. He might just be allergic to you, hon. That does happen. I should go to his place with some chicken soup or something. Where does he live?"

She smiled sweetly. I didn't know if she actually fancied Walt or if she just pretended because she hated me. Either way, the idea of turning her into an earthworm was becoming more appealing.

Before I could do anything rash, a familiar voice behind me said, "Hello, Sadie."

The other girls let out a collective gasp. My pulse quickened from "slow walk" to "fifty-meter dash." I turned and found that—yes, indeed—the god Anubis had crashed our dance.

He had the nerve to look amazing, as usual. He's *so* annoying that way. He wore skinny black trousers with black leather boots, and a biker's jacket over an Arcade Fire T-shirt. His dark hair was naturally disheveled as if he'd just woken up, and I fought the urge to run my fingers through it. His brown eyes glittered with amusement. Either he was happy to see me, or he enjoyed seeing me flustered.

"Oh . . . my . . . god," Drew whimpered. "Who . . ."

Anubis ignored her (bless him for that) and held out his elbow for me—a sweet old-fashioned gesture. "May I have this dance?"

"I suppose," I said, as noncommittally as I could.

I looped my arm through his, and we left the Plastic Bags behind us, all of them muttering, "Oh my god! Oh my god!"

No, actually, I wanted to say. *He's my amazingly hot boy god. Find your own.*

The uneven paving stones made for a dangerous dance floor. All around us, kids were tripping over each other. Anubis didn't help matters, as all the girls turned and gawked at him as he led me through the crowd.

I was glad Anubis had my arm. My emotions were so jumbled, I felt dizzy. I was ridiculously happy that he was here. I felt crushingly guilty that poor Walt was at home alone while I strolled arm in arm with Anubis. But I was relieved that Walt and Anubis weren't both here together. That would've been *beyond* awkward. The relief made me feel guiltier, and so on. Gods of Egypt, I was a mess.

As we reached the middle of the dance floor, the band suddenly switched from a dance number to a love ballad.

"Was that your doing?" I asked Anubis.

He smiled, which wasn't much of an answer. He put one hand on my hip and clasped my other hand, like a proper gentleman. We swayed together.

I'd heard of dancing on air, but it took me a few steps to realize we were actually levitating—a few millimeters off the ground, not enough for anyone to notice, just enough for us to glide across the stones while others stumbled.

A few meters away, Carter looked quite awkward as Lacy showed him how to slow-dance. [Really, Carter, it isn't quantum physics.]

I gazed up at Anubis's warm brown eyes and his exquisite lips. He'd kissed me once—for my birthday, last spring—and I'd never quite got over it. You'd think a god of death would have cold lips, but that wasn't the case at all.

I tried to clear my head. I knew Anubis must be here for

some reason, but it was awfully hard to focus.

"I thought . . . Um," I gulped and barely managed not to drool on myself.

Oh, brilliant, Sadie, I thought. *Let's try for a complete sentence, now, shall we?*

"I thought you could only appear in places of death," I said.

Anubis laughed gently. "This *is* a place of death, Sadie. The Battle of Brooklyn Heights, 1776. Hundreds of American and British troops died right where we're dancing."

"How romantic," I muttered. "So we're dancing on their graves?"

Anubis shook his head. "Most never received proper burials. That's why I decided to visit you here. These ghosts could use a night of entertainment, just like your initiates."

Suddenly, spirits were twirling all around us—luminous apparitions in eighteenth-century clothes. Some wore the red uniforms of British regulars. Others had ragtag militia outfits. They pirouetted with lady ghosts in plain farm dresses or fancy silk. A few of the posh women had piles of curly hair that would have made even Drew jealous. The ghosts seemed to be dancing to a different song. I strained my ears and could faintly hear violins and a cello.

None of the regular mortals seemed to notice the spectral invasion. Even my friends from Brooklyn House were oblivious. I watched as a ghostly couple waltzed straight through Carter and Lacy. As Anubis and I danced, Brooklyn Academy seemed to fade and the ghosts became more real.

One soldier had a musket wound in his chest. A British

officer had a tomahawk sticking out of his powdered wig. We danced between worlds, waltzing side by side with smiling, gruesomely slaughtered phantoms. Anubis certainly knew how to show a girl a good time.

"You're doing it again," I said. "Taking me out of phase, or whatever you call it."

"A little," he admitted. "We need privacy to talk. I promised you I'd visit in person—"

"And you did."

"—but it's going to cause trouble. This may be the last time I can see you. There's been grumbling about our situation."

I narrowed my eyes. Was the god of the dead blushing?

"Our situation," I repeated.

"Us."

The word set my ears buzzing. I tried to keep my voice even. "As far as I'm aware, there *is* no official 'us.' Why would this be the last time we can talk?"

He was definitely blushing now. "Please, just listen. There's so much I need to tell you. Your brother has the right idea. The shadow of Apophis is your best hope, but only one person can teach you the magic you need. Thoth may guide you somewhat, but I doubt he'll reveal the secret spells. It's too dangerous."

"Hold on, hold on." I was still reeling from the comment about *us*. And the idea that this might be the last time I saw Anubis. . . . That sent my brain cells into panic mode, thousands of tiny Sadies running around in my skull, screaming and waving their arms.

I tried to focus. "You mean Apophis *does* have a shadow? It could be used to execrate—"

"Please don't use that word." Anubis grimaced. "But yes, all intelligent entities have souls, so all of them have shadows, even Apophis. I know this much, being the guide of the dead. I have to make souls my business. Could his shadow be used against him? In theory, yes. But there are many dangers."

"Naturally."

Anubis twirled me through a pair of colonial ghosts. Other students watched us, whispering as we danced, but their voices sounded distant and distorted, as if they were on the far side of a waterfall.

Anubis studied me with a sort of tender regret. "Sadie, I wouldn't set you on this path if there was another way. I don't want you to die."

"I can agree with that," I said.

"Even *talking* about this sort of magic is forbidden," he warned. "But you need to know what you're dealing with. The *sheut* is the least understood part of the soul. It's . . . how to explain . . . a soul of last resort, an afterimage of the person's life force. You've heard that the souls of the wicked are destroyed in the Hall of Judgment—"

"When Ammit devours their hearts," I said.

"Yes." Anubis lowered his voice. "We say that this completely destroys the soul. But that's not true. The shadow lingers. Occasionally, not often, Osiris has decided to, ah, *review* a judgment. If someone was found guilty, but new evidence comes to light, there must be a way to retrieve a soul from oblivion."

I tried to grasp that. My thoughts felt suspended in midair like my feet, not able to connect with anything solid. "So . . . you're saying the shadow could be used to, um, *reboot* a soul? Like a computer's backup drive?"

Anubis looked at me strangely.

"Ugh, I'm sorry." I sighed. "I've been spending too much time with my geeky brother. He speaks like a computer."

"No, no," Anubis said. "It's actually a good analogy. I'd just never thought of it that way. Yes, the soul isn't completely destroyed until the shadow is destroyed, so in extreme cases, with the right magic, it's possible to reboot the soul using the *sheut*. Conversely, if you were to destroy a god's shadow, or even Apophis's shadow as part of an ex—um, the sort of spell you mentioned—"

"The *sheut* would be infinitely more powerful than a regular statue," I guessed. "We could destroy him, possibly without destroying ourselves."

Anubis glanced around us nervously. "Yes, but you can see why this sort of magic is secret. The gods would never want such knowledge in the hands of a mortal magician. This is w hy we always hide our shadows. If a magician were able to capture a god's *sheut* and use it to threaten us—"

"Right." My mouth felt dry. "But I'm on your side. I'd only use the spell on Apophis. Surely Thoth will understand that."

"Perhaps." Anubis didn't sound convinced. "Start with Thoth, at least. Hopefully he'll see the need to assist you. I fear, though, you may still need better guidance—more *dangerous* guidance."

I gulped. "You said only one person could teach us the magic. Who?"

"The only magician crazy enough to ever research such a spell. His trial is tomorrow at sunset. You'll have to visit your father before then."

"Wait. What?"

Wind blew through the pavilion. Anubis's hand tightened on mine.

"We have to hurry," he said. "There's more I need to tell you. Something is happening with the spirits of dead. They're being . . . Look, there!"

He pointed to a pair of nearby specters. The woman danced barefoot in a simple white linen dress. The man wore breeches and a frock coat like a Colonial farmer, but his neck was canted at a funny angle, as if he'd been hanged. Black mist coiled around the man's legs like ivy. Another three waltz steps, and he was completely engulfed. The murky tendrils pulled him into the ground, and he disappeared. The woman in white kept dancing by herself, apparently unaware that her partner had been consumed by evil fingers of smog.

"What—what was *that?*" I asked.

"We don't know," Anubis said. "As Apophis grows stronger, it's happening more frequently. Souls of the dead are disappearing, being drawn farther down into the Duat. We don't know where they're going."

I almost stumbled. "My mother. Is she all right?"

Anubis gave me a pained look, and I knew the answer. Mum had warned me—we might never see her again unless we discovered a way to defeat Apophis. She'd sent me that message urging me to find the serpent's shadow. It *had* to be connected to her dilemma somehow.

"She's missing," I guessed. My heart pounded against my ribs. "It's got something to do with this business about shadows, hasn't it?"

"Sadie, I wish I knew. Your father is—he's trying his best to find her, but—"

The wind interrupted him.

Have you ever stuck your hand out of a moving car and felt the air push against you? It was a bit like that, but ten times more powerful. A wedge of force pushed Anubis and me apart. I staggered backward, my feet no longer levitating.

"Sadie . . ." Anubis reached out, but the wind pushed him farther away.

"Stop that!" said a squeaky voice between us. "No public displays of affection on *my* watch!"

The air took on human form. At first it was just a faint silhouette. Then it became more solid and colorful. Before me stood a man in an old-fashioned aviator's outfit—leather helmet, goggles, scarf, and a bomber's jacket, like photos I'd seen of the Royal Air Force pilots during World War II. He wasn't flesh and blood, though. His form swirled and shifted. I realized he was put together from blown rubbish: specks of dirt, scraps of paper, bits of dandelion fuzz, dried leaves—all churning about, but held together in such a tight collage by the wind that from a distance he might have passed for a normal mortal.

He wagged his finger at Anubis. "This is the final insult, boy!" His voice hissed like air from a balloon. "You have been warned *numerous* times."

"Hold on!" I said. "Who are you? And Anubis is hardly a boy. He's five thousand years old."

"Exactly," the aviator snapped. "A mere child. And I didn't give you permission to speak, girl!"

The aviator exploded. The blast was so powerful, my ears popped and I fell on my bum. Around me, the other mortals— my friends, teachers, and all the students—simply collapsed. Anubis and the ghosts seemed unaffected. The aviator formed again, glaring down at me.

I struggled to my feet and tried to summon my staff from the Duat. No such luck.

"What have you done?" I demanded.

"Sadie, it's all right," Anubis said. "Your friends are only unconscious. Shu just lowered the air pressure."

"Shoe?" I demanded. "Shoe who?"

Anubis pressed his fingers to his temples. "Sadie . . . this is Shu, my great-grandfather."

Then it struck me: Shu was one of those ridiculous godly names I'd heard before. I tried to place it. "Ah. The god of . . . flip-flops. No, wait. Leaky balloons. No—"

"Air!" Shu hissed. "God of the air!"

His body dissolved into a tornado of debris. When he formed again, he was in Ancient Egyptian costume—bare-chested with a white loincloth and a giant ostrich feather sprouting from his braided headband.

He changed back into RAF clothes.

"Stick with the pilot's outfit," I said. "The ostrich feather really doesn't work for you."

Shu made an unfriendly whooshing sound. "I'd *prefer* to be invisible, thank you very much. But you mortals have polluted the air so badly, it's getting harder and harder. It's *dreadful* what you've done, the last few millennia! Haven't you people heard of 'Spare the Air' days? Carpooling? Hybrid engines? And don't get me started on cows. Did you know that every cow belches and farts over a hundred gallons of methane a day? There are one and a half billion cows in the world. Do you have *any* idea what that does to my respiratory system?"

"Uh . . ."

From his jacket pocket, Shu produced an inhaler and puffed on it. "Shocking!"

I raised an eyebrow at Anubis, who looked mortally embarrassed (or perhaps immortally embarrassed).

"Shu," he said. "We were just talking. If you'll let us finish—"

"Oh, *talking*!" Shu bellowed, no doubt releasing his own share of methane. "While holding hands, and dancing, and other degenerate behavior. Don't play innocent, boy. I've been a chaperone before, you know. I kept your grandparents apart for eons."

Suddenly I remembered the story of Nut and Geb, the sky and earth. Ra had commanded Nut's father, Shu, to keep the two lovers apart so they would never have children who might someday usurp Ra's throne. That strategy hadn't worked, but apparently Shu was still trying.

The air god waved his hand in disgust at the unconscious

mortals, some of whom were just starting to groan and stir. "And now, Anubis, I find you in this den of iniquity, this morass of questionable behavior, this . . . this—"

"School?" I suggested.

"Yes!" Shu nodded so vigorously, his head disintegrated into a cloud of leaves. "You heard the decree of the gods, boy. You've become *entirely* too close to this mortal. You are hereby banned from further contact!"

"What?" I shouted. "That's ridiculous! Who decreed this?"

Shu made a sound like a blown-out tire. Either he was laughing or giving me a windy raspberry. "The entire council, girl! Led by Lord Horus and Lady Isis!"

I felt as if I were dissolving into scraps of rubbish myself.

Isis and Horus? I couldn't believe it. Stabbed in the back by my two supposed friends. Isis and I were going to have words about this.

I turned to Anubis, hoping he'd tell me it was a lie.

He raised his hands miserably. "Sadie, I was trying to tell you. Gods are not allowed to become directly . . . um, *involved* with mortals. That's only possible when a god inhabits a human form, and . . . and as you know, I've never worked that way."

I gritted my teeth. I wanted to argue that Anubis had quite a *nice* form, but he'd told me often that he could only manifest in dreams, or in places of death. Unlike other gods, he'd never taken a human host.

It was so bloody *unfair*. We hadn't even dated properly. One kiss six months ago, and Anubis was grounded from seeing me forever?

"You can't be serious." I'm not sure who made me angrier—the fussy air god chaperone or Anubis himself. "You're not really going to let them rule you like this?"

"He has no choice!" Shu cried. The effort made him cough so badly, his chest exploded into dandelion fluff. He took another blast from his inhaler. "Brooklyn ozone levels—deplorable! Now, off with you, Anubis. No more contact with this mortal. It is *not* proper. And as for you, girl, stay away from him! You have more important things to do."

"Oh, yes?" I said. "And what about you, Mr. Trash Tornado? We're preparing for war, and the most important thing you can do is keep people from waltzing?"

The air pressure rose suddenly. Blood roared in my head.

"See here, girl," Shu growled. "I've already helped you more than you deserve. I heeded that Russian boy's prayer. I brought him here all the way from St. Petersburg to speak with you. So, shoo!"

The wind blasted me backward. The ghosts blew away like smoke. The unconscious mortals began to stir, shielding their faces from the debris.

"Russian boy?" I shouted over the gale. "What on earth are you talking about?"

Shu disbanded into rubbish and swirled around Anubis, lifting him off his feet.

"Sadie!" Anubis tried to fight his way toward me, but the storm was too strong. "Shu, at least let me tell her about Walt! She has a right to know!"

I could barely hear him above the wind. "Did you say, *Walt?*" I shouted. "What about him?"

Anubis said something I couldn't make out. Then the flurry of debris completely obscured him.

When the wind died, both gods were gone. I stood alone on the dance floor, surrounded by dozens of kids and adults who were starting to wake up.

I was about to run to Carter to make sure he was all right. [Yes, Carter, honestly I was.]

Then, at the edge of the pavilion, a young man stepped into the light.

He wore a gray military outfit with a wool coat too heavy for the warm September night. His enormous ears seemed to be the only things holding up his oversized hat. A rifle was slung across his shoulder. He couldn't have been more than seventeen; and though he was definitely not from any of the schools at the dance, he looked vaguely familiar.

St. Petersburg, Shu had said.

Yes. I'd met this boy briefly last spring. Carter and I had been running from the Hermitage Museum. This boy had tried to stop us. He'd been disguised as a guard, but revealed himself as a magician from the Russian nome—one of the servants of the evil Vlad Menshikov.

I grabbed my staff from the Duat—successfully this time. The boy raised his hands in surrender.

"Nyet!" he pleaded. Then, in halting English, he said: "Sadie Kane. We . . . need . . . to talk."

6. Amos Plays with Action Figures

HIS NAME WAS LEONID, and we agreed not to kill each other.

We sat on the steps of the gazebo and talked while the students and teachers struggled to wake up around us.

Leonid's English was not good. My Russian was nonexistent, but I understood enough of his story to be alarmed. He'd escaped the Russian nome and somehow convinced Shu to whisk him here to find me. Leonid remembered me from our invasion of the Hermitage. Apparently I'd made a strong impression on the young man. No surprise. I am rather memorable.

[Oh, stop laughing, Carter.]

Using words, hand gestures, and sound effects, Leonid tried to explain what had happened in St. Petersburg since the death of Vlad Menshikov. I couldn't follow it all, but this much I understood: *Kwai, Jacobi, Apophis, First Nome, many deaths, soon, very soon.*

Teachers began corralling students and calling parents. Apparently they feared the mass blackout might have been caused by bad punch or hazardous gas (Drew's perfume, perhaps) and they'd decided to evacuate the area. I suspected we'd have police and paramedics on the scene shortly. I wanted to be gone before then.

I dragged Leonid over to meet my brother, who was stumbling around, rubbing his eyes.

"What happened?" Carter asked. He scowled at Leonid. "Who—?"

I gave him the one-minute version: Anubis's visit, Shu's intervention, the Russian's appearance. "Leonid has information about an impending attack on the First Nome," I said. "The rebels will be after him."

Carter scratched his head. "You want to hide him at Brooklyn House?"

"No," I said. "I've got to take him to Amos straightaway."

Leonid choked. "Amos? He turn into Set—eat face?"

"Amos will *not* eat your face," I assured him. "Jacobi's been telling you stories."

Leonid still looked uneasy. "Amos not become Set?"

How to explain without making it sound worse? I didn't know the correct Russian for: *He was possessed by Set but it wasn't his fault, and he's much better now.*

"No Set," I said. "Good Amos."

Carter studied the Russian. He looked at me with concern. "Sadie, what if this is a trap? You *trust* this guy?"

"Oh, I can handle Leonid. He doesn't want me to morph him into a banana slug, do you, Leonid?"

"*Nyet*," Leonid said solemnly. "No banana slug."

"There, you see?"

"What about visiting Thoth?" Carter asked. "That can't wait."

I saw the worry in his eyes. I imagined he was thinking the same thing I was: our mum was in trouble. The spirits of the dead were disappearing, and it had something to do with the shadow of Apophis. We had to find the connection.

"You visit Thoth," I said. "Take Walt. And, uh, keep an eye on him, all right? Anubis wanted to tell me something about him, but there wasn't time. And in Dallas, when I looked at Walt in the Duat . . ."

I couldn't make myself finish. Just thinking about Walt wrapped in mummy linen brought tears to my eyes.

Fortunately, Carter seemed to get the general idea. "I'll keep him safe," he promised. "How will you get to Egypt?"

I pondered that. Leonid had apparently flown here via Shu Airways, but I doubted that fussy aviator god would be willing to help me, and I didn't want to ask.

"We'll risk a portal," I said. "I know they've been a bit wonky, but it's just one quick jump. What could go wrong?"

"You could materialize inside a wall," Carter said. "Or wind up scattered through the Duat in a million pieces."

"Why, Carter, you care! But really, we'll be fine. And we haven't got much choice."

I gave him a quick hug—I know, horribly sentimental, but I wanted to show solidarity. Then, before I could change my mind, I took Leonid's hand and raced across campus.

My head was still spinning from my talk with Anubis.

How dare Isis and Horus keep us apart when we weren't even together! And what had Anubis wanted to tell me about Walt? Perhaps he'd wanted to end our ill-fated relationship and give his blessing for me to date Walt. (Lame.) Or perhaps he wanted to declare his undying love and fight Walt for my affections. (Highly unlikely, nor would I appreciate being fought over like a basketball.) Or perhaps—most probable—he'd wanted to break some bad news.

Anubis had visited Walt on several occasions that I knew of. They'd both been rather tight-lipped about what was discussed, but since Anubis was the guide of the dead, I assumed he'd been preparing Walt for death. Anubis might have wanted to warn me that the time was nigh—as if I needed another reminder.

Anubis: off-limits. Walt: at death's door. If I lost both of the guys I liked, well . . . there wasn't much point in saving the world.

All right, that was a *slight* exaggeration. But only slight.

On top of that, my mum was in trouble, and Sarah Jacobi's rebels were planning some horrible attack on my uncle's headquarters.

Why, then, did I feel so . . . *hopeful?*

An idea started to tug at me—a tiny glimmer of possibility. It wasn't just the prospect that we might find a way to defeat the serpent. Anubis's words kept playing in my mind: *The shadow lingers. There must be a way to retrieve a soul from oblivion.*

If a shadow could be used to bring back a mortal soul that had been destroyed, could it do the same for a god?

I was so lost in thought, I barely noticed when we reached the fine arts building. Leonid stopped me.

"This for portal?" He pointed to a block of carved limestone in the courtyard.

"Yes," I said. "Thanks."

Long story short: when I started at BAG, I reckoned it would be good to have an Egyptian relic close by for emergencies. So I did the logical thing: I borrowed a chunk of limestone frieze from the nearby Brooklyn Museum. Honestly, the museum had enough rocks. I didn't think they'd miss this one.

I'd left a facsimile in its place and asked Alyssa to present the actual Egyptian frieze to her art teacher as her class project—an attempt to simulate an ancient art form. The teacher had been duly impressed. He'd installed "Alyssa's" artwork in the courtyard outside his classroom. The carving showed mourners at a funeral, which I thought appropriate for a school setting.

It wasn't a powerful or important piece of art, but all relics of Ancient Egypt have some amount of power, like magical batteries. With the right training, a magician can use them to jump-start spells that would otherwise be impossible, such as opening portals.

I'd got rather good at this particular magic. Leonid watched my back as I began to chant.

Most magicians wait for "auspicious moments" to open gates. They spend years memorizing a timetable of important anniversaries like the time of day each god was born, the alignment of the stars, and whatnot. I suppose I should have worried about such things, but I didn't. Given the thousands of years of Egyptian history, there were so *many* auspicious moments that I simply chanted until I hit one. Of course, I had to hope my portal didn't open during an *inauspicious* moment. That could have caused all sorts of nasty side effects—but what's life without taking a few risks?

(Carter is shaking his head and muttering. I have no idea why.)

The air rippled in front of us. A circular doorway appeared—a swirling vortex of golden sand—and Leonid and I jumped through.

I'd like to say my spell worked perfectly and we ended up in the First Nome. Sadly, I was a bit off the mark.

The portal spit us out roughly a hundred meters above Cairo. I found myself free-falling through the cool night air toward the city lights below.

I didn't panic. I could have cast any number of spells to get out of this situation. I could have even assumed the form of a kite (the bird of prey, not the kind with a string), although that wasn't my favorite way to travel. Before I could decide on a plan of action, Leonid grabbed my hand.

The direction of the wind changed. Suddenly we were gliding over the city in a controlled descent. We set down softly in the desert just outside the city limits near a cluster of ruins that I knew from experience hid an entrance to the First Nome.

I looked at Leonid in amazement. "You summoned the power of Shu!"

"Shu," he said grimly. "Yes. Necessary. I do . . . forbidden."

I smiled with delight. "You clever boy! You learned the path of the gods on your own? I knew there was a reason I didn't turn you into a banana slug."

Leonid's eyes widened. "No banana slug! Please!"

"It was a compliment, silly," I said. "Forbidden is good! Sadie likes forbidden! Now, come on. You need to meet my uncle."

No doubt Carter would describe the underground city in excruciating detail, with exact measurements of each room, boring history on every statue and hieroglyph, and background notes on the construction of the magical headquarters of the House of Life.

I will spare you that pain.

It's big. It's full of magic. It's underground.

There. Sorted.

At the bottom of the entry tunnel, we crossed a stone bridge over a chasm, where I was challenged by a *ba*. The glowing bird spirit (with the head of a famous Egyptian I probably should've known) asked me a question: *What color are the eyes of Anubis?*

Brown. *Duh.* I suppose he was trying to trick me with an easy question.

The *ba* let us pass into the city proper. I hadn't visited in six months, and I was distressed to see how few magicians were about. The First Nome had never been crowded. Egyptian magic had withered over the centuries as fewer and fewer young initiates learned the arts. But now most shops in the central cavern were closed. At the market stalls, no one was haggling over the price of *ankhs* or scorpion venom. A bored-looking amulet salesman perked up as we approached, then slumped as we passed by.

Our footsteps echoed in the silent tunnels. We crossed one of the subterranean rivers, then wound our way through the library quarter and the Chamber of Birds.

(Carter says I should tell you why it's called that. It's a cave full of all sorts of birds. Again—*duh*. [Carter, why are you banging your head against the table?])

I brought my Russian friend down a long corridor, past a sealed tunnel that had once led up to the Great Sphinx of Giza, and finally to the bronze doors of the Hall of Ages. It was my uncle's hall now, so I strolled right in.

Impressive place? Certainly. If you filled it with water, the hall would've been large enough for a pod of whales. Running down the middle, a long blue carpet glittered like the River Nile. Along either side marched rows of columns, and between them shimmered curtains of light displaying scenes from Egypt's past—all sorts of horrible, wonderful, heart-wrenching events.

I tried to avoid looking at them. I knew from experience that those images could be dangerously absorbing. Once I'd made the mistake of touching the lights, and the experience had almost turned my brain into oatmeal.

The first section of light was gold—the Age of the Gods. Farther along, the Old Kingdom glowed silver, then the Middle Kingdom in coppery brown, and so on.

Several times as we walked, I had to pull Leonid back from scenes that caught his eye. Honestly, I wasn't much better.

I got teary-eyed when I saw a vision of Bes entertaining the other gods by doing cartwheels in a loincloth. (I cried because I missed seeing him so full of life, I mean, though the sight of Bes in a loincloth *is* enough to make anyone's eyes burn.)

We passed the bronze curtain of light for the New Kingdom. I stopped abruptly. In the shifting mirage, a thin man in priestly robes held a wand and a knife over a black bull. The man muttered as if blessing the animal. I couldn't tell much about the scene, but I recognized the man's face—a beaky nose, high forehead, thin lips that twisted in a wicked smile as he ran the knife along the poor animal's throat.

"That's him," I muttered.

I walked toward the curtain of light.

"*Nyet.*" Leonid grabbed my arm. "You tell me the lights are bad, stay away."

"You—you're right," I said. "But that's Uncle Vinnie."

I was positive it was the same face that had appeared in the wall at the Dallas Museum, but how could that be? The scene I was looking at must have happened thousands of years ago.

"Not Vinnie," Leonid said. "Khaemwaset."

"Sorry?" I wasn't sure if I'd heard him correctly, or even in what language he'd spoken. "Is that a name?"

"He is . . ." Leonid slipped into Russian, then sighed in exasperation. "Too difficult to explain. Let us see Amos, who will not eat my face."

I forced myself to look away from the image. "Good idea. Let's keep going."

At the end of the hall, the curtains of red light for the Modern Age changed to dark purple. Supposedly this marked the beginning of a new age, though none of us knew exactly what sort of era it would be. If Apophis destroyed the world, I guessed it would be the Age of Extremely Short Lives.

I'd expected to see Amos sitting at the foot of the pharaoh's throne. That was the traditional place for the Chief Lector, symbolizing his role as the pharaoh's main advisor. Of course, the pharaohs rarely needed advising these days, as they'd all been dead for several thousand years.

The dais was empty.

That stumped me. I'd never considered where the Chief Lector hung out when he wasn't on display. Did he have a dressing room, possibly with his name and a little star on the door?

"There." Leonid pointed.

Once again, my clever Russian friend was right. On the back wall, behind the throne, a faint line of light shone along the floor—the bottom edge of a door.

"A creepy secret entrance," I said. "Well done, Leonid."

On the other side, we found a sort of war room. Amos and a young woman in camouflage clothes stood at opposite ends of a large table inlaid with a full-color world map. The table's surface was crowded with tiny figurines—painted ships, monsters, magicians, cars, and markers with hieroglyphs.

Amos and the camouflage girl were so engrossed in their work, moving figurines across the map, they didn't notice us at first.

Amos wore traditional linen robes. With his barrel-shaped figure, they made him look a bit like Friar Tuck, except with darker skin and cooler hair. His braided locks were decorated with gold beads. His round glasses flashed as he studied the map. Draped around his shoulders was the leopard-skin cape of the Chief Lector.

As for the young woman . . . oh, gods of Egypt. It was *Zia*.

I'd never seen her in modern clothes before. She wore camouflage cargo pants, hiking boots, and an olive-colored tank top that flattered her coppery skin. Her black hair was longer than I remembered. She looked so much more grown-up and gorgeous than she'd been six months ago, I was glad Carter hadn't come along. He would've had difficulty picking up his jaw from the floor.

[Yes, you would have, Carter. She looked quite stunning, in a Commando Girl sort of way.]

Amos moved one of the figurines across the map. "Here," he told Zia.

"All right," she said. "But that leaves Paris undefended."

I cleared my throat. "Are we interrupting?"

Amos turned and broke into a grin. "Sadie!"

He crushed me in a hug, then rubbed my head affectionately.

"Ow," I said.

He chuckled. "I'm sorry. It's just so good to see you." He glanced at Leonid. "And this is—"

Zia cursed. She wedged herself between Amos and Leonid. "He's one of the Russians! Why is *he* here?"

"Calm down," I told her. "He's a friend."

I explained about Leonid's appearance at the dance. Leonid

tried to help, but he kept slipping into Russian.

"Wait," Amos said. "Let's make this easier."

He touched Leonid's forehead. *"Med-wah."*

In the air above us, the hieroglyph for *Speak* burned red:

"There," Amos said. "That should help."

Leonid's eyebrows shot up. "You speak Russian?"

Amos smiled. "Actually for the next few minutes, we'll all be speaking Ancient Egyptian, but it will sound to each of us like our native tongue."

"Brilliant," I said. "Leonid, you'd best make the most of your time."

Leonid took off his army cap and fidgeted with the brim. "Sarah Jacobi and her lieutenant, Kwai . . . they mean to attack you."

"We know that," Amos said dryly.

"No, you don't understand!" Leonid's voice trembled with fear. "They are evil! They are working with Apophis!"

Perhaps it was a coincidence, but when he said that name, several figurines on the world map sparked and melted. My heart felt much the same way.

"Hold on," I said. "Leonid, how do you know this?"

His ears turned pink. "After the death of Menshikov, Jacobi and Kwai came to our nome. We gave them refuge. Soon Jacobi took over, but my comrades did not object. They, ah, hate the Kanes very much." He looked at me guiltily. "After you broke into our headquarters last spring . . . well, the other Russians blame you for Menshikov's death and the rise of Apophis. They blame you for everything."

"Quite used to that," I said. "You didn't feel the same?"

He pinched his oversized cap. "I saw your power. You defeated the *tjesu-heru* monster. You could have destroyed me, but you didn't. You did not seem evil."

"Thanks for that."

"After we met, I became curious. I began reading old scrolls, learning to channel the power of the god Shu. I have always been a good air elementalist."

Amos grunted. "That took courage, Leonid. Exploring the path of the gods on your own in the middle of the Russian nome? You were brave."

"I was foolhardy." Leonid's forehead was damp with sweat. "Jacobi has killed magicians for lesser crimes. One of my friends, an old man named Mikhail, he once made the mistake of saying all Kanes might not be bad. Jacobi arrested him for treason. She gave him to Kwai, who does magic with—with lightning . . . terrible things. I heard Mikhail screaming in the dungeon for three nights before he died."

Amos and Zia exchanged grave looks. I had a feeling this wasn't the first time they'd heard about Kwai's torture methods.

"I'm so sorry," Amos said. "But how can you be sure Jacobi and Kwai are working for Apophis?"

The young Russian glanced at me for reassurance.

"You can trust Amos," I promised. "He'll protect you."

Leonid chewed his lip. "Yesterday I was in one of the

chambers deep under the Hermitage, a place I thought was secret. I was studying a scroll to summon Shu—very forbidden magic. I heard Jacobi and Kwai approaching, so I hid. I overheard the two of them speaking, but their voices were . . . splintered. I don't know how to explain."

"They were possessed?" Zia asked.

"Worse," Leonid said. "They were each channeling dozens of voices. It was like a war council. I heard many monsters and demons. And presiding over the meeting was one voice, deeper and more powerful than the rest. I'd never heard anything like it, as if darkness could speak."

"Apophis," Amos said.

Leonid had gone very pale. "Please understand, most magicians in St. Petersburg, they are not evil. They are only scared and desperate to survive. Jacobi has convinced them she will save them. She has misled them with lies. She says the Kanes are demons. But she and Kwai . . . *they* are the monsters. They are no longer human. They have set up a camp at Abu Simbel. From there, they will lead the rebels against the First Nome."

Amos turned to his map. He traced his finger south along the River Nile to a small lake. "I sense nothing at Abu Simbel. If they are there, they've managed to hide themselves completely from my magic."

"They are there," Leonid promised.

Zia scowled. "Under our very noses, within easy striking distance. We should've killed the rebels at Brooklyn House when we had the chance."

Amos shook his head. "We are servants of Ma'at—order

and justice. We don't kill our enemies for things they might do in the future."

"And now our enemies will kill us," Zia said.

On the table map, two more figurines sparked and melted in Spain. A miniature ship broke into pieces off the coast of Japan.

Amos grimaced. "More losses."

He chose a cobra figurine from Korea and pushed it toward the shipwreck. He swept away the melted magicians from Spain.

"What *is* that map?" I asked.

Zia moved a hieroglyph token from Germany to France. "Iskandar's war map. As I once told you, he was an expert at statuary magic."

I remembered. The old Chief Lector had been so good, he'd made a replica of Zia herself . . . but I decided not to bring that up.

"Those tokens stand for actual forces," I guessed.

"Yes," Amos said. "The map shows us our enemy's movements, at least most of them. It also allows us to send our forces by magic to where they are needed."

"And, uh, how are we doing?"

His expression told me all I needed to know.

"We are spread too thin," Amos said. "Jacobi's followers strike wherever we are weakest. Apophis sends his demons to terrorize our allies. The attacks seem coordinated."

"Because they are," Leonid said. "Kwai and Jacobi are under the serpent's control."

I shook my head in disbelief. "How could Kwai and Jacobi be so stupid? Don't they understand Apophis is going to destroy the world?"

"Chaos is seductive," Amos said. "No doubt Apophis has made them promises of power. He whispers in their ears, convincing them they are too important to be destroyed. They believe they can make a new world better than the old, and the change is worth any price—even mass annihilation."

I couldn't grasp how anyone could be so deluded, but Amos spoke as if he understood. Of course, Amos had been through this. He'd been possessed by Set, god of evil and Chaos. Compared to Apophis, Set was a minor nuisance, but he'd still been able to turn my uncle—one of the most powerful magicians in the world—into a helpless puppet. If Carter and I hadn't defeated Set and forced him to return to the Duat . . . well, the consequences wouldn't have been pretty.

Zia picked up a falcon figurine. She moved it toward Abu Simbel, but the little statue began to steam. She was forced to drop it.

"They've put up powerful wards," she said. "We won't be able to eavesdrop."

"They will attack in three days," Leonid said. "At the same time, Apophis will rise—at dawn on the autumn equinox."

"*Another* equinox?" I grumbled. "Didn't that *last* bit of nastiness happen on one of those? You Egyptians have an unhealthy obsession with equinoxes."

Amos gave me a stern look. "Sadie, as I'm sure you're aware, the equinox is a time of great magic significance, when day and night are equal. Besides, the autumn equinox marks the last day before darkness overtakes the light. It is the anniversary of Ra's retreat into the heavens. I feared that Apophis might make his move at that time. It's a most inauspicious day."

"Inauspicious?" I frowned. "But inauspicious is bad. Why would they . . . oh."

I realized for the forces of Chaos, our bad days must've been their good days. That meant they probably had a lot of good days.

Amos leaned on his staff. His hair seemed to be turning gray before my eyes. I remembered Michel Desjardins, the last Chief Lector, and how quickly he had aged. I couldn't bear the idea of that happening to Amos.

"We don't have the strength to defeat our enemies," he said. "I will have to use other means."

"Amos, no," Zia said. "Please."

I wasn't sure what they were talking about. Zia sounded horrified, and anything that scared her, I didn't want to know about.

"Actually," I said, "Carter and I have a plan."

I told them about our idea of using Apophis's own shadow against him. Perhaps saying this in front of Leonid was reckless, but he had risked his life to warn us about Sarah Jacobi's plans. He had trusted me. The least I could do was return the favor.

When I finished explaining, Amos gazed at his map. "I've never heard of such magic. Even if it's possible—"

"It *is*," I insisted. "Why else would Apophis delay his Doomsday attack so he could track down and destroy every scroll by this fellow Setne? Apophis is afraid we'll figure out the spell and stop him."

Zia crossed her arms. "But you can't. You just said all copies were destroyed."

"We'll ask Thoth for help," I said. "Carter's on his way there now. And in the meantime . . . I have an errand to run. I may be able to test our theory about shadows."

"How?" Amos asked.

I told him what I had in mind.

He looked as if he wanted to object, but he must've seen the defiance in my eyes. We're related, after all. He knows how stubborn Kanes can be when they set their minds to something.

"Very well," he said. "First you must eat and rest. You can leave at dawn. Zia, I want you to go with her."

Zia looked startled. "Me? But I might . . . I mean, is it wise?"

Again I got the feeling I'd missed an important conversation. What had Amos and Zia been discussing?

"You'll be fine," Amos assured her. "Sadie will need your help. And I will arrange for someone else to watch Ra during the day."

She looked quite nervous, which wasn't like her. Zia and I had had our differences in the past, but she'd never been short of confidence. Now I almost felt worried for her.

"Cheer up," I told her. "It'll be a laugh. Quick trip to the Netherworld, fiery lake of doom. What could go wrong?"

7. I Get Strangled by an Old Friend

SO, YEAH.

Sadie goes off on a side adventure with some guy, leaving me to do the boring work of figuring out how to save the world. Why does this sound familiar? Oh, right. That's the way Sadie always is. If it's time to move forward, you can count on her to veer sideways on some ADHD tangent of her own.

[Why are you thanking me, Sadie? That wasn't a compliment.]

After the Brooklyn Academy dance, I was pretty miffed. Bad enough being forced to slow-dance with Sadie's friend Lacy. But passing out on the dance floor, waking up with Lacy snoring in my armpit, and then finding out I'd missed visits from two gods—that was just embarrassing.

After Sadie and the Russian guy left, I got our crew back to Brooklyn House. Walt was confused to see us so soon. I pulled him and Bast aside for a quick conference on the terrace. I explained what Sadie had told me about Shu, Anubis, and the Russian dude Leonid.

"I'll take Freak to Memphis," I said. "Be back as soon as I talk to Thoth."

"I'm going with you," Walt said.

Sadie had told me to take him along, of course, but looking at him now, I had second thoughts. Walt's cheeks were sunken. His eyes were glassy. I was alarmed by how much worse he looked since just yesterday. I know this is horrible, but I couldn't help thinking about Egyptian burial practices—how they'd pack a body with embalming salts to slowly dry it up from the inside. Walt looked like he'd been started on that process.

"Look, man," I said, "Sadie asked me to keep you safe. She's worried about you. So am I."

He clenched his jaw. "If you plan on using a shadow for your spell, you'll have to capture it with that figurine. You'll need a *sau*, and I'm the best you've got."

Unfortunately, Walt was right. Neither Sadie nor I had the skill to capture a shadow, if that was even possible. Only Walt had that kind of charm-making talent.

"All right," I muttered. "Just . . . keep your head down. I don't want my sister going nuclear on me."

Bast poked Walt's arm, the way a cat might nudge a bug to see if it was still alive. She sniffed his hair.

"Your aura is weak," Bast said, "but you should be all right to travel. Try not to exert yourself. No magic unless absolutely necessary."

Walt rolled his eyes. "Yes, Mother."

Bast seemed to like that.

"I'll watch the other kittens," she promised. "Er, I mean initiates. You two be careful. I don't have much love for Thoth, but I don't want you caught up in his problems."

"What problems?" I asked.

"You'll see. Just come back to me. All this guard duty is cutting into my nap schedule!"

She shooed us toward Freak's stable and headed back downstairs, muttering something about catnip.

We hitched up the boat. Freak squawked and buzzed his wings, anxious to go. He looked like he'd gotten a good rest. Besides, he knew that a journey meant more frozen turkeys for him.

Soon we were flying over the East River.

Our ride through the Duat seemed bumpier than usual, like airplane turbulence, except with ghostly wailing and heavy fog. I was glad I'd had a light dinner. My stomach churned.

The boat shuddered as Freak brought us out of the Duat. Below us spread a different nighttime landscape—the lights of Memphis, Tennessee, curving along the banks of the Mississippi River.

On the shoreline rose a glassy black pyramid—an abandoned sports arena that Thoth had appropriated for his home. Bursts of multicolored light peppered the air, reflections rippling across the pyramid. At first I thought Thoth was hosting a fireworks exhibition. Then I realized his pyramid was under attack.

Clambering up the sides was a gruesome assortment of

demons—humanoid figures with chicken feet or paws or insect legs. Some had fur. Some had scales or shells like tortoises. Instead of heads, many had weapons or tools sprouting from their necks—hammers, swords, axes, chain saws, even a few screwdrivers.

At least a hundred demons were climbing toward the top, digging their claws into the seams of the glass. Some tried to smash their way through, but wherever they struck, the pyramid flickered with blue light, repelling their attacks. Winged demons swirled through the air, screeching and diving at a small group of defenders.

Thoth stood at the peak. He looked like a scruffy college lab assistant in a white medical coat, jeans, and T-shirt, a day-old beard, and wild Einstein hair—which doesn't sound very intimidating, but you should see him in combat. He threw glowing hieroglyphs like grenades, causing iridescent explosions all around him. Meanwhile his assistants, a troop of baboons and long-beaked birds called ibises, engaged the enemy. The baboons slammed basketballs into the demons, sending them toppling back down the pyramid. The ibises ran between the monsters' legs, jabbing their beaks in the most sensitive places they could find.

As we flew closer, I lowered my vision into the Duat. The scene there was even scarier. The demons were connected by red coils of energy that formed one massive translucent serpent. The monster encircled the entire pyramid. At the top, Thoth shone in his ancient form—a giant, white-kilted man with the head of an ibis, hurling bolts of energy at his enemies.

Walt whistled. "How can the mortals not notice a battle like that?"

I wasn't sure, but I remembered some of the recent disaster news. Huge storms had been causing floods all along the Mississippi River, including here in Memphis. Hundreds of people had been displaced. Magicians might be able to see what was really happening, but any regular mortals still in the city probably thought this was just a major thunderstorm.

"I'll help Thoth," I said. "You stay in the boat."

"No," Walt said. "Bast said I should use magic only in an emergency. This qualifies."

I knew Sadie would kill me if I let Walt get hurt. On the other hand, Walt's tone told me he wasn't going to back down. He can be almost as stubborn as my sister when he wants to be.

"Fine," I said. "Hold on."

A year ago, if I'd faced a fight like this, I would have curled into a ball and tried to hide. Even our battle at the Red Pyramid last Christmas seemed minor compared to dive-bombing an army of demons with no backup except one sick guy and a slightly dysfunctional griffin.

But a lot had happened in the past year. Now this was just another bad day in the life of the Kane family.

Freak came screaming down out of the night sky and banked hard to the right, shooting across the side of the pyramid. He gulped down smaller demons and shredded the larger ones with his buzz-saw wings. Some that survived got run over by our boat.

As Freak began to climb again, Walt and I jumped out, scrambling for footing on the glassy slope. Walt threw an amulet. In a flash of light, a golden sphinx appeared, with a lion's body and the head of a woman. After our experience at the Dallas Museum, I didn't much care for sphinxes, but thankfully this one was on our side.

Walt jumped on its back and rode into battle. The sphinx snarled and pounced on a reptilian demon, tearing it to pieces. Other monsters scattered. I couldn't blame them. A massive gold lion would have been scary enough, but the growling woman's head made it even more horrifying, with merciless emerald eyes, a shining Egyptian crown, and a fanged mouth with way too much lipstick.

As for me, I summoned my *khopesh* from the Duat. I called on the power of Horus, and the glowing blue avatar of the war god formed around me. Soon I was encased in a twenty-foot-tall hawk-headed apparition.

I stepped forward. The avatar mirrored my movements. I swiped my sword at the nearest demons, and the avatar's massive glowing blade plowed them down like bowling pins. Two of the monsters actually had bowling pins for heads, so I guess that was appropriate.

The baboons and ibises were slowly making headway against the surge of demons. Freak flew around the pyramid, snapping up winged demons or smacking them out of the air with his boat.

Thoth kept flinging hieroglyphic grenades.

"Bloated!" he cried. The corresponding hieroglyph flew

through the air, bursting against a demon's chest in a spray of light. Instantly, the demon swelled like a water balloon and rolled screaming down the pyramid.

"Flat!" Thoth blasted another demon, who collapsed and shriveled into a monster-shaped doormat.

"Intestinal problems!" Thoth yelled. The poor demon who got zapped with that one turned green and doubled over.

I waded through monsters, tossing them aside and slicing them to dust. Everything was going great until a winged demon did a kamikaze dive into my chest. I toppled backward, slamming against the pyramid with such force that I lost my concentration. My magical armor dissolved. I would've skidded all the way down the pyramid if the demon hadn't grabbed my throat and held me in place.

"Carter Kane," he hissed. "You are stupidly persistent."

I recognized that face—like an anatomy-class cadaver with muscle and sinew but no skin. His lidless eyes glowed red. His fangs were bared in a murderous grin.

"You," I grunted.

"Yes," the demon chuckled, his claws tightening around my neck. "Me."

Face of Horror—Set's lieutenant from the Red Pyramid, and the secret mouthpiece of Apophis. We'd killed him in the shadow of the Washington Monument, but I guess that didn't mean anything. Now he was back, and, judging by his rasping voice and glowing red eyes, he was still possessed by my least favorite snake.

I didn't remember his being able to fly, but now leathery bat wings sprouted from his shoulders. He straddled me with his chicken legs, his hands digging into my windpipe. His breath smelled like fermented juice and skunk spray.

"I could have killed you many times," the demon said. "But you interest me, Carter."

I tried to fight him off. My arms had turned to lead. I could barely hold my sword.

Around us, the sounds of battle became muted. Freak flew overhead, but his wings beat so sluggishly, I could actually see them. A hieroglyph exploded in slow motion like dye in water. Apophis was dragging me deeper into the Duat.

"I can feel your turmoil," said the demon. "Why do you fight this hopeless battle? Don't you realize what will happen?"

Images raced through my mind.

I saw a landscape of shifting hills and fiery geysers. Winged demons turned in the sulfurous sky. Spirits of the dead skittered across the hills, wailing in desperation and clawing for handholds. They were all being pulled in the same direction— toward a blot of darkness on the horizon. Whatever it was, its gravity was as powerful as a black hole. It sucked in the spirits, bending the hills and plumes of fire toward it. Even the demons in the air struggled.

Huddled in the shelter of a cliff, the glowing white form of a woman tried to anchor herself against the dark current. I wanted to cry. The woman was my mother. Other ghosts flew past her, wailing helplessly. My mom tried to reach out, but she couldn't save them.

The scene shifted. I saw the Egyptian desert at the edge

of Cairo under a blazing sun. Suddenly the sands erupted. A giant red serpent rose from the Underworld. He lunged at the sky and somehow, impossibly, swallowed the sun in a single gulp. The world darkened. Frost spread across the dunes. Cracks appeared in the ground. The landscape crumbled. Whole neighborhoods of Cairo sank into chasms. A red ocean of Chaos swelled up from the Nile, dissolving the city and desert, washing away pyramids that had stood for millennia. Soon there was nothing left but a boiling sea under a starless black sky.

"No gods can save you, Carter." Apophis sounded almost sympathetic. "This fate has been decreed since the beginning of time. Yield to me, and I will spare you and those you love. You will ride the Sea of Chaos. You will be master of your own destiny."

I saw an island floating across the boiling ocean—a small patch of green earth like an oasis. My family and I could be together on that island. We could survive. We could have anything we wanted just by imagining it. Death would mean nothing.

"All I ask is a token of good will," Apophis urged. "Give me Ra. I know you hate him. He represents everything that is wrong with your mortal world. He has grown senile, rotten, weak, and useless. Surrender him to me. I will spare you. Think on this, Carter Kane. Have the gods promised you anything as fair?"

The visions faded. Face of Horror grinned down at me, but suddenly his features contorted in pain. A fiery hieroglyph burned across his forehead—the symbol for *desiccate*—and the demon crumbled to dust.

I gasped for breath. My throat felt like it was packed with hot coals.

Thoth stood over me, looking grim and tired. His eyes swirled with kaleidoscopic colors, like portals to another world.

"Carter Kane." He offered me a hand and helped me up.

All the other demons were gone. Walt stood at the peak of the pyramid with the baboons and ibises, who were climbing over the golden sphinx lady like she was a merry-go-round animal. Freak hovered nearby, looking full and happy from eating so many demons.

"You shouldn't have come," Thoth chided. He brushed demon dust off his T-shirt, which had a flaming heart logo and the words HOUSE OF BLUES. "It was much too dangerous, especially for Walt."

"You're welcome," I croaked. "It looked like you needed help."

"The demons?" Thoth waved dismissively. "They'll be back just before sunrise. They've been attacking every six hours for the past week. Quite annoying."

"Every six hours?" I tried to imagine that. If Thoth had been fighting off an army like that several times a day for a week . . . I didn't see how even a god could have that much power.

"Where are the other gods?" I asked. "Shouldn't they be helping you?"

Thoth wrinkled his nose as if he smelled a demon with

intestinal problems. "Perhaps you and Walt should come inside. Now that you're here, we have a lot to talk about."

I'll say this for Thoth. He knew how to decorate a pyramid.

The former arena's basketball court was still there, no doubt so his baboons could play. (Baboons love basketball.) The JumboTron still hung from the ceiling, flashing a series of hieroglyphs that announced things like: GO TEAM! DEFENSE! and THOTH 25—DEMONS 0 in Ancient Egyptian.

The stadium seating had been replaced with a series of tiered balconies. Some were lined with computer stations, like mission control for a rocket launch. Others had chemistry tables cluttered with beakers, Bunsen burners, vials of smoking goo, jars of pickled organs, and stranger things. The nosebleed section was devoted to scroll cubbies—a library easily as big as the one in the First Nome. And behind the left backboard rose a three-story-tall whiteboard covered in computations and hieroglyphs.

Hanging from the girders, instead of championship banners and retired numbers, were black tapestries embroidered with gold incantations.

Courtside was Thoth's living area—a free-standing gourmet kitchen, a plush collection of couches and easy chairs, piles of books, buckets of Legos and Tinker Toys, a dozen flat-screen TVs showing different news programs and documentaries, and a small forest of electric guitars and amplifiers—everything a scatterbrained god needed to be able to do twenty things at once.

Thoth's baboons took Freak into the locker room to groom him and let him rest. I think they were worried he might eat the ibises, since they did look a bit like turkeys.

Thoth turned to Walt and me, looking us over critically. "You need rest. Then I'll fix you some dinner."

"We don't have time," I said. "We have to—"

"Carter Kane," Thoth scolded. "You've just battled Apophis, gotten the Horus knocked out of you, been dragged through the Duat and half-strangled. You're no good to anyone until you get some sleep."

I wanted to protest, but Thoth pressed his hand to my forehead. Weariness washed over me.

"Rest," Thoth insisted.

I collapsed on the nearest couch.

I'm not sure how long I slept, but Walt got up first. When I woke, he and Thoth were deep in conversation.

"No," Thoth said. "It's never been done. And I'm afraid you don't have time. . . ." He faltered when he noticed me sitting up. "Ah. Good, Carter. You're awake."

"What did I miss?"

"Nothing," he said, a little too cheerily. "Come and eat."

His kitchen counter was laden with fresh-cut brisket, sausage, ribs, and cornbread, plus an industrial-sized dispenser of ice tea. Thoth had once told me that barbecue was a form of magic, and I guess he was right. The smell of food made me temporarily forget my troubles.

I scarfed down a brisket sandwich and drank two glasses of tea. Walt nibbled on a rib, but he didn't seem to have much of an appetite.

Meanwhile Thoth picked up a Gibson guitar. He struck a power chord that shook the arena floor. He'd gotten better since I'd last heard him. The chord actually sounded like a chord, not like a mountain goat being tortured.

I gestured around with a piece of cornbread. "This place is looking good."

Thoth chuckled. "Better than my last headquarters, eh?"

The first time Sadie and I had crossed paths with the god of knowledge, he'd been holed up at a local university campus. He had tested our worth by sending us on a quest to trash Elvis Presley's house (long story), but hopefully we were past the testing phase now. I preferred hanging out courtside eating barbecue.

Then I thought about the visions Face of Horror had shown me—my mother in danger, a darkness swallowing the souls of the dead, the world dissolving in a sea of Chaos—except for one small island floating across the waves. The memory kind of killed my appetite.

"So . . ." I pushed my plate away. "Tell me about the demon attacks. And what were you saying to Walt?"

Walt stared at his half-eaten pork rib.

Thoth strummed a minor chord. "Where to start . . . ? The attacks began seven days ago. I'm cut off from the other gods. They haven't come to my rescue, I imagine, because they're having similar problems. Divide and conquer—Apophis understands that basic military principle. Even if my brethren *could* help me . . . well, they have other priorities. Ra was recently brought back, as you may recall."

Thoth gave me a hard look, like I was an equation he

couldn't balance. "The sun god must be guarded on his nightly journey. That takes a lot of godpower."

My shoulders sagged. I didn't need one more thing to feel guilty about. I also didn't think it was fair of Thoth to act so critical of me. Thoth had been on our side, more or less, about bringing back the sun god. Maybe seven days of demon attacks had started to change his mind.

"Can't you just leave?" I asked.

Thoth shook his head. "Perhaps you can't see so deeply into the Duat, but the power of Apophis has completely encircled this pyramid. I am quite stuck."

I gazed up at the arena's ceiling, which suddenly seemed much lower. "Which means . . . we're stuck too?"

Thoth waved aside the question. "*You* should be able to pass back through. The serpent's net is designed to catch a god. You and Walt aren't large or important enough to be caught."

I wondered if that were true, or if Apophis was allowing me to come and go—to have the choice of surrendering Ra.

You interest me, Carter, Apophis had said. *Yield to me, and I will spare you.*

I took a deep breath. "But, Thoth, if you're on your own . . . I mean, how much longer can you last?"

The god brushed at his lab coat, which was covered with scribbles in a dozen languages. The word *time* fluttered off his sleeve. Thoth caught it, and suddenly he was checking a gold pocket watch.

"Let's see. Judging from the weakening of the pyramid's defenses and the rate at which my power is being expended,

I'd say I could withstand nine more attacks, or just over two days, which would take us to dawn on the equinox. Ha! That can't be a coincidence."

"And then?" Walt asked.

"Then my pyramid will be breached. My minions will be killed. I'm guessing Doomsday will happen all over, in fact. The fall equinox would be a sensible time for Apophis to rise. He'll probably cast me into the abyss, or possibly scatter my essence across the universe in a billion pieces. Hmm . . . the physics of a god's death." His pocket watch turned into a pen. He scribbled something on the neck of his guitar. "That would make an excellent research paper."

"Thoth," Walt prompted. "Tell Carter what you told me, about why you're being targeted."

"I thought that was obvious," Thoth said. "Apophis wants to distract me from helping you. That *is* why you've come, isn't it? To find out about the serpent's shadow?"

For a moment I was too stunned to speak. "How did you know?"

"*Please.*" Thoth played a Jimi Hendrix riff, then set down his guitar. "I *am* the god of knowledge. I knew sooner or later you'd come to the conclusion that your only hope of victory was a shadow execration."

"A shadow execration," I repeated. "That's an actual spell with an actual name? It could work?"

"In theory."

"And you didn't volunteer this information—*why?*"

Thoth snorted. "Knowledge of any value can't be given. It

must be sought and earned. You're a teacher now, Carter. You should know this."

I wasn't sure whether to strangle him or hug him. "So, I'm seeking the knowledge. I'm earning the knowledge. How do I defeat Apophis?"

"I'm so glad you asked!" Thoth beamed at me with his multicolored eyes. "Unfortunately, I can't tell you."

I glanced at Walt. "Do you want to kill him, or should I?"

"Now, now," Thoth said. "I can guide you a little. But you'll have to connect the freckles, as they say."

"Dots," I said.

"Yes," he said. "You're on the right track. The *sheut* could be used to destroy a god, or even Apophis himself. And yes, like all sentient beings, Apophis has a shadow, though he keeps that part of his soul well hidden and well guarded."

"So where is it?" I asked. "How do we use it?"

Thoth spread his hands. "The second question I can't answer. The first question I'm not allowed to answer."

Walt shoved his plate aside. "I've been trying to get it out of him, Carter. For a god of knowledge, he isn't very helpful."

"Come on, Thoth," I said. "Can't we do a quest for you or something? Couldn't we blow up Elvis's house again?"

"Tempting," the god said. "But you must understand, giving a mortal the location of an immortal's shadow—even Apophis's—would be a grave crime. The other gods already think I'm a sell-out. Over the centuries, I've divulged too many secrets to mankind. I taught you the art of writing. I taught you magic and founded the House of Life."

"Which is why magicians still honor you," I said. "So help us one more time."

"And give humans knowledge that could be used to destroy the gods?" Thoth sighed. "Can you understand why my brethren might object to such a thing?"

I clenched my fists. I thought about my mother's spirit huddling beneath a cliff, fighting to stay put. The dark force *had* to be Apophis's shadow. Apophis had shown me that vision to make me despair. As his power grew, his shadow grew stronger too. It was pulling in the spirits of the dead, consuming them.

I could guess the shadow was somewhere in the Duat, but that didn't help. It was like saying *somewhere in the Pacific Ocean*. The Duat was huge.

I glared at Thoth. "Your other option is not to help us and let Apophis destroy the world."

"Point taken," he admitted, "which is why I'm still talking to you. There *is* a way you could find the shadow's location. Long ago, when I was young and naïve, I wrote a book—a field study, of sorts—called the Book of Thoth."

"Catchy name," Walt muttered.

"*I* thought so!" Thoth said. "At any rate, it described every form and disguise each god can take, their most secret hiding places—all sorts of embarrassing details."

"Including how to find their shadows?" I asked.

"No comment. At any rate, I never meant for humans to read the book, but it was stolen in ancient times by a crafty magician."

"Where is it now?" I asked. Then I held up my hands. "Wait . . . let me guess. You can't tell us."

"Honestly, I don't know," Thoth said. "This crafty magician hid the book. Fortunately he died before he could take full advantage of it, but he *did* use its knowledge to formulate a number of spells, including the shadow execration. He wrote down his thoughts in a special variation of the Book of Overcoming Apophis."

"Setne," I said. "That's the magician you're talking about."

"Indeed. His spell was only theoretical, of course. Even *I* never had that knowledge. And as you know, all copies of his scroll have now been destroyed."

"So it's hopeless," I said. "Dead end."

"Oh, no," Thoth said. "You could ask Setne himself. He wrote the spell. He hid the Book of Thoth that, ahem, may or may not describe the shadow's location. If he were so inclined, he could help you."

"But hasn't Setne been dead for thousands of years?"

Thoth grinned. "Yes. And that's only the first problem."

Thoth told us about Setne, who'd apparently been pretty famous in Ancient Egypt—like Robin Hood, Merlin, and Attila the Hun rolled into one. The more I heard, the less I wanted to meet him.

"He was a pathological liar," Thoth said. "A scoundrel, a traitor, a thief, and a brilliant magician. He prided himself on stealing books of knowledge, including mine. He battled monsters, adventured in the Duat, conquered gods, and broke into sacred tombs. He created curses that couldn't be lifted and unearthed secrets that should have stayed buried. He was quite the evil genius."

Walt tugged at his amulets. "Sounds like you admire him."

The god gave him a sidelong grin. "Well, I appreciate the pursuit of knowledge, but I couldn't endorse Setne's methods. He'd stop at nothing to possess the secrets of the universe. He wanted to be a god, you see—not the *eye* of a god. A full-fledged immortal."

"Which is impossible," I guessed.

"Hard, not impossible," Thoth said. "Imhotep, the first mortal magician—he was made a god after his death." Thoth turned toward his computers. "That reminds me, I haven't seen Imhotep in millennia. I wonder what he's up to. Perhaps I should Google him—"

"Thoth," Walt said, "concentrate."

"Right. So, Setne. He created this spell for destroying any being—even a god. I could never endorse such knowledge falling into the hands of a mortal, but hypothetically speaking, if you needed the spell to defeat Apophis, you might be able to convince *Setne* to teach you the enchantment and lead you to the shadow of Apophis."

"Except Setne's dead," I said. "We keep coming back to that."

Walt sat up. "Unless . . . you're suggesting we find his spirit in the Underworld. But if Setne was so evil, wouldn't Osiris have condemned him in the Hall of Judgment? Ammit would've eaten his heart, and he would have ceased to exist."

"Normally, yes," Thoth said. "But Setne is a special case. He's quite . . . persuasive. Even before the court of the Underworld, he was able to, ah, manipulate the legal system. Many times, Osiris sentenced him to oblivion, but Setne always managed to evade punishment. He got a lighter sentence, or he made a plea bargain, or he simply escaped. He's managed to survive— as a spirit, at least—all these eons."

Thoth turned his swirling eyes toward me. "But recently, Carter Kane, your father became Osiris. He's been cracking down on rebellious ghosts, trying to restore Ma'at to the Underworld. The next time the sun sets, approximately fourteen hours from now, Setne is scheduled for a new trial. He will come before your father. And this time—"

"My dad won't let him go." I felt like the demon's hands were closing around my throat again.

My father was fair but stern. He didn't take excuses from anyone. All the years we'd traveled together, I could never even get away with leaving my shirt untucked. If Setne was as bad as Thoth said, my father would show him no mercy. He'd toss this guy's heart to Ammit the Devourer like it was a doggie biscuit.

Walt's eyes shone with excitement. He looked more animated than I'd seen him in a long time. "We can plead with your dad," he said. "We can get Setne's trial delayed, or ask for a reduced sentence in exchange for Setne's help. The laws of the Underworld allow that."

I frowned. "How do you know so much about dead people's court?"

I regretted saying that immediately. I realized that he'd probably been preparing himself to face that courtroom. Maybe that's what he'd been discussing with Thoth earlier.

I'm afraid you don't have much time, Thoth had said.

"Sorry, man," I said.

"It's okay," Walt said. "But we have to try. If we can convince your dad to spare Setne—"

Thoth laughed. "That would be amusing, wouldn't it? If Setne got off yet again, because his evil ways were the only thing that might save the world?"

"Hilarious," I said. The brisket sandwich wasn't sitting well in my stomach. "So you're suggesting we go to my father's court and try to save the ghost of an evil psychotic magician. Then we ask this ghost to lead us to Apophis's shadow and teach us how to destroy it, while trusting that he won't escape, kill us, or betray us to the enemy."

Thoth nodded enthusiastically. "You'd have to be crazy! I certainly hope you are."

I took a deep breath. "I guess I'm crazy."

"Excellent!" Thoth cheered. "One more thing, Carter. To make this work, you'll need Walt's help, but he's running out of time. His only chance—"

"It's fine," Walt snapped. "I'll tell him myself."

Before I could ask what he meant, the overtime buzzer blared from the arena's speakers.

"It's almost dawn," Thoth said. "You two had better leave, before the demons return. Good luck. And by all means, give Setne my regards—if you live that long, of course."

8. My Sister, The Flowerpot

THE RIDE BACK WASN'T FUN.

Walt and I held on to the boat while our teeth chattered and our eyes jiggled. The magic fog had turned the color of blood. Ghostly voices whispered angrily, like they'd decided to riot and loot the ethereal world.

Sooner than I expected, Freak pushed his way out of the Duat. We found ourselves over the New Jersey dockyards, our boat trailing steam as Freak bobbed wearily through the air. In the distance, the Manhattan skyline gleamed gold in the sunrise.

Walt and I hadn't spoken during the trip. The Duat tends to put a damper on conversation. Now he regarded me sheepishly.

"I should explain some things," he said.

I can't pretend I wasn't curious. As his sickness had progressed, Walt had gotten more and more secretive. I wondered what he'd been talking about with Thoth.

But it wasn't my business. After Sadie learned my secret

name last spring and got a free tour of my innermost thoughts, I'd become sensitive about respecting people's privacy.

"Look, Walt, it's your personal life," I said. "If you don't want to tell—"

"But it's not just personal. You need to know what's going on. I—I won't be around much longer."

I gazed down at the harbor, the Statue of Liberty passing below us. For months I'd known Walt was dying. It never got easier to accept. I remembered what Apophis had said at the Dallas Museum: Walt wouldn't live long enough to see the end of the world.

"Are you sure?" I asked. "Isn't there some way—?"

"Anubis is sure," he said. "I've got until sunset tomorrow, at the very latest."

I didn't want to hear another impossible deadline. By sunset tonight, we had to save the ghost of an evil magician. By sunset tomorrow, Walt would die. And the sunrise after that, if we were really lucky, we could look forward to Doomsday.

I never liked being thwarted. Whenever I felt like something was impossible, I usually tried even harder out of sheer stubbornness.

But at this point, I felt like Apophis was having a good laugh at my expense.

Oh, you're not a quitter? he seemed to be asking. *How about now? What if we give you a few more impossible tasks? Are you a quitter now?*

Anger made a small hard knot in my gut. I kicked the side of the boat and nearly broke my foot.

Walt blinked. "Carter, it's—"

"*Don't* say it's all right!" I snapped. "It's *not* all right."

I wasn't mad at him. I was mad at the unfairness of his stupid curse, and the fact that I kept failing people who depended on me. My parents had died to give Sadie and me a chance to save the world, which we were close to botching. In Dallas, dozens of good magicians had died because they'd tried to help me. Now we were about to lose Walt.

Sure, he was important to Sadie. But I relied on him just as much. Walt was my unofficial lieutenant at Brooklyn House. The other kids listened to him. He was a calming presence in every crisis, the deciding vote in every debate. I could trust him with any secret—and even with making the execration statue of Apophis, which I couldn't tell my uncle about. If Walt died . . .

"I won't let it happen," I said. "I refuse."

Wild thoughts ran through my mind: Maybe Anubis was lying to Walt about his imminent death, trying to push Walt away from Sadie. (Okay, unlikely. Sadie wasn't that much of a prize.)

[Yeah, Sadie, I really said that. Just checking to see if you were still paying attention.]

Maybe Walt could beat the odds. People survived cancer miraculously. Why not ancient curses? Maybe we could put him in suspended animation like Iskandar had done for Zia, until we found an antidote. Sure, his family had been searching for a cure unsuccessfully for centuries. Jaz, our best healer, had tried everything with no luck. But maybe we'd overlooked something.

"Carter," Walt said. "Will you let me finish? We've got to make plans."

"How can you be so calm?" I demanded.

Walt fingered his *shen* necklace, the twin of the one he'd given Sadie. "I've known about my curse for years. I won't let it stop me from doing what I need to. One way or another, I'm going to help you beat Apophis."

"How?" I said. "You just told me—"

"Anubis has an idea," Walt said. "He's been helping me make sense of my powers."

"You mean . . ." I glanced at Walt's hands. Several times I'd seen him turn objects to ashes simply by touching them, the way he'd done to that criosphinx in Dallas. The power didn't come from any of his magic items. None of us understood it, and as Walt's disease progressed, he seemed less and less able to control it, which made me think twice about giving the guy a high five.

Walt flexed his fingers. "Anubis thinks he understands why I have that ability. And there's more. He thinks there might be a way to extend my life."

That was such good news that I let out a shaky laugh. "Why didn't you say so? He can cure you?"

"No," Walt said. "Not a cure. And it's risky. It's never been done before."

"That's what you were talking to Thoth about."

Walt nodded. "Even if Anubis's plan works, there could be . . . side effects. You might not like it." He lowered his voice. "Sadie might not like it."

Unfortunately, I had a vivid imagination. I envisioned Walt turning into some sort of undead creature—a withered mummy, a ghostly *ba*, or a disfigured demon. In Egyptian magic, side effects could be pretty extreme.

I tried not to let my emotions show. "We want you to live. Don't worry about Sadie."

I could tell from Walt's eyes that he worried about Sadie a lot. Seriously, what did he *see* in my sister?

[Stop hitting me, Sadie. I'm just being honest.]

Walt flexed his fingers. Maybe it was my imagination, but I thought I detected wisps of gray steam curling from his hands, as if just talking about his strange power had made it turn active.

"I won't make the decision yet," Walt said. "Not until I'm on my last breath. I want to talk to Sadie first, explain to her . . ."

He rested his hand on the side of the boat. That was a mistake. The woven reeds turned gray under his touch.

"Walt, stop!" I yelped.

He jerked his hand away, but it was too late. The boat crumbled to ashes.

We lunged for the ropes. Thankfully they did not crumble— maybe because Walt was paying more attention now. Freak squawked as the boat disappeared, and suddenly Walt and I were dangling under the griffin's belly, holding on to the ropes for dear life and bonking into each other as we flew above the skyscrapers of Manhattan.

"Walt!" I yelled over the wind. "You *really* need to get a handle on that power!"

"Sorry!" he shouted back.

My arms were aching, but somehow we made it to Brooklyn House without plummeting to our deaths. Freak set us down on the roof, where Bast was waiting, her mouth agape.

"Why are you swinging from ropes?" she demanded.

"Because it's so fun," I growled. "What's the news?"

Behind the chimneys, a frail voice warbled: "Ha-lllooooo!"

The ancient sun god Ra popped out. He gave us a toothless grin and hobbled around the roof, muttering, "Weasels, weasels. Cookie, cookie, cookie!" He reached into the folds of his loincloth and tossed cookie crumbs in the air like confetti—and yes, it was just as disgusting as it sounds.

Bast tensed her arms, and her knives shot into her hands. Probably just an involuntary reflex; but she looked tempted to use those blades on someone—anyone. She reluctantly slipped the blades back into her sleeves.

"The news?" she said. "I'm on babysitting duty, thanks to your Uncle Amos, who asked me for a favor. And Sadie's *shabti* is waiting for you downstairs. Shall we?"

Explaining Sadie and her *shabti* would take a whole separate recording.

My sister had no talent for crafting magical statues. That didn't stop her from trying. She'd gotten this harebrained idea that she could create the perfect *shabti* to be her avatar, speak with her voice, and do all her chores like a remote-controlled robot. All her previous attempts had exploded or gone haywire, terrorizing Khufu and the initiates. Last week she'd created a magical Thermos with googly eyes that levitated around the room, yelling, "Exterminate! Exterminate!" until it smacked me in the head.

Sadie's latest *shabti* was Sadie Junior—a gardener's nightmare.

Not being much of an artist, Sadie had fashioned a vaguely human figure out of red ceramic flowerpots, held together by magic, string, and duct tape. The face was an upside-down pot with a smiley face drawn in black marker.

"About time." The pot creature was waiting in my room when Walt and I came in. Its mouth didn't move, but Sadie's voice echoed from inside the face pot as if she were trapped within the *shabti*. That thought made me happy.

"Stop smiling!" she ordered. "I can see you, Carter. Oh . . . and, uh, hullo, Walt."

The pot monster made squeaky grinding noises as it stood up straight. One clunky arm rose and tried to fix Sadie's nonexistent hair. Leave it to Sadie to be self-conscious around boys, even when she's made out of pots and duct tape.

We traded stories. Sadie told us about the impending attack on the First Nome that was supposed to go down at sunrise on the equinox, and the alliance between Sarah Jacobi's forces and Apophis. Wonderful news. Just great.

In return, I told Sadie about our visit with Thoth. I shared the visions Apophis had shown me about our mother's precarious situation in the Duat (which made the pot monster shudder) and the end of the world (which didn't seem to surprise her at all). I didn't tell Sadie about Apophis's offer to spare me if I gave up Ra. I didn't feel comfortable announcing that with Ra just outside the door, singing songs about cookies. But I told her about the evil ghost Setne, whose trial would start at sunset in the Hall of Judgment.

"Uncle Vinnie," Sadie said.

"Pardon?" I asked.

"The face that spoke to me at the Dallas Museum," she said. "It was obviously Setne himself. He warned me that we would need his help to understand the shadow execration spell. He said we'd have to 'pull some strings' and free him before sunset tonight. He meant the trial. We'll have to convince Dad to free him."

"I did mention that Thoth said he's a murderous psychopath, right?"

The pot monster made a clucking sound. "Carter, it'll be fine. Befriending psychopaths is one of our specialties."

She turned her flowerpot head toward Walt. "You'll be coming along, I hope?"

Her tone had a hint of reproach, like she was still upset that Walt hadn't attended the school dance/mass blackout party.

"I'll be there," he promised. "I'm fine."

He shot me a warning look, but I wasn't going to contradict him. Whatever he and Anubis were plotting, I could wait for him to explain it to Sadie. Jumping in the middle of the whole Sadie-Walt-Anubis drama sounded about as much fun as diving into a food processor.

"Right," Sadie said. "We'll meet you two at the Hall of Judgment before sunset tonight. That should give us time to finish up."

"Finish up?" I asked. "And who is *us*?"

It's hard to read expressions on a smiley-face pot, but Sadie's hesitation told me enough. "You aren't in the First Nome anymore," I guessed. "What are you doing?"

"A small errand," Sadie said. "I'm off to see Bes."

I frowned. Sadie went to see Bes in his nursing home almost every week, which was fine and all, but why now? "Uh, you do understand we're in a hurry."

"It's necessary," she insisted. "I've got an idea that might help us with our shadow project. Don't fret. Zia's with me."

"Zia?" It was my turn to feel self-conscious. If I were a flowerpot, I would've checked my hair. "That's why Bast is watching Ra today? Why exactly are you and Zia—?"

"Stop worrying," Sadie chided. "I'll take good care of her. And no, Carter, she hasn't been talking about you. I have no idea how she feels about you."

"*What?*" I wanted to punch Sadie Junior in her ceramic face. "I didn't say anything like that!"

"Now, now," she chided. "I don't think Zia cares what you wear. It's not a date. Just please brush your teeth for once."

"I'm going to kill you," I said.

"Love you too, brother, dear. Ta!"

The pottery creature crumbled into pieces, leaving a mound of shards and a red clay face smiling up at me.

Walt and I joined Bast outside my room. We leaned on the rail overlooking the Great Room while Ra skipped back and forth on the balcony, singing nursery songs in Ancient Egyptian.

Down below, our initiates were getting ready for the school

day. Julian had a breakfast sausage sticking out of his mouth as he rummaged through his backpack. Felix and Sean were arguing over who stole whose math textbook. Little Shelby was chasing the other ankle-biters with a fistful of crayons that shot rainbow-colored sparks.

I'd never had a big family, but living at Brooklyn House, I felt like I had a dozen brothers and sisters. Despite the craziness, I enjoyed it . . . which made my next decision even harder.

I told Bast about our plan to visit the Hall of Judgment.

"I don't like it," she said.

Walt managed a laugh. "Is there a plan you'd like better?"

She tilted her head. "Now that you mention it, no. I don't like plans. I'm a cat. Still, if half the things I've heard about Setne are true—"

"I know," I said. "But it's our only shot."

She wrinkled her nose. "You don't want me to come along? You're sure? Maybe I could get Nut or Shu to watch Ra—"

"No," I said. "Amos is going to need help at the First Nome. He doesn't have the numbers to fend off an attack from both the rebel magicians and Apophis."

Bast nodded. "I can't enter the First Nome, but I can patrol outside. If Apophis shows himself, I will engage him in battle."

"He'll be at full strength," Walt warned. "He's getting stronger by the hour."

She lifted her chin defiantly. "I've fought him before, Walt Stone. I know him better than anyone. Besides, I owe it to Carter's family. And to Lord Ra."

"Kitty!" Ra appeared behind us, patted Bast on the head, and skipped away. "Meow, meow, meow!"

Watching him prance around, I wanted to scream and throw things. We'd risked everything to revive the old sun god, hoping we'd get a divine pharaoh who could stand toe-to-toe with Apophis. Instead we got a wrinkly, bald troll in a loincloth.

Give me Ra, Apophis had urged. *I know you hate him.*

I tried to put it out of my mind, but I couldn't quite shake that image of an island in the Sea of Chaos—a personal paradise where the people I loved would be safe. I knew it was a lie. Apophis would never deliver on that promise. But I could understand how Sarah Jacobi and Kwai might be tempted.

Besides, Apophis knew how to strike a nerve. I *did* resent Ra for being so weak. Horus agreed with me.

We don't need the old fool. The war god's voice spoke inside my head. *I'm not saying you should give him to Apophis, but he is useless. We should put him aside and take the throne of the gods for ourselves.*

He made it sound so tempting—such an obvious solution.

But, no. If Apophis wanted me to give up Ra, then Ra must be valuable in some way. The sun god still had a role to play. I just had to figure out what it was.

"Carter?" Bast frowned. "I know you're worried about me, but your parents saved me from the abyss for a reason. Your mother foresaw that I would make a difference in the final battle. I will fight Apophis to the death if necessary. He won't get past me."

I wavered. Bast had already helped us so much. She had almost been destroyed fighting the crocodile god Sobek. She'd enlisted her friend Bes to help us, and then seen him reduced to an empty shell. She'd helped us restore her old master, Ra, to the world, and now she was stuck babysitting him. I didn't want to ask her to face Apophis again, but she was right. She knew the enemy better than anyone—except maybe Ra, when he was in his right mind.

"All right," I said. "But Amos will need more help than you can give, Bast. He'll need magicians."

Walt frowned. "Who? After the disaster in Dallas, we don't have many friends left. We could contact São Paulo and Vancouver—they're still with us—but they won't be able to spare many people. They'll be worried about protecting their own nomes."

I shook my head. "Amos needs magicians who know the path of the gods. He needs *us*. All of us."

Walt digested that silently. "You mean, abandon Brooklyn House."

Below us, the ankle-biters shrieked with joy as Shelby tried to tag them with her sparking crayons. Khufu sat on the fire-place mantel eating Cheerios, watching ten-year-old Tucker bounce a basketball off the statue of Thoth. Jaz was putting a bandage on Alyssa's forehead. (Probably she'd been attacked by Sadie's rogue Thermos, which was still on the loose.) In the middle of all this, Cleo was sitting on the sofa, engrossed in a book.

Brooklyn House was the first real home some of them had

ever known. We'd promised to keep them safe and teach them to use their powers. Now I was about to send them unprepared into the most dangerous battle of all time.

"Carter," Bast said, "they're not ready."

"They *have* to be," I said. "If the First Nome falls, it's all over. Apophis will attack us in Egypt, at the source of our power. We have to stand together with the Chief Lector."

"One last battle." Walt gazed sadly at the Great Room, maybe wondering whether or not he'd die before that battle happened. "Should we break the news to others?"

"Not yet," I said. "The rebel magicians' attack on the First Nome won't happen until tomorrow. Let the kids have one last day at school. Bast, when they come home this afternoon, I want you to lead them to Egypt. Use Freak, use whatever magic you have to. If all goes well in the Underworld, Sadie and I will join you before the attack."

"If all goes well," Bast said dryly. "Yes, that happens a lot."

She glanced over at the sun god, who was trying to eat the doorknob to Sadie's room. "What about Ra?" she asked. "If Apophis is going to attack in two days . . ."

"Ra has to keep making his nightly journey," I said. "That's part of Ma'at. We can't mess with it. But on the morning of the equinox, he'll need to be in Egypt. He'll have to face Apophis."

"Like *that*?" Bast gestured toward the old god. "In his loincloth?"

"I know," I admitted. "It sounds crazy. But Apophis still thinks Ra is a threat. Maybe facing Apophis in battle will remind Ra who he is. He might rise to the challenge and become . . . what he used to be."

Walt and Bast didn't answer. I could tell from their expressions that they didn't buy it. Neither did I. Ra was gumming Sadie's doorknob with intent to kill, but I didn't think he'd be much good against the Lord of Chaos.

Still, it felt good to have a plan of action. That was much better than standing around, dwelling on the hopelessness of our situation.

"Use today to organize," I told Bast. "Gather up the most valuable scrolls, amulets, weapons—anything we can use to help the First Nome. Let Amos know you're coming. Walt and I will head to the Underworld and meet Sadie. We'll rendezvous with you in Cairo."

Bast pursed her lips. "All right, Carter. But be careful of Setne. However bad you think he is? He's ten times worse."

"Hey, we defeated the god of evil," I reminded her.

Bast shook her head. "Set is a god. He doesn't change. Even with a god of Chaos, you can pretty much predict how he'll act. Setne, on the other hand . . . he has both power *and* human unpredictability. Don't trust him. Swear to me."

"That's easy," I said. "I promise."

Walt folded his arms. "So how are we going to get to the Underworld? Portals are unreliable. We're leaving Freak here, and the boat is destroyed—"

"I have another boat in mind," I said, trying to believe it was a good idea. "I'm going to summon an old friend."

S
A
D
I
E

9. Zia Breaks Up a Lava Fight

I'D BECOME QUITE AN EXPERT at visiting the godly nursing home—which was a sad statement on my life.

The first time Carter and I found our way there, we had traveled the River of Night, plunged down a fiery waterfall, and almost died in a lake of lava. Since then, I'd discovered I could simply call on Isis to transport me, as she could open doorways to many locations in the Duat. Honestly, though, dealing with Isis was almost as annoying as swimming through fire.

After my *shabti* conversation with Carter, I joined Zia on a limestone cliff overlooking the Nile. It was already midday in Egypt. Getting over portal-lag had taken me longer than I'd expected. After changing into more sensible clothes, I'd had a quick lunch and one more strategy talk with Amos deep in the Hall of Ages. Then Zia and I had climbed back to the surface. Now we stood at a ruined shrine to Isis on the river just south

150

of Cairo. It was a good place to summon the goddess, but we didn't have much time.

Zia still wore her combat outfit—camouflage cargo pants and an olive tank top. Her staff was slung over her back, and her wand hung at her belt. She rummaged through her pack, checking her supplies one last time.

"What did Carter say?" she asked.

[That's right, brother dear. I stepped out of earshot before I contacted you, so Zia didn't hear any of those teasing comments. Honestly, I'm not *that* mean.]

I told her what we'd discussed, but I couldn't bring myself to share how my mum's spirit was in danger. I'd known about the problem in general terms since I'd spoken with Anubis, of course, but the knowledge that our mother's ghost was huddled under a cliff somewhere in the Duat, resisting the pull of the serpent's shadow—well, that bit of information had lodged in my chest like a bullet. If I tried to touch it, I feared it would go straight to my heart and kill me.

I explained about my villainous ghost friend Uncle Vinnie, and how we intended to solicit his help.

Zia looked appalled. "Setne? As in *the* Setne? Does Carter realize—?"

"Yep."

"And Thoth suggested this?"

"Yep."

"And you're actually going along with it?"

"Yep."

She gazed down the Nile. Perhaps she was thinking of

her home village, which had stood on the banks of this river until it was destroyed by the forces of Apophis. Perhaps she was imagining her entire homeland crumbling into the Sea of Chaos.

I expected her to tell me that our plan was insane. I thought she might abandon me and go back to the First Nome.

But I suppose she had got used to the Kane family—poor girl. She must've known by now that *all* our plans were insane.

"Fine," she said. "How do we reach this . . . nursing home of the gods?"

"Just a mo'." I closed my eyes and concentrated.

Yoo-hoo, Isis? I thought. *Anyone home?*

Sadie, the goddess answered immediately.

In my mind she appeared as a regal woman with dark braided hair. Her dress was gossamer white. Her prismatic wings shimmered like sunlight rippling through clear water.

I wanted to smack her.

Well, well, I said. *If it isn't my good friend who decides whom I can and can't date.*

She had the nerve to look surprised. *Are you speaking of Anubis?*

Right, first try! I should've left it at that since I needed Isis's help. But seeing her floating there all shiny and queenly made me angrier than ever. *Where do you get the nerve, eh? Going behind my back, lobbying to keep Anubis away from me. How is that your business?*

Surprisingly, Isis kept her temper. *Sadie, there are things you don't understand. There are rules.*

Rules? I demanded. *The world is about to end, and you're worried about which boys are socially acceptable for me?*

Isis steepled her fingers. *The two issues are more connected than you realize. The traditions of Ma'at must be followed, or Chaos wins. Immortals and mortals can only interact in specific, limited ways. Besides, you cannot afford to be distracted. I'm doing you a favor.*

A favor! I said. *If you want to do me a real favor, we need passage to the Fourth House of the Night—the House of Rest, Sunny Acres, or whatever you want to call it. After that, you can butt out of my private life!*

Perhaps that was rude of me, but Isis had stepped over the line. Besides, why should I act proper with a goddess who had previously rented space in my head? Isis should have known me better!

The goddess sighed. *Sadie, proximity to the gods is dangerous. It must be regulated with utmost care. You know this. Your uncle is still tainted from his experience with Set. Even your friend Zia is struggling.*

What do you mean? I asked.

If you join with me, you'll understand, Isis promised. *Your mind will be clear. It's past time we united again and combined our strength.*

There it was: the sales pitch. Every time I called on Isis, she tried to persuade me to meld with her as we'd done before—mortal and god inhabiting one body, acting with a single will. Each time, I said no.

So, I ventured, *proximity to the gods is dangerous, but you're anxious to join forces with me again. I'm glad you're looking out for my safety.*

Isis narrowed her eyes. *Our situation is different, Sadie. You need my strength.*

Certainly it was tempting. Having the full power of a goddess at my command was quite a rush. As the Eye of Isis, I would feel confident, unstoppable, completely without fear. One could get addicted to such power—and that was the problem.

Isis could be a good friend, but her agenda wasn't always best for the mortal world—or for Sadie Kane.

She was driven by her loyalty to her son Horus. She'd do anything to see him on the throne of the gods. She was ambitious, vengeful, power-hungry, and envious of anyone who might have more magic than she did.

She claimed my mind would be clearer if I let her in. What she really meant was that I'd start seeing things her way. It would be harder to separate my thoughts from hers. I might even come to believe she was right by keeping Anubis and me apart. (Horrifying idea.)

Unfortunately, Isis had a point about joining forces. Sooner or later we'd have to. There was no other way I'd have the power to challenge Apophis.

But now wasn't the time. I wanted to remain Sadie Kane as long as possible—just my own wonderful self without any godly hitchhiker.

Soon, I told Isis. *I have things to do first. I need to be sure my decisions are my own. Now, about that doorway to the House of Rest . . .*

Isis was quite good at looking hurt and disapproving at the same time, which must have made her an impossible mother. I almost felt sorry for Horus.

Sadie Kane, she said, *you are my favorite mortal, my chosen magician. And still you do not trust me.*

I didn't bother to contradict her. Isis knew how I felt.

The goddess spread her arms in resignation. *Very well. But the path of the gods is the only answer. For all the Kanes, and for that one.* She nodded in Zia's direction. *You will need to advise her, Sadie. She must learn the path quickly.*

What do you mean? I asked again. I really wished she would stop talking in riddles. Gods are so annoying that way.

Zia was a much more experienced magician than I was. I didn't know how I could advise her. Besides, Zia was a fire elementalist. She tolerated us Kanes, but she had never shown the slightest interest in the path of the gods.

Good luck, Isis said. *I will await your call.*

The image of the goddess rippled and vanished. When I opened my eyes, a square of darkness the size of a doorway hovered in the air.

"Sadie?" Zia asked. "You were silent for so long, I was getting worried."

"No need." I tried for a smile. "Isis just likes to talk. Next stop, the Fourth House of the Night."

I'll be honest. I never quite understood the difference between the swirling sand portals that magicians can summon with artifacts and the doors of darkness that gods are able to conjure. Perhaps the gods use a more advanced wireless network. Perhaps they simply have better aim.

Whatever the reason, Isis's portal worked much more reliably than the one I'd created to get to Cairo. It deposited us right in the lobby of Sunny Acres.

As soon as we stepped through, Zia scanned our surroundings and frowned. "Where is everyone?"

Good question. We'd arrived at the correct godly nursing home—the same potted plants, the same massive lobby with windows looking out on the Lake of Fire, the same rows of limestone columns plastered with tacky posters of smiling seniors and mottos like: *These Are Your Golden Centuries!*

But the nurses' station was unattended. IV poles were clustered in one corner like they were having a conference. The sofas were empty. The coffee tables were littered with half-played games of checkers and senet. Ugh, I *hate* senet.

I stared at an empty wheelchair, wondering where its occupant had gone, when suddenly the chair burst into flames, collapsing in a pile of charred leather and half-melted steel.

I stumbled backward. Behind me, Zia held a ball of white-hot fire in her hand. Her eyes were as wild as a cornered animal's.

"Are you mad?" I yelled. "What are you—?"

She lobbed her second fireball at the nurses' station. A vase full of daisies exploded in a shower of flaming petals and pottery shards.

"Zia!"

She didn't seem to hear me. She summoned another fireball and took aim at the sofas.

I should have run for cover. I wasn't prepared to die saving badly upholstered furniture. Instead, I lunged at her and grabbed her wrist. "Zia, stop it!"

She glared at me with flames in her eyes—and I mean that quite literally. Her irises had become disks of orange fire.

This was terrifying, of course, but I stood my ground. Over the past year I'd got rather used to surprises—what with my cat being a goddess, my brother turning into a falcon, and Felix producing penguins in the fireplace several times a week.

"Zia," I said firmly. "We can't burn down the nursing home. What's got into you?"

A look of confusion passed over her face. She stopped struggling. Her eyes returned to normal.

She stared at the melted wheelchair, then the smoldering remains of the bouquet on the carpet. "Did I—?"

"Decide those daisies needed to die?" I finished. "Yes, you did."

She extinguished her fireball, which was lucky, as it was starting to bake my face. "I'm sorry," she muttered. "I—I thought I had it under control. . . ."

"Under control?" I let go of her hand. "You mean to say you've been throwing *a lot* of random fireballs lately?"

She still looked bewildered, her gaze drifting around the lobby. "N-no . . . maybe. I've been having blackouts. I come to, and I don't remember what I've done."

"Like just now?"

She nodded. "Amos said . . . at first he thought it might be a side effect of my time in that tomb."

Ah, the tomb. For months, Zia had been trapped in a

watery sarcophagus while her *shabti* ran about impersonating her. The Chief Lector Iskandar had thought this would protect the real Zia—from Set? From Apophis? We still weren't sure. At any rate, it didn't strike me as the most brilliant idea for a supposedly wise two-thousand-year-old magician to have come up with. During her slumbers, Zia had endured horrible nightmares about her village burning and Apophis destroying the world. I suppose that might lead to some nasty posttraumatic stress.

"You said Amos thought that *at first*," I noted. "There's more to the story, then?"

Zia gazed at the melted wheelchair. The light from outside turned her hair the color of rusted iron.

"He was here," she murmured. "He was here for eons, trapped."

I took a moment to process that. "You mean Ra."

"He was miserable and alone," she said. "He had been forced to abdicate his throne. He left the mortal world and lost the will to live."

I stamped out a smoldering daisy on the carpet. "I don't know, Zia. He looked quite happy when we woke him up, singing and grinning and so on."

"No." Zia walked toward the windows, as if drawn by the lovely view of brimstone. "His mind is still sleeping. I've spent time with him, Sadie. I've watched his expressions while he naps. I've heard him whimpering and mumbling. That old body is a cage, a prison. The true Ra is trapped inside."

She was starting to worry me now. Fireballs I could deal with. Incoherent rambling—not so much.

"I suppose it makes sense you'd have sympathy with Ra," I ventured. "You're a fire elementalist. He's a fiery sort of god. You were trapped in that tomb. Ra was trapped in a nursing home. Perhaps that's what caused your blackout just now. This place reminded you of your own imprisonment."

That's right—Sadie Kane, junior psychologist. And why not? I'd spent enough time diagnosing my crazed mates Liz and Emma back in London.

Zia stared out at the burning lake. I had the feeling that my attempt at therapy might not have been so therapeutic.

"Amos tried to help me," she said. "He knows what I'm going through. He cast a spell on me to focus my mind, but . . ." She shook her head. "It's been getting worse. This is the first day in weeks that I *haven't* taken care of Ra, and the more time I spend with him, the fuzzier my thoughts get. When I summon fire now, I have trouble controlling it. Even simple spells I've done for years—I channel too much power. If that happens during a blackout . . ."

I understood why she sounded frightened. Magicians have to be careful with spells. If we channel too much power, we might inadvertently exhaust our reserves. Then the spell would tap directly into the magician's life force—with unpleasant consequences.

You will need to advise her, Isis had told me. *She must learn the path quickly.*

An uncomfortable thought began to form. I remembered Ra's delight when he had first met Zia, the way he'd tried to give her his last remaining scarab beetle. He'd babbled on and on about zebras . . . possibly meaning Zia. And now Zia was starting to empathize with the old god, even trying to burn down the nursing home where he'd been trapped for so long.

That couldn't be good. But how could I advise her when I had no idea what was happening?

Isis's warnings rattled around in my head: The path of the gods was the answer for all the Kanes. Zia was struggling. Amos was still tainted by his time with Set.

"Zia . . ." I hesitated. "You said Amos knows what you're going through. Is that why he asked Bast to watch Ra today? To give you time away from the sun god?"

"I—I suppose."

I tried to steady my breathing. Then I asked the harder question: "In the war room, Amos said he might have to use other means to fight his enemies. He hasn't . . . um, he hasn't been having trouble with Set?"

Zia wouldn't meet my eyes. "Sadie, I promised him—"

"Oh, gods of Egypt! He's *calling* on Set? Trying to channel his power, after all Set did to him? Please, no."

She didn't answer, which was an answer in itself.

"He'll be overwhelmed!" I cried. "If the rebel magicians find out that the Chief Lector is meddling with the god of evil, just as they suspected—"

"Set isn't just the god of evil," Zia reminded me. "He is Ra's lieutenant. He defended the sun god against Apophis."

"You think that makes it all better?" I shook my head in disbelief. "And now Amos thinks you're having trouble with Ra? Does he think Ra is trying to . . ." I pointed to Zia's head.

"Sadie, please . . ." Her voice trailed off in misery.

I suppose it wasn't fair for me to press her. She seemed even more confused than I was.

Still, I hated the idea of Zia being disoriented so close to our final battle—blacking out, throwing random fireballs, losing control of her own power. Even worse was the possibility that Amos had some sort of link with Set—that he might actually have *chosen* to let that horrible god back into his head.

The thought tied my gut into *tyets*—Isis knots.

I imagined my old enemy Michel Desjardins scowling. *Ne voyez-vous pas, Sadie Kane? This is what comes from the path of the gods. This is why the magic was forbidden.*

I kicked the melted remains of the wheelchair. One bent wheel squeaked and wobbled.

"We'll have to table that conversation," I decided. "We're running out of time. Now . . . where have all the old folks gone?"

Zia pointed out the window. "There," she said calmly. "They're having a beach day."

We made our way down to the black sand beach by the Lake of Fire. It wouldn't have been my top vacation spot, but elderly gods were lounging on deck chairs under brightly colored umbrellas. Others snored on beach towels or sat in their wheelchairs and stared at the boiling vista.

One shriveled bird-headed goddess in a one-piece bathing suit was building a sand pyramid. Two old men—I assumed they were fire gods—stood waist-deep in the blazing surf, laughing and splashing lava in each other's faces.

Tawaret the caretaker beamed when she saw us.

"Sadie!" she called. "You're early this week! And you've brought a friend."

Normally, I wouldn't have stood still as an upright grinning female hippo charged toward me for a hug, but I'd got used to Tawaret.

She'd traded her high heels for flip-flops. Otherwise she was dressed in her usual white nurse's uniform. Her mascara and lipstick were tastefully done, for a hippo, and her luxuriant black hair was pinned under a nurse's cap. Her ill-fitting blouse opened over an enormous belly—possibly a sign of permanent pregnancy, as she was the goddess of childbirth, or possibly a sign of eating too many cupcakes. I'd never been entirely sure.

She embraced me without crushing me, which I greatly appreciated. Her lilac perfume reminded me of my Gran, and the tinge of sulfur on her clothes reminded me of Gramps.

"Tawaret," I said, "this is Zia Rashid."

Tawaret's smile faded. "Oh . . . Oh, I see."

I'd never seen the hippo goddess so uneasy. Did she somehow know that Zia had melted her wheelchair and torched her daisies?

As the silence got awkward, Tawaret recovered her smile. "Sorry, yes. Hello, Zia. It's just that you look . . . well, never mind! Are you a friend of Bes's too?"

"Uh, not really," Zia admitted. "I mean, I suppose, but—"

"We're here on a mission," I said. "Things in the upper world have gone a bit wonky."

I told Tawaret about the rebel magicians, Apophis's plans

for attack, and our mad scheme to find the serpent's shadow and stomp it to death.

Tawaret mashed her hippoish hands together. "Oh, dear. Doomsday tomorrow? Bingo night was supposed to be Friday. My poor darlings will be so disappointed. . . ."

She glanced down the beach at her senile charges, some of whom were drooling in their sleep or eating black sand or trying to talk to the lava.

Tawaret sighed. "I suppose it would be kinder not to tell them. They've been here for eons, forgotten by the mortal world. Now they have to perish along with everyone else. They don't deserve such a fate."

I wanted to remind her that *no one* deserved such a fate— not my friends, not my family, and certainly not a brilliant young woman named Sadie Kane, who had her whole life ahead of her. But Tawaret was so kindhearted, I didn't want to sound selfish. She didn't seem concerned for herself at all, just the fading gods she cared for.

"We're not giving up yet," I promised.

"But this plan of yours!" Tawaret shuddered, causing a tsunami of jiggling hippo flesh. "It's impossible!"

"Like reviving the sun god?" I asked.

She conceded that with a shrug. "Very well, dear. I'll admit you've done the impossible before. Nevertheless . . ." She glanced at Zia, as if my friend's presence still made her nervous. "Well, I'm sure you know what you're doing. How can I help?"

"May we see Bes?" I asked.

"Of course . . . but I'm afraid he hasn't changed."

She led us down the beach. The past few months I'd visited Bes at least once a week, so I knew many of the elderly gods by sight. I spotted Heket the frog goddess perched atop a beach umbrella as if it were a lily pad. Her tongue shot out to catch something from the air. Did they have flies in the Duat?

Farther on, I saw the goose god Gengen-Wer, whose name—I kid you not—meant the Great Honker. The first time Tawaret told me that, I almost spewed tea. His Supreme Honkiness was waddling along the beach, squawking at the other gods and startling them out of their sleep.

Yet every time I visited, the crowd changed. Some gods disappeared. Others popped up—gods of cities that no longer existed; gods who had only been worshiped for a few centuries before being replaced by others; gods so old, they'd forgot their own names. Most civilizations left behind pottery shards or monuments or literature. Egypt was so old, it had left behind a landfill's worth of deities.

Halfway down the beach, we passed the two old codgers who'd been playing in the lava. Now they were wrestling waist-deep in the lake. One pummeled the other with an *ankh* and warbled, "It's *my* pudding! My pudding!"

"Oh dear," Tawaret said. "Fire-embracer and Hot Foot are at it again."

I choked back a laugh. "Hot Foot? What sort of godly name is that?"

Tawaret studied the fiery surf, as if looking for a way to navigate through it without getting incinerated. "They're gods from the Hall of Judgment, dear. Poor things. There used to be forty-two of them, each in charge of judging a different crime. Even in the old days, we could never keep them all straight. Now . . ." She shrugged. "They're quite forgotten, sadly. Fire-embracer, the one with the *ankh*—he used to be the god of robberies. I'm afraid it made him paranoid. He always thinks Hot Foot has stolen his pudding. I'll have to break up the fight."

"Let me," Zia said.

Tawaret stiffened. "You, my . . . dear?"

I got the feeling she was going to say something other than *dear.*

"The fire won't bother me," Zia assured her. "You two go ahead."

I wasn't sure how Zia could be so confident. Perhaps she simply preferred swimming in flames to seeing Bes in his present state. If so, I couldn't blame her. The experience was unsettling.

Whatever the case, Zia strode toward the surf and waded straight in like a flame-retardant *Baywatch* lifeguard.

Tawaret and I continued along the beach. We reached the dock where Ra's sun boat had anchored the first time Carter and I had visited this place.

Bes sat at the end of the pier in a comfy leather chair, which Tawaret must have brought down especially for him. He wore a fresh red-and-blue Hawaiian shirt and khaki shorts. His face was thinner than it had been last spring, but otherwise he looked unchanged—the same scraggly nest of black hair, the same bristly mane that passed for a beard, the same lovably grotesque face that reminded me of a pug dog's.

But Bes's soul was gone. He stared vacantly at the lake, not reacting at all when I knelt next to him and gripped his furry hand.

I remembered the first time he'd saved my life—picking me up in a limo full of rubbish, driving me to Waterloo Bridge, then scaring away two gods who had been chasing me. He had jumped out of the car wearing nothing but a Speedo and screamed, "Boo!"

Yes, he'd been a true friend.

"Dear Bes," I said, "we're going to try to help you."

I told him everything that had happened since my last visit. I knew he couldn't hear me. Since his secret name had been stolen, his mind simply wasn't there. But talking to him made me feel better.

Tawaret sniffled. I knew she had loved Bes forever, though Bes hadn't always returned her feelings. He couldn't have had a better caretaker.

"Oh, Sadie . . ." The hippo goddess wiped away a tear. "If you truly could help him, I—I'd do anything. But how is it possible?"

"Shadows," I said. "This bloke Setne . . . he found a way to use shadows for an execration spell. If the *sheut* is a backup copy of the soul, and if Setne's magic could be used in reverse . . ."

Tawaret's eyes widened. "You believe you could use Bes's shadow to bring him back?"

"Yes." I knew it sounded mad, but I *had* to believe. Saying it aloud to Tawaret, who cared about Bes even more than I did . . . well, I simply couldn't let her down. Besides, if we could do this for Bes, then who knew? Perhaps we could use the same magic to get the sun god Ra back in fighting shape. First things first, however. I intended to keep my promise to the dwarf god.

"Here's the tricky bit," I said. "I'm hoping you can help me locate Bes's shadow. I don't know much about gods and their *sheuts* and whatnot. I understand that you often hide them?"

Tawaret shifted nervously, her feet creaking on the pier boards. "Um, yes . . ."

"I'm hoping they're a bit like secret names," I forged on. "Since I can't ask Bes where he keeps his shadow, I thought I'd ask the person who was closest to him. I thought you'd have the best chance of knowing."

Seeing a hippo blush is quite odd. It almost made Tawaret look delicate—in a massive sort of way.

"I—I saw his shadow once," she admitted. "During one of our best moments together. We were sitting on the temple wall in Saïs."

"Sorry?"

"A city in the Nile Delta," Tawaret explained. "The home of a friend of ours—the hunting goddess Neith. She liked to invite Bes and me on her hunting excursions. We would, ah, flush her prey for her."

I imagined Tawaret and Bes, two gods with super-ugly powers, plowing through the marshes hand in hand, yelling "Boo!" to scare up bevies of quail. I decided to keep that image to myself.

"At any rate," Tawaret continued, "one night after dinner,

Bes and I were sitting alone on the walls of Neith's temple, watching the moon rise over the Nile."

She gazed at the dwarf god with such adoring eyes, I couldn't help but imagine myself on that temple wall, sharing a romantic evening with Anubis . . . no, Walt . . . no . . . Gah! My life was horrid.

I sighed unhappily. "Go on, please."

"We talked about nothing in particular," Tawaret remembered. "We held hands. That was all. But I felt so close to him. Just for a moment, I looked at the mud-brick wall next to us, and I saw Bes's shadow in the torchlight. Normally gods don't keep their shadows so close. He must've trusted me a great deal to reveal it. I asked him about it, and he laughed. He said, 'This is a good place for my shadow. I think I'll leave it here. That way it can always be happy, even when I'm not.'"

The story was so sweet and sad, I could hardly bear it.

Down the shore, the old god Fire-embracer shrieked something about pudding. Zia was standing in the surf, trying to keep the two gods apart as they splashed her with lava from both sides. Amazingly, it didn't seem to bother her.

I turned to Tawaret. "That night in Saïs—how long ago was it?"

"A few thousand years."

My heart sank. "Any chance the shadow would still be there?"

She shrugged helplessly. "Saïs was destroyed centuries ago. The temple is gone. Farmers pulled down the ancient buildings and used the mud bricks for fertilizer. Most of the land has reverted to marshes."

Blast. I'd never been a fan of Egyptian ruins. From time to time, I'd been tempted to pull down a few temples myself. But just this once, I wished the ruins had survived. I wanted to cuff those farmers.

"Then there's no hope?" I asked.

"Oh, there's always hope," Tawaret said. "You could search the area, calling on Bes's shadow. You're his friend. It might appear to you if it's still there. And if Neith is still in the area, she might be able to help. That is, if she doesn't hunt you instead . . ."

I decided not to dwell on that possibility. I had enough problems. "We'll have to try. If we can find the shadow and puzzle out the proper spell—"

"But, Sadie," the goddess said, "you have so little time. You have to stop Apophis! How can you help Bes, too?"

I looked at the dwarf god. Then I bent down and kissed his bumpy forehead. "I made a promise," I said. "Besides, we'll need him if we're going to win."

Did I really believe that? I knew Bes couldn't scare Apophis away simply by yelling "Boo!" no matter how ghastly he looked in his Speedo. In the sort of battle we were facing, I wasn't sure one more god would even make a difference. And I was even less sure that this reverse shadow idea could work on Ra. But I had to try with Bes. If the world ended the day after tomorrow, I would *not* go to my death without first knowing I'd done everything I could to save my friend.

Of all the goddesses I'd met, Tawaret was the most likely to understand my motives.

She put her hands protectively on Bes's shoulders. "In that

case, Sadie Kane, I wish you luck—for Bes, and for all of us."

I left her on the dock, standing behind Bes as if the two gods were enjoying a romantic sunset together.

On the beach, I rejoined Zia, who was brushing ashes out of her hair. Except for a few burn holes in her trousers, she looked perfectly fine.

She gestured at Fire-embracer and Hot Foot, who were once again playing nice in the lava. "They're not so bad," Zia said. "They just needed some attention."

"Like pets," I said. "Or my brother."

Zia actually smiled. "Did you find the information you need?"

"I think so," I said. "But first, we need to get to the Hall of Judgment. It's almost time for Setne's trial."

"How do we get there?" Zia asked. "Another doorway?"

I stared across the Lake of Fire, pondering that problem. I remembered the Hall of Judgment being on an island somewhere on this lake, but Duat geography is a bit dodgy. For all I knew, the hall was on a totally different level of the Duat, or the lake was six billion miles wide. I didn't fancy the idea of walking around the shore through unknown territory, or taking a swim. And I certainly didn't feel like arguing with Isis again.

Then I saw something across the fiery waves—the silhouette of a familiar steamboat approaching, twin smokestacks trailing luminous gold smoke and a paddle wheel churning through the lava.

My brother—bless his heart—was absolutely mad.

"Problem solved," I told Zia. "Carter will give us a ride."

10. "Take Your Daughter to Work Day" Goes Horribly Wrong

As THEY APPROACHED THE DOCK, Carter and Walt waved at us from the bow of the *Egyptian Queen*. Next to them stood the captain, Bloodstained Blade, who looked quite dashing in his riverboat pilot's uniform, except for the fact that his head was a blood-speckled double-sided ax.

"That's a demon," Zia said nervously.

"Yes," I agreed.

"Is it safe?"

I raised an eyebrow at her.

"Of course not," she muttered. "I'm traveling with the Kanes."

The crew of glowing orbs zipped around the boat, pulling lines and lowering the gangplank.

Carter looked tired. He wore jeans and a rumpled shirt with specks of barbecue sauce on it. His hair was wet and flat on one side as if he'd fallen asleep in the shower.

Walt looked much better—well, really, there was no

contest. He wore his usual sleeveless shirt and workout pants, and managed a smile for me even though his posture made it obvious he was in pain. The *shen* charm on my necklace seemed to heat up, or perhaps that was just my body temperature rising.

Zia and I climbed the gangplank. Bloodstained Blade bowed, which was quite unnerving, as his head could've sliced a watermelon in half.

"Welcome aboard, Lady Kane." His voice was a metallic hum from the edge of his frontal blade. "I am at your service."

"Thanks ever so," I said. "Carter, may I speak with you?"

I grabbed his ear and pulled him toward the deckhouse.

"Ow!" he complained as I dragged him along. I suppose doing that in front of Zia wasn't nice, but I thought I might as well give her pointers on how best to handle my brother.

Walt and Zia followed us into the main dining room. As usual, the mahogany table was laden with platters of fresh food. The chandelier illuminated colorful wall murals of Egyptian gods, the gilded columns, and the ornately molded ceiling.

I let go of Carter's ear and snarled, "Have you lost your mind?"

"Ow!" he yelled again. "What is your problem?"

"My problem," I said, lowering my voice, "is that you summoned this boat again and its demon captain, who Bast warned would slit our throats if he ever got the opportunity!"

"He's under a magic binding," Carter argued. "He was *fine* last time."

"Last time *Bast* was with us," I reminded him. "And if you think I trust a demon named Bloodstained Blade farther than I can—"

"Guys," Walt interrupted.

Bloodstained Blade entered the dining room, dipping his ax head under the doorframe. "Lord and Lady Kane, the journey is short from here. We will arrive at the Hall of Judgment in approximately twenty minutes."

"Thanks, BSB," Carter said as he rubbed his ear. "We'll join you on deck soon."

"Very good," said the demon. "What are your orders when we arrive?"

I tensed, hoping Carter had thought ahead. Bast had warned us that demons needed very clear instructions to stay under control.

"You'll wait for us while we visit the Hall of Judgment," Carter announced. "When we return, you'll take us where we wish to go."

"As you say." Bloodstained Blade's tone had a hint of disappointment—or was that my imagination?

After he left, Zia frowned. "Carter, in this case I agree with Sadie. How can you trust that creature? Where did you get this ship?"

"It belonged to our parents," Carter said.

He and I shared a look, silently agreeing that was enough said. Our mum and dad had sailed this riverboat up the Thames to Cleopatra's Needle the night Mum had died releasing Bast from the abyss. Afterward, Dad had sat in this very room, grieving, with only the cat goddess and the demon captain for company.

Bloodstained Blade had accepted us as his new masters. He'd followed our orders before, but that was little comfort. I didn't trust him. I didn't like being on this ship.

On the other hand, we needed to get to the Hall of Judgment. I was hungry and thirsty, and I supposed I could endure a twenty-minute voyage if it meant enjoying a chilled Ribena and a plate of tandoori chicken with naan.

The four of us sat around the table. We ate while we compared stories. All in all, it was quite possibly the most awkward double date in history. We had no shortage of dire emergencies to talk about, but the tension in the room was as thick as Cairo smog.

Carter hadn't seen Zia in person for months. I could tell he was trying not to stare. Zia was clearly uncomfortable sitting so close to him. She kept leaning away, which no doubt hurt his feelings. Perhaps she was just worried about having another fireball-throwing episode. As for me, I was elated to be next to Walt, but at the same time, I was desperately worried about him. I couldn't forget how he'd looked wrapped in glowing mummy linen, and I wondered what Anubis had wanted to tell me about Walt's situation. Walt tried to hide it, but he was obviously in great pain. His hands trembled as he picked up his peanut butter sandwich.

Carter told me about the pending evacuation of Brooklyn House, which Bast was overseeing. My heart nearly broke when I thought of little Shelby, wonderful silly Felix, shy Cleo, and all the rest going off to defend the First Nome against an impossible attack, but I knew Carter was right. There was no other choice.

Carter kept hesitating, as if waiting for Walt to contribute information. Walt stayed silent. Clearly he was holding some-thing back. Somehow or other, I'd have to get Walt alone and grill him for details.

In return, I told Carter about our visit to the House of Rest. I shared my suspicions that Amos might be calling on Set for extra power. Zia didn't contradict me, and the news didn't sit well with my brother. After several minutes of swearing and pacing the room, he finally calmed down enough to say, "We can't let that happen. He'll be destroyed."

"I know," I said. "But we can best help him by moving forward."

I didn't mention Zia's blackout in the nursing home. In Carter's present state of mind, I thought that might be too much for him. But I did tell him what Tawaret had said about the possible location of Bes's shadow.

"The ruins of Saïs . . ." He frowned. "I think Dad men-tioned that place. He said there wasn't much left. But even if we could find the shadow, we don't have time. We've got to stop Apophis."

"I made a promise," I insisted. "Besides, we *need* Bes. Think of it as a trial run. Saving his shadow will give us a chance to practice this sort of magic before we try it on Apophis—um, in reverse, of course. It might even give us a way to revive Ra."

"But—"

"She's got a point," Walt interrupted.

I'm not sure who was more surprised—Carter, or me.

"Even if we get Setne's help," Walt said, "trapping a shadow in a statue is going to be difficult. I'd feel better if we could try it on a friendly target first. I could show you how it's done while—while I still have time."

"Walt," I said, "please, don't talk like that."

"When you face Apophis," he continued, "you'll have only one chance to get the spell right. It would be better to have some practice."

When you face Apophis. He said it so calmly, but his meaning was clear: he wouldn't be around when that happened.

Carter nudged his half-eaten pizza. "I just . . . I don't see how we can do it all in time. I know this is a personal mission for you, Sadie, but—"

"She has to," Zia said gently. "Carter, you once went off on a personal mission in the middle of a crisis, didn't you? That worked out." She put her hand on Carter's. "Sometimes you have to follow your heart."

Carter looked like he was trying to swallow a golf ball. Before he could say anything, the ship's bell sounded.

In the corner of the dining room, a loudspeaker crackled with Bloodstained Blade's voice: "My lords and ladies, we have reached the Hall of Judgment."

The black temple looked just as I remembered. We made our way up the steps from the dock and passed between rows of obsidian columns that marched into the gloom.

Sinister-looking scenes of Underworld life glittered on the floor and in friezes circling the pillars—black designs on black stone. Despite the reed torches that burned every few meters, the air was so hazy with volcanic ash, I couldn't see far in front of us.

As we moved deeper into the temple, voices whispered around us. Out of the corner of my eye, I saw groups of spirits drifting across the pavilion—ghostly shapes camouflaged in the smoky air. Some moved aimlessly—crying softly or tearing at their clothes in despair. Others carried armfuls of papyrus scrolls. These ghosts looked more solid and purposeful, as if they were waiting for something.

"Petitioners," Walt said. "They've brought their case files, hoping for an audience with Osiris. He was gone so long . . . there must be a real backlog of cases."

Walt's step seemed lighter. His eyes looked more alert, his body less weighed down by pain. He was so close to death, I'd feared this trip to the Underworld might be hard for him, but if anything he seemed more at ease than the rest of us.

"How do you know?" I asked.

Walt hesitated. "I'm not sure. It just seems . . . correct."

"And the ghosts without scrolls?"

"Refugees," he said. "They're hoping this place will protect them."

I didn't ask what from. I remembered the ghost at the Brooklyn Academy dance who'd been engulfed in black tendrils and dragged underground. I thought about the vision Carter had described—our mother huddled beneath a cliff somewhere in the Duat, resisting the pull of a dark force in the distance.

"We need to hurry." I started to forge ahead, but Zia grabbed my arm.

"There," she said. "Look."

The smoke parted. Twenty meters ahead stood a massive set of obsidian doors. In front of them, an animal the size of a greyhound sat on its haunches—an oversized jackal with thick black fur, fluffy pointed ears, and a face somewhere between a fox and a wolf. Its moon-colored eyes glittered in the darkness.

It snarled at us, but I wasn't put off. I may be biased, but I think jackals are cute and cuddly, even if they *were* known for digging up graves in Ancient Egypt.

"It's just Anubis," I said hopefully. "This is where we met him last time."

"That's not Anubis," Walt warned.

"Of course it is," I told him. "Watch."

"Sadie, don't," Carter said, but I walked toward the guardian.

"Hullo, Anubis," I called. "It's just me, Sadie."

The cute fuzzy jackal bared his fangs. His mouth began to froth. His adorable yellow eyes sent an unmistakable message: *One more step, and I'll chew your head off.*

I froze. "Right . . . that's not Anubis, unless he's having a really bad day."

"This is where we met him before," Carter said. "Why isn't he here?"

"It's one of his minions," Walt ventured. "Anubis must be . . . elsewhere."

Again, he sounded awfully sure, and I felt a strange pang of jealousy. Walt and Anubis seemed to have spent more time talking with each other than with me. Walt was suddenly an expert on all things deathly. Meanwhile, I couldn't even be *near* Anubis without invoking the wrath of his chaperone— Shu, the god of hot air. It wasn't bloody fair!

Zia moved next to me, gripping her staff. "So, what now? Do we have to defeat it to pass?"

I imagined her lobbing some of her daisy-destroying fireballs. That's all we needed—a yelping, flaming jackal running through my father's courtyard.

"No," Walt said, stepping forward. "It's just a gatekeeper. It needs to know our business."

"Walt," Carter said, "if you're wrong . . ."

Walt raised his hands and slowly approached the jackal. "I am Walt Stone," he said. "This is Carter and Sadie Kane. And this is Zia . . ."

"Rashid," Zia supplied.

"We have business at the Hall of Judgment," Walt said.

The jackal snarled, but it sounded more inquisitive, not so *chew-your-head-off* hostile.

"We have testimony to offer," Walt continued. "Information relevant to the trial of Setne."

"Walt," Carter whispered, "when did you become a junior lawyer?"

I shushed him. Walt's plan seemed to be working. The jackal tilted its head as if listening, then rose and padded away into the darkness. The obsidian double doors swung open silently.

"Well done, Walt," I said. "How did you . . . ?"

He faced me, and my heart did a somersault. Just for a moment I thought he looked like . . . No. Obviously my mixed-up emotions were playing with my mind. "Um, how did you know what to say?"

Walt shrugged. "I took a guess."

Just as quickly as they'd opened, the doors began to close.

"Hurry!" Carter warned. We sprinted into the courtroom of the dead.

At the start of the autumn semester—my first experience in an American school—our teacher had asked us to write down our parents' contact information and what they did for a living, in case they could help with career day. I had never heard of career day. Once I understood what it was, I couldn't stop giggling.

Could your dad come talk about his work? I imagined the headmistress asking.

Possibly, Mrs. Laird . . . I'd say. Except he's dead, you see. Well, not completely dead. He's more of a resurrected god. He judges mortal spirits and feeds the hearts of the wicked to his pet monster. Oh, and he has blue skin. I'm sure he'd make quite an impression on career day, for all those students aspiring to grow up and become Ancient Egyptian deities.

The Hall of Judgment had changed since my last visit. The room tended to mirror the thoughts of Osiris, so it often looked like a ghostly replica of my family's old apartment in Los Angeles, from the happier times when we all lived together.

Now, possibly because Dad was on duty, the place was fully Egyptian. The circular chamber was lined with stone pillars carved in lotus flower designs. Braziers of magic fire washed the walls in green and blue light. In the center of the room stood the scales of justice, two large golden saucers balanced from an iron T.

Kneeling before the scales was the ghost of a man in a pinstriped suit, nervously reciting from a scroll. I understood why he was tense. On either side of him stood a large reptilian demon with green skin, a cobra head, and a wicked-looking pole arm poised over the ghost's head.

Dad sat at the far end of the room on a golden dais, with a blue-skinned Egyptian attendant at his side. Seeing my father in the Duat was always disorienting, because he appeared to be two people at once. On one level, he looked like he had in life—a handsome, muscular man with chocolate-brown skin, a bald scalp, and a neatly trimmed goatee. He wore an elegant silk suit and a dark traveling coat, like a businessman about to board a private jet.

On a deeper level of reality, however, he appeared as Osiris, god of the dead. He was dressed as a pharaoh in sandals, an embroidered linen kilt, and rows of gold and coral neckbands on his bare chest. His skin was the color of a summer sky. Across his lap lay a crook and flail—the symbols of Egyptian kingship.

As strange as it was seeing my father with blue skin and a skirt, I was so happy to be near him again, I quite forgot about the court proceedings.

"Dad!" I ran toward him.

(Carter says I was foolish, but Dad *was* the king of the court, wasn't he? Why shouldn't I be allowed to run up to say hello?)

I was halfway across when the snake demons crossed their pole arms and blocked my path.

"It's all right," Dad said, looking a bit startled. "Let her through."

I flew into his arms, knocking the crook and flail out of his lap.

He hugged me warmly, chuckling with affection. For a moment I felt like a little girl again, safe in his embrace. Then he held me at arm's length, and I could see how weary he was. He had bags under his eyes. His face was gaunt. Even the powerful blue aura of Osiris, which normally surrounded him like the corona of a star, flickered weakly.

"Sadie, my love," he said in a strained voice. "Why have you come? I'm *working*."

I tried not to feel hurt. "But, Dad, this is important!"

Carter, Walt, and Zia approached the dais. My father's expression turned grim.

"I see," he said. "First let me finish this trial. Children, stand here on my right. And please, don't interrupt."

My dad's attendant stamped his foot. "My lord, this is most irregular!"

He was an odd-looking fellow—an elderly blue Egyptian man with a huge scroll in his arms. Too solid to be a ghost, too blue to be human, he was almost as decrepit as Ra, wearing nothing but a loincloth, sandals, and an ill-fitting wig. I suppose that glossy black wedge of fake hair was meant to look manly in an Ancient Egyptian sort of way, but along with the kohl eyeliner and the rouge on his cheeks, the old boy looked like a grotesque Cleopatra impersonator.

The roll of papyrus he held was simply enormous. Years ago, I'd gone to synagogue with my friend Liz, and the Torah they kept there was *tiny* in comparison.

"It's all right, Disturber," my father told him. "We may continue now."

"But, my lord—" The old man (was his name really Disturber?) became so agitated he lost control of his scroll. The bottom dropped out and unraveled, bouncing down the steps like a papyrus carpet.

"Oh, bother, bother, bother!" Disturber struggled to reel in his document.

My father suppressed a smile. He turned back to the ghost in the pinstriped suit, who was still kneeling at the scales. "My apologies, Robert Windham. You may finish your testimony."

The ghost bowed and scraped. "Y-yes, Lord Osiris."

He referred to his notes and began rattling off a list of crimes he wasn't guilty of—murder, theft, and selling cattle under false pretenses.

I turned to Walt and whispered, "He's a modern chap, isn't he? What's he doing in Osiris's court?"

I was a bit troubled to find that Walt once again had an answer.

"The afterlife looks different to every soul," he said,

"depending on what they believe. For that guy, Egypt must've made a strong impression. Maybe he read the stories when he was young."

"And if someone doesn't believe in *any* afterlife?" I asked.

Walt gave me a sad look. "Then that's what they experience."

On the other side of the dais, the blue god Disturber hissed at us to be quiet. Why is it when adults try to silence kids, they always make more noise than the noise they're trying to stop?

The ghost of Robert Windham seemed to be winding down his testimony. "I haven't given false witness against my neighbors. Um, sorry, I can't read this last line—"

"Fish!" Disturber yelped crossly. "Have you stolen any fish from the holy lakes?"

"I lived in Kansas," the ghost said. "So . . . no."

My father rose from his throne. "Very well. Let his heart be weighed."

One of the snake demons produced a linen parcel the size of a child's fist.

Next to me, Carter inhaled sharply. "His *heart* is in there?"

"Shh!" Disturber said so loudly his wig almost fell off. "Bring forth the Destroyer of Souls!"

On the far wall of the chamber, a doggy door burst open. Ammit ran into the room in great excitement. The poor dear wasn't very coordinated. His miniature lion chest and forearms were sleek and agile, but his back half was a stubby and much-less-agile hippo bum. He kept sliding sideways, swerving into pillars, and knocking over braziers. Each time he crashed, he shook his lion's mane and crocodile snout and yipped happily.

(Carter is scolding me, as always. He says Ammit is female. I'll admit I can't prove it either way, but I've always thought of Ammit as a boy monster. He's much too hyper to be otherwise, and the way he marks his territory . . . but never mind.)

"There's my baby!" I cried, quite carried away. "There's my Poochiekins!"

Ammit ran at me and leaped into my arms, nuzzling me with his rough snout.

"My lord Osiris!" Disturber lost the bottom of his scroll again, which unraveled around his legs. "This is an outrage!"

"Sadie," Dad said firmly, "please do not refer to the Devourer of Souls as Poochiekins."

"Sorry," I muttered, and let Ammit down.

One of the snake demons set Robert Windham's heart on the scales of justice. I'd seen many pictures of Anubis performing this duty, and I wished he were here now. Anubis would've been *much* more interesting to watch than some snake demon.

On the opposite scale, the Feather of Truth appeared. (Don't get me started on the Feather of Truth.)

The scales wavered. The two saucers stopped, just about even. The pinstriped ghost sobbed with relief. Ammit whimpered disappointedly.

"Most impressive," my father said. "Robert Windham, you have been found sufficiently virtuous, despite the fact you were an investment banker."

"Red Cross donations, baby!" the ghost yelled.

"Yes, well," Dad said dryly, "you may proceed to the afterlife."

A door opened to the left of the dais. The snake demons hauled Robert Windham to his feet.

"Thank you!" he yelled, as the demons escorted him out. "And if you need any financial advice, Lord Osiris, I still believe in the long term viability of the market—"

The door shut behind him.

Disturber sniffed indignantly. "Horrible man."

My father shrugged. "A modern soul who appreciated the ancient ways of Egypt. He couldn't have been all bad." Dad turned to us. "Children, this is Disturber, one of my advisors and gods of judgment."

"Sorry?" I pretended not to have heard. "Did you say he's *disturbed?*"

"Disturber is my name!" the god shouted angrily. "I judge those who are guilty of losing their temper!"

"Yes." Despite my father's weariness, his eyes sparkled with amusement. "That was Disturber's traditional duty, although now that he's my last minister, he helps me with all my cases. There used to be forty-two judgment gods for different crimes, you see, but—"

"Like Hot Foot and Fire-embracer," Zia said.

Disturber gasped. "How do you know of them?"

"We saw them," Zia said. "In the Fourth House of the Night."

"You—saw—" Disturber almost dropped his scroll altogether. "Lord Osiris, we must save them immediately! My brethren—"

"We will discuss it," Dad promised. "First, I want to hear what brings my children to the Duat."

We took turns explaining: the rebel magicians and their secret alliance with Apophis, their impending attack on the First Nome, and our hope to find a new sort of execration spell that might stop Apophis for good.

Some of our news surprised and troubled our father—like the fact that many magicians had fled the First Nome, leaving it so poorly defended that we'd sent our initiates from Brooklyn House to help, and that Amos was flirting with the powers of Set.

"No," Dad said. "No, he can't! These magicians who've abandoned him—inexcusable! The House of Life must rally to the Chief Lector." He began to rise. "I should go to my brother—"

"My lord," Disturber said, "you are not a magician anymore. You are Osiris."

Dad grimaced, but he eased back into his throne. "Yes. Yes, of course. Please, children, continue."

Some of our news Dad already knew. His shoulders slumped when we mentioned the spirits of the dead who were disappearing, and the vision of our mum lost somewhere in the deep Duat, fighting against the pull of a dark force that Carter and I were certain was the shadow of Apophis.

"I have searched for your mother everywhere," Dad said despondently. "This force that is taking the spirits—whether it's the serpent's shadow or something else—I cannot stop it. I can't even *find* it. Your mother . . ."

His expression turned brittle as ice. I understood what he was feeling. For years he had lived with guilt because he couldn't prevent our mum's death. Now she was in danger again, and even though he was the lord of the dead, he felt helpless to save her.

"We can find her," I promised. "All of this is connected, Dad. We have a plan."

Carter and I explained about the *sheut*, and how it might be used for a king-sized execration spell.

My father sat forward. His eyes narrowed. "Anubis *told* you this? He revealed the nature of the *sheut* to a mortal?"

His blue aura flickered dangerously. I'd never been scared of my dad, but I'll admit I took a step back. "Well . . . it wasn't just Anubis."

"Thoth helped," Carter said. "And some of it we guessed—"

"Thoth!" my father spat. "This is dangerous knowledge, children. Much too dangerous. I won't have you—"

"Dad!" I shouted. I think I surprised him, but my patience had finally snapped. I'd had quite enough of gods telling me what I *shouldn't* or *couldn't* do. "Apophis's shadow is what's drawing the souls of the dead. It has to be! It's feeding on them, getting stronger as Apophis prepares to rise."

I hadn't really processed that idea before, but as I spoke the words, they felt like the truth—horrifying, but the truth.

"We've got to find the shadow and capture it," I insisted. "Then we can use it to banish the serpent. It's our only chance—unless you want us to use a *standard* execration. We've got the statue ready to go for that, don't we, Carter?"

Carter patted his backpack. "The spell will kill us," he said. "And it probably won't work. But if that's our only option . . ."

Zia looked horrified. "Carter, you didn't tell me! You made a statue of—of *him*? You'd sacrifice yourself to—"

"No," our father said. The anger drained out of him. He slumped forward and put his face in his hands. "No, you're right, Sadie. A small chance is better than none. I just couldn't bear it if you . . ." He sat up and took a breath, trying to regain his composure. "How can I help? I assume you came here for a reason, but you're asking for magic I don't possess."

"Yes, well," I said, "that's the tricky part."

Before I could say more, the sound of a gong reverberated through the chamber. The main doors began to open.

"My lord," Disturber said, "the next trial begins."

"Not now!" my father snapped. "Can't it be delayed?"

"No, my lord." The blue god lowered his voice. "This is *his* trial. You know . . ."

"Oh, by the twelve gates of the night," Dad cursed. "Children, this trial is very serious."

"Yes," I said. "Actually, that's what—"

"We'll talk afterward," Dad cut me off. "And please, whatever you do, don't speak to the accused or make eye contact with him. This spirit is particularly—"

The gong sounded again. A troop of demons marched in, surrounding the accused. I didn't have to ask who he was.

Setne had arrived.

The guards were intimidating enough—six red-skinned warriors with guillotine blades for heads.

Even without them, I could tell Setne was dangerous from

all the magical precautions. Glowing hieroglyphs spiraled around him like the rings of Saturn—a collection of anti-magic symbols like: *Suppress, Dampen, Stay, Shut up, Powerless,* and *Don't even think about it.*

Setne's wrists were bound together with pink strips of cloth. Two more pink bands were tied around his waist. One was fastened around his neck, and two more connected his ankles so he shuffled as he walked. To the casual observer, the pink ribbons might've looked like the Hello Kitty incarceration play set, but I knew from personal experience that they were some of the most powerful magic bonds in the world.

"The Seven Ribbons of Hathor," Walt whispered. "I wish I could make some of those."

"I've got some," Zia murmured. "But the recharge time is *really* long. Mine won't be ready until December."

Walt looked at her in awe.

The guillotine demons fanned out on either side of the accused.

Setne himself didn't look like trouble, certainly not some-one worthy of so much security. He was quite small—not *Bes* small, mind you, but still a diminutive man. His arms and legs were scrawny. His chest was a xylophone of ribs. Yet he stuck out his chin and smiled confidently as if he owned the world—which isn't easy when one is wearing only a loincloth and some pink ribbons.

Without a doubt, his face was the same one I'd seen in the wall at the Dallas Museum, and again in the Hall of Ages. He'd been the priest who sacrificed that bull in the shimmer-ing vision from the New Kingdom.

He had the same hawkish nose, heavy-lidded eyes, and thin cruel lips. Most priests from ancient times were bald, but Setne's hair was dark and thick, slicked back with oil like a 1950s tough boy. If I'd seen him in Piccadilly Circus (with more clothes on, hopefully) I would've steered clear, assuming he was handing out advertisements or trying to sell scalped tickets to a West End show. Sleazy and annoying? Yes. Dangerous? Not really.

The guillotine demons pushed him to his knees. Setne seemed to find that amusing. His eyes flickered over the room, registering each one of us. I tried not to make eye contact, but it was difficult. Setne recognized me and winked. Somehow I knew that he could read my jumbled emotions quite well, and that he found them funny.

He inclined his head toward the throne. "Lord Osiris, all this fuss for me? You shouldn't have."

My father didn't answer. With a grim expression, he gestured at Disturber, who shuffled through his scroll until he found the proper spot.

"Setne, also known as Prince Khaemwaset—"

"Oh, wow . . ." Setne grinned at me, and I fought the urge to smile back. "Haven't heard *that* name in a while. That's ancient history, right there!"

Disturber huffed. "You stand accused of heinous crimes! You have blasphemed against the gods four thousand and ninety-two times."

"Ninety-one," Setne corrected. "That crack about Lord Horus—that was just a misunderstanding." He winked at Carter. "Am I right, pal?"

How in the world did he know about Carter and Horus?

Disturber shuffled his scroll. "You have used magic for evil purposes, including twenty-three murders—"

"Self-defense!" Setne tried to spread his hands, but the ribbons restrained him.

"—including one incident where you were *paid* to kill with magic," Disturber said.

Setne shrugged. "That was self-defense for my employer."

"You plotted against three separate pharaohs," Disturber continued. "You tried to overthrow the House of Life on six occasions. Most grievous of all, you robbed the tombs of the dead to steal books of magic."

Setne laughed easily. He glanced at me as if to say, *Can you believe this guy?*

"Look, Disturber," he said, "that *is* your name, right? A handsome, intelligent judgment god like you—you've got to be overworked and underappreciated. I feel for you, I really do. You've got better things to do than dig up my old history. Besides, all these charges—I answered them already in my previous trials."

"Oh." Disturber looked confused. He adjusted his wig self-consciously and turned to my dad. "Should we let him go, then, my lord?"

"No, Disturber." Dad sat forward. "The prisoner is using divine words to influence your mind, warping the most sacred magic of Ma'at. Even in his bindings, he is dangerous."

Setne examined his fingernails. "Lord Osiris, I'm flattered, but honestly, these charges—"

"Silence!" Dad thrust his hand toward the prisoner. The swirling hieroglyphs glowed brighter around him. The Ribbons of Hathor tightened.

Setne began to choke. His smug expression melted, replaced by absolute hatred. I could feel his anger. He wanted to kill my father, kill us all.

"Dad!" I said. "Please, don't!"

My father frowned at me, clearly unhappy with the interruption. He snapped his fingers, and Setne's bonds eased. The ghost magician coughed and retched.

"Khaemwaset, son of Ramses," my father said calmly, "you have been sentenced to oblivion more than once. The first time you managed to plead for a reduced sentence, volunteering to serve the pharaoh with your magic—"

"Yes," Setne croaked. He tried to recover his poise, but his smile was twisted with pain. "I'm skilled labor, my lord. It would be a crime to destroy me."

"Yet you escaped en route," my father said. "You killed your guards and spent the next three hundred years sowing Chaos across Egypt."

Setne shrugged. "It wasn't *that* bad. Just a bit of fun."

"You were captured and sentenced again," my father continued, "three more times. In each instance, you connived your way to freedom. And since the gods have been absent from the world, you've run amok, doing as you pleased, committing crimes and terrorizing mortals."

"My lord, that's unfair," Setne protested. "First of all, I *missed* you gods. Honestly, it was a dull few millennia without you. As for these so-called crimes, well, some people might say the French Revolution was a first-class party! I know *I* enjoyed myself. And Archduke Ferdinand? A total bore. If you knew him, you would've assassinated him too."

"Enough!" Dad said. "You are done. I am the host of Osiris now. I will not tolerate the existence of a villain like you, even as a spirit. This time you are out of tricks."

Ammit yipped excitedly. The guillotine guards chopped their blades up and down as if they were clapping. Disturber cried, "Hear, hear!"

As for Setne . . . he threw back his head and laughed.

My father looked stunned, then outraged. He raised his hand to tighten the Ribbons of Hathor, but Setne said, "Wait, my lord. Here's the thing. I'm *not* out of tricks. Ask your children over there. Ask their friends. Those kids need my help."

"No more lies," my father growled. "Your heart shall be weighed, *again*, and Ammit will devour—"

"Dad!" I shrieked. "He's right! We *do* need him."

My father turned toward me. I could practically see the grief and rage roiling inside him. He'd lost his wife again. He was powerless to assist his brother. A battle for the end of the world was about to begin, and his children were on the front line. Dad *needed* to serve justice on this ghost magician. He needed to feel that he could do something right.

"Dad, please, listen," I said. "I know it's dangerous. I know you'll hate this. But we came here because of Setne. What we told you earlier about our plan—Setne's got the knowledge we need."

"Sadie's right," Carter said. "Please, Dad. You asked how you could help. Give us custody of Setne. He's the key to defeating Apophis."

At the sound of that name, a cold wind blew through the courtroom. The braziers sputtered. Ammit whimpered and put his paws over his snout. Even the guillotine demons shuffled nervously.

"No," Dad said. "Absolutely not. Setne is influencing you with his magic. He is a servant of Chaos."

"My lord," Setne said, his tone suddenly soft and respectful, "I'm a lot of things, but a servant of the snake? No. I don't want the world destroyed. There's nothing in that for me. Listen to the girl. Let her tell you her plan."

The words worked their way into my mind. I realized Setne was using magic, commanding me to speak. I steeled myself against the urge. Sadly, Setne was ordering me to do something I loved—talk. It all came spilling out: How we'd tried to save the Book of Overcoming Apophis in Dallas, how Setne had spoken with me there, how we'd found the shadow box and struck on the idea of using the *sheut*. I explained my hopes to revive Bes and destroy Apophis.

"It's impossible," Dad said. "Even if it wasn't, Setne can't be trusted. I would never release him, especially not to my children. He'd kill you at the first opportunity!"

"Dad," Carter said, "we're not children anymore. We can do this."

The agony in my father's face was hard to bear. I forced back my tears and approached the throne.

"Dad, I know you love us." I gripped his hand. "I know you want to protect us, but you risked everything to give us a chance at saving the world. Now it's time we did that. This is the only way."

"She's right." Setne managed to sound regretful, as if he were sorry he might get a reprieve. "Also, my lord, it's the only way to save the spirits of the dead before the shadow of Apophis destroys them all—including your wife."

My father's face turned from sky blue to deep indigo. He gripped the throne like he wanted to tear off the armrests.

I thought Setne had gone too far.

Then my father's hands relaxed. The anger in his eyes changed to desperation and hunger.

"Guards," he said, "give the prisoner the Feather of Truth. He will hold it while he explains himself. If he lies, he will perish in flames."

One of the guillotine demons plucked the feather from the scales of justice. Setne looked unconcerned as the glowing plume was placed in his hands.

"Right!" he began. "So your kids are correct. I did create a shadow execration spell. In theory, it could be used to destroy a god—or even Apophis. I never tried. Unfortunately, it can only be cast by a living magician. I died before I could test it. Not that I wanted to kill any gods, my lord. I was just thinking I'd use it to blackmail them into doing my bidding."

"Blackmail . . . the gods," Dad growled.

Setne smiled guiltily. "This was back in my misguided youth. Anyway, I recorded the formula in several copies of the Book of Overcoming Apophis."

Walt grunted. "Which have all been destroyed."

"Okay," Setne said, "but my original notes would still be in the margins of the Book of Thoth that I . . . that I stole. See? Being honest. I guarantee you even Apophis hasn't found that book. I hid it too well. I can show you where it is. The book will explain how to find the shadow of Apophis, how to capture it, and how to cast the execration."

"Can't you just tell us how?" Carter asked.

Setne pouted. "Young master, I'd *love* to. But I don't have the whole book memorized. And it's been millennia since I wrote that spell. If I told you one wrong word in the incantation, well . . . we wouldn't want any mistakes. But I can lead you to the book. Once we get it—"

"*We?*" Zia asked. "Why can't you just give us directions to the book? Why do you need to come along?"

The ghost grinned. "Because, doll, I'm the only one who can retrieve it. Traps, curses . . . you know. Besides, you'll need my help deciphering the notes. The spell is complicated! But don't worry. All you gotta do is keep these Ribbons of Hathor on me. It's Zia, right? You've got experience using them."

"How did you know—?"

"If I cause you any trouble," Setne continued, "you can tie me up good like a Harvest Day present. But I won't try to escape—at least not until I lead you to the Book of Thoth and then get you safely to the shadow of Apophis. Nobody knows the deepest levels of the Duat like I do. I'm your best hope for a guide."

The Feather of Truth didn't react. Setne didn't go up in flames, so I guessed he wasn't lying.

"Four of us," Carter said. "One of him."

"Except he killed his guards last time," Walt pointed out.

"So we'll be more careful," Carter said. "All of us together should be able to keep him under control."

Setne winced. "Oh, except . . . see, Sadie's got her little side task, doesn't she? She's gotta find the shadow of Bes. And actually, it's a good idea."

I blinked. "It is?"

"Absolutely, doll," Setne said. "We don't have much time. More specifically, your friend Walt there doesn't have much time."

I wanted to kill the ghost, except he was already dead. I suddenly hated that smug smile.

I gritted my teeth. "Go on."

"Walt Stone—sorry, pal, but you won't survive long enough to get the Book of Thoth, travel to the shadow of Apophis, and use the spell. There just isn't time left on your clock. But getting Bes's shadow—that won't take as long. It'll be a good test of the magic. If it works, great! If it doesn't . . . well, we've only lost one dwarf god."

I wanted to stomp his face, but he gestured for patience.

"What I'm thinking," he said, "is we split up. Carter and Zia, you two go with me to get the Book of Thoth. Meanwhile, Sadie takes Walt to the ruins of Saïs to find the dwarf's shadow. I'll give you some notes on how to capture it, but the spell is just theory. In practice, you'll need Walt's charm-making skill to pull it off. He'll have to improvise if anything goes wrong. If Walt succeeds, then Sadie will know how to capture a shadow. If Walt dies afterward—and I'm sorry, but casting a spell like that will probably do him in—then Sadie can rendezvous with us in the Duat, and we'll hunt down the snake's shadow. Everybody wins!"

I wasn't sure whether to weep or scream. I only managed to keep my calm because I sensed that Setne would find any reaction extremely funny.

He faced my father. "What do you say, Lord Osiris? It's a chance to get your wife back, defeat Apophis, restore Bes's soul, save the world! All I ask is that when I come back, the court take my good deeds into consideration when you sentence me. How fair is that, huh?"

The chamber was silent except for the crackling fires in the braziers.

Finally Disturber seemed to shake himself out of a trance. "My lord . . . what is your ruling?"

Dad looked at me. I could tell he hated this plan. But Setne had tempted him with the one thing he couldn't pass up: a chance to save our mum. The vile ghost had promised me one last day alone with Walt, which I wanted more than anything, and a chance to save Bes, which was a close second. He'd put Carter and Zia together and promised them a chance to save the world.

He'd put hooks in all of us and reeled us in like fish from a sacred lake. But despite the fact that I knew we were being played, I couldn't find a reason to say no.

"We have to, Dad," I said.

He lowered his head. "Yes, we do. May Ma'at protect us all."

"Oh, we'll have fun!" Setne said cheerfully. "Shall we get going? Doomsday isn't gonna wait!"

11. Don't Worry, Be Hapi

TYPICAL.

Sadie and Walt go off looking for a friendly shadow, while Zia and I escort a psychotic murderous ghost to his heavily trapped stash of forbidden magic. Gee, who got the better end of that deal?

The *Egyptian Queen* burst out of the Underworld and into the Nile like a breaching whale. Its paddle wheel churned through the blue water. Its smokestacks billowed golden smoke into the desert air. After the gloom of the Duat, the sunlight was blinding. Once my eyes adjusted, I saw we were chugging downriver, heading north, so we must have surfaced somewhere to the south of Memphis.

On either side, marshy green riverbanks columned with palm trees stretched into the humid haze. A few houses dotted the landscape. A battered pickup truck rumbled down the riverfront road. A sailboat glided by on our port side. No one paid us any attention.

I wasn't sure exactly where we were. It could've been anywhere along the Nile. But judging from the position of the sun, it was already late morning. We'd eaten and slept in my father's realm, figuring we wouldn't be able to close our eyes once we had custody of Setne. It hadn't felt like much of a rest, but obviously we'd spent more time down under than I realized. The day was slipping by. Tomorrow at dawn, the rebels would attack the First Nome, and Apophis would rise.

Zia stood next to me at the bow. She'd showered and changed into a spare set of combat clothes—a camo tank top, olive cargo pants tucked into her boots. Maybe that doesn't sound glamorous, but in the morning sunlight she was beautiful. Best of all, she was here in person—not a reflection in the scrying bowl, not a *shabti*. When the wind changed directions I caught the scent of her lemon shampoo. Our forearms touched as we leaned against the rail, but she didn't seem to mind. Her skin was feverishly warm.

"What are you thinking?" I asked.

She had trouble focusing on me. Up close, the flecks of green and black in her amber eyes were sort of hypnotizing. "I was thinking about Ra," she said. "Wondering who's taking care of him today."

"I'm sure he's fine."

But I felt a little disappointed. Personally, I was thinking about the moment when Zia had taken my hand in the dining room last night: *Sometimes you have to follow your heart.* This might be our last day on earth. If it was, I should really tell Zia how I felt about her. I mean, I thought she knew, but I didn't *know* that she knew, so . . . Oh, man. Headache.

I started to say, "Zia—"

Setne materialized next to us. "All better!"

In the daylight, he looked almost like flesh-and-blood, but when he turned in a circle, showing off his new clothes, his face and hands flickered holographically. I'd given him permission to put on something besides the loincloth. In fact, I'd insisted. But I hadn't expected an outfit so mind-boggling.

Maybe he was trying to live up to Sadie's nickname for him: Uncle Vinnie. He wore a black suit jacket with padded shoulders, a red T-shirt, a crisp pair of jeans, and blindingly white running shoes. Around his neck was a heavy gold chain of interlocking *ankhs*. On each pinky he wore a ring the size of a jawbreaker, with the symbol of power—*was*—set in diamonds. His hair was combed back with even more grease. His eyes were lined with kohl. He looked like the Ancient Egyptian Mafia.

Then I noticed something missing from his ensemble. He didn't seem to be wearing the Ribbons of Hathor.

I'll admit: I panicked. I yelled the command word Zia had taught me: *"Tās!"*

The symbol for *Bind* flared in Setne's face:

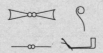

The Ribbons of Hathor reappeared around his neck, wrists, ankles, chest, and waist. They expanded aggressively, cocooning Setne in a pink tornado until he was wrapped tight as a mummy, with nothing showing but his eyes.

"Mm!" he protested.

I took a deep breath. Then I snapped my fingers. The bindings shrank back to their normal size.

"What was *that* for?" Setne demanded.

"I didn't see the ribbons."

"You didn't . . ." Setne laughed. "Carter, Carter, Carter. Come on, pal. That's just an illusion—a cosmetic change. I can't *really* get out of these things."

He held out his wrists. The ribbons vanished, then reappeared. "See? I'm just concealing them, 'cause pink doesn't go with my outfit."

Zia snorted. "Nothing goes with that outfit."

Setne shot her an irritated look. "No need to get personal, doll. Just relax, okay? You saw what happens—one word from you, and I'm tied up good. No problems."

His tone sounded so reasonable. Setne was no problem. Setne would cooperate. I could just relax.

In the back of my mind, the voice of Horus said, *Careful.*

I raised my mental guard. Suddenly I was aware of hieroglyphs floating in the air around me—half-visible wisps of smoke. I willed them to disappear, and they fizzled like gnats in a bug zapper. "Stop it with the magic words, Setne. I'll relax when our business is done and you're back in my dad's custody. Now, where are we going?"

A moment of surprise passed over Setne's face. He hid it with a smile. "Sure, no problem. Glad to see that *path of the gods* magic is working out for you. How you doing in there, Horus?"

Zia snarled impatiently. "Just answer the question, you maggot, before I burn that smile off your face."

She thrust out her hand. Flames wreathed her fingers.

"Zia, whoa," I said.

I'd seen her get angry before, but the *burn-your-smile-off* tactic seemed a little harsh even for her.

Setne didn't seem concerned. From his jacket, he pulled a strange white comb—were those human finger bones?—and brushed his greasy hair.

"Poor Zia," he said. "The old man is getting to you, isn't he? Having any trouble with, ah, temperature control yet? I've seen a few people in your situation spontaneously combust. Not pretty."

His words obviously rattled Zia. Her eyes seethed with loathing, but she closed her fist and extinguished the flames. "You vile, despicable—"

"Take it easy, doll," Setne said. "I'm just expressing concern. As for where we're going—south of Cairo, the ruins of Memphis."

I wondered what he'd meant about Zia. I decided this wasn't the time to ask. I didn't want Zia's flaming fingers in *my* face.

I tried to recall what I knew about Memphis. I remembered it was one of the old capitals of Egypt, but it had been destroyed centuries ago. Most of the ruins were buried under modern Cairo. Some were scattered in the desert to the south. My dad had probably taken me to excavation sites in that area once or twice, but I didn't have any clear recollection. After a few years, all the dig sites sort of blended together.

"Where exactly?" I demanded. "Memphis was a big place."

Setne wiggled his eyebrows. "You got that right. Man, the

times I used to have in Gamblers' Alley . . . but never mind. The less you know, pal, the better. We don't want our snaky Chaos friend gleaning information from your mind, do we? Speaking of which, it's a miracle he hasn't already seen your plans and sent some nasty monster to stop you. You seriously need to work on your mental defenses. Reading your mind is *way* too easy. As for your girlfriend here . . ."

He leaned toward me with a grin. "Would you like to know what *she's* thinking?"

Zia understood the Ribbons of Hathor better than I did. Instantly, the band around Setne's neck tightened and became a lovely pink collar with a leash. Setne gagged and clawed at his throat. Zia grabbed the other end of the lead.

"Setne, you are I are going to the wheelhouse," she announced. "You will give the captain *exact* information about where we're going, or you'll never breathe again. Understood?"

She didn't wait for a response. He couldn't have given one anyway. She dragged him across the deck and up the stairs like a very bad dog.

As soon as they'd disappeared into the pilot's house, someone next to me chuckled. "Remind me not to get on *her* bad side."

Horus's instincts kicked in. Before I knew what was happening, I'd summoned my *khopesh* from the Duat and was resting the curved edge against my visitor's throat.

"Really?" said the god of Chaos. "This is how you greet an old friend?"

Set leaned casually against the rail in a black three-piece suit and a matching porkpie hat. The outfit was striking against his bloodred skin. The last time I'd seen him, he'd been bald. Now he had braided cornrows decorated with rubies. His black eyes glittered behind small round glasses. With a chill, I realized he was impersonating Amos.

"Stop that." I pressed my blade against his throat. "Stop mocking my uncle!"

Set looked offended. "Mocking? My dear boy, imitation is the sincerest form of flattery! Now, please, can we talk like civilized semi-divine beings?"

With one finger he pushed the *khopesh* away from his neck. I lowered my blade. Now that I was over my initial shock, I had to admit I was curious about what he wanted.

"Why are you here?" I demanded.

"Oh, pick a reason. The world ends tomorrow. Perhaps I wanted to say good-bye." He grinned and waved. "Bye! Or perhaps I wanted to explain. Or give you a warning."

I glanced toward the wheelhouse. I couldn't see Zia. No alarm bells were ringing. No one else seemed to have noticed that the god of evil had just materialized on our boat.

Set followed my gaze. "How about that Setne, huh? I love that guy."

"You would," I muttered. "Was he named after you?"

"Nah. *Setne* is just his nickname. His real name is Khaemwaset, so you can see why he likes Setne better. I hope he doesn't kill you right away. He's a lot of fun . . . until he kills you."

"Is that what you wanted to explain?"

Set adjusted his glasses. "No, no. It's the thing with Amos. You've got the wrong idea."

"You mean that you possessed him and tried to destroy him?" I asked. "That you almost shattered his mind? And that now you want to do it again?"

"The first two—true. The last one—no. Amos called *me*, kid. You gotta understand, I could never have invaded his mind in the first place if he didn't share some of my qualities. He *understands* me."

I clenched my sword. "I understand you, too. You're evil."

Set laughed. "You figure that out all by yourself? The god of evil is evil? Sure I am, but not *pure* evil. Not *pure* Chaos, either. After I spent some time in Amos's head, he understood. I'm like that improvisational jazz he loves—chaos within order. That's our connection. And I'm still a god, Carter. I'm . . . what do you call it? The *loyal opposition*."

"Loyal. Yeah, right."

Set gave me a sly smile. "Okay, I want to rule the world. Destroy anyone who gets in my way? Of course. But that snake Apophis—he takes things too far. He wants to pull the whole of creation down into a big soupy primordial mess. Where's the fun in that? If it comes down to Ra or Apophis, I fight on Ra's side. That's why Amos and I have a deal. He's learning the path of Set. I'm going to help him."

My arms trembled. I wanted to cut Set's head off, but I wasn't sure I had the strength. I also wasn't sure it would hurt him. I knew from Horus that gods tended to laugh off simple injuries like decapitation.

"You expect me to believe you'll cooperate with Amos?" I asked. "Without trying to overpower him?"

"Sure, I'll *try*. But you should have more faith in your uncle.

He's stronger than you think. Who do you think sent me here to explain?"

An electric charge went through my body. I wanted to believe Amos had everything under control, but this was *Set* talking. He did remind me a lot of the ghost magician Setne—and that wasn't a good thing.

"You've done your explaining," I said. "Now you can leave."

Set shrugged. "Okay, but it does seem like there was one more thing . . ." He tapped his chin. "Oh, right. The warning."

"The warning?" I repeated.

"Because usually when Horus and I fight, it would be *me* who was responsible for what's about to kill you. But this time, it's not. I thought you should know. Apophis is *so* copying my moves, but like I said . . ." He took off his porkpie hat and bowed, the rubies glittering in his cornrows. "Imitation is flattery."

"What are you—?"

The riverboat lurched and groaned as if we'd hit a sandbar. Up in the wheelhouse, the alarm bell *ding*ed. The glowing crew orbs zipped around the deck in a panic.

"What's happening?" I grabbed the rail.

"Oh, that'd be the giant hippo," Set said casually. "Good luck!"

He disappeared in a cloud of red smoke as a monstrous shape rose from the Nile.

You might not think a hippo could inspire terror. Screaming "Hippo!" doesn't have the same impact as screaming "Shark!"

But I'm telling you—as the *Egyptian Queen* careened to one side, its paddle wheel lifting completely out of the water, and I saw that monster emerge from the deep, I nearly discovered the hieroglyphs for *accident in my pants.*

The creature was easily as big as our riverboat. Its skin glistened purple and gray. As it rose near the bow, it fixed its eyes on me with unmistakable malice and opened a maw the size of an airplane hangar. Its bottom peglike teeth were taller than me. Looking down the creature's throat, I felt like I was seeing a bright pink tunnel straight to the Underworld. The monster could have eaten me right there, along with the front half of the boat. I would have been too paralyzed to react.

Instead, the hippo bellowed. Imagine someone revving a dirt bike, then blowing a trumpet. Now imagine those sounds amplified twenty times, coming at you in a blast of breath that smells of rotten fish and pond scum. That's what a giant hippo's war cry is like.

Somewhere behind me, Zia yelled, "Hippo!" Which I thought was a little late.

She stumbled toward me over the rocking deck, the tip of her staff on fire. Our ghostly pal Setne floated behind her, grinning with delight.

"There it is!" Setne shook his diamond pinky rings. "Told ya Apophis would send a monster to kill you."

"You're so smart!" I shouted. "Now, how do we stop it?"

"BRRRAAHHHHH!" The hippo shoved its face against the *Egyptian Queen.* I tumbled backward and slammed against the deckhouse.

Out of the corner of my eye I saw Zia blast a column of fire at the creature's face. The flames went straight up its left nostril, which just made the hippo mad. It snorted smoke and bashed the ship harder, catapulting Zia into the river.

"No!" I staggered to my feet. I tried to summon the avatar of Horus, but my head was throbbing. My focus was shot.

"Want some advice?" Setne wafted next to me, unaffected by the rocking of the ship. "I could give you a spell to use."

His evil smile didn't exactly fill me with confidence.

"Just stay put!" I pointed at his hands and yelled, *"Tas!"*

The Ribbons of Hathor tied his wrists together.

"Oh, come on!" he complained. "How am I supposed to comb my hair like this?"

The hippo peered at me over the rail—its eye like a greasy black dinner plate. Up in the wheelhouse, Bloodstained Blade rang the alarm bell and shouted at the crew, "Hard to port! Hard to port!"

Somewhere over the side, I heard Zia choking and splashing, which at least meant she was alive, but I had to keep the hippo away from her and give the *Egyptian Queen* time to disengage. I grabbed my sword, charged up the tilting deck, and leaped straight onto the monster's head.

My first discovery: hippos are slippery. I scrambled for a handhold—not easy while wielding a sword—and almost slid off the other side of the hippo's head before I hooked my free arm around its ear.

The hippo roared and shook me like a dangle earring. I caught a glimpse of a fishing boat sailing calmly by as if nothing were wrong. The crew orbs of the *Egyptian Queen* zipped around a large crack in the stern. Just for a moment, I saw Zia floundering in the water, about twenty yards downstream. Then her head went under. I summoned all my strength and drove my sword into the hippo's ear.

"BRRRAAHHHHH!" The monster thrashed its head. I lost my grip and went sailing across the river like a three-point shot.

I would've hit the water hard, but at the last second I changed into a falcon.

I know . . . that sounds crazy. *Oh, by the way, I just happened to change into a falcon.* But it was fairly easy magic for me, since the falcon was Horus's sacred animal. Suddenly, instead of falling, I was soaring over the Nile. My vision was so sharp I could see field mice in the marshes. I could see Zia struggling in the water, as well as every bristle on the hippo's massive snout.

I dove at the monster's eye, raking it with my claws. Unfortunately it was heavily lidded and covered with some kind of membrane. The hippo blinked and bellowed in annoyance, but I could tell that I hadn't done any real damage.

The monster snapped at me. I was much too fast. I flew to the ship and perched on the wheelhouse roof, trying to catch my breath. The *Egyptian Queen* had managed to turn. It was slowly putting distance between itself and the monster, but the hull had taken serious damage. Smoke billowed from the cracks in the stern. We were listing to starboard, and Bloodstained Blade kept ringing his alarm bell, which was really annoying.

Zia was working to stay afloat, but she'd drifted farther

downstream from the hippo and didn't seem to be in immediate danger. She tried to summon fire—which isn't easy to do when you're floundering in a river.

The hippo lumbered back and forth, apparently looking for the pesky bird that had poked it in the eye. The monster's ear was still bleeding, though my sword was no longer there—maybe at the bottom of the river somewhere. Finally the hippo turned its attention to the ship.

Setne materialized next to me. His arms were still tied, but he looked like he was enjoying himself. "You ready for that advice now, pal? I can't cast the spell myself 'cause I'm dead and all, but I can tell you what to say."

The hippo charged. It was less than fifty yards away, closing fast. If it hit the ship at that speed, the *Egyptian Queen* would break into kindling.

Time seemed to slow down. I tried to gather my focus. Emotions are bad for magic, and I was completely panicked; but I knew I'd only get one shot at this. I spread my wings and flew straight at the hippo. Halfway there, I transformed back into a human, dropped like a stone, and summoned the avatar of Horus.

If it hadn't worked, I would've ended my life as an insignificant grease spot on the chest of a charging hippo.

Thankfully, the blue aura flickered around me. I landed in the river encased in the glowing body of a twenty-foot-tall hawk-headed warrior. Compared to the hippo, I was still tiny, but I got its attention when I drove my fist into its snout.

That worked really well for about two seconds. The monster

forgot all about the ship. I sidestepped and made it turn toward me, but I was way too slow. Wading through the river in avatar form was about as easy as running through a room full of bouncy balls.

The monster lunged. It twisted its head and clamped its mouth around my waist. I staggered, trying to break free, but its jaws were like a vise grip. Its teeth sank into the magical shielding. I didn't have my sword. All I could do was pummel its head with my glowing blue fists, but my power was fading rapidly.

"Carter!" Zia screamed.

I had maybe ten seconds to live. Then the avatar would collapse, and I'd be swallowed or bitten in half.

"Setne!" I yelled. "What's that spell?"

"Oh, *now* you want the spell," Setne called from the ship. "Repeat after me: *Hapi, u-ha ey pwah.*"

I didn't know what that meant. Setne might've been tricking me into self-destructing or transforming into a chunk of Swiss cheese. But I was out of options. I shouted: *"Hapi, u-ha ey pwah!"*

Blue hieroglyphs—brighter than I'd ever summoned— blazed above the hippo's head:

Seeing them written out, I suddenly understood their meaning: *Hapi, arise and attack.* But what did *that* mean?

At least they distracted the hippo. It let go of me and

snapped at the hieroglyphs. My avatar failed. I plunged into the water, my magic exhausted, my defenses gone—just tiny little Carter Kane in the shadow of a sixteen-ton hippo.

The monster swallowed the hieroglyphs and snorted. It shook its head as if it had just gulped down a chili pepper.

Great, I thought. *Setne's awesome magic summoned an appetizer for the devil hippo.*

Then, from the boat, Setne yelled, "Wait for it! Three, two, one . . ."

The Nile boiled around me. A huge mass of brown seaweed erupted beneath me and lifted me skyward. Instinctively I held on, slowly realizing that the seaweed wasn't seaweed. It was *hair* on top of a colossal head. The giant man rose from the Nile, higher and higher, until the hippo looked almost cute in comparison. I couldn't tell much about the giant from the top of his head, but his skin was darker blue than my father's. He had shaggy brown hair full of river muck. His belly was hugely swollen, and he seemed to be wearing nothing but a loincloth made of fish scales.

"*BRRRAAHHHHH!*" The hippo lunged, but the blue giant grabbed its bottom teeth and stopped it cold. The force of the impact nearly shook me off his head.

"Yay!" the blue giant bellowed. "Hippo toss! I love this game!" He swung his arms in a golf swing motion and launched the monster out of the water.

Few things are stranger than watching a giant hippo fly. It careened wildly, kicking its stubby legs as it sailed over the marshlands. Finally it crashed into a limestone cliff in the distance, causing a minor avalanche. Boulders collapsed on top of the hippo. When the dust settled, there was no sign of the monster. Cars kept driving down the river road. Fishing boats went about their business, as if blue giants fighting hippos was nothing remarkable on this stretch of the Nile.

"Fun!" the blue giant cheered. "Now, who summoned me?"

"Up here!" I yelled.

The giant froze. He carefully patted his scalp until he found me. Then he picked me up with two fingers, waded over to the riverbank, and gently set me down.

He pointed to Zia, who was struggling to reach the shore, and the *Egyptian Queen*, which was drifting downstream, listing and smoking from the stern. "Are those friends of yours?"

"Yes," I said. "Could you help them?"

The giant grinned. "Be right back!"

A few minutes later the *Egyptian Queen* was safely moored. Zia sat next to me on the shore, wringing Nile water out of her hair.

Setne hovered next to us, looking quite smug, even though his arms were still tied. "So maybe *next time* you'll trust me, Carter Kane!" He nodded at the giant, who loomed over us, still grinning like he was *really* excited to be here. "May I present my old friend Hapi!"

The blue giant waved at us. "Hi!"

His eyes were completely dilated. His teeth were brilliant white. A mass of stringy brown hair fell around his shoulders, and his skin rippled in different shades of watery blue. His belly was much too big for his body. It sagged over his fish-scale skirt like he was either pregnant or had swallowed a blimp. He was, without a doubt, the tallest, fattest, bluest, most cheerful hippie giant I had ever met.

I tried to place his name, but I couldn't.

"Hapi?" I asked.

"Why, yes, I am happy!" Hapi beamed. "I'm always happy because I'm Hapi! Are you happy?"

I glanced at Setne, who seemed to find this terribly amusing.

"Hapi is the god of the Nile," the ghost explained. "Along with his other duties, Hapi is the provider of bountiful harvests and all good things, and so he is always—"

"Happy," I guessed.

Zia frowned up at the giant. "Does he have to be so big?"

The god laughed. Immediately he shrank down to human size, though the crazy cheerful look on his face was still pretty unnerving.

"So!" Hapi rubbed his hands with anticipation. "Anything else I can do for you kids? It's been centuries since anybody summoned me. Since they built that stupid Aswan Dam, the Nile doesn't flood every year like it used to. Nobody depends on me anymore. I could *kill* those mortals!"

He said this with a smile, as if he'd suggested bringing the mortals some home-baked cookies.

I did some quick thinking. It's not often a god offers to do you favors—even if that god is psychotically over-caffeinated. "Actually, yes," I said. "See, Setne suggested I summon you to deal with the hippo, but—"

"Oh, Setne!" Hapi chuckled and pushed the ghost playfully. "I *hate* this guy. Absolutely despise him! He's the only magician who ever learned my secret name. Ha!"

Setne shrugged. "It was nothing, really. And I gotta say, you came in handy many times back in the old days."

"Ha, ha!" Hapi's smile became painfully wide. "I'd love to rip off your arms and legs, Setne. That would be amazing!"

Setne's expression remained calm, but he drifted a little farther away from the smiling god.

"Um, anyway," I said. "We're on a quest. We need to find this magic book to defeat Apophis. Setne was leading us to the ruins of Memphis, but now our boat is busted. Do you think—?"

"Oh!" Hapi clapped excitedly. "The world is going to end tomorrow. I forgot!"

Zia and I exchanged looks.

"Right . . ." I said. "So, if Setne told you exactly where we were going, could you take us there? And, um, if he won't tell you, then you could rip his limbs off. That would be fine."

"Yay!" Hapi cried.

Setne gave me a murderous look. "Yeah, sure. We're going to the *serapeum*—the temple of the Apis Bull."

Hapi smacked his knee. "I should have figured! Brilliant place to hide something. That's pretty far inland, but sure, I can send you there if you want. And just so you know, Apophis has demons scouring the riverbanks. You'd never get to Memphis without my help. You'd get torn into a million pieces!"

He seemed genuinely pleased to share that news.

Zia cleared her throat. "Okay, then. We'd love your help."

I turned toward the *Egyptian Queen*, where Bloodstained Blade stood at the railing, awaiting further orders. "Captain," I called, "wait here and continue repairing the ship. We'll—"

"Oh, the ship can go too!" Hapi interrupted. "That's no problem."

I frowned. I wasn't sure how the river god was going to move the ship, especially since he'd told us Memphis was inland, but I decided not to ask.

"Belay that order," I called to the captain. "The ship is coming with us. Once we reach Memphis, you'll continue repairs and await further orders."

The captain hesitated. Then he bowed his ax-blade head. "I obey, my lord."

"Great!" Hapi said.

He held out his palm, which contained two slimy black orbs like fish eggs. "Swallow these. One each."

Zia wrinkled her nose. "What are they?"

"They'll take you where you want to go!" the god promised. "They're Hapi pills."

I blinked. "What now?"

The ghost Setne cleared his throat. He looked like he was trying not to laugh. "Yeah, you know. Hapi invented them. So that's what they're called."

"Just eat them!" Hapi said. "You'll see."

Reluctantly, Zia and I took the pills. They tasted even worse than they looked. Instantly, I felt dizzy. The world shimmered like water.

"It was nice to meet you!" Hapi cried, his voice turning murky and distant. "You do realize you're walking into a trap, don't you? Okay! Good luck!"

With that, my vision went blue, and my body melted into liquid.

12. Bulls with Freaking Laser Beams

BEING LIQUIDATED IS NOT FUN. I will never be able to walk by another LIQUIDATION SALE sign without getting seasick and feeling like my bones are turning to tapioca.

I know I'm going to sound like a public service announcement here, but for all you kids at home: if somebody offers you Hapi pills, just say, "No!"

I felt myself seeping inland through the mud, traveling at incredible speed. When I hit the hot sand, I evaporated, rising above the ground as a cloud of moisture, pushed west by the winds into the desert. I couldn't exactly see, but I could feel the movement and the heat. My molecules agitated as the sun dispersed me.

Suddenly the temperature dropped again. I sensed cool stone around me—a cave or an underground room, maybe. I coalesced into moisture, splashed to the floor as a puddle, then rose and solidified into Carter Kane once more.

For my next trick, I buckled to my knees and lost my breakfast.

Zia stood near me, hugging her stomach. We seemed to be in the entry tunnel of a tomb. Below us, stone steps led into the darkness. A few feet above, desert sunlight blazed.

"That was *horrible*," Zia gasped.

I could only nod. Now I understood the science lesson my dad had once taught me in homeschooling—matter has three forms: solid, liquid, and gas. In the last few minutes I'd been all three. And I didn't like it.

Setne materialized just outside the doorway, smiling down at us. "So, did I come through again, or what?"

I didn't remember loosening his bonds, but his arms were now free. That would've worried me more if I hadn't felt so sick.

Zia and I were still wet and muddy from our swim in the Nile, but Setne looked immaculate—jeans and T-shirt freshly pressed, Elvis hair perfect, not even a spot on his white running shoes. That disgusted me so much, I staggered into the sunlight and threw up on him. Unfortunately, my stomach was mostly empty and he was a ghost, so nothing much happened.

"Hey, pal!" Setne adjusted his golden *ankh* necklace and straightened his jacket. "Some respect, all right? I did you a favor."

"A favor?" I gulped back the horrible taste in my mouth. "Don't—*ever*—"

"Never Hapi again," Zia finished for me. "Never."

"Aw, c'mon!" Setne spread his hands. "That was a smooth trip! Look, even your ship made it."

I squinted. Mostly we were surrounded by flat, rocky desert, like the surface of Mars; but beached on a nearby sand dune was a slightly broken riverboat—the *Egyptian Queen*. The stern wasn't on fire anymore, but the ship looked like it had taken more damage in transit. A section of railing was broken. One of the smokestacks was leaning dangerously. For some reason, a huge slimy tarp of fish scales was hanging off the pilot's house like a snagged parachute.

Zia muttered, "Oh, gods of Egypt—please don't let that be Hapi's loincloth."

Bloodstained Blade stood at the bow, facing our direction. He had no expression, being an ax head, but from the way his arms were crossed, I could tell he was not a Hapi camper.

"Can you fix the ship?" I called to him.

"Yes, my lord," he hummed. "Given a few hours. Sadly, we seem to be stuck in the middle of a desert."

"We'll worry about that later," I said. "Get the ship repaired. Wait here for us to return. You'll receive more instructions at that time."

"As you say." Bloodstained Blade turned and started humming at the glowing orbs in a language I didn't understand. The crew stirred into a flurry of activity.

Setne smiled. "See? Everything's good!"

"Except we're running out of time." I looked at the sun. I figured it was one or two in the afternoon, and we still had a lot to do before Doomsday tomorrow morning. "Where does that tunnel go? What's a *serapeum*? And why did Hapi say it was a trap?"

"So many questions," Setne said. "Come on, you'll see. You're gonna love this place!"

I did not love this place.

The steps down led to a wide hall chiseled from golden bedrock. The barreled ceiling was so low, I could touch it without stretching my arms. I could tell that archaeologists had been here, from the bare electric bulbs that cast shadows across the arches. Metal beams braced the walls, but the cracks in the ceiling didn't help me feel safe. I'd never been comfortable in enclosed spaces.

Every thirty feet or so, square alcoves opened up on either side of the main hall. Each niche held a massive freestanding stone sarcophagus.

After passing the fourth such coffin, I stopped. "Those things are way too big for humans. What's in there?"

"Bull," Setne said.

"Excuse me?"

Setne's laugh echoed through the hall. I figured that if there were any sleeping monsters in this place, they were awake now.

"These are the burial chambers for the Apis Bull." Setne gestured around him proudly. "I built all this, you know, back when I was Prince Khaemwaset."

Zia ran her hand along the white stone lid of the

sarcophagus. "The Apis Bull. My ancestors thought it was an incarnation of Osiris in the mortal world."

"Thought?" Setne snorted. "It *was* his incarnation, doll. At least some of the time—like on festival days and whatnot. We took our Apis Bull seriously back then."

He patted the coffin like he was showing off a used car. "This bad boy here? He had the perfect life. All the food he could eat. Got a harem of cows, burnt offerings, a special gold cloth for his back—all the perks. Only had to show himself in public a few times a year for big festivals. When he turned twenty-five, he got slaughtered in a big ceremony, mummified like a king, and put down here. Then a new bull took his place. Nice gig, huh?"

"Killed at twenty-five," I said. "Sounds awesome."

I wondered how many mummified bulls were down that hallway. I didn't want to find out. I liked being right here, where I could still see the exit and the sunlight outside. "So why is this place called a—what was it?"

"Serapeum," Zia answered. Her face was illuminated with golden light—probably just the electrical bulbs reflecting off the stone, but it seemed like she was glowing. "Iskandar, my old teacher—he told me about this place. The Apis Bull was a vessel for Osiris. In later times, the names were merged: Osiris-Apis. Then the Greeks shorted it to Serapis."

Setne sneered. "Stupid Greeks. Moving in on our territory. Taking over our gods. I'm telling you, I got no love for those guys. But yeah, that's how it happened. This place became known as a *serapeum*—a house for dead bull gods. Me, I wanted to call it the Khaemwaset Memorial of Pure Awesomeness, but my dad wouldn't go for it."

"Your dad?" I asked.

Setne waved aside the question. "Anyway, I hid the Book of Thoth down here before I died because I knew no one would ever disturb it. You'd have to be frothing-at-the-mouth crazy to mess with the sacred tomb of the Apis Bull."

"Great." I felt like I was turning back into liquid.

Zia frowned at the ghost. "Don't tell me—you hid the book in one of these sarcophagi with a mummified bull, and the bull will come to life if we disturb it?"

Setne winked at her. "Oh, I did better than that, doll. Archaeologists have discovered *this* part of the complex." He gestured at the electric lights and metal support beams. "But I'm gonna take you on a *behind-the-scenes* tour."

The catacombs seemed to go on forever. Hallways split off in different directions, all of them lined with sarcophagi for holy cows. After descending a long slope, we ducked through a secret passage behind an illusionary wall.

On the other side, there were no electric lights. No steel beams braced the cracked ceiling. Zia summoned fire at the tip of her staff and burned away a canopy of cobwebs. Our footprints were the only marks on the dusty floor.

"Are we close?" I asked.

Setne chuckled. "It's just getting good."

He led us farther into the maze. Every so often, he stopped to deactivate traps with a command or a touch. Sometimes he made me do it—supposedly because he couldn't cast certain spells, being dead—though I got the feeling he thought it would be incredibly funny if I failed and died.

"How come you can touch some things but not other things?" I asked. "You seem to have a real selective ability."

Setne shrugged. "I don't make the rules of the spirit world, pal. We can touch money and jewelry. Picking up trash and messing with poison spikes, no. We get to leave that dirty work to the living."

Whenever the traps were disabled, hidden hieroglyphs glowed and vanished. Sometimes we had to jump over pits that opened in the floor, or swerve when arrows shot from the ceiling. Paintings of gods and pharaohs peeled off the walls, formed into ghostly guardians, and faded. The whole time, Setne kept a running commentary.

"That curse would've made your feet rot off," he explained. "This one over here? That summons a plague of fleas. And this one—oh, man. This is one of my favorites. It turns you into a dwarf! I hate those short little guys."

I frowned. Setne was shorter than me, but I decided to let it go.

"Yes, indeed," he continued. "You're lucky to have me along, pal. Right now, you'd be a flea-bitten dwarf with no feet. And you haven't even seen the worst of it! Right this way."

I wasn't sure how Setne remembered so many details about this place from so long ago, but he was obviously proud of these catacombs. He must have relished designing horrible traps to kill intruders.

We turned down another corridor. The floor sloped again. The ceiling got so low, I had to stoop. I tried to stay calm, but I was having trouble breathing. All I could think about were those tons of stone over my head, ready to collapse at any moment.

Zia took my hand. The tunnel was so narrow, we were walking single file; but I glanced back at her.

"You okay?" I asked.

She mouthed the words: *Watch him.*

I nodded. Whatever trap Hapi had warned us about, I had a feeling we hadn't seen it yet, even though we were surrounded by traps. We were alone with a murderous ghost, deep underground in his home territory. I didn't have my *khopesh* anymore. For some reason I hadn't been able to summon it from the Duat. And I couldn't use my warrior avatar in such a tiny tunnel. If Setne turned on us, my options would be limited.

Finally the corridor widened. We reached a dead end—a solid wall flanked by two statues of my dad . . . I mean, Osiris.

Setne turned. "Okay, here's the score, you guys. I'm gonna have to cast a disenchantment to open this wall. The spell takes a few minutes. I don't want you freaking out halfway through and wrapping me in pink ribbons, or things could get ugly. Half-finished magic right here, and this whole tunnel could collapse on top of us."

I managed to avoid screaming like a little girl—but only barely.

Zia cranked the fire on her staff to white-hot. "Careful, Setne. I know what a proper disenchantment sounds like.

If I suspect you're casting anything else, I'll blast you into ectoplasmic dust."

"Relax, doll." Setne cracked his knuckles. His diamond pinky rings flashed in the firelight. "You gotta keep that scarab under control, or you're gonna turn *yourself* into ashes."

I frowned. "Scarab?"

Setne glanced back and forth between us and laughed. "You mean she hasn't told you? And you haven't figured it out? You *kids* today! I *love* the ignorance!"

He turned toward the wall and began to chant. Zia's fire ebbed to a cooler red flame. I gave her a questioning look.

She hesitated—then touched the base of her throat. She hadn't been wearing a necklace before. I was sure of that. But when she touched her throat, an amulet blinked into existence—a glittering golden scarab on a gold chain. She must have hidden it with a glamor—a magical illusion like Setne had done with the Ribbons of Hathor.

The scarab looked metal, but I realized I'd seen it before, and I'd seen it *alive*. Back when Ra had imprisoned Apophis in the Underworld, he'd given up part of his soul—his incarnation as Khepri, scarab of the morning sun—to keep his enemy confined. He'd buried Apophis under a landslide of living beetles.

By the time Sadie and I had found that prison last spring, millions of scarabs had been reduced to desiccated shells. When Apophis broke free, only one golden beetle survived: the last remnant of Khepri's power.

Ra had tried to swallow that scarab. (Yes, disgusting. I know.) When that didn't work . . . he'd offered it to Zia.

I didn't remember Zia taking the scarab, but somehow I knew that amulet was the same bug.

"Zia—"

She shook her head adamantly. "Later."

She gestured at Setne, who was in the middle of his spell.

Okay, probably not a good time to talk. I didn't want the tunnel coming down on us. But my mind was reeling.

You haven't figured it out? Setne had taunted me.

I knew Ra was fascinated with Zia. She was his favorite babysitter. Setne mentioned that Zia was having temperature control problems. *The old man is getting to you,* he'd said. And Ra had given Zia that scarab—literally a piece of his soul— as if she were his high priestess . . . or maybe someone even more important.

The tunnel rumbled. The dead-end wall dissolved into dust, revealing a chamber beyond.

Setne glanced back at us with a smile. "Showtime, kids."

We followed him into a circular room that reminded me of the library at Brooklyn House. The floor was a sparkling mosaic of pastures and rivers. On the walls, painted priests were adorning painted cows with flowers and feathery head-dresses for some kind of festival, while Ancient Egyptians waved palm fronds and shook bronze noisemakers called *sistrums.* The domed ceiling depicted Osiris on his throne, passing judgment over a bull. For an absurd moment, I wondered if Ammit devoured the hearts of wicked cows, and if he liked the beefy taste.

In the middle of the chamber, on a coffin-shaped pedestal, stood a life-sized statue of the Apis Bull. It was made of dark stone—basalt, maybe—but painted so skillfully, it looked alive. Its eyes seemed to follow me. Its hide glistened black except for a small white diamond on the front of its chest, and over its back was a gold blanket cut and embroidered to resemble hawk's wings. Between its horns sat a Frisbee of gold—a sun disk crown. Beneath that, sticking out of the bull's forehead like a curly unicorn horn, was a rearing cobra.

A year ago I would've said, "Freaky, but at least it's just a statue." Now, I'd had lots of experience with Egyptian statues coming to life and trying to stomp the *ankh* out of me.

Setne didn't seem worried. He strolled right up to the stone bull and patted its leg. "The Shrine of Apis! I built this chamber just for my chosen priests and me. Now all we have to do is wait."

"Wait for what?" Zia asked. Being a smart girl, she was hanging back by the entrance with me.

Setne checked his nonexistent watch. "It won't be long. Just a timer, sort of. Come on in! Make yourself comfortable."

I edged my way inside. I waited for the doorway to solidify behind me, but it stayed open. "You sure the book is still here?"

"Oh, yeah." Setne walked around the statue, checking the base. "I just need to remember which of these panels on the dais is going to pop open. I wanted to make this entire room out of gold, you know? That would've been much cooler. But Dad cut back on my funding."

"Your dad." Zia stepped next to me and slipped her hand into mine, which I didn't mind. The golden scarab necklace glinted around her neck. "You mean Ramses the Great?"

Setne's mouth twisted in a cruel sneer. "Yeah, that's how his PR department branded him. Me, I liked to call him Ramses II, or Ramses Number Two."

"Ramses?" I said. "Your dad is *the* Ramses?"

I suppose I hadn't processed how Setne fit into Egyptian history. Looking at this scrawny little guy with his greasy hair, his shoulder-padded jacket, and his ridiculous bling, I couldn't believe he was related to a ruler so famous. Even worse, it made him related to *me*, since our mom's side of the family traced its magic heritage from Ramses the Great.

(Sadie says she can see the family resemblance between Setne and me. [Shut up, Sadie.])

I guess Setne didn't like my looking surprised. He stuck his beaky nose in the air. "You should know what it's like, Carter Kane—growing up in the shadow of a famous dad. Always trying to live up to his legend. Look at you, son of the great Dr. Julius Kane. You finally make a name for yourself as a big-shot magician, what does your dad do? He goes and becomes a god."

Setne laughed coldly. I'd never felt any resentment toward my father before; I'd always thought it was cool being Dr. Kane's son. But Setne's words rolled over me, and anger started to build in my chest.

He's playing with you, said the voice of Horus.

I knew Horus was right, but that didn't make me feel better.

"Where's the book, Setne?" I asked. "Enough delays."

"Don't warp your wand, pal. It won't be much longer." He gazed at the picture of Osiris on the ceiling. "There he is! The blue dude himself. I'm telling you, Carter, you and I are a lot alike. I can't go anywhere in Egypt without seeing my dad's face, either. Abu Simbel? There's Papa Ramses glaring down at me—four copies of him, each sixty feet tall. It's like a nightmare. Half the temples in Egypt? He commissioned them and put up statues of himself. Is it any wonder I wanted to be the world's *biggest* magician?" He puffed up his scrawny chest. "And I made it, too. What I don't understand, Carter Kane, is why you haven't taken the pharaoh's throne yet. You've got Horus on your side, itching for power. You should merge with the god, become the pharaoh of the world, and, ah . . ." He patted the Apis statue. "Take the bull by the horns."

He's right, Horus said. *This human has wisdom.*

Make up your mind, I complained.

"Carter, don't listen to him," Zia said. "Setne, whatever you're up to—stop. Now."

"What *I'm* up to? Look, doll—"

"Don't call me that!" Zia said.

"Hey, I'm on your side," Setne promised. "The book's right here in the dais. As soon as the bull moves—"

"The bull *moves?*" I asked.

Setne narrowed his eyes. "Didn't I mention that? I got the idea from this holiday we used to have in the old days, the Festival of Sed. Awesome fun! You ever been to that Running of the Bulls in, what is it, Spain?"

"Pamplona," I said. Another wave of resentment got the best of me. My dad had taken me to Pamplona once, but he hadn't let me go out in the street while the bulls were running through town. He'd said it was too dangerous—as if his secret life as a magician weren't *way* more dangerous than that.

"Right, Pamplona," Setne agreed. "Well, you know where that tradition started? Egypt. The pharaoh would do this ritual race with the Apis Bull to renew his kingly power, prove his strength, get blessed by the gods—all that junk. In later times, it became just a charade, no real danger. But at the beginning, it was the real thing. Life and death."

On the word *death*, the bull statue moved. He bent his legs stiffly. Then he lowered his head and glared at me, snorting out a cloud of dust.

"Setne!" I reached for my sword, but of course it wasn't there. "Make that thing stop, or I'll wrap you in ribbons so fast—"

"Oh, I wouldn't do that," Setne warned. "See, I'm the only one who can pick up the book without getting zapped by about sixteen different curses."

Between the bull's horns, its golden sun disk flashed. On its forehead, the cobra writhed to life, hissing and spitting gobs of fire.

Zia drew her wand. Was it my imagination, or was her scarab necklace starting to steam? "Call off that creature, Setne. Or I swear—"

"I can't, doll. Sorry." He grinned at us from behind the bull's dais. He didn't look very sorry. "This is part of the security system, see? If you want the book, you've got to distract the bull and get it out of here, while I open the dais and grab the Book of Thoth. I have complete faith in you."

The bull pawed his pedestal and leaped off. Zia pulled me back into the hallway.

"That's it!" Setne shouted. "Just like the Sed Festival. Prove you're worthy of the pharaoh's throne, kid. Run or die!"

The bull charged.

A sword would've been really nice. I would've settled for a matador's cape and a spear. Or an assault rifle. Instead, Zia and I ran back through the catacombs and quickly realized that we were lost. Letting Setne lead us into the maze had been a stupid idea. I should've dropped breadcrumbs or marked the walls with hieroglyphs or something.

I hoped the tunnels would be too narrow for the Apis Bull. No such luck. I heard rock walls rumbling behind us as the bull shouldered his way through. There was another sound I liked even less—a deep hum followed by an explosion. I didn't know what that was, but it was good incentive to run faster.

We must have passed through a dozen halls. Each had twenty or thirty sarcophagi. I couldn't believe how many Apises had been mummified down here—centuries' worth of bull. Behind us, our monstrous stone friend bellowed as he smashed his way through the tunnels.

I glanced back once and was sorry I did. The bull was closing fast, the cobra on his forehead spewing fire.

"This way!" Zia cried.

She pulled me down a side corridor. At the far end, what looked like daylight spilled from an open doorway. We sprinted toward it.

I was hoping for an exit. Instead we stumbled into another circular chamber. There was no bull statue in the middle, but spaced around the circumference were four giant stone sarcophagi. The walls were painted with pictures of bovine paradise—cows being fed, cows frolicking in meadows, cows being worshipped by silly little humans. The daylight streamed from a shaft in the domed ceiling, twenty feet above. A beam of sunshine sliced through the dusty air and hit the middle of the floor like a spotlight, but there was no way we could use the shaft to escape. Even if I turned into a falcon, the opening was too narrow, and I wasn't about to leave Zia alone.

"Dead end," she said.

"HRUUUFF!" The Apis Bull loomed in the doorway, blocking our exit. His hood ornament cobra hissed.

We backed into the room until we stood in the warm sunlight. It seemed cruel to die here, stuck under thousands of tons of rock but able to see the sun.

The bull pawed the floor. He took a step forward, then hesitated, as if the sunlight bothered him.

"Maybe I can talk to him," I said. "He's connected to Osiris, right?"

Zia looked at me like I was crazy—which I was—but I didn't have any better ideas.

She readied her wand and staff. "I'll cover you."

I stepped toward the monster and showed my empty hands. "Nice bull. I'm Carter Kane. Osiris is my dad, sort of. How about we call a truce and—"

The cobra spewed fire in my face.

It would've turned me into an extra-crispy Carter, but Zia shouted a command. As I stumbled backward, her staff absorbed the blast, sucking in the flames like a vacuum cleaner. She sliced the air with her wand, and a shimmering red wall of fire erupted around the Apis Bull. Unfortunately, the bull just stood there and glared at us, completely unharmed.

Zia cursed. "We seem to be at an impasse with the fire magic."

The bull lowered its horns.

My war god instincts took control. "Take cover!"

Zia dove one way. I dove the other. The bull's sun disk glowed and hummed, then shot a golden beam of heat right where we'd been standing. I barely made it behind a sarcophagus. My clothes were steaming. The bottoms of my shoes were melted. Where the beam had hit, the floor was blackened and bubbling, as if the rock had reached boiling point.

"Cows with laser beams?" I protested. "That's *completely* unfair!"

"Carter!" Zia called from across the room. "You okay?"

"We'll have to split up!" I shouted back. "I'll distract it. You get out of here!"

"What? No!"

The bull turned toward the sound of her voice. I had to move fast.

My avatar wouldn't be much good in an enclosed space like this, but I needed the war god's strength and speed. I summoned the power of Horus. Blue light flickered around me. My skin felt as thick as steel, my muscles as powerful as hydraulic pistons. I rose to my feet, smashed my fists into the sarcophagus, and reduced it to a pile of stone and mummy dust. I picked up a chunk of the lid—a three-hundred-pound stone shield—and charged at the bull.

We smashed into each other. Somehow I held my ground, but it took every bit of my magical strength. The bull bellowed and pushed. The cobra spit flames that rolled over the top of my shield.

"Zia, get out of here!" I shouted.

"I'm not leaving you!"

"You've got to! I can't—"

The hairs on my arms stood up even before I heard the humming sound. My slab of stone disintegrated in a flash of gold, and I flew backward, crashing into another sarcophagus.

My vision blurred. I heard Zia shout. When my eyes could focus again, I saw her standing in the middle of the room, wrapped in sunlight, chanting a spell I didn't recognize. She'd gotten the bull's attention, which had probably saved my life. But before I could cry out, the bull aimed his sun disk and shot a superheated laser beam straight at Zia.

"No!" I screamed.

The light blinded me. The heat sucked all the oxygen out of my lungs. There was no way Zia could have survived that hit.

But when the golden light faded, Zia was still there. Around her burned a massive shield shaped like . . . like a scarab shell. Her eyes glowed with orange fire. Flames swirled around her. She looked at the bull and spoke a deep rasping voice that definitely wasn't hers: "I am Khepri, the rising sun. I will not be denied."

Only later did I realize that she'd spoken in Ancient Egyptian.

She thrust out her hand. A miniature comet shot toward the Apis Bull and the monster burst into flames, turning and stomping, suddenly panicked. His legs crumbled. He collapsed and broke into a smoking pile of charred rubble.

The room was suddenly quiet. I was afraid to move. Zia was still wreathed in fire, and it seemed to be getting hotter—burning yellow, then white. She stood as if in a trance. The golden scarab around her neck was definitely smoking now.

"Zia!" My head throbbed, but I managed to rise.

She turned toward me and hefted another fireball.

"Zia, no!" I said. "It's me. Carter."

She hesitated. "Carter . . . ?" Her expression turned to confusion, then fear. The orange flames faded in her eyes, and she collapsed in the pool of sunlight.

I ran to her. I tried to gather her in my arms, but her skin was too hot to touch. The golden scarab had left a nasty burn on her throat.

"Water," I muttered to myself. "I need water."

I'd never been good at divine words, but I shouted: *"Maw!"*

The symbol blazed above us:

Several cubic gallons of water materialized in midair and crashed down on us. Zia's face steamed. She coughed and spluttered, but she didn't wake. Her fever still felt dangerously high.

"I'll get you out of here," I promised, lifting her in my arms.

I didn't need the strength of Horus. I had so much adrenaline coursing through my body, I didn't feel any of my own injuries. I ran right by Setne when he passed me in the hall.

"Hey, pal!" He turned and jogged along next to me, waving a thick papyrus scroll. "Good job! I got the Book of Thoth!"

"You almost killed Zia!" I snapped. "Get us out of here—NOW!"

"Okay, okay," Setne said. "Calm down."

"I'm taking you back to my dad's courtroom," I growled. "I'm going to *personally* stuff you down Ammit's mouth, like a branch into a wood chipper."

"Whoa, big man." Setne led me up a sloping passage back to the electrical lighting of the excavated tunnels. "How about we get you out of here first, huh? Remember, you still need me to decipher this book and find the serpent's shadow. Then we'll see about the wood chipper, okay?"

"She can't die," I insisted.

"Right, I got that." Setne led me through more tunnels, picking up speed. Zia seemed to weigh nothing. My headache had disappeared. Finally we burst into the sunlight and ran for the *Egyptian Queen*.

I'll admit I wasn't thinking straight.

When we got back on board, Bloodstained Blade reported on the ship's repairs, but I barely heard him. I plowed right past him and carried Zia inside to the nearest cabin. I set her on the bed and rummaged through my pack for medical supplies—a water bottle, some magic salve Jaz had given me, a few written charms. I was no *rekhet* like Jaz. My healing powers consisted mostly of bandages and aspirin, but I began to work.

"Come on," I mumbled. "Come on, Zia. You're going to be fine."

She was so warm, her drenched clothes had almost dried. Her eyes were rolled back in her head. She started muttering, and I could've sworn she said, "Dung balls. Time to roll the dung balls."

It might've been funny—except for the fact that she was dying.

"That's Khepri talking," Setne explained. "He's the divine dung beetle, rolling the sun across the sky."

I didn't want to process that—the idea that the girl I liked had been possessed by a dung beetle and was now having dreams about pushing a giant sphere of flaming poo across the sky.

But there was no question: Zia had used the path of the gods. She'd called on Ra—or at least one of his incarnations, Khepri.

Ra had chosen her, the way Horus had chosen me.

Suddenly it made sense that Apophis had destroyed Zia's village when she was young, and that the old Chief Lector Iskandar had gone to such lengths to train her and then hide her in a magical sleep. If she held the secret to reawakening the sun god . . .

I dabbed some ointment on her throat. I pressed a cold washcloth to her forehead, but it didn't seem to help.

I turned to Setne. "Heal her!"

"Oh, um . . ." He winced. "See, healing magic isn't really

my thing. But at least you've got the Book of Thoth! If she dies, it wasn't for nothing—"

"If she dies," I warned, "I will . . . I will . . ." I couldn't think of a torture painful enough.

"I see you need some time," Setne said. "No problem. How about I go tell your captain where we're heading? We should get back to the Duat, back onto the River of Night as soon as possible. Do I have your permission to give him orders?"

"Fine," I snapped. "Just get out of my sight."

I don't know how much time passed. Zia's fever seemed to subside. She started breathing more easily and slipped into a gentler sleep. I kissed her forehead and stayed by her side, holding her hand.

I was dimly aware of the ship's moving. We dropped into a momentary free-fall, then hit water with a shudder and a loud splash. I felt a river rolling under the hull once again, and from the tingling in my gut, I guessed we were back in the Duat.

The door creaked open behind me, but I kept my eyes on Zia.

I waited for Setne to say something—probably to brag about how well he'd done navigating us back to the River of Night—but he stayed silent.

"Well?" I asked.

The sound of splintering wood made me jump.

Setne wasn't at the door. Instead, Bloodstained Blade loomed over me, his ax head having just split the doorframe. His fists were clenched.

He spoke in an angry, cold hum: "Lord Kane, it's time to die."

241

13. A Friendly Game of Hide-and-Seek (with Bonus Points for Painful Death!)

I SEE. LEAVE OFF WITH THE AX-MURDERING DEMON. Trying to make my part of the story seem boring, eh? Carter, you are *such* an attention hog.

Well, as you were cruising down the Nile in a lavishly appointed riverboat, Walt and I were traveling in a bit less style.

From the realm of the dead, I ventured another conversation with Isis to negotiate a doorway into the Nile Delta. Isis must have been cross with me (I can't imagine why) because she deposited Walt and me waist-deep in a swamp, our feet completely stuck in the mud.

"Thanks!" I yelled at the sky.

I tried to move but couldn't. Clouds of mosquitoes gathered around us. The river was alive with bubbling and splashing noises, which made me think of pointy-toothed tiger fish and the water elementals Carter had once described to me.

"Any ideas?" I asked Walt.

Now that he was back in the mortal world, he seemed to have lost his vitality. He looked . . . I suppose the phrase would be *hollowed out*. His clothes fit more loosely. The whites of his eyes were tinted an unhealthy yellow. His shoulders hunched, as if the amulets around his neck weighed him down. Seeing him like this made me want to cry—which is not something I do easily.

"Yeah," he said, digging through his bag. "I have just the thing."

He brought out a *shabti*—a white wax figurine of a crocodile.

"Oh, you didn't," I said. "You wonderfully naughty boy."

Walt smiled. For a moment he almost looked like his old self. "Everyone was abandoning Brooklyn House. I figured it wasn't right to leave him behind."

He tossed the figurine in the river and spoke a command word. Philip of Macedonia erupted from the water.

Being surprised by a giant crocodile in the Nile is something you usually want to avoid, but Philip was a welcome sight. He smiled at me with his massive croc teeth, his pink eyes gleaming and his white scaly back floating just above the surface.

Walt and I grabbed hold. In no time, Philip had pulled us free of the muck. Soon we were perched on his back, making our way upriver. I rode in front, straddling Philip's shoulders. Walt sat behind at Philip's midsection. Philip was such a roomy crocodile that this left considerable space between Walt and me—possibly more than I would've preferred. Nevertheless we had a lovely ride, except for being drenched, caked in mud, and swarmed by mosquitoes.

The landscape was a maze of waterways, grassy islands, reed beds, and muddy shoals. It was impossible to tell where the river ended and the land began. Occasionally in the distance we saw plowed fields or the rooftops of small villages, but mostly we had the river to ourselves. We saw several crocodiles, but they all steered clear of us. They would have been quite insane to bother Philip.

Like Carter and Zia, we'd got a late start leaving the Underworld. I was alarmed at how far the sun had already climbed in the sky. The heat turned the air into a soupy haze. My shirt and trousers were soaked through. I wished I'd brought a change of clothes, though it wouldn't have made much difference, as my pack was damp, too. Also, with Walt around, there was no place to change.

After a while, I got bored with watching the Delta. I turned and sat cross-legged, facing Walt. "If we had some wood, we could start a campfire on Philip's back."

Walt laughed. "I don't think he'd like that. Plus, I'm not sure we want to send up smoke signals."

"You think we're being watched?"

His expression turned serious. "If I were Apophis, or even Sarah Jacobi . . ."

He didn't need to finish that thought. Any number of villains wanted us dead. Of *course* they'd be looking for us.

Walt rummaged through his collection of necklaces. I didn't notice the gentle curves of his mouth at all, or how his shirt clung to his chest in the humid air. No—all business, that's me.

He chose an amulet shaped like an ibis—Thoth's sacred animal. Walt whispered to it and threw it into the air. The charm expanded into a beautiful white bird with a long curved beak and black-tipped wings. It circled above us, buffeting my face with wind, then flew off slowly and gracefully over the wetlands. It reminded me of a stork from those old cartoons— the birds who bring babies in bundles. For some ridiculous reason, that thought made me blush.

"You're sending it to scout ahead?" I guessed.

Walt nodded. "It'll look for the ruins of Saïs. Hopefully they're close by."

Unless Isis sent us to the wrong end of the Delta, I thought.

Isis didn't reply, which was proof enough she was miffed.

We glided upstream on Crocodile Cruise Line. Normally I wouldn't have felt uncomfortable having so much face time with Walt, but there was so much to say, and no good way to say it. Tomorrow morning, one way or another, our long fight against Apophis would be over.

Of course I was worried about *all* of us. I'd left Carter with the sociopathic ghost of Uncle Vinnie. I hadn't even got up the courage to tell him that Zia occasionally became a fireball-lobbing maniac. I worried about Amos and his struggle with Set. I worried about our young initiates, virtually alone at the First Nome and no doubt terrified. I felt heartbroken for my father, who sat on his Underworld throne grieving for our mother—yet again—and of course I feared for my mother's spirit, on the verge of destruction somewhere in the Duat.

More than anything, I was concerned about Walt. The rest of us had *some* chance of surviving, however slim. Even if we prevailed, Walt was doomed. According to Setne, Walt might not even survive our trip to Saïs.

I didn't need anyone to tell me that. All I had to do was lower my vision into the Duat. A gray sickly aura swirled around Walt, growing weaker and weaker. How long, I wondered, before he turned into the mummified vision I'd seen in Dallas?

Then again, there was the *other* vision I'd seen at the Hall of Judgment. After talking to the jackal guardian, Walt had turned to me, and just for a moment, I thought he was . . .

"Anubis wanted to be there," Walt interrupted my thoughts. "I mean, in the Hall of Judgment—he wanted to be there for you, if that's what you were wondering about."

I scowled. "I was wondering about *you*, Walt Stone. You're running out of time, and we haven't had a proper talk about it."

Even saying *that* much was difficult.

Walt trailed his feet in the water. He'd set his shoes to dry on Philip's tail. Boys' feet are not something I find attractive, especially when they've just been removed from mucky trainers. However, Walt's feet were quite nice. His toes were almost the same color as the swirling silt in the Nile.

(Carter is complaining about my comments on Walt's feet. Well, *pardon me*. It was easier to focus on his toes than on the sad look on his face!)

"Tonight at the latest," he said. "But, Sadie, it's okay."

Anger swelled inside me, taking me quite by surprise.

"Stop it!" I snapped. "It's not anywhere *close* to okay! Oh, yes, you've told me how grateful you are to have known me, and learned magic at Brooklyn House, and helped with the fight against Apophis. All very noble. But it's not—" My voice broke. "It's not okay."

I pounded my fist on Philip's scaly back, which wasn't fair to the crocodile. Yelling at Walt wasn't fair either. But I was tired of tragedy. I wasn't *designed* for all this loss and sacrifice and horrible sadness. I wanted to throw my arms around Walt, but there was a wall between us—this knowledge that he was doomed. My feelings for him were so mixed up, I didn't know whether I was driven by simple attraction, or guilt, or (dare I say it) love—or stubborn determination not to lose someone else I cared about.

"Sadie . . ." Walt gazed across the marshes. He looked quite helpless, and I suppose I couldn't blame him. I was being rather impossible. "If I die for something I believe in . . . that's okay with me. But death doesn't have to be the end. I've been talking with Anubis, and—"

"Gods of Egypt, not *that* again!" I said. "*Please* don't talk about him. I know exactly what he's been telling you."

Walt looked startled. "You do? And . . . you don't like the idea?"

"Of course not!" I yelled.

Walt looked absolutely crestfallen.

"Oh, come off it!" I said. "I know Anubis is the guide for

the dead. He's been preparing you for the afterlife. He's told you that it'll be right. You'll die a noble death, get a speedy trial, and go straight into Ancient Egyptian Paradise. Bloody wonderful! You'll be a ghost like my poor mother. Perhaps it's not the end of the world for *you*. If it makes you feel better about your fate, then fine. But I don't want to hear about it. I don't need another . . . another person I can't be with."

My face was burning. It was bad enough that my mother was a spirit. I could never properly hug her again, never go shopping with her, never get advice about *girl* sorts of things. Bad enough that I'd been cut off from Anubis—that horribly frustrating gorgeous god who'd wrapped my heart into knots. Deep down, I'd always known a relationship with him was impossible given our age difference—five thousand years or so—but having the other gods decree him off-limits just rubbed salt in the wound.

Now to think of Walt as a spirit, out of reach as well—that was simply too much.

I looked up at him, afraid my bratty behavior would have made him feel even worse.

To my surprise, he broke into a smile. Then he laughed.

"What?" I demanded.

He doubled over, still laughing, which I found quite inconsiderate.

"You find this funny?" I shouted. "Walt Stone!"

"No . . ." He hugged his sides. "No, it's just . . . You don't understand. It's not like that."

"Well, then, what *is* it like?"

He got control of himself. He seemed to be collecting his thoughts when his white ibis dived out of the sky. It landed on Philip's head, flapped its wings, and cawed.

Walt's smile melted. "We're here. The ruins of Saïs."

Philip carried us ashore. We put on our shoes and waded across the marshy ground. In front of us stretched a forest of palm trees, hazy in the afternoon light. Herons flew overhead. Orange-and-black bees hovered over the papyrus plants.

One bee landed on Walt's arm. Several more circled his head.

Walt looked more perplexed than worried. "The goddess who's supposed to live around here, Neith . . . didn't she have something to do with bees?"

"No idea," I admitted. For some reason, I felt the urge to speak quietly.

[Yes, Carter. It *was* a first for me. Thanks for asking.]

I peered through the palm forest. In the distance, I thought I saw a clearing with a few clumps of mud brick sticking above the grass like rotten teeth.

I pointed them out to Walt. "The remains of a temple?"

Walt must have felt the same instinct for stealth that I did. He crouched in the grass, trying to lower his profile. Then he glanced back nervously at Philip of Macedonia. "Maybe we shouldn't have a three-thousand-pound crocodile trampling through the woods with us."

"Agreed," I said.

He whispered a command word. Philip shrank back to a

small wax statuette. Walt pocketed our croc, and we began sneaking toward the ruins.

The closer we got, the more bees filled the air. When we arrived at the clearing, we found an entire colony swarming like a living carpet over a cluster of crumbling mud-brick walls.

Next to them, sitting on a weathered block of stone, a woman leaned on a bow, sketching in the dirt with an arrow.

She was beautiful in a severe way—thin and pale with high cheekbones, sunken eyes, and arched eyebrows, like a super-model walking the line between glamorous and malnourished. Her hair was glossy black, braided on either side with flint arrowheads. Her haughty expression seemed to say: *I'm much too cool to even look at you.*

There was nothing glamorous about her clothes, however. She was dressed for the hunt in desert-colored fatigues—beige, brown, and ochre. Several knives hung from her belt. A quiver was strapped to her back, and her bow looked like quite a serious weapon—polished wood carved with hieroglyphs of power.

Most disturbing of all, she seemed to be waiting for us.

"You're noisy," she complained. "I could've killed you a dozen times already."

I glanced at Walt, then back at the huntress. "Um . . . thanks? For not killing us, I mean."

The woman snorted. "Don't thank me. You'll have to do better than that if you want to survive."

I didn't like the sound of that, but generally speaking, I don't ask heavily armed women to elaborate on such statements.

Walt pointed to the symbol the huntress was drawing in the dirt—an oval with four pointy bits like legs.

"You're Neith," Walt guessed. "That's your symbol—the shield with crossed arrows."

The goddess raised her eyebrows. "Think much? Of *course* I'm Neith. And, yes, that's my symbol."

"It looks like a bug," I said.

"It's not a bug!" Neith glowered. Behind her, the bees became agitated, crawling over the mud bricks.

"You're right," I decided. "Not a bug."

Walt wagged his finger as if he'd just had a thought. "The bees . . . I remember now. That was one name for your temple—the House of the Bee."

"Bees are tireless hunters," Neith said. "Fearless warriors. I like bees."

"Uh, who doesn't?" I offered. "Charming little . . . buzzers. But you see, we're here on a mission."

I began to explain about Bes and his shadow.

Neith cut me off with a wave of her arrow. "I know why you're here. The others told me."

I moistened my lips. "The others?"

"Russian magicians," she said. "They were terrible prey. After that, a few demons came by. They weren't much better. They all wanted to kill you."

I moved a step closer to Walt. "I see. And so you—"

"Destroyed them, of course," Neith said.

Walt made a sound somewhere between a grunt and a whimper. "Destroyed them because . . . they were evil?" he said hopefully. "You knew the demons and those magicians were working for Apophis, right? It's a conspiracy."

"Of course it's a conspiracy," Neith said. "They're *all* in on it—the mortals, the magicians, the demons, the tax collectors. But I'm on to them. Anyone who invades my territory pays." She gave me a hard smile. "I take trophies."

From under the collar of her army jacket, she dug out a necklace. I winced, expecting to see some grisly bits of . . . well, I don't even want to say. Instead, the cord was strung with ragged squares of cloth—denim, linen, silk.

"Pockets," Neith confided, a wicked gleam in her eyes.

Walt's hands went instinctively to the sides of his workout pants. "You, um . . . took their *pockets*?"

"Do you think me cruel?" Neith asked. "Oh, yes, I collect the pockets of my enemies."

"Horrifying," I said. "I didn't know demons had pockets."

"Oh, yes." Neith glanced in either direction, apparently to be sure no one was eavesdropping. "You just have to know where to look."

"Right . . ." I said. "So anyway, we've come to find Bes's shadow."

"Yes," the goddess said.

"And I understand you're a friend of Bes and Tawaret's."

"That's true. I like them. They're ugly. I don't think they're in the conspiracy."

"Oh, definitely not! So could you, perhaps, show us where Bes's shadow is?"

"I could. It dwells in my realm—in the shadows of ancient times."

"In the . . . what now?"

I was *so* sorry I asked.

Neith nocked her arrow and shot it toward the sky. As it sailed upward, the air rippled. A shockwave spread across the landscape, and I felt momentarily dizzy.

When I blinked, I found that the afternoon sky had turned a more brilliant blue, striped with orange clouds. The air was crisp and clean. Flocks of geese flew overhead. The palm trees were taller; the grass was greener—

[Yes, Carter, I know it sounds silly. But the grass really *was* greener on the other side.]

Where the mud-brick ruins had been, a proud temple now stood. Walt, Neith, and I were just outside the walls, which rose ten meters and gleamed brilliant white in the sun. The whole complex must have been at least a kilometer square. Halfway down the left wall, a gate glittered with gold filigree. A road lined with stone sphinxes led to the river, where sailboats were docked.

Disorienting? Yes. But I'd had a similar experience once before, when I'd touched the curtains of light in the Hall of Ages.

"We're in the past?" I guessed.

"A shadow of it," Neith said. "A memory. This is my refuge. It may be your burial ground, unless you survive the hunt."

I tensed. "You mean . . . you hunt *us*? But we're not your enemy! Bes is your friend. You should be helping us!"

"Sadie's right," Walt said. "*Apophis* is your enemy. He's going to destroy the world tomorrow morning."

Neith snorted. "The end of the world? I've seen *that* coming for eons. You soft mortals have ignored the warning signs, but I'm prepared. I've got an underground bunker stockpiled with food, clean water, and enough weapons and ammunition to hold off a zombie army."

Walt knit his eyebrows. "A zombie army?"

"You never know!" Neith snapped. "The point is, I'll survive the apocalypse. I can live off the land!" She jabbed a finger at me. "Did you know the palm tree has six different edible parts?"

"Um—"

"And I'll never be bored," Neith continued, "since I'm also the goddess of weaving. I have enough twine for a millennium of macramé!"

I had no reply, as I wasn't sure what macramé was.

Walt raised his hands. "Neith, that's great, but Apophis is rising tomorrow. He'll swallow the sun, plunge the world into darkness, and let the whole earth crumble back into the Sea of Chaos."

"I'll be safe in my bunker," Neith insisted. "If you can prove to me that you're friend and not foe, maybe I'll help you with Bes. Then you can join me in the bunker. I'll teach you survival skills. We'll eat rations and weave new clothes from the pockets of our enemies!"

Walt and I exchanged looks. The goddess was a nutter. Unfortunately, we needed her help.

"So you want to hunt us," I said. "And we're supposed to survive—"

"Until sunset," she said. "Evade me that long, and you can live in my bunker."

"I've got a counteroffer," I said quickly. "No bunker. If we win, you help us find Bes's shadow, but you'll also fight on our side against Apophis. If you're really a war goddess and a huntress and all that, you should enjoy a good battle."

Neith grinned. "Done! I'll even give you a five-minute head start. But I should warn you: I never lose. When I kill you, I'll take your pockets!"

"You drive a hard bargain," I said. "But fine."

Walt elbowed me. "Um, Sadie—"

I shot him a warning look. As I saw it, there was no way we could escape this hunt, but I *did* have an idea that might keep us alive.

"We've begun!" Neith cried. "You can go anywhere in my territory, which is basically the entire delta. It doesn't matter. I'll find you."

Walt said, "But—"

"Four minutes, now," Neith said.

We did the only sensible thing. We turned and ran.

"What is macramé?" I yelled as we barreled through the rushes.

"A kind of weaving," Walt said. "Why are we talking about this?"

"Dunno," I admitted. "Just cur—"

The world turned upside down—or rather, I did. I found myself hanging in a scratchy twine net with my feet in the air.

"*That's* macramé," Walt said.

"Lovely. Get me down!"

He pulled a knife from his pack—practical boy—and managed to free me, but I reckoned we'd lost most of our head start.

The sun was lower on the horizon, but how long would we have to survive—thirty minutes? An hour?

Walt rifled through his pack and briefly considered the white wax crocodile. "Philip, maybe?"

"No," I said. "We can't fight Neith head-on. We have to avoid her. We can split—"

"Tiger. Boat. Sphinx. Camels. No invisibility," Walt muttered, examining his amulets. "Why don't I have an amulet for invisibility?"

I shuddered. The last time I'd tried invisibility, it hadn't gone very well. "Walt, she's a hunting goddess. We probably couldn't fool her with any sort of concealment spell, even if you had one."

"Then what?" he asked.

I put my finger on Walt's chest and tapped the one amulet he wasn't considering—a necklace that was the twin to mine.

"The *shen* amulets?" He blinked. "But how can those help?"

"We split up and buy time," I said. "We can share thoughts through the amulets, yes?"

"Well . . . yes."

"And they can teleport us to each other's side, right?"

Walt frowned. "I—I designed them for that, but—"

"If we split up," I said, "Neith will have to choose one of us to track. We get as far apart as possible. If she finds me first, you teleport me out of danger with the amulet. Or vice versa. Then we split up again, and we keep at it."

"That's brilliant," Walt admitted. "If the amulets will work quickly enough. And if we can keep the mental connection. And if Neith doesn't kill one of us before we can call for help. And—"

I put my finger to his lips. "Let's just leave it at 'That's brilliant.'"

He nodded, then gave me a hasty kiss. "Good luck."

The silly boy shouldn't do things like that when I need to stay focused. He dashed off to the north and, after a dazed moment, I ran south.

Squishy combat boots are not the best for sneaking around.

I considered wading into the river, thinking perhaps the water would obscure my trail, but I didn't want to go for a swim without knowing what was under the surface—crocs, snakes, evil spirits. Carter once told me that most Ancient Egyptians couldn't swim, which had seemed ridiculous to me at the time. How could people living next to a river not swim? Now I understood. No one in his right mind would want to take a dip in that water.

(Carter says a swim in the Thames or the East River would be almost as bad for your health. All right, fair point. [Now shut up, brother dear, and let me get back to the brilliant Sadie-saves-the-day part.])

I ran along the banks, crashing through reeds, jumping straight over a sunning crocodile. I didn't bother to check if it was chasing me. I had bigger predators to worry about.

I'm not sure how long I ran. It seemed like miles. As the riverbank widened, I veered inland, trying to stay under the cover of the palm trees. I heard no signs of pursuit, but I had a constant itch in the middle of my shoulder blades where I expected an arrow.

I stumbled through a clearing where some Ancient Egyptians in loincloths were cooking over an open fire next to a small thatched hut. Perhaps the Egyptians were just shadows from the past, but they looked real enough. They seemed quite startled to see a blond girl in combat clothes stumble into their encampment. Then they saw my staff and wand and immediately groveled, putting their heads to the dirt and mumbling something about *Per Ankh*—the House of Life.

"Um, yes," I said. "*Per Ankh* official business. Carry on. Bye."

Off I raced. I wondered if I would appear on a temple wall painting someday—a blond Egyptian girl with purple highlights running sideways through the palm trees, screaming "Yikes!" in hieroglyphics as Neith chased after me. The thought of some poor archaeologist trying to figure that out almost lifted my spirits.

I reached the edge of the palm forest and stumbled to a stop. Before me, plowed fields spread into the distance. Nowhere to run or hide.

I turned back.

THUNK!

An arrow hit the nearest palm tree with such force that dates rained down on my head.

Walt, I thought desperately, *now, please*.

Twenty meters away, Neith rose from the grass. She had smeared river mud on her face. Palm fronds stuck from her hair like bunny ears.

"I've hunted feral pigs with more skill than you," she complained. "I've hunted *papyrus* plants with more skill!"

Now, Walt, I thought. *Dear, dear Walt. Now.*

Neith shook her head in disgust. She nocked an arrow. I felt a tugging sensation in my stomach, as if I were in a car and the driver suddenly slammed on the brakes.

I found myself sitting in a tree next to Walt, on the lowest bough of a large sycamore.

"It worked," he said.

Wonderful Walt!

I kissed him properly—or as properly as possible given our situation. There was a sweet smell about him I hadn't noticed before, as if he'd been eating lotus blossoms. I imagined that old school rhyme: "Walt and Sadie / sitting in a tree / K-I-S-S-I-N-G." Fortunately, anyone who might tease me was still five thousand years in the future.

Walt took a deep breath. "Is that a thank-you?"

"You look better," I noticed. His eyes weren't as yellow. He seemed to be moving with less pain. This should have delighted me, but instead it made me worried. "That lotus smell . . . did you drink something?"

"I'm okay." He looked away from me. "We'd better split up and try again."

That didn't make me any less worried, but he was right. We had no time to chat. We both jumped to the ground and headed off in opposite directions.

The sun was almost touching the horizon. I began to feel hopeful. Surely we wouldn't have to hold out much longer.

I almost stumbled into another macramé net, but fortunately I was on the lookout for Neith's arts and crafts projects. I sidestepped the trap, pushed through a stand of papyrus plants, and found myself back at Neith's temple.

The golden gates stood open. The wide avenue of sphinxes led straight into the complex. No guards . . . no priests. Maybe Neith had killed them all and collected their pockets, or perhaps they were all down in the bunker, preparing for a zombie invasion.

Hmm. I reckoned that the last place Neith might look for me was in her home base. Besides, Tawaret had seen Bes's shadow up on those ramparts. If I could find the shadow without Neith's help, all the better.

I ran for the gates, keeping a suspicious eye on the sphinxes. None of them came alive. Inside the massive courtyard were two freestanding obelisks tipped with gold. Between them glowered a statue of Neith in Ancient Egyptian garb. Shields and arrows had been piled around her feet like spoils of war.

I scanned the surrounding walls. Several stairways led up to the ramparts. The setting sun cast plenty of long shadows, but I didn't see any obvious dwarf silhouettes. Tawaret had suggested I call to the shadow. I was about to try when I heard Walt's voice in my mind: *Sadie!*

It's awfully hard to concentrate when someone's life depends on you.

I grasped the *shen* amulet and muttered, "Come on. Come on."

I pictured Walt standing next to me, preferably without

an arrow in him. I blinked—and there he was. He almost knocked me down with a hug.

"She—she would've killed me," Walt gasped. "But she wanted to talk first. She said she liked our trick. She was proud to slay us and take our pockets."

"Super," I said. "Split up again?"

Walt glanced over my shoulder. "Sadie, look."

He pointed to the northwest corner of the walls, where a tower jutted from the ramparts. As the sky turned red, shadows slowly melted from the side of the tower, but one shadow remained—the silhouette of a stout little man with frizzy hair.

I'm afraid we forgot our plan. Together, we ran to the steps and climbed the wall. In no time, we were standing on the parapets, staring at the shadow of Bes.

I realized we must have been in the exact spot where Tawaret and Bes had held hands on the night Tawaret had described. Bes had told the truth—he'd left his shadow here so it could be happy, even when he wasn't.

"Oh, Bes . . ." My heart felt like it was shrinking into a wax *shabti*. "Walt, how do we capture it?"

A voice behind us said, "You don't."

We turned. A few meters away, Neith stood on the ramparts. Two arrows were nocked in her bow. At this range, I imagined she'd have no trouble hitting us both at once.

"A good try," she admitted. "But I always win the hunt."

14. Fun with Split Personalities

AN EXCELLENT TIME TO CALL ON ISIS?

Perhaps. But even if Isis had answered, I doubted I could summon any magic faster than Neith could shoot. And on the off chance I actually defeated the huntress, I had the feeling Neith would consider it cheating if I used another goddess's power against her. She'd probably decide I was part of the Russian/zombie/tax collector conspiracy.

As mad as Neith was, we needed her help. She'd be much more useful shooting arrows at Apophis than sitting in her bunker making jackets out of our pockets and knotted twine.

My mind raced. How to win over a hunter? I didn't know much about hunters, except for old Major McNeil, Gramps's friend from the pensioners' home, who used to tell stories constantly about . . . Ah.

"It's a shame, really," I blurted out.

Neith hesitated, as I'd hoped she would.

"What is?" she asked.

"Six edible parts of a palm tree." I laughed. "It's seven actually."

Neith frowned. "Impossible!"

"Oh, yes?" I raised my eyebrows. "Have *you* ever lived off the land in Covent Garden? Have *you* ever trekked through the wilds of Camden Lock and lived to tell about it?"

Neith's bow dipped ever so slightly. "I do not know those places."

"I thought not!" I said triumphantly. "Oh, the stories we could've shared, Neith. The tips for survival. Once I went for a whole week on nothing but stale biscuits and the juice of the Ribena."

"Is that a plant?" Neith asked.

"With every nutrient you need for survival," I said. "If you know where to buy—I mean harvest it."

I lifted my wand, hoping she would see this as a dramatic move, not a threat. "Why once, in my bunker at Charing Cross Station, I stalked the deadly prey known as Jelly Babies."

Neith's eyes widened. "They are dangerous?"

"Horrible," I agreed. "Oh, they seem small alone, but they always appear in great numbers. Sticky, fattening—quite deadly. There I was, alone with only two quid and a Tube pass, beset by Jelly Babies, when . . . Ah, but never mind. When the Jelly Babies come for you . . . you will find out on your own."

She lowered her bow. "Tell me. I must know how to hunt Jelly Babies."

I looked at Walt gravely. "How many months have I trained you, Walt?"

"Seven," he said. "Almost eight."

"And have I ever deemed you worthy of hunting Jelly Babies with me?"

"Uh . . . no."

"There you have it!" I knelt and began tracing on the rampart floor with my wand. "Even Walt is not ready for such knowledge. I could draw for you here a picture of the dreaded Jelly Baby, or even—gods forbid!—the Jacob's Digestive Cream. But that knowledge might destroy a lesser hunter."

"I am the goddess of hunting!" Neith inched closer, staring in awe at the glowing markings—apparently not realizing I was making protective hieroglyphs. "I must know."

"Well . . ." I glanced at the horizon. "First, you must understand the importance of timing."

"Yes!" Neith said eagerly. "Tell me of this."

"For instance . . ." I tapped the hieroglyphs and activated my spell. "It's sunset. We're still alive. We win."

Neith's expression hardened. "Trickery!"

She lunged at me, but the protective glyphs flared, pushing back the goddess. She raised her bow and shot her arrows.

What happened next was surprising on many levels. First, the arrows must have been heavily enchanted, because they sailed right through my defenses. Second, Walt lunged forward with impossible speed. Faster than I could scream (which I did), Walt snatched the arrows out of the air. They crumbled to gray dust, scattering in the wind.

Neith stepped back in horror. "It's *you*. This is unfair!"

"We won," Walt said. "Honor your agreement."

A look passed between them that I didn't quite understand—some sort of contest of wills.

Neith hissed through clenched teeth. "Very well. You may go. When Apophis rises, I will fight at your side. But I will not forget how you trespassed on my territory, child of Set. And you—"

She glared at me. "I lay this hunter's curse upon you: someday you will be tricked by *your* prey as I have been tricked today. May you be set upon by a pack of wild Jelly Babies!"

With that terrifying threat, Neith dissolved into a pile of twine.

"Child of Set?" I narrowed my eyes at Walt. "What exactly—?"

"Look out!" he warned. All around us, the temple began to crumble. The air rippled as the magic shockwave contracted, transforming the landscape back to present-day Egypt.

We barely made it to the base of the stairs. The last walls of the temple were reduced to a pile of worn mud bricks, but the shadow of Bes was still visible against them, slowly fading as the sun went down.

"We need to hurry," Walt said.

"Yes, but how do we capture it?"

Behind us, someone cleared his throat.

Anubis leaned against a nearby palm tree, his expression grim. "I'm sorry to intrude. But, Walt . . . it's time."

Anubis was sporting the formal Egyptian look. He wore a golden neck collar, a black kilt, sandals, and pretty much nothing else. As I've mentioned before, not many boys could pull off this look, especially with kohl eyeliner, but Anubis managed.

Suddenly his expression turned to alarm. He sprinted toward us. For a moment I had an absurd vision of myself on the cover of one of Gran's old romance novels, where the damsel wilts into the arms of one half-dressed beefy guy while another stands by, casting her longing looks. Oh, the horrible choices a girl must make! I wished I'd had a moment to clean up. I was still covered in dried river muck, twine, and grass, like I'd been tarred and feathered.

Then Anubis pushed past me and gripped Walt's shoulders. Well . . . that was unexpected.

I quickly realized, however, that he'd stopped Walt from collapsing. Walt's face was beaded with sweat. His head drooped, and his knees gave out as if someone had cut the last string holding him together. Anubis lowered him gently to the ground.

"Walt, stay with me," Anubis urged. "We have business to finish."

"Business to finish?" I cried. I'm not sure what came over me, but I felt as if I'd just been Photoshopped out of my own book cover. And if there was one thing I wasn't used to, it was being ignored. "Anubis, what are you *doing* here? What is going on with you two? *And what bloody business?*"

Anubis frowned at me, as if he'd forgot my presence. That didn't do much to help my mood. "Sadie—"

"I tried to tell her," Walt groaned. Anubis helped him sit up, though Walt still looked awful.

"I see," Anubis said. "Couldn't get a word in edgewise, I guess?"

Walt managed a weak smile. "You should've seen her talking to Neith about Jelly Babies. She was like . . . I don't know, a verbal freight train. The goddess never stood a chance."

"Yes, I saw," Anubis said. "It was endearing, in an annoying sort of way."

"I beg your pardon?" I wasn't sure which of them to slap first.

"And when she turns red like that," Anubis added, as if I were some interesting specimen.

"Cute," Walt agreed.

"So have you decided?" Anubis asked him. "This is our last chance."

"Yes. I can't leave her."

Anubis nodded and squeezed his shoulder. "Neither can I. But the shadow, first?"

Walt coughed, his face contorting in pain. "Yes. Before it's too late."

I can't pretend I was thinking clearly, but one thing was obvious: these two had been talking behind my back *much* more than I'd realized. What on earth had they been telling each other about me? Forget Apophis swallowing the sun—*this* was my ultimate nightmare.

How could they *both* not leave me? Hearing that from a dying boy and a god of death sounded quite ominous. They'd formed some sort of conspiracy. . . .

Oh, lord. I was beginning to think like Neith. Soon I'd be huddled in an underground bunker eating army rations and cackling as I sewed together the pockets of all the boys who'd jilted me.

With difficulty, Anubis helped Walt over to the shadow of Bes, now rapidly disappearing in the twilight.

"Can you do it?" Anubis asked.

Walt murmured something I couldn't make out. His hands were shaking, but he pulled a block of wax from his bag and began kneading it into a *shabti.* "Setne tried to make it sound so complicated, but I see now. It's simple. No wonder the gods wanted this knowledge kept out of mortal hands."

"Excuse me," I interrupted.

They both looked at me.

"Hi, I'm Sadie Kane," I said. "I don't mean to barge in on your chummy conversation, but what in *blazes* are you doing?"

"Capturing Bes's shadow," Anubis told me.

"But . . ." I couldn't seem to make words come out. So much for being a verbal freight train. I'd become a verbal train wreck. "But if that's the business you were talking about, then what was all that about *deciding,* and *leaving me,* and—"

"Sadie," Walt said, "we're going to lose the shadow if I don't act now. You need to watch the spell, so you can do this with the shadow of the serpent."

"You are *not* going to die, Walt Stone. I forbid it."

"It's a simple incantation," he continued, quite ignoring my plea. "A regular summons, with the words *shadow of Bes* substituted for *Bes.* After the shadow is absorbed, you'll need a binding spell to anchor it. Then—"

"Walt, stop it!"

He was shivering so badly, his teeth chattered. How could he think about giving me a magic lesson now?

"—then for the execration," he said, "you'll need to be in front of Apophis. The ritual is exactly the same as normal. Setne lied about that part—there's nothing special about his enchantment. The only hard part is finding the shadow. For Bes, just reverse the spell. You should be able to cast it from a distance, since it's a beneficial spell. The shadow will *want* to help you. Send out the *sheut* to find Bes, and it should . . . should bring him back."

"But—"

"Sadie." Anubis put his arms around me. His brown eyes were full of compassion. "Don't make him talk more than he has to. He needs his strength for this spell."

Walt began to chant. He raised the lump of wax, which now resembled a miniature Bes, and pressed it against the shadow on the wall.

I sobbed. "But he'll die!"

Anubis held me. He smelled of temple incense—copal and amber and other ancient fragrances.

"He was born under the shadow of death," Anubis said. "That's why we understand each other. He would've collapsed long before now, but Jaz gave him one last potion to hold off the pain—to give him a final burst of energy in an emergency."

I remembered the sweet smell of lotus on Walt's breath. "He took it just now. When we were running from Neith."

Anubis nodded. "It's worn off. He'll only have enough energy to finish this spell."

"No!" I meant to scream and hit him, but I'm afraid I rather melted and wept instead. Anubis sheltered me in his arms, and I sniveled like a little girl.

I have no excuse. I simply couldn't stand the thought of losing Walt, even to bring back Bes. Just once, couldn't I succeed at something without a massive sacrifice?

"You have to watch," Anubis told me. "Learn the spell. It's the only way to save Bes. And you'll need the same enchantment to capture the serpent's shadow."

"I don't care!" I cried, but I did watch.

As Walt chanted, the figurine absorbed the shadow of Bes like a sponge soaking up liquid. The wax turned as black as kohl.

"Don't worry," Anubis said gently. "Death won't be the end for him."

I pounded on his chest without much force. "I don't want to hear that! You shouldn't even be here. Didn't the gods put a restraining order on you?"

"I'm not supposed to be near you," Anubis agreed, "because I have no mortal form."

"How, then? There's no graveyard. This isn't *your* temple."

"No," Anubis admitted. He nodded at Walt. "Look."

Walt finished his spell. He spoke a single command word: "*Hi-nehm.*"

The hieroglyph for *Join together* blazed silver against the dark wax:

It was the same command I'd used to repair the gift shop in Dallas, the same command Uncle Amos had used last Christmas when he had demonstrated how to put a broken saucer back together. And with horrible certainty, I knew it would be the last spell Walt ever cast.

He slumped forward. I ran to his side. I cradled his head in my arms. His breathing was ragged.

"Worked," he muttered. "Now . . . send the shadow to Bes. You'll have to—"

"Walt, please," I said. "We can get you to the First Nome. Their healers might be able to—"

"No, Sadie . . ." He pressed the figurine into my hands. "Hurry."

I tried to concentrate. It was almost impossible, but I managed to reverse the wording of an execration. I channeled power into the figurine and imagined Bes as he once was. I urged the shadow to find its master, to reawaken his soul. Instead of erasing Bes from the world, I tried to draw him back into the picture, this time with permanent ink.

The wax statue turned to smoke and disappeared.

"Did—did it work?" I asked.

Walt didn't answer. His eyes were closed. He lay perfectly still.

"Oh, please . . . no." I hugged his forehead, which was rapidly cooling. "Anubis, do something!"

No answer. I turned, and Anubis was gone.

"Anubis!" I screamed so loudly it echoed off the distant cliffs. I set Walt down as gently as I could. I stood and turned in a full circle, my fists clenched. "That's it?" I shouted at the empty air. "You take his soul and leave? I *hate* you!"

Suddenly Walt gasped and opened his eyes.

I sobbed with relief.

"Walt!" I knelt next to him.

"The gate," he said urgently.

I didn't know what he meant. Perhaps he'd had some sort of near-death vision? His voice sounded clearer, free of pain, but still weak. "Sadie, hurry. You know the spell now. It will work on . . . on the serpent's shadow."

"Walt, what happened?" I brushed the tears from my face. "What gate?"

He pointed feebly. A few meters away, a door of darkness hovered in the air. "The whole quest was a trap," he said. "Setne . . . I see his plan now. Your brother needs your help."

"But what about you? Come with me!"

He shook his head. "I'm still too weak. I will do my best to summon reinforcements for you in the Duat—you'll need them—but I can barely move. I'll meet you at sunrise, at the First Nome, if—if you're sure you don't hate me."

"Hate you?" I was completely baffled. "Why on earth would I hate you?"

He smiled sadly—a smile that wasn't quite like him.

"Look," he said.

It took me a moment to understand his meaning. A cold feeling washed over me. How had Walt survived? Where was Anubis? And what had they been conspiring about?

Neith had called Walt a child of Set, but he wasn't. Set's only child was Anubis.

I tried to tell her, Walt had said.

He was born under the shadow of death, Anubis had told me. *That's why we understand each other.*

I didn't want to, but I lowered my vision into the Duat. Where Walt lay, I saw a different person, like a superimposed image . . . a young man lying weak and pale, in a gold neckband and black Egyptian kilt, with familiar brown eyes and a sad smile. Deeper still, I saw the glowing gray radiance of a god—the jackal-headed form of Anubis.

"Oh . . . no, no." I got up and stumbled away from him. From *them*. Too many puzzle pieces fell together at once. My head was spinning. Walt's ability to turn things to dust . . . it was the path of Anubis. He'd been channeling the god's power for months. Their friendship, their discussions, the *other* way Anubis hinted at for saving Walt . . .

"What have you done?" I stared at him in horror. I wasn't even sure what to call him.

"Sadie, it's me," Walt said. "Still me."

In the Duat, Anubis spoke in unison: "Still me."

"No!" My legs trembled. I felt betrayed and cheated. I felt as if the world was already crumbling into the Sea of Chaos.

"I can explain," he said in two voices. "But Carter needs your help. Please, Sadie—"

"Stop it!" I'm not proud of how I acted, but I turned and fled, leaping straight through the doorway of darkness. At the moment I didn't even care where it led, as long as it was away from that deathless creature I had thought I loved.

15. I Become a Purple Chimpanzee

JELLY BABIES? SERIOUSLY?

I hadn't heard that part. My sister never ceases to amaze me—[and no, Sadie, that's not a compliment, either.]

Anyway, while Sadie was having her supernatural guy drama, I was confronting an ax-murdering riverboat captain who apparently wanted to change his name to Even-More-Bloodstained Blade.

"Back down," I told the demon. "That's an order."

Bloodstained Blade made a humming sound that might've been laughter. He swung his head to the left—kind of an Elvis Presley dance move—and smashed a hole in the wall. Then he faced me again, splinters all over his shoulders.

"I have other orders," he hummed. "Orders to kill!"

He charged like a bull. After the mess we'd just been through in the *serapeum*, a bull was the last thing I wanted to deal with.

I thrust out my fist. *"Ha-wi!"*

The hieroglyph for *Strike* glowed between us:

A blue fist of energy slammed into Bloodstained Blade, pushing him out the door and straight through the wall of the opposite stateroom. A hit like that would have knocked out a human, but I could hear BSB digging out from the rubble, humming angrily.

I tried to think. It would've been nice to keep smashing him with that hieroglyph over and over, but magic doesn't work that way. Once spoken, a divine word can't be used again for several minutes, sometimes even hours.

Besides, divine words are top-of-the-line magic. Some magicians spend years mastering a single hieroglyph. I'd learned the hard way that saying too many will burn through your energy really fast, and I didn't have much to spare.

First problem: keep the demon away from Zia. She was still half-conscious and totally defenseless. I summoned as much magic as I could and said: *"N'dah!"*—*Protect.*

Blue light shimmered around her. I had a horrible flashback to when I found Zia in her watery tomb last spring. If she woke up encased in blue energy and thought she was imprisoned again . . .

"Oh, Zia," I said, "I didn't mean—"

"KILL!" Bloodstained Blade rose from the wreckage of the opposite room. A feather pillow was impaled on his head, raining goose fluff all over his uniform.

I dashed into the hall and headed for the stairs, glancing back to be sure the captain was following me and not going after Zia. Lucky me—he was right on my tail.

I reached the deck and yelled, "Setne!"

The ghost was nowhere to be seen. The crew lights were going crazy, buzzing around frantically, bonking into walls, looping around the smokestacks, lowering and raising the gangplank for no apparent reason. I guess without Bloodstained Blade to give them directions, they were lost.

The riverboat careened down the River of Night, weaving drunkenly in the current. We slipped between two jagged rocks that would have pulverized the hull, then dropped over a cataract with a jaw-rattling *thunk*. I glanced up at the wheelhouse and saw no one steering. It was a miracle that we hadn't crashed already. I had to get the boat under control.

I ran for the stairs.

When I was halfway there, Bloodstained Blade appeared out of nowhere. He sliced his head across my gut, ripping open my shirt. If I'd had a larger belly—no, I don't want to think about it. I stumbled backward, pressing my hand against my navel. He'd only grazed the skin, but the sight of blood on my fingers made me feel faint.

Some warrior, I scolded myself.

Fortunately, Bloodstained Blade had embedded his ax head

in the wall. He was still trying to tug it free, grumbling, "New orders: *Kill Carter Kane. Take him to the Land of Demons. Make sure it's a one-way trip.*"

The Land of Demons?

I bolted up the stairs and into the wheelhouse.

All around the boat, the river churned into whitewater rapids. A pillar of stone loomed out of the fog and scraped against our starboard side, ripping off part of the railing. We twisted sideways and picked up speed. Somewhere ahead of us, I heard the roar of millions of tons of water cascading into oblivion. We were rushing toward a waterfall.

I looked around desperately for the shore. It was hard to see through the thick fog and gloomy gray light of the Duat, but a hundred yards or so off the bow, I thought I saw fires burning, and a dark line that might've been a beach.

The Land of Demons sounded bad, but not as bad as dropping off a waterfall and getting smashed to pieces. I ripped the cord off the alarm bell and lashed the pilot's wheel in place, pointing us toward the shore.

"Kill Kane!"

The captain's well-polished boot slammed me in the ribs and sent me straight through the port window. Glass shattered, raking my back and legs. I bounced off a hot smokestack and landed hard on the deck.

My vision blurred. The cut across my stomach stung. My legs felt like they'd been used for a tiger's chew toy, and judging from the hot pain in my side, I may have broken some ribs in the fall.

All in all, not my best combat experience.

Hello? Horus spoke in my mind. *Any intention of calling for help, or are you happy to die on your own?*

Yeah, I snapped back at him. *The sarcasm is real helpful.*

Truthfully, I didn't think I had enough energy left to summon my avatar, even with Horus's help. My fight with the Apis Bull had nearly tapped me out, and that was before I got chased by an ax demon and kicked out a window.

I could hear Bloodstained Blade stomping his way back down the stairs. I tried to rise, and almost blacked out from the pain.

A weapon, I told Horus. *I need a weapon.*

I reached into the Duat and pulled out an ostrich feather. "Really?" I yelled.

Horus didn't answer.

Meanwhile the crew lights zipped around in a panic as the boat barreled toward the shore. The beach was easier to see now—black sand littered with bones and plumes of volcanic gas shooting from fiery crevices. Oh, good. Just the sort of place I wanted to crash land.

I dropped the ostrich feather and reached into the Duat again.

This time I pulled out a pair of familiar weapons—the crook and flail, symbols of the pharaoh. The crook was a gold-and-red shepherd's rod with a curved end. The flail was a pole arm with three wicked-looking spiked chains. I'd seen lots of similar weapons. Every pharaoh had a set. But *these* looked disturbingly like the original pair—the weapons of the sun god that I'd found last spring buried in Zia's tomb.

"What are these doing here?" I demanded. "These should be with Ra."

Horus remained silent. I got the feeling he was as surprised as I was.

Bloodstained Blade stormed around the side of the wheel-house. His uniform was ripped and covered in feathers. His blades had some new nicks, and he'd gotten the emergency bell wrapped around his left boot so it clanged as he walked. But he still looked better than me.

"Enough," he hummed. "I have served the Kanes too long!"

Toward the bow of the ship, I heard the *crank, crank, crank* of the gangplank lowering. I glanced over and saw Setne strolling calmly across as the river churned beneath him. He stopped at the edge of the plank and waited as the boat raced toward the black sand beach. He was preparing to jump to safety. And tucked under his arm was a large papyrus scroll— the Book of Thoth.

"Setne!" I screamed.

He turned and waved, smiling pleasantly. "It'll be fine, Carter! I'll be right back!"

"*Tas!*" I yelled.

Instantly the Ribbons of Hathor encased him, scroll and all, and Setne pitched overboard into the water.

I hadn't planned on that, but I didn't have time to worry about it. Bloodstained Blade charged, his left foot going *clump, BONG!*, *clump, BONG!* I rolled sideways as his ax head cut the floor, but he recovered more quickly than I could. My ribs felt like they'd been dipped in acid. My arm was too weak to lift Ra's flail. I raised the crook for defense, but I had no idea how to use it.

Bloodstained Blade loomed over me, humming with evil glee. I knew I couldn't evade another attack. I was about to become two separate halves of Carter Kane.

"We are done!" he bellowed.

Suddenly, he erupted in a column of fire. His body vaporized. His metal ax head dropped, impaling itself in the deck between my feet.

I blinked, wondering if this was some sort of demon trick, but Bloodstained Blade was truly and completely gone. Beside the ax head, all that remained were his polished boots, a slightly melted alarm bell, and some charred goose feathers floating in the air.

A few feet away, Zia leaned against the wheelhouse. Her right hand was wrapped in flames.

"Yes," Zia muttered to the smoking ax blade. "We're done."

She extinguished her fire, then stumbled over and embraced me. I was so relieved I could almost ignore the searing pain in my side.

"You're okay," I said, which sounded dumb under the circumstances, but she rewarded me with a smile.

"Fine," she said. "Had a moment of panic. Woke up with blue energy all around me, but—"

I happened to glance behind her, and my stomach turned inside out.

"Hold on!" I yelled.

The *Egyptian Queen* rammed into the shore at full speed.

I now understand the whole thing about wearing seat belts.

Hanging on did absolutely no good. The boat ran aground with such force, Zia and I shot into the air like human cannonballs. The hull cracked apart behind us with an almighty *ka-blam!* The landscape hurtled toward my face. I had half a second to contemplate whether I would die by smacking into the ground or falling into a flaming crevice. Then, from above me, Zia grabbed my arm and hoisted me skyward.

I caught a glimpse of her, grim-faced and determined, holding on to me with one hand and hanging from the talons of a giant vulture with the other. Her amulet. I hadn't thought about it in months, but Zia had a vulture amulet. She'd somehow managed to activate it, because she's just awesome that way.

Unfortunately, the vulture wasn't strong enough to hold two people aloft. It could only slow our fall, so instead of being smashed flat, Zia and I rolled hard against the black sandy soil, tumbling over each other right to the edge of a fiery crevice.

My chest felt like it had been stomped flat. Every muscle in my body ached, and I had double vision. But to my amazement, the sun god's crook and flail were clasped tightly in my right hand. I hadn't even realized I still had them.

Zia must've been in better shape than me (of course, I'd seen roadkill in better shape than me). She found the strength to drag me away from the fissure and down toward the beach.

"Ouch," I said.

"Lie still." She spoke a command word, and her vulture shrank back into a charm. She rummaged through her backpack.

She brought out a small ceramic jar and began rubbing blue paste on the cuts, burns, and bruises that covered my upper body. The pain in my side eased immediately. The wounds disappeared. Zia's hands were smooth and warm. The magical unguent smelled like blossoming honeysuckle. It wasn't the worst experience I'd had all day.

She scooped another dollop of salve and looked at the long cut across my stomach. "Um . . . you should do this part."

She scraped the salve onto my fingers and let me apply it. The gash mended. I sat up slowly and took care of the glass cuts on my legs. Inside my chest, I swear I could feel my ribs mending. I took a deep breath and was relieved to find it didn't hurt.

"Thank you," I said. "What is that stuff?"

"Nefertem's Balm," she said.

"It's a bomb?"

Her laughter made me feel almost as good as the salve. "*Healing* balm, Carter. It's made of blue lotus flower, coriander, mandrake, ground malachite, and a few other special ingredients. Very rare, and this is my only jar. So don't get injured anymore."

"Yes, ma'am."

I was pleased that my head had stopped spinning. My double vision was returning to normal.

The *Egyptian Queen* wasn't in such good shape. The remains of the hull were scattered across the beach—boards and railings, ropes and glass, mixed with the bones that had already been there. The wheelhouse had imploded. Fire curled from the broken windows. The fallen smokestacks bubbled golden smoke into the river.

As we watched, the stern cracked off and slid underwater, dragging the glowing orbs of light with it. Maybe the magical crew was bound to the boat. Maybe they weren't even alive. But I still felt sorry for them as they disappeared under the murky surface.

"We won't be going back that way," I said.

"No," Zia agreed. "Where are we? What happened to Setne?"

Setne. I'd almost forgotten about that ghostly scumbag. I would've been fine with his sinking to the bottom of the river, except that he'd taken the Book of Thoth.

I scanned the beach. To my surprise, I spotted a slightly battered pink mummy about twenty yards down the shore, squirming and struggling through the flotsam, apparently trying to inchworm his way to freedom.

I pointed him out to Zia. "We could leave him like that, but he's got the Book of Thoth."

She gave me one of those cruel smiles that made me glad she wasn't my enemy. "No hurry. He won't get far. How about a picnic?"

"I like the way you think."

We spread out our supplies and tried to clean up as best we

could. I busted out some bottled water and protein bars—yeah, look at me, the Boy Scout.

We ate and drank and watched our gift-wrapped pink ghost try to crawl away.

"How did we get here, exactly?" Zia asked. Her golden scarab still glittered at her throat. "I remember the *serapeum*, the Apis Bull, the room with the sunlight. After that, it's fuzzy."

I described what had happened as best I could—her magic scarab shield, her suddenly awesome powers from Khepri, the way she'd fried the Apis Bull and almost combusted herself. I explained how I'd gotten her back to the ship, and how Bloodstained Blade had turned psycho.

Zia winced. "You granted Setne permission to give Bloodstained Blade orders?"

"Yeah. Maybe not my best idea."

"And he brought us here—to the Land of Demons, the most dangerous part of the Duat."

I'd heard of the Land of Demons, but I didn't know much about it. At the moment, I didn't want to learn. I'd already escaped death so many times today, I just wanted to sit here, rest, and talk with Zia—and maybe enjoy watching Setne struggle to get somewhere in his cocoon.

"You, uh, feeling okay?" I asked Zia. "I mean, about the stuff with the sun god . . ."

She gazed across the pitted landscape of black sand, bones, and fire. Not many people can look good in the light of super-heated volcanic gas plumes. Zia managed.

"Carter, I wanted to tell you, but I didn't understand what was happening to me. I was frightened."

"It's okay," I said. "I was the Eye of Horus. I understand."

Zia pursed her lips. "Ra is different, though. He's much older, much more dangerous to channel. And he's trapped in that old husk of a body. He can't restart his cycle of rebirth."

"That's why he needs you," I guessed. "He woke up talking about *zebras*—you. He offered you that scarab when he first met you. He wants you to be his host."

A crevice spewed fire. The reflection in Zia's eyes reminded me of how she'd looked when she merged with Khepri—her pupils filled with orange flames.

"When I was entombed in that . . . that sarcophagus," Zia said, "I almost lost my mind, Carter. I still have nightmares. And when I tap into Ra's power, I have the same sense of panic. He feels imprisoned, helpless. Reaching out to him is like . . . it's like trying to save somebody who's drowning. They grab on to you and take you down with them." Zia shook her head. "Maybe that doesn't make sense. But his power tries to escape through me, and I can barely control it. Every time I black out, it gets worse."

"Every time?" I said. "Then you've blacked out before?"

She explained what had happened in the House of Rest when she'd tried to destroy the nursing home with her fireballs. Just a minor little detail Sadie forgot to tell me.

"Ra is too powerful," she said. "I'm too weak to control him. In the catacombs with the Apis Bull, I might've killed you."

"But you didn't," I said. "You saved my life—*again*. I know it's hard, but you can control the power. Ra needs to break out of his prison. The whole shadow magic idea that Sadie wants to try with Bes? I get the feeling that won't work with Ra. The sun god needs *rebirth*. You understand what that's like. I think that's why he gave you Khepri, the rising sun." I pointed to her scarab amulet. "You're the key to bringing him back."

Zia took a bite of her protein bar. "This tastes like Styrofoam."

"Yeah," I admitted. "Not as good as Macho Nachos. I still owe you that date at the mall food court."

She laughed weakly. "I wish we could do that right now."

"Usually girls aren't so eager to go out with me. Um . . . not that I've ever asked—"

She leaned over and kissed me.

I'd imagined this many times, but I was so unprepared, I didn't act very cool about it. I dropped my protein bar and breathed in her cinnamon fragrance. When she pulled away, I was gaping like a fish. I said something like "Hum-uh-huh."

"You are kind, Carter," she said. "And funny. And despite the fact you were just pushed out a window and hurled from an explosion, you're even handsome. You've also been very patient with me. But I'm afraid. I've never been able to hold on to anyone I cared about—my parents, Iskandar. . . . If I'm too weak to control the power of Ra and I end up hurting you—"

"No," I said immediately. "No, you won't, Zia. Ra didn't choose you because you're weak. He chose you because you're strong. And, um . . ." I looked down at the crook and flail lying at my side. "These just sort of appeared. . . . I think they showed up for a reason. You should take them."

I tried to hand them over, but she curled my fingers around them.

"Keep them," she said. "You're right: they didn't appear by accident, but they appeared in *your* hands. They may be Ra's, but Horus must be pharaoh."

The weapons seemed to heat up, or maybe that was because Zia was holding my hands. The idea of using the crook and flail made me nervous. I'd lost my *khopesh*—the sword used by the pharaoh's guards—and gained the weapons of the pharaoh himself. Not just any pharaoh, either . . . I was holding the implements of Ra, the first king of the gods.

Me, Carter Kane, a homeschooled fifteen-year-old who was still learning how to shave and could barely dress himself for a school dance—somehow I'd been deemed worthy of the most powerful magic weapons in creation.

"How can you be sure?" I asked. "How could these be for me?"

Zia smiled. "Maybe I'm getting better at understanding Ra. He needs Horus's support. I need you."

I tried to think of what to say, and whether I had the nerve to ask for another kiss. I'd never pictured my first date being on a bone-littered riverbank in the Land of Demons, but at that moment there was no place I'd rather be.

Then I heard a *bonk*—the sound of someone's head hitting a thick piece of wood. Setne let out a muffled curse. He'd managed to inchworm himself right into a broken section of keel. Dazed and off-balance, he rolled into the water and started to sink.

"We'd better fish him out," I said.

"Yes," Zia agreed. "We don't want the Book of Thoth to get damaged."

We hauled Setne onto the beach. Zia carefully dispelled just the ribbons around his chest so she could pull the Book of Thoth out from under his arm. Thankfully, the papyrus scroll appeared intact.

Setne said, "Mmm-hmmpfh!"

"Sorry, not interested," I said. "We've got the book, so we'll be leaving you now. I don't feel like being stabbed in the back anymore or listening to your lies."

Setne rolled his eyes. He shook his head vigorously, mumbling what was probably a very good explanation of why he'd been within his rights to turn my demon servant against me.

Zia opened the scroll and studied the writing. After a few lines, she began to frown. "Carter, this is . . . really dangerous stuff. I'm only skimming, but I see descriptions of the gods' secret palaces, spells to make them reveal their true names, information on how to recognize all the gods no matter what form they try to take . . ."

She looked up fearfully. "With knowledge like this, Setne could have caused *a lot* of damage. The only good thing . . . as far as I can tell, most of these spells can only be used by a living magician. A ghost wouldn't be able to cast them."

"Maybe that's why he kept us alive this long," I said. "He needed our help to get the book. Then he planned on tricking us into casting the spells he wanted."

Setne mumbled in protest.

"Can we find Apophis's shadow without him?" I asked Zia.

"Mm-mm!" Setne said, but I ignored him.

Zia studied a few more lines. "Apophis . . . the *sheut* of Apophis. Yes, here it is. It lies in the Land of Demons. So we're in the right place. But this map . . ." She showed me part of the scroll, which was so dense with hieroglyphs and pictures, I couldn't even tell it *was* a map. "I have no idea how to read it. The Land of Demons is huge. From what I've read, it's constantly shifting, breaking apart, and reforming. And it's full of demons."

"Imagine that." I tried to swallow the bitter taste from my mouth. "So we'll be as out-of-place here as demons are in the mortal world. We won't be able to go anywhere unseen, and everything that meets us will want to kill us."

"Yes," Zia agreed. "And we're running out of time."

She was right. I didn't know exactly what time it was in the mortal world, but we had descended into the Duat in the late afternoon. By now, the sun might have gone down. Walt wasn't supposed to survive past sunset. For all I knew, he might be dying right now, and my poor sister . . . No. It was too painful to think about.

But at dawn tomorrow, Apophis would rise. The rebel magicians would attack the First Nome. We didn't have the luxury to roam around a hostile land, fighting everything in our path until we found what we were looking for.

I glared down at Setne. "I'm guessing you can guide us to the shadow."

He nodded.

I turned to Zia. "If he does or says anything you don't like, incinerate him."

"With pleasure."

I commanded the ribbons to release just his mouth.

"Holy Horus, pal!" he complained. "Why did you tie me up?"

"Well, let's see . . . maybe because you tried to get me *killed?*"

"Aw, that?" Setne sighed. "Look, pal, if you're going to overreact every time I try to kill you—"

"*Overreact?*" Zia summoned a white-hot fireball into her hand.

"Okay, okay!" Setne said. "Look, that demon captain was going to turn on you anyway. I just helped things along. And I did it for a reason! We needed to get here, to the Land of Demons, right? Your captain would never have agreed to set that course unless he thought he could kill you. This is his homeland! Demons don't *ever* bring mortals here unless they're for snacks."

I had to remember Setne was a master liar. Whatever he told me was complete and utter Apis-quality bull. I steeled my willpower against his words, but it was still difficult not to find them reasonable.

"So you were going to let Bloodstained Blade kill me," I said, "but it was for a good cause."

"Aw, I knew you could take him," Setne said.

Zia held up the scroll. "And that's why you were running away with the Book of Thoth?"

"Running? I was going to scout ahead! I wanted to find the shadow so I could lead you there! But that's not important. If you let me go, I can still bring you to the shadow of Apophis, and I can get you there unseen."

"How?" Zia asked.

Setne sniffed indignantly. "I've been practicing magic since your ancestors were in diapers, doll. And while it's true I can't do all the mortal spells I'd like . . ." He glanced wistfully at the Book of Thoth. "I *have* picked up some tricks only ghosts can do. Untie me and I'll show you."

I looked at Zia. I could tell we were thinking the same thing: terrible idea, but we didn't have a better one.

"I can't believe we're seriously considering this," she grumbled.

Setne grinned. "Hey, you're being smart. This is your best shot. Besides, I *want* you to succeed! Like I said, I don't want Apophis destroying *me*. You won't regret it."

"I'm pretty sure I will." I snapped my fingers, and the Ribbons of Hathor unraveled.

Setne's brilliant plan? He turned us into demons.

Well, okay . . . it was actually just a glamor, so we *looked* like demons, but it was the best illusion magic I'd ever seen.

Zia took one look at me and started to giggle. I couldn't see my own face, but she told me I now had a massive bottle opener for a head. I *did* notice that my skin was fuchsia, and I had hairy bowed legs like a chimpanzee.

I didn't blame Zia for laughing, but she didn't look much

better. She was now a big muscular girl demon with bright green skin, a zebra-hide dress, and the head of a piranha.

"Perfect," Setne said. "You'll blend right in."

"What about you?" I asked.

He spread his hands. He was still wearing his jeans, white sneakers, and black jacket. His diamond pinky rings and gold *ankh* chain flashed in the volcanic firelight. The only difference was that his red T-shirt now read: GO, DEMONS!

"You can't improve on perfection, pal. This outfit works anywhere. The demons won't even bat an eye—assuming they have eyes. Now, come on!"

He drifted inland, not waiting to see if we would follow.

Every once in a while, Setne checked the Book of Thoth for directions. He explained that the shadow would be impossible to find in this moving landscape without consulting the book, which served as a combination compass, tourist's guide, and Farmer's Almanac timetable.

He promised us it would be a short journey, but it seemed pretty long to me. Any more time in Demon Land, and I'm not sure I would have come out sane. The landscape was like an optical illusion. We spotted a vast mountain range in the distance, then walked fifty feet and discovered the mountains were so tiny, we could jump over them. I stepped into a small puddle and suddenly found myself drowning in a flooded sinkhole fifty feet wide. Huge Egyptian temples crumbled and rearranged themselves as if some invisible giant were playing with blocks. Limestone cliffs erupted out of nowhere, already carved with monumental statues of grotesque monsters. The stone faces turned and watched us as we passed.

Then there were the demons. I'd seen lots of them under Camelback Mountain, where Set built his red pyramid, but here in their native environment, they were even larger and more horrible. Some looked like torture victims, with gaping wounds and twisted limbs. Others had insect wings, or multiple arms, or tentacles made from darkness. As for their heads, pretty much every zoo animal and Swiss Army knife attachment was well represented.

The demons roamed in hordes across the dark landscape. Some built fortresses. Others tore them down. We saw at least a dozen large-scale battles. Winged demons circled through the smoky air, occasionally snatching up unsuspecting smaller monsters and carrying them off.

But none of them bothered us.

As we stumbled along, I became more and more aware of the presence of Chaos. A cold churning started in my gut, spreading through my limbs like my blood cells were turning to ice. I'd felt this before at the prison of Apophis, when Chaos sickness had almost killed me, but this place seemed even more poisonous.

After a while, I realized everything in the Land of Demons was being pulled in the direction we were traveling. The whole landscape was bending and crumbling, the fabric of matter unweaving. I knew the same force was pulling at the molecules of my body.

Zia and I should have died. But as bad as the cold and the nausea were, I sensed that they should have been worse. Something was protecting us, an invisible layer of warmth keeping the Chaos at bay.

It is her, said the voice of Horus, with grudging respect. *Ra sustains us.*

I looked at Zia. She still appeared to be a piranha-headed green she-demon, but the air around her shimmered like vapor off a hot road.

Setne kept glancing back. Each time, he seemed surprised to find us still alive. But he shrugged and kept going.

The demons became fewer and farther between. The landscape got even more twisted. Rock formations, sand dunes, dead trees, even pillars of fire all leaned toward the horizon.

We came to a cratered field, peppered with what looked like huge black lotus blossoms. They rose up quickly, spread their petals, and burst. Only when we got closer did I realize they were knots of shadowy tendrils, like Sadie had described at the Brooklyn Academy dance. Each time one burst, it spit out a spirit that had been dragged from the upper world. These ghosts, no more than pale bits of mist, clawed desperately for something to anchor them, but they were quickly dispersed and sucked away in the same direction we were traveling.

Zia frowned at Setne. "You're not affected?"

The ghost magician turned. For once his expression was grim. His color was paler, his clothes and jewelry bleached out. "Let's just keep moving, huh? I hate this place."

I froze. Ahead of us stood a cliff I recognized—the same one I'd seen in the vision Apophis had shown me. Except now there were no spirits huddled in its shelter.

"My mother was there," I said.

Zia seemed to understand. She took my hand. "It might be a different cliff. The landscape is always changing."

Somehow I knew it was the same place. I had the feeling Apophis had left it intact just to taunt me.

Setne twisted his pinky rings. "The serpent's shadow feeds on spirits, pal. None of them last long. If your mom was here—"

"She was strong," I insisted. "A magician, like you. If you can fight it, she could too."

Setne hesitated. Then he shrugged. "Sure, pal. We're close now. Better keep going."

Soon I heard a roar in the distance. The horizon glowed red. We seemed to be moving faster, as if we'd stepped on an automated walkway.

Then we came over the crest of a hill, and I saw our destination.

"There you go," Setne said. "The Sea of Chaos."

Before us spread an ocean of mist, fire, or water—it was impossible to tell which. Grayish-red matter churned, boiling and smoking, surging just like my stomach. It stretched as far as I could see—and something told me it had no end.

The ocean's edge wasn't so much a beach as a reverse waterfall. Solid ground poured into the sea and disappeared. A house-sized boulder trundled over the hill to our right, slid down the beach, and dissolved in the surf. Chunks of solid ground, trees, buildings, and statues constantly flew over our heads and sailed into the ocean, vaporizing as they touched the waves. Even the demons weren't immune. A few winged ones strayed over the beach, realized too late that they'd flown too close, and disappeared screaming into the swirling misty soup.

It was pulling us, too. Instead of walking forward, I was

instinctively backpedaling now, just to stay in one place. If we got any closer, I was afraid I wouldn't be able to stop.

Only one thing gave me hope. A few hundred yards to the north, jutting into the waves, was a single solid strip of land like a jetty. At the far end rose a white obelisk like the Washington Monument. The spire glowed with light. I had a feeling it was ancient—even older than the gods. As beautiful as the obelisk was, I couldn't help thinking of Cleopatra's Needle on the banks of the River Thames, where my mother had died.

"We can't go down there," I said.

Setne laughed. "The Sea of Chaos? That's where we all came from, pal. Haven't you heard how Egypt was formed?"

"It rose from this sea," Zia said, almost in a trance. "Ma'at appeared from Chaos—the first land, creation from destruction."

"Yep," Setne said. "The two great forces of the universe. And there they are."

"That obelisk is . . . the first land?" I asked.

"Dunno," Setne said. "I wasn't there. But it's the *symbol* of Ma'at, for sure. Everything else, that's Apophis's power, always chewing away at creation, always eating and destroying. You tell me, which force is more powerful?"

I tried to swallow. "Where is Apophis's shadow?"

Setne chuckled. "Oh, it's here. But to see it, to catch it, you'll have to cast the spell from out there—at the edge of the jetty."

"We'll never make it," Zia said. "One false step—"

"Sure," Setne agreed cheerfully. "It'll be fun!"

16. Sadie Rides Shotgun
(Worst. Idea. Ever.)

HERE'S SOME FREE ADVICE: Don't walk toward Chaos.

With every step, I felt like I was being dragged into a black hole. Trees, boulders, and demons flew past us and were sucked into the ocean, while lightning flickered through the red-gray mist. Under our feet, chunks of the ground kept cracking and sliding into the tide.

I grasped the crook and flail in one hand and held Zia's hand with the other. Setne whistled and floated along beside us. He tried to act cool, but from the way his colors were fading and his greased hair pointed toward the ocean like a comet's tail, I figured he was having a tough time holding his ground.

Once I lost my balance. I almost tumbled into the surf, but Zia pulled me back. A few steps later, a fish-headed demon flew out of nowhere and slammed into me. He grabbed my leg, trying desperately to avoid getting sucked in. Before I could decide whether or not to help him, he lost his grip and disappeared into the sea.

The most horrible thing about the journey? Part of me was tempted to give up and let Chaos draw me in. Why keep struggling? Why not end the pain and the worry? So what, if Carter Kane dissolved into trillions of molecules?

I knew those thoughts weren't really mine. The voice of Apophis was whispering in my head, tempting me as it had before. I concentrated on the glowing white obelisk—our lighthouse in the storm of Chaos. I didn't know if that spire was really the first part of creation, or how that myth jibed with the Big Bang, or with God creating the world in seven days, or whatever else people might believe. Maybe the obelisk was just a manifestation of something larger—something my mind couldn't comprehend. Whatever the case, I knew the obelisk stood for Ma'at, and I had to focus on it. Otherwise I was lost.

We reached the base of the jetty. The rocky path felt reassuringly solid under my feet, but the pull of Chaos was strong on either side. As we inched forward, I remembered photos I'd seen of construction workers building skyscrapers back in the old days, fearlessly walking across girders six hundred feet in the air with no safety harnesses.

I felt like that now, except I wasn't fearless. The winds buffeted me. The jetty was ten feet wide, but I still felt like I was going to lose my balance and pitch into the waves. I tried not to look down. The stuff of Chaos churned and crashed against the rocks. It smelled like ozone, car exhaust, and formaldehyde mixed together. The fumes alone were almost enough to make me pass out.

"Just a little farther," Setne said.

His form flickered unevenly. Zia's green demon disguise blinked in and out. I held up my arm and saw my glamor shimmering in the wind, threatening to collapse. I didn't mind losing the shocking-purple bottle-opening chimp look, but I hoped the wind would tear away only the illusion, not my actual skin.

Finally, we reached the obelisk. It was carved with tiny hieroglyphs, thousands of them, white on white, so they were almost impossible to read. I spotted the names of gods, enchantments to invoke Ma'at, and some divine words so powerful, they almost blinded me. Around us, the Sea of Chaos heaved. Each time the wind blew, a glowing shield in the shape of a scarab flickered around Zia—the magical carapace of Khepri, sheltering us all. I suspected it was the only thing keeping us from instant death.

"What now?" I asked.

"Read the spell," Setne said. "You'll see."

Zia handed me the scroll. I tried to find the right lines, but I couldn't see straight. The glyphs blurred together. I should have anticipated this problem. Even when I *wasn't* standing next to the Sea of Chaos, I'd never been good at incantations. I wished Sadie were there.

[Yes, Sadie. I actually said that. Don't gasp so loud.]

"I—I can't read it," I admitted.

"Let me help." Zia traced her finger down the scroll. When she found the hieroglyphs she wanted, she frowned.

"This is a simple summoning spell." She glared at Setne.

"You said the magic was complicated. You said we'd need your help. How could you lie while holding the Feather of Truth?"

"I didn't lie!" Setne protested. "The magic *is* complicated for me. I'm a ghost! Some spells—like summoning spells—I can't cast at all. And you *did* need my help to find the shadow. You needed the Book of Thoth for that, and you needed me to interpret it. Otherwise, you'd still be shipwrecked at the river."

I hated to admit it, but I said, "He's got a point."

"Sure I do," Setne said. "Now that you're here, the rest isn't so bad. Just force the shadow to show itself, and then I—er—you can capture it."

Zia and I exchanged a nervous look. I imagined she felt the same way I did. Standing at the edge of creation, facing an endless Sea of Chaos, the *last* thing I wanted to do was cast a spell that would summon part of Apophis's soul. It was like shooting off a flare gun, signaling, *Hey, big nasty shadow! Here we are! Come and kill us!*

I didn't see that we had much choice, though.

Zia did the honors. It was an easy invocation, the kind a magician might use to summon a *shabti*, or an enchanted dust mop, or pretty much any minor creature from the Duat.

When Zia finished, a tremor spread in all directions, as if she'd dropped a massive stone into the Sea of Chaos. The disturbance rippled up the beach and over the hills.

"Um . . . what was that?" I asked.

"Distress signal," Setne said. "I'm guessing the shadow just called on the forces of Chaos to protect it."

"Wonderful," I said. "We'd better hurry, then. Where's the—? Oh . . ."

The *sheut* of Apophis was so large, it took me a moment to understand what I was looking at. The white obelisk seemed to cast a shadow across the sea; but as the shadow darkened, I realized that it wasn't the silhouette of the obelisk. Rather, the shadow writhed across the surface of the water like the body of a giant snake. The shadow grew until the head of the serpent almost reached the horizon. It lashed across the sea, darting its tongue, and biting at nothing.

My hands shook. My insides felt like I'd just chugged a big glass of Chaos water. The serpent's shadow was so massive, radiating so much power, that I didn't see how we could possibly capture it. What had I been thinking?

Only one thing kept me from total panic.

The serpent wasn't completely free. Its tail seemed to be anchored to the obelisk, as if someone had driven a spike to keep it from escaping.

For a disturbing moment, I felt the serpent's thoughts. I saw things from Apophis's point of view. It was trapped by the white obelisk—seething and in pain. It hated the world of mortals and gods, which pinned it down and constricted its freedom. Apophis despised creation the way I might despise a rusty nail driven through my foot, keeping me from walking.

All Apophis wanted was to snuff out the obelisk's blinding light. He wanted to annihilate the earth, so he could go back to the darkness and swim forever in the unrestricted expanses of Chaos. It took all of my willpower not to feel sorry for the poor little world-destroying, sun-devouring serpent.

"Well," I said hoarsely. "We found the shadow. Now what do we do with it?"

Setne chuckled. "Oh, I can take it from here. You guys did great. *Tas!*"

If I hadn't been so distracted, I might have seen what was coming, but I didn't. My demon glamor suddenly turned into solid bands of mummy linen, covering my mouth first, then wrapping around my body with blinding speed. I toppled and fell, completely encased except for my eyes. Zia hit the rocks next to me, also cocooned. I tried to breathe, but it was like inhaling through a pillow.

Setne leaned over Zia. He carefully extracted the Book of Thoth from beneath her bindings and tucked it under his arm. Then he smiled down at me.

"Oh, Carter, Carter." He shook his head as if he were mildly disappointed. "I like you, pal. I really do. But you are *way* too trusting. After that business on the riverboat, you *still* gave me permission to cast a glamor spell on you? Come on! Changing a glamor into a straitjacket is *sooo* easy."

"Mmm!" I grunted.

"What's that?" Setne cupped his ear. "Hard to talk when you're all bound up, isn't it? Look, it's nothing personal. I couldn't cast that invocation spell myself, or I would have done it ages ago. I needed you two! Well . . . one of you, anyway. I figured I'd be able to kill either you or your girlfriend along the way, make the other one easier for me to handle. I never thought *both* of you would survive this far. Impressive!"

I wriggled and almost toppled into the water. For some reason, Setne pulled me back to safety.

"Now, now," he chided. "No point killing yourself, pal. Your plan isn't ruined. I'm just going to alter it. I'll trap the shadow. That part I can do myself! But instead of casting the execration, I'll blackmail Apophis, see? He'll destroy only what I *let* him destroy. Then he retreats back into Chaos, or his shadow gets stomped, and the big snake goes bye-bye."

"Mmm!" I protested, but it was getting harder to breathe.

"Yeah, yeah." Setne sighed. "This is the part where you say, 'You're mad, Setne! You'll never get away with it!' But the thing is, I will. I've been getting away with impossible stuff for thousands of years. I'm sure the snake and I can come to a deal. Oh, I'll let him kill Ra and the rest of the gods. Big deal. I'll let him destroy the House of Life. I'll *definitely* let him tear down Egypt and every cursed statue of my dad, Ramses. I want that blowhard erased from existence! But the whole mortal world? Don't worry about it, pal. I'll spare most of it. I've gotta have someplace to rule, don't I?"

Zia's eyes flared orange. Her bonds started to smoke, but they held her fast. Her fire receded, and she slumped against the rocks.

Setne laughed. "Nice try, doll. You guys sit tight. If you make it through the big shake-up, I'll come back and get you. Maybe you can be my jesters or something. You two crack me up! But in the meantime, I'm afraid we're done here. No miracle's gonna drop from the sky and save you."

A rectangle of darkness appeared in the air just above the ghost's head. Sadie dropped out of it.

I'll say this for my sister: she has great timing, and she's quick on the draw. She crashed into the ghost and sent him sprawling. Then she noticed us wrapped up like presents, quickly realized what was going on, and turned toward Setne.

"*Tas!*" she yelled.

"Noooo!" Setne was wrapped in pink ribbons until he looked like a forkful of spaghetti.

Sadie stood and stepped back from Setne. Her eyes were puffy like she'd been crying. Her clothes were covered in dried mud and leaves.

Walt wasn't with her. My heart sank. I was almost glad my mouth was covered, because I wouldn't have known what to say.

Sadie took in the scene—the Sea of Chaos, the serpent's writhing shadow, the white obelisk. I could tell she felt the pull of Chaos. She braced her feet, leaning away from the sea like the anchorperson in a tug-of-war. I knew her well enough to tell she was steeling herself, pushing her emotions back inside and forcing her sorrow down.

"Hullo, brother dear," she said in a shaky voice. "Need some help?"

She managed to dispel the glamor on us. She looked surprised to find me holding Ra's crook and flail. "How in the world—?"

Zia briefly explained what we'd been up to—from the fight with the giant hippo through Setne's most recent betrayals.

"All that," Sadie marveled, "and you had to drag my brother along too? You poor girl. But how can we even survive here? The Chaos power . . ." She focused on Zia's scarab pendant. "Oh. I really am thick. No wonder Tawaret looked at you strangely. You're channeling the power of Ra."

"Ra chose me," Zia said. "I didn't want this."

Sadie got very quiet—which wasn't like her.

"Sis," I said, as gently as possible, "what happened to Walt?"

Her eyes were so full of pain that I wanted to apologize for even asking. I hadn't seen her look like that since . . . well, since our mom died, when Sadie was little.

"He's not coming," she said. "He's . . . gone."

"Sadie, I'm so sorry," I said. "Are you—?"

"I'm fine!" she snapped.

Translation: *I'm most definitely not fine, but if you ask again I'll stuff wax in your mouth.*

"We have to hurry," she continued, trying to modulate her voice. "I know how to capture the shadow. Just give me the figurine."

I had a moment of panic. Did I still *have* the statue of Apophis that Walt had made? Coming all the way here and forgetting it would've been a major bonehead move.

Fortunately, it was still at the bottom of my pack.

I handed it to Sadie, who stared at the careful red carving of the coiled serpent, the hieroglyphs of binding around the name *Apophis*. I imagined she was thinking of Walt, and all the effort he'd put into making it.

She knelt at the edge of the jetty, where the obelisk's base met the shadow.

"Sadie," I said.

She froze. "Yeah?"

My mouth felt like it was full of glue. I wanted to tell her to forget the whole thing.

Seeing her at the obelisk, with that massive shadow coiling

toward the horizon . . . I just knew something would go wrong. The shadow would attack. The spell would backfire somehow.

Sadie reminded me so much of our mom. I couldn't shake the impression that we were repeating history. Our parents had tried to restrain Apophis once before, at Cleopatra's Needle, and our mom had died. I'd spent years watching my dad deal with his guilt. If I stood by now while Sadie got hurt . . .

Zia took my hand. Her fingers were trembling, but I was grateful for her presence. "This will work," she promised.

Sadie blew a strand of hair from her face. "Listen to your girlfriend, Carter. And stop distracting me."

She sounded exasperated, but there was no irritation in her eyes. Sadie understood my concerns as clearly as she knew my secret name. She was just as scared as I was, but in her own annoying way, she was trying to reassure me.

"May I continue?" she asked.

"Good luck," I managed.

Sadie nodded.

She touched the figurine to the shadow and began to chant.

I was afraid the waves of Chaos might dissolve the figurine, or, worse, pull Sadie in. Instead, the serpent's shadow began to thrash. Slowly it shrank, writhing and snapping its mouth as if it were being hit with a cattle prod. The figurine absorbed the darkness. Soon the shadow was completely gone, and the statue was midnight black. Sadie spoke a simple binding spell on the figurine: "*Hi-nehm.*"

A long hiss escaped from the sea—almost like a sigh of relief—and the sound echoed across the hills. The churning waves turned a lighter shade of red, as if some murky sediment had been dredged away. The pull of Chaos seemed to lessen just slightly.

Sadie stood. "Right. We're ready."

I stared at my sister. Sometimes she teased me that she'd eventually catch up to me in age and be my older sibling. Looking at her now, with that determined glint in her eyes and the confidence in her voice, I could almost believe her. "That was amazing," I said. "How did you know the spell?"

She scowled. Of course, the answer was obvious: she'd watched Walt do the same spell on Bes's shadow . . . before whatever happened to Walt.

"The execration will be easy," she said. "We have to be facing Apophis, but otherwise it's the same spell we've been practicing."

Zia prodded Setne with her foot. "That's another thing this maggot lied about. What should we do with him? We'll have to get the Book of Thoth out of those bindings, obviously, but after that should we shove him into the drink?"

"MMM!" Setne protested.

Sadie and I exchanged looks. We silently agreed that we couldn't dissolve Setne—even as horrible as he was. Maybe we'd seen too many awful things over the past few days, and we didn't need to see any more. Or maybe we knew that Osiris had to be the one to decide Setne's punishment, since we had promised to bring the ghost back to the Hall of Judgment.

Maybe, standing next to the obelisk of Ma'at, surrounded by the Sea of Chaos, we both realized that restraining ourselves from vengeance is what made us different from Apophis. Rules had their place. They kept us from unraveling.

"Drag him along," Sadie said. "He's a ghost. Can't be *that* heavy."

I grabbed his feet, and we made our way back down the jetty. Setne's head bonked against the rocks, but that didn't concern me. It took all my concentration to keep putting one foot in front of the other. Moving away from the Sea of Chaos was even harder than moving toward it.

By the time we reached the beach, I was exhausted. My clothes were drenched in sweat. We trudged across the sand and finally crested the hill.

"Oh . . ." I uttered some words that were *definitely* not divine.

In the cratered field below us, demons had gathered—hundreds of them, all marching in our direction. As Setne had guessed, the shadow *had* sent a distress signal to the forces of Apophis, and the call had been answered. We were trapped between the Sea of Chaos and a hostile army.

At this point, I was starting to wonder, *Why me?*

All I wanted was to infiltrate the most dangerous part of the Duat, steal the shadow of the primordial Lord of Chaos, and save the world. Was that too much to ask?

The demons were maybe two football fields away, closing rapidly. I estimated that there were at least three or four hundred of them, and more kept pouring onto the field. Several dozen winged monsters were even closer, spiraling lower and lower overhead. Against this army, we had two Kanes, Zia, and a gift-wrapped ghost. I didn't like those odds.

"Sadie, can you make a gate to the surface?" I asked.

She closed her eyes and concentrated. She shook her head. "No signal from Isis. Possibly we're too close to the Sea of Chaos."

That was a scary thought. I tried to summon the avatar of Horus. Nothing happened. I guess I should have known it would be hard to channel his powers down here, especially after I had asked him for a weapon back on the ship, and the best he could do was an ostrich feather.

"Zia?" I said. "Your powers from Khepri are still working. Can you get us out of here?"

She clutched her scarab amulet. "I don't think so. All Khepri's energy is being spent shielding us from Chaos. He can't do any more."

I considered running back to the white obelisk. Maybe we could use it to open a portal. But I quickly dismissed the idea. The demons would be on us before we ever got there.

"We're not going to get out of this," I decided. "Can we cast the execration on Apophis right now?"

Zia and Sadie spoke in unison: "No."

I knew they were right. We had to stand face-to-face with Apophis for the spell to work. But I couldn't believe we'd come all this way, just to be stopped now.

"At least we can go out fighting." I unhooked the crook and flail from my belt.

Sadie and Zia readied their staffs and wands.

Then, at the other end of the field, a wave of confusion spread through the demons' ranks. They slowly began turning away from us, running in different directions. Behind the demon army, fireballs lit the sky. Plumes of smoke rose from newly opened craters in the ground. A battle seemed to be breaking out at the wrong end of the field.

"Who are they fighting?" I asked. "Each other?"

"No." Zia pointed, a smile spreading across her face. "Look."

It was hard to see through the hazy air, but a wedge of combatants was slowly forcing its way through the back ranks of the demons. Their numbers were smaller—maybe a hundred or so—but the demons gave way to them. Those that didn't were cut down, trampled, or blown up like fireworks.

"It's the gods!" Sadie said.

"That's impossible," I said. "The gods wouldn't march into the Duat to rescue us!"

"Not the big gods, no." She grinned at me. "But the old forgotten ones from the House of Rest would! Anubis *said* he was calling for reinforcements."

"Anubis?" I was really confused now. When had she seen Anubis?

"There!" Sadie shouted. "Oh—!"

She seemed to forget how to speak. She just waved her finger toward our new friends. The battle lines opened momentarily. A sleek black car barreled into combat. The driver had to be a maniac. He plowed down demons, going out of his way to hit them. He jumped over fiery crevices and spun in circles, flashing his lights and honking his horn. Then he came straight at us, until the front ranks of demons started to scatter. Only a few brave winged demons had the nerve to chase him.

As the car got closer, I could see it was a Mercedes limo. It climbed the hill, trailed by bat demons, and screeched to a stop in a cloud of red dust. The driver's door opened, and a small hairy man in a blue Speedo stepped out.

I had never been so happy to see someone so ugly.

Bes, in all his horrible warty glory, climbed onto the roof of his car. He turned to face the bat demons. His eyes bulged. His mouth opened impossibly wide. His hair stood out like porcupine quills, and he yelled, "BOO!"

The winged demons screamed and disintegrated.

"Bes!" Sadie ran toward him.

The dwarf god broke into a grin. He slid down to the hood, so he was almost Sadie's height when she hugged him.

"There's my girl!" he said. "And, Carter, get your sorry hide over here!"

He hugged me, too. I didn't even mind him rubbing his knuckles on my head.

"And, Zia Rashid!" Bes cried generously. "I got a hug for you too—"

"I'm good," Zia said, stepping back. "Thanks."

Bes bellowed with laughter. "You're right. Time for warm and fuzzy later. We gotta get you guys out of here!"

"The—the shadow spell?" Sadie stammered. "It actually worked?"

"Of course it worked, you crazy kid!" Bes thumped his hairy chest, and suddenly he was wearing a chauffeur's uniform. "Now, get in the car!"

I turned to grab Setne . . . and my heart nearly stopped. "Oh, holy Horus . . ." The magician was gone. I scanned the terrain in every direction, hoping he'd just inchwormed away. There was no sign of him.

Zia blasted fire at the spot where he'd been lying. Apparently, the ghost hadn't merely become invisible, because there was no scream.

"Setne was right there!" Zia protested. "Tied up in the Ribbons of Hathor! How could he just disappear?"

Bes frowned. "Setne, eh? I hate that weasel. Have you got the serpent's shadow?"

"Yeah," I said, "but Setne has the Book of Thoth."

"Can you cast the execration without it?" Bes asked.

Sadie and I exchanged looks.

"Yes," we both said.

"Then we'll have to worry about Setne later," Bes said. "We don't have much time!"

I guess if you have to travel through the Land of Demons, a limo is the way to go. Unfortunately, Bes's new sedan was no cleaner than the one we'd left at the bottom of the Mediterranean last spring. I wondered if he pre-ordered them already littered with old Chinese-food containers, stomped-on magazines, and dirty laundry.

Sadie rode shotgun. Zia and I climbed in back. Bes slammed the accelerator and played a game of hit-the-demon.

"Five points if you can hit that bloke with the cleaver head!" Sadie screamed.

Boom! Cleaver-head went flying over the hood.

Sadie applauded. "Ten points if you can hit those two dragonfly things at once."

Boom, boom! Two very large bugs hit the windshield.

Sadie and Bes laughed like crazy. Me, I was too busy yelling, "Crevice! Look out! Flaming geyser! Go left!"

Call me practical. I wanted to live. I grabbed Zia's hand and tried to hang on.

As we approached the heart of the battle, I could see the gods pushing back the demons. It looked like the entire Sunny Acres Godly Retirement Community had unleashed their geriatric wrath on the forces of darkness. Tawaret the hippo goddess was in the lead, wearing her nurse's outfit and high heels, swinging a flaming torch in one hand and a hypodermic needle in the other. She bonked one demon on the head, then injected another in the rump, causing him to pass out immediately.

Two old guys in loincloths were hobbling around, throwing fireballs into the sky and incinerating flying demons. One of the old dudes kept screaming, "My pudding!" for no apparent reason.

Heket the frog goddess leaped around the battlefield, knocking out monsters with her tongue. She seemed to have a special fondness for the demons with insect heads. A few yards away, the senile cat goddess Mekhit was smashing demons with her walker, yelling, "Meow!" and hissing.

"Should we help them?" Zia asked.

Bes chuckled. "They don't need help. This is the most fun

they've had in centuries. They have a purpose again! They're going to cover our retreat while I get *you* to the river."

"But we don't have a ship anymore!" I protested.

Bes raised a furry eyebrow. "You sure about that?" He slowed the Mercedes and rolled down the window. "Hey, sweetie! You okay here?"

Tawaret turned and gave him a huge hippo smile. "We're fine, honeycakes! Good luck!"

"I'll be back!" he promised. He blew her a kiss, and I thought Tawaret was going to faint from happiness.

The Mercedes peeled out.

"Honeycakes?" I asked.

"Hey, kid," Bes growled, "do I criticize *your* relationships?"

I didn't have the guts to look at Zia, but she squeezed my hand. Sadie stayed quiet. Maybe she was thinking about Walt.

The Mercedes leaped one last flaming chasm and slammed to a stop on the beach of bones.

I pointed to the wreckage of the *Egyptian Queen*. "See? No boat."

"Oh, yeah?" Bes asked. "Then what's that?"

Upriver, light blazed in the darkness.

Zia inhaled sharply. "Ra," she said. "The sun boat approaches."

As the light got closer, I saw she was right. The gold-and-white sail gleamed. Glowing orbs flitted around the deck of a boat. The crocodile-headed god Sobek stood at the bow, knocking aside random river monsters with a big pole. And sitting in a fiery throne in the middle of the sun barque was the old god Ra.

"Hallllloooooo!" he yelled across the water. "We have cooooookies!"

Sadie kissed Bes on the cheek. "You're brilliant!"

"Hey, now," the dwarf mumbled. "You're gonna make Tawaret jealous. It just so happened the timing was right. If we'd missed the sun boat, we'd have been out of luck."

That thought made me shudder.

For millennia, Ra had followed this cycle—sailing into the Duat at sunset, traveling along the River of Night until he emerged into the mortal world again at sunrise. But it was a one-way trip, and the boat kept to a tight schedule. As Ra passed through the various Houses of the Night, their gates closed until the next evening, making it easy for mortal travelers like us to get stranded. Sadie and I had experienced that once before, and it hadn't been fun.

As the sun boat drifted toward the shore, Bes gave us a lopsided grin. "Ready, kids? I got a feeling things up in the mortal world aren't going to be pretty."

That was the first unsurprising thing I'd heard all day.

The glowing lights extended the boat's gangplank, and we climbed aboard for what might be the last sunrise in history.

17. Brooklyn House
Goes to War

I WAS SORRY TO LEAVE THE LAND OF DEMONS.

[Yes, Carter, I'm quite serious.]

After all, I'd had a rather successful visit there. I'd saved Zia and my brother from that horrid ghost Setne. I'd captured the serpent's shadow. I'd witnessed the Charge of the Old Folks' Brigade in all its glory, and most of all, I'd been reunited with Bes. Why wouldn't I have fond memories of the place? I might even take a beach holiday there someday, rent a cabana on the Sea of Chaos. Why not?

The flurry of activity also distracted me from less pleasant thoughts. But once we arrived at the riverbank and I had a few moments to breathe, I started thinking about how I'd learned the spell to rescue Bes's shadow. My elation turned to despair.

Walt—oh, Walt. What had he done?

I remembered how lifeless and cold he'd been, cradled in my arms amid the mud-brick ruins. Then suddenly he had opened his eyes and gasped.

Look, he'd said to me.

On the surface, I'd seen Walt as I'd always known him. But in the Duat . . . the boy god Anubis shimmered, his ghost-gray aura sustaining Walt's life.

Still me, they had said in unison. Their double voice had made my skin tingle.

I'll meet you at sunrise, they had promised, *at the First Nome, if you're sure you don't hate me.*

Did I hate him? Or was it *them*? Gods of Egypt, I wasn't even sure what to call him anymore! I certainly didn't know how I felt, or if I wanted to see him again.

I tried to put those thoughts aside. We still needed to defeat Apophis. Even with his captured shadow, there was no guarantee we would succeed in casting the spell. I doubted Apophis would stand idly by while we tried to obliterate him from the universe. And it was entirely possible that the execration would require more magic than Carter and I had, combined. If we burned up, my dilemma with Walt would hardly be a problem.

Nevertheless, I couldn't stop thinking about him/them— the way their warm brown eyes merged together so perfectly, and how natural Anubis's smile looked on Walt's face.

Argh! This was *not* helpful.

We climbed aboard the sun barque—Carter, Zia, Bes, and me. I was relieved beyond words that my favorite dwarf would be accompanying us to our final battle. I needed a reliably ugly god in my life right now.

At the bow, our old enemy Sobek regarded me with a crocodile smile, which I suppose was the only kind of smile he had.

"So . . . the little Kane children have returned."

"So," I snapped, "the crocodile god wants his teeth kicked in."

Sobek threw back his scaly green head and laughed. "Well said, girl! You have iron in your bones."

I suppose that was meant as a compliment. I chose to sneer at him and turn away.

Sobek only respected strength. In our first encounter, he had drowned Carter in the Rio Grande and smacked me across the Texas-Mexico border. We hadn't got much chummier since. From what I'd heard, he had only agreed to join our side because Horus and Isis had threatened him with extreme bodily harm. That didn't say much about his loyalty.

The glowing crew orbs fluttered around me, humming in my mind—little happy greetings of: *Sadie. Sadie. Sadie.* Once upon a time, they had *also* wanted to kill me; but since I'd awakened their old master Ra, they'd become quite friendly.

"Yes, hullo, boys," I muttered. "Lovely to see you. Excuse me."

I followed Carter and Zia to the fiery throne. Ra gave us a toothless grin. He was still as old and wrinkly as ever, but something seemed different about his eyes. Before, his gaze had always slid over me as if I were part of the scenery. Now, he actually focused on my face.

He held out a plate of macaroons and chocolate biscuits, which were a bit melted from the heat of his throne. "Cookies? Wheee!"

"Uh, thanks." Carter took a macaroon.

Naturally, I opted for the chocolate. I hadn't eaten a proper meal since we'd left our father's court.

Ra set down the platter and wobbled to his feet. Bes tried to help, but Ra waved him off. He tottered toward Zia.

"Zia," he warbled happily, as if singing a nursery rhyme. "Zia, Zia, Zia."

With a jolt, I realized it was the first time I'd heard him use her actual name.

He reached out to touch her scarab amulet. Zia backed away nervously. She glanced at Carter for reassurance.

"It's okay," Carter promised.

She took a deep breath. She unclasped her necklace and pressed it into the old man's hands. A warm glow expanded from the scarab, enveloping both Zia and Ra in a brilliant golden light.

"Good, good," Ra said. "Good . . ."

I expected the old god to get better. Instead, he began to crumble.

It was one of the most alarming things I'd seen in a very alarming day. First his ears fell off and melted to dust. Then his skin started turning to sand.

"What's happening?" I cried. "Shouldn't we do something?"

Carter's eyes widened with horror. His mouth opened, but no words came out.

Ra's smiling face dissolved. His arms and legs cracked apart like a desiccated sand sculpture. His particles scattered across the River of Night.

Bes grunted. "That was fast." He didn't seem particularly shocked. "Usually it takes longer."

I stared at him. "You've seen this *before*?"

Bes gave me a crooked grin. "Hey, I took my turns working on the sun barque in the old days. We've *all* seen Ra go through his cycle. But it's been a long, long time. Look."

He pointed at Zia.

The scarab had disappeared from her hands, but golden light still radiated around her like a full-body halo. She turned toward me with a brilliant smile. I'd never seen her so at ease, so pleased.

"I see now." Her voice was much richer, a chorus of tones descending in octaves through the Duat. "It's all about balance, isn't it? My thoughts and his. Or is it mine and hers . . . ?"

She laughed like a child on her first bike ride. "Rebirth, at last! You were right, Sadie and Carter! After so many eons in the darkness, I am finally reborn through Zia's compassion. I'd forgot what it is like to be young and powerful."

Carter stepped back. I couldn't blame him. The memory of Walt and Anubis merging was still fresh in my mind, so I had a sense what Carter was feeling; it was more than a little creepy hearing Zia describe herself in the third person.

I lowered my vision deeper into the Duat. In Zia's place stood a tall man in leather and bronze armor. In some ways, he still looked like Ra. He was still bald. His face was still wrinkled and weathered with age, and he had the same kindly smile (only with teeth). Now, though, his posture was straight. His body rippled with muscles. His skin glowed like molten gold. He was the world's buffest, most golden grandpa.

Bes knelt. "My lord Ra."

"Ah, my small friend." Ra ruffled the dwarf god's hair. "Rise! It's good to see you."

At the bow, Sobek came to attention, holding his long iron staff like a rifle. "Lord Ra! I knew you would return."

Ra chuckled. "Sobek, you old reptile. You would snap me up for dinner if you thought you could get away with it. Horus and Isis kept you in line?"

Sobek cleared his throat. "As you say, my king." He shrugged. "I can't help my nature."

"No matter," Ra said. "We'll need your strength soon enough. Are we approaching sunrise?"

"Yes, my king." Sobek pointed ahead of us.

I saw light at the end of the tunnel—literally. As we neared the end of the Duat, the River of Night widened. The exit gates stood about a kilometer ahead, flanked by statues of the sun god. Past that, daylight glowed. The river turned to clouds and poured into the morning sky.

"Very good," Ra said. "Steer us to Giza, Lord Sobek."

"Yes, my king." The croc god thrust his iron staff into the water, poling us along like a gondolier.

Carter still hadn't moved. The poor boy stared at the sun god with a mixture of fascination and shock.

"Carter Kane," Ra said with affection, "I know this is difficult for you, but Zia cares for you greatly. Nothing about her feelings has changed."

I coughed. "Ah . . . request? Please don't kiss him."

Ra laughed. His image rippled, and I saw Zia in front of me again.

"It's all right, Sadie," she promised. "Now would not be the time."

Carter turned awkwardly. "Um . . . I'll just . . . be over there." He bumped into the mast, then staggered toward the stern of the boat.

Zia knit her brow in concern. "Sadie, go take care of him, will you? We'll be reaching the mortal world soon. I must stay vigilant."

For once, I didn't argue. I went to check on my brother.

He was sitting by the tiller in crash position, his head between his knees.

"All right?" I asked. Stupid question, I know.

"She's an old man," he muttered. "The girl I like is a buff old man with a voice deeper than mine. I kissed her on the beach, and now . . ."

I sat next to him. The glowing orbs fluttered around us in excitement as the ship approached the daylight.

"Kissed her, eh?" I said. "Details, please."

I thought he might feel better if I could get him talking. I'm not sure if it worked, but at least it got his head out from between his knees. He told me about his journey with Zia through the *serapeum*, and the destruction of the *Egyptian Queen*.

Ra—I mean Zia—stood at the bow between Sobek and Bes, very carefully *not* looking back at us.

"So you told her it was all right," I summed up. "You encouraged her to help Ra. And now you're having second thoughts."

"Do you blame me?" he asked.

"We've both hosted gods ourselves," I said. "It doesn't have to be permanent. And she's still Zia. Besides, we're heading into battle. If we don't survive, do you want to spend your last few hours pushing her away?"

He studied my expression. "What happened to Walt?"

Ah . . . *touché*. At times, it seemed that Carter knew *my* secret name as well as I knew his.

"I . . . I don't know exactly. He's alive, but only because—"

"He's hosting Anubis," Carter finished.

"You knew?"

He shook his head. "Not until I saw that look on your face. But it makes sense. Walt has a knack for . . . whatever it is. That gray obliteration touch. Death magic."

I couldn't answer. I'd come back here to comfort Carter and reassure him that everything would be all right. Now, somehow, he'd managed to turn the tables.

He put his hand briefly on my knee. "This could work, sis. Anubis can keep Walt alive. Walt could live a normal life."

"You call that *normal*?"

"Anubis has never had a human host. This is his chance to have an actual body, to be flesh and blood."

I shivered. "Carter, it isn't like Zia's situation. *She* can separate at any time."

"So let me get this straight," Carter said. "The two guys you liked—one who was dying and one who was off-limits because he's a god—are now one guy, who isn't dying and isn't off-limits. And you're complaining."

"Don't make me sound ridiculous!" I shouted. "I'm not ridiculous!"

The three gods looked back at me. All right. Fine. I *did* sound ridiculous.

"Look," Carter said, "let's agree to freak out about this later, okay? Assuming we don't die."

I took a shaky breath. "Deal."

I helped my brother up. Together we joined the gods at the bow as the sun boat emerged from the Duat. The River of Night disappeared behind us, and we sailed across the clouds.

The Egyptian landscape spread out red and gold and green in the dawn. To the west, sandstorms swirled across the desert. To the east, the Nile snaked its way through Cairo. Directly below us, at the edge of the city, three pyramids rose on the plains of Giza.

Sobek struck his staff against the bow of the ship. He shouted like a herald: "At last, Ra has truly returned! Let his people rejoice! Let his throngs of worshippers assemble!"

Perhaps Sobek said that as a formality, or to suck up to Ra, or possibly just to make the old sun god feel worse. Whatever the case, nobody down below was assembling. Definitely nobody was rejoicing.

I'd seen this vista many times, but something was wrong. Fires burned across the city. The streets seemed strangely deserted. There were no tourists, no humans at all around the pyramids. I'd never seen Giza so empty.

"Where is everyone?" I asked.

Sobek hissed in disgust. "I should have known. The weak

humans are in hiding, or scared away because of the unrest in Egypt. Apophis has planned this well. His chosen battleground will be clear of mortal annoyances."

I shivered. I'd heard about the troubles in Egypt lately, along with all the strange natural disasters, but I hadn't thought of it as part of Apophis's plan.

If this was his chosen battleground . . .

I focused more closely on the plains of Giza. Peering into the Duat, I realized the area wasn't empty after all. Encircling the base of the Great Pyramid was an enormous serpent formed from a swirling tornado of red sand and darkness. His eyes were burning points of light. His fangs were forks of lightning. Wherever he touched, the desert boiled, and the pyramid itself shook with a horrible resonance. One of the oldest structures in human history was about to crumble.

Even from high above, I could feel the presence of Apophis. He radiated panic and fear so strongly, I could sense the mortals across Cairo cowering in their homes, afraid to go out. The whole land of Egypt was holding its breath.

As we watched, Apophis reared his massive cobra head. He struck at the desert floor, biting a house-sized crater in the sand. Then he recoiled as if he'd been stung, and hissed with anger. At first, I couldn't tell what he was fighting. I called on Isis's bird-of-prey sight and spotted a small lithe figure in a leopard-skin leotard, knives flashing in both hands as she leaped with inhuman agility and speed, striking at the serpent and evading his bite. All by herself, Bast was holding Apophis at bay.

My mouth tasted like old pennies. "She's alone. Where are the others?"

"They await the pharaoh's orders," Ra said. "Chaos has left them divided and confused. They will not march to battle without a leader."

"Then lead them!" I demanded.

The sun god turned. His form shimmered, and for a moment I saw Zia in front of me instead. I wondered if she would blast me to cinders. I had a feeling that would be quite easy for her now.

"I will face my old enemy," she said calmly, still with Ra's voice. "I won't let my loyal cat fight alone. Sobek, Bes— attend me."

"Yes, my king," Sobek said.

Bes cracked his knuckles. His chauffeur's outfit vanished, replaced by only his Dwarf Pride Speedo. "Chaos . . . get ready to meet Ugly."

"Wait," Carter said. "What about us? We've got the serpent's shadow."

The ship was descending rapidly now, coming in for a landing just south of the pyramids.

"First things first, Carter." Zia pointed to the Great Sphinx, which stood about three hundred meters from the pyramids. "You and Sadie must help your uncle."

Between the Sphinx's paws, a trail of smoke rose from a tunnel entrance. My heart missed a beat. Zia had once told us how that tunnel was sealed to keep archaeologists from finding their way into the First Nome. Obviously, the tunnel had been forced open.

"The First Nome is about to fall," Zia said. Her form shifted again, and it was the sun god standing before me. I really wished he/she/they would make up their mind.

"I will hold off Apophis as long as I can," Ra said. "But if you don't help your uncle and your friends immediately, there will be no one left to save. The House of Life will crumble."

I thought about poor Amos and our young initiates, surrounded by a mob of rebel magicians. We couldn't let them be slaughtered.

"She's right," I said. "Er, *he's* right. Whichever."

Carter nodded reluctantly. "You'll need these, Lord Ra."

He offered the sun god the crook and flail, but Ra shook his head. Or Zia shook her head. Gods of Egypt, this is confusing!

"When I told you the gods waited for their pharaoh," Ra said, "I meant you, Carter Kane, the Eye of Horus. I am here to fight my old enemy, not to assume the throne. That is your destiny. Unite the House of Life, rally the gods in my name. Never fear, I will hold Apophis until you come."

Carter stared at the crook and flail in his hands. He looked every bit as terrified as he had when Ra had crumbled to sand.

I couldn't blame him. Carter had just been ordered to assume the throne of creation and lead an army of magicians and gods into battle. A year ago, even six months ago, the idea of my brother's being given that kind of responsibility would've horrified me as well.

Strangely, I didn't mind it now. Thinking of Carter as the

pharaoh was actually comforting. I'm sure I'll regret saying this, and I'm sure Carter will never let me forget it, but the truth was I'd been relying on my brother ever since we'd moved to Brooklyn House. I'd come to depend on his strength. I trusted him to make the right decisions, even when he didn't trust himself. When I had learned his secret name, I'd seen one very clear trait woven into his character: leadership.

"You're ready," I told him.

"Indeed," Ra agreed.

Carter looked up, a bit stunned, but I suppose he could tell I wasn't teasing him—not this time.

Bes punched him in the shoulder. "'Course you're ready, kid. Now, stop wasting time and go save your uncle!"

Looking at Bes, I tried not to get teary-eyed. I'd already lost him once.

As for Ra, he seemed so confident, but still he was confined to the form of Zia Rashid. She was a strong magician, yes, but she was new to this hosting business. If she wavered even slightly, or overextended herself . . .

"Good luck, then." Carter swallowed. "I hope . . ."

He faltered. I realized the poor boy was trying to say good-bye to his girlfriend, possibly for the last time, and he couldn't even kiss her without kissing the sun god.

Carter began to change shape. His clothes, his pack, even the crook and flail melted into plumage. His form shrank until he was a brown-and-white falcon. Then he spread his wings and dove off the side of the boat.

"Oh, I hate this part," I muttered.

I called on Isis and invited her in: *Now. It's time to act as one.*

Immediately her magic flowed into me. It felt as if someone had switched on enough hydroelectric generators to light up a nation and channeled all that power straight into me. I turned into a kite (the bird) and soared into the air.

For once, I had no problem turning back to human. Carter and I rendezvoused at the feet of the Great Sphinx and studied the newly blasted tunnel entrance. The rebels hadn't been too subtle. Stone blocks the size of cars had been reduced to rubble. The surrounding sand had blackened and melted to glass. Either Sarah Jacobi's crew had used a *ha-di* spell or several sticks of dynamite.

"This tunnel . . ." I said. "Doesn't the other end open just across from the Hall of Ages?"

Carter nodded grimly. He pulled out the crook and flail, which were now glowing with ghostly white fire. He plunged into the darkness. I summoned my staff and wand and followed him inside.

As we descended, we saw evidence of battle. Explosions had scorched the walls and steps. One portion of the ceiling had buckled. Carter was able to clear a path with the strength of Horus, but as soon as we were through, the tunnel collapsed behind us. We wouldn't be exiting that way.

Below us, I heard the sounds of combat—divine words being cast; fire, water, and earth magic clashing. A lion roared. Metal clanged on metal.

A few meters farther, and we found the first casualty. A young man in a tattered gray military uniform was propped against the wall, holding his stomach and wheezing painfully.

"Leonid!" I cried.

My Russian friend was pale and bloody. I put my hand on his forehead. His skin was cold.

"Below," he gasped. "Too many. I try—"

"Stay here," I said, which I realized was silly, since he could hardly move. "We'll be back with help."

He nodded bravely, but I looked at Carter and knew we were thinking the same thing. Leonid might not last that long. His uniform coat was soaked with blood. He kept his hand over his gut, but he'd clearly been savaged—either by claws or knives or some equally horrible magic.

I cast a *Slow* spell on Leonid, which would at least steady his breathing and stem the flow of blood, but it wouldn't help much. The poor boy had risked his life to escape St. Petersburg. He'd come all the way to Brooklyn to warn me about the impending attack. Now he'd tried to defend the First Nome against his former masters, and they'd cut him down and walked right over him, leaving him to suffer a lingering death.

"We *will* be back," I promised again.

Carter and I stumbled on.

We reached the bottom of the steps and were instantly thrown into battle. A *shabti* lion leaped at my face.

Isis reacted faster than I could have. She gave me a single word to speak: *"Fah!"*

And the hieroglyph for *Release* shimmered in the air:

The lion shrank to a wax statuette and bounced harmlessly off my chest.

All around us, the corridor was in mayhem. In either direction our initiates were locked in combat with enemy magicians. Directly in front of us, a dozen rebels had formed a wedge blocking the doors to the Hall of Ages, and our friends seemed to be trying to get past them.

For a moment, that seemed backward to me. Shouldn't our side be defending the doors? Then I realized what must have happened. The attack on the sealed tunnel had surprised our allies. They'd rushed to help Amos, but by the time they'd got to the doors, the enemies were already inside. Now this lot was keeping our reinforcements from reaching Amos, while our uncle was inside the hall, possibly alone, facing Sarah Jacobi and her elite hit squad.

My pulse raced. I charged into battle, flinging spells from Isis's incredibly diverse menu. It felt good to be a goddess again, I must admit, but I had to keep careful track of my energy. If I let Isis have free reign, she would destroy our enemies in seconds, but she would also burn me up in the process. I had to temper her inclination to rend the puny mortals to pieces.

I threw my wand like a boomerang and hit a large, bearded magician who was yelling in Russian as he fought sword-to-sword against Julian.

The Russian disappeared in a golden flash. Where he'd been standing, a hamster squeaked in alarm and scurried away. Julian grinned at me. His sword blade was smoking and the turn-ups of his trousers were on fire, but otherwise he looked all right.

"About time!" he said.

Another magician charged him, and we had no further time to chat.

Carter waded forward, swinging his flail and crook as if he had trained with them all his life. An enemy magician summoned a rhino—which I thought quite rude, considering the tight space we were in. Carter lashed it with his flail, and each spiked chain became a rope of fire. The rhino crumbled, cut into three pieces, and melted into a pile of wax.

Our other friends weren't doing too badly, either. Felix used an ice spell that I'd never seen before—encasing his enemies in big fluffy snowmen, complete with carrot noses and pipes. His army of penguins waddled around him, pecking at enemy magicians and stealing their wands.

Alyssa was fighting with another earth elementalist, but this Russian woman was clearly outmatched. She'd probably never faced the power of Geb before. Each time the Russian summoned a stone creature or tried to throw boulders, her attacks dissolved into rubble. Alyssa snapped her fingers, and the floor turned to quicksand under her opponent's feet. The Russian sank up to her shoulders, quite stuck.

At the north end of the corridor, Jaz crouched next to Cleo, tending her arm, which had been turned into a sunflower.

Cleo had got off better than her opponent, though. At her feet lay a human-sized volume of the novel *David Copperfield*, which I had a feeling had once been an enemy magician.

(Carter tells me David Copperfield *is* a magician. He finds this funny for some reason. Just ignore him. I do.)

Even our ankle-biters had got into the act. Young Shelby had scattered her crayons down the hallway to trip the enemy. Now she was wielding her wand like a tennis racket, running between the legs of adult magicians, swatting them on the bottom and yelling, "Die, die, die!"

Aren't children adorable?

She swatted a large metal warrior, a *shabti* no doubt, and he transformed into a rainbow-colored potbellied pig. If we lived through the day, I had a bad feeling Shelby would want to keep it.

Some of the First Nome residents were helping us, but depressingly few. A handful of tottering old magicians and desperate merchants threw talismans and deflected spells.

Slowly but surely, we waded toward the doors, where the main wedge of enemies seemed to be focused on a single attacker.

When I realized who it was, I was tempted to turn *myself* into a hamster and scamper away, squeaking.

Walt had arrived. He ripped through the enemy line with his bare hands—throwing one rebel magician down the hallway with inhuman strength, touching another and instantly encasing the man in mummy linen. He grabbed the staff of a third rebel, and it crumbled to dust. Finally he swept his hand toward the remaining enemies, and they shrank to the size of dolls. Canopic jars—the sort used to bury a mummy's internal organs—sprang up around each of the tiny magicians, sealing them in with lids shaped like animal heads. The poor magicians yelled desperately, banging on the clay containers and wobbling about like a line of very unhappy bowling pins.

Walt turned to our friends. "Is everyone all right?"

He looked like normal old Walt—tall and muscular with a confident face, soft brown eyes, and strong hands. But his clothes had changed. He wore jeans, a dark Dead Weather T-shirt, and a black leather jacket—Anubis's outfit, sized up to fit Walt's physique. All I had to do was lower my vision into the Duat, just a bit, and I saw Anubis standing there in all his usual annoying gorgeousness. Both of them—occupying the same space.

"Get ready," Walt told our troops. "They've sealed the doors, but I can—"

Then he noticed me, and his voice faltered.

"Sadie," he said. "I—"

"Something about opening the doors?" I demanded.

He nodded mutely.

"Amos is in there?" I asked. "Fighting Kwai and Jacobi and who knows what else?"

He nodded again.

"Then stop staring at me and *open the doors*, you annoying boy!"

I was talking to both of them. It felt quite natural. And it felt good to let my anger out. I'd deal with those two—that one—whatever he was—later. Right now, my uncle needed me.

Walt/Anubis had the nerve to smile.

He put his hand on the doors. Gray ash spread across the surface. The bronze crumbled to dust.

"After you," he told me, and we charged into the Hall of Ages.

18. Death Boy to the Rescue

THE GOOD NEWS: Amos wasn't entirely alone.

The bad news: his backup was the god of evil.

As we poured into the Hall of Ages, our rescue attempt sputtered to a stop. We hadn't expected to see a deadly aerial ballet with lightning and knives. The normal floating hieroglyphs that filled the room were gone. The holographic curtains on either side of the hall flickered weakly. Some had collapsed altogether.

As I'd suspected, an assault team of enemy magicians had locked themselves in here with Amos, but it looked like they were regretting their choice.

Hovering midair in the center of the hall, Amos was cloaked in the strangest avatar I'd ever seen. A vaguely human form swirled around him—part sandstorm, part fire, rather like the giant Apophis we'd seen upstairs, except a lot happier. The giant red warrior laughed as he fought, spinning a ten-meter black iron staff with careless force. Suspended in his chest, Amos copied the giant's moves, his face beaded with sweat. I couldn't tell if Amos was directing Set or trying to restrain him. Possibly both.

Enemy magicians flew circles around him. Kwai was easy to spot, with his bald head and blue robes, darting through the air like one of those martial arts monks who could defy gravity. He shot bolts of red lightning at the Set avatar, but they didn't seem to have much effect.

With her spiky black hair and flowing white robes, Sarah Jacobi looked like the Schizophrenic Witch of the West, especially as she was surfing about on a storm cloud like a flying carpet. She held two black knives like barbershop razors, which she threw over and over in a horrific juggling act, launching them into the Set avatar, then catching them as they returned to her hands. I'd seen knives like that before—*netjeri* blades, made from meteoric iron. They were mostly used in funeral ceremonies, but they seemed to work quite well as weapons. With every strike, they disrupted the avatar's sandy flesh a little more, slowly wearing it down. As I watched her throw her knives, anger clenched inside me like a fist. Some instinct told me that Jacobi had stuck my Russian friend Leonid with those knives before leaving him to die.

The other rebels weren't quite as successful with their attacks, but they were certainly persistent. Some blasted Set with gusts of wind or water. Others launched *shabti* creatures, like giant scorpions and griffins. One fat bloke was pelting Amos with bits of cheese. Honestly, I'm not sure I would have chosen a Cheese Master for my elite hit squad, but perhaps Sarah Jacobi got peckish during her battles.

Set seemed to be enjoying himself. The giant red warrior slammed his iron staff into Kwai's chest and sent him spiraling through the air. He kicked another magician into the holographic curtains of the Roman Age, and the poor man collapsed with smoke coming out his ears, his mind probably overloaded with visions of toga parties.

Set thrust his free hand toward the Cheese Master. The fat magician was swallowed in a sandstorm and began to scream, but just as quickly, Set retracted his hand. The storm died. The magician dropped to the floor like a rag doll, unconscious but still alive.

"Bah!" the red warrior bellowed. "Come on, Amos, let me have *some* fun. I only wanted to strip the flesh from his bones!"

Amos's face was tight with concentration. Clearly he was doing his best to control the god, but Set had many other enemies to play with.

"Pull!" The red god shot lightning at a stone sphinx and blasted it to dust. He laughed insanely and swatted his staff at Sarah Jacobi. "This is fun, little magicians! Don't you have any more tricks?"

I'm not sure how long we stood in the doorway, watching the battle. Probably not more than a few seconds, but it seemed like an eternity.

Finally Jaz choked back a sob. "Amos . . . he's possessed again."

"No," I insisted. "No, this is different! He's in control."

Our initiates gazed at me with disbelief. I understood their panic. I remembered better than anyone how Set had nearly broken my uncle's sanity. It was hard to comprehend that Amos would ever willingly channel the red god's power. Yet he was doing the impossible. He was winning.

Still, even the Chief Lector couldn't channel that much power for long.

"Look at him!" I pleaded. "We have to help him! Amos isn't possessed. He's controlling Set!"

Walt frowned. "Sadie, that—that's impossible. Set can't be controlled."

Carter raised his crook and flail. "Obviously he *can* be, because Amos is doing it. Now, are we going to war, or what?"

We charged forward, but we'd hesitated too long. Sarah Jacobi had noticed our presence. She yelled down at her followers: "Now!"

She may have been evil, but she was not a fool. Their assault on Amos thus far had simply been to distract him and weaken him. On her cue, the real attack began. Kwai blasted lightning at Amos's face just as the other magicians drew out magic ropes and threw them at the Set avatar.

The red warrior staggered as the ropes tightened all at once, lashing around his legs and arms. Sarah Jacobi sheathed her knives and produced a long black lariat. Sailing her storm cloud above the avatar, she deftly lassoed his head and pulled the noose tight.

Set roared with outrage, but the avatar began to shrink. Before we could even close the distance, Amos was kneeling on the floor of the Hall of Ages, surrounded by only the thinnest of glowing red shields. Magical ropes now bound him tight. Sarah Jacobi stood behind him, holding the black lasso like a leash. One of her *netjeri* blades was pressed against Amos's neck.

"Stop!" she commanded us. "This ends *now*."

My friends hesitated. The rebel magicians turned and faced us warily.

Isis spoke in my mind: *Regrettable, but we must let him die. He hosts Set, our old enemy.*

That's my uncle! I replied.

He has been corrupted, Isis said. *He is already gone.*

"No!" I yelled. Our connection wavered. You can't share the mind of a god and have a disagreement. To be the Eye, you must act in perfect unison.

Carter seemed to be having similar trouble with Horus. He summoned the hawk warrior avatar, but almost immediately it dissipated and dropped Carter to the floor.

"Come on, Horus!" he growled. "We *have* to help."

Sarah Jacobi's laugh sounded like metal scraped through sand.

"Do you see?" She pulled tight on the noose around Amos's neck. "*This* is what comes from the path of the gods! Confusion. Chaos. *Set* himself in the Hall of Ages! Even you misguided fools cannot deny this is wrong!"

Amos clawed at his throat. He growled in outrage, but it was Set's voice that spoke. "I try to do something nice, and *this* is my thanks? You should have let me kill them, Amos!"

I stepped forward, careful to make no sudden movements.

"Jacobi, you don't understand. Amos is channeling Set's power, but he's in control. He could have killed you, but he didn't. Set was a lieutenant of Ra. He's a useful ally, properly managed."

Set snorted. "Useful, yes! I don't know about the *properly managed* business. Let me go, puny magicians, so I can crush you!"

I glared at my uncle. "Set! Not helping!"

Amos's expression changed from anger to concern. "Sadie!" he said with his own voice. "Go: fight Apophis. Leave me here!"

"No," I said. "You're the Chief Lector. We'll fight for the House of Life."

I didn't look behind me, but I hoped that my friends would agree. Otherwise my last stand would be very, very short.

Jacobi sneered. "Your uncle is a servant of Set! You and your brother are sentenced to death. The rest of you, lay down your weapons. As your new Chief Lector, I will give you amnesty. Then we will battle Apophis together."

"You're in *league* with Apophis!" I yelled.

Jacobi's face turned stony cold. "Treason."

She thrust out her staff. "*Ha-di.*"

I raised my wand, but Isis wasn't helping me this time. I was just Sadie Kane, and my defenses were slow. The explosion ripped through my weak shields and threw me backward into a curtain of light. Images from the Age of the Gods crackled around me—the founding of the world, the crowning of Osiris, the battle between Set and Horus—like having sixty different movies downloaded into my brain while being electrocuted. The light shattered, and I lay on the floor, dazed and drained.

"Sadie!" Carter charged toward me, but Kwai blasted him with a bolt of red lightning. Carter fell to his knees. I didn't even have the strength to cry out.

Jaz ran toward him. Little Shelby yelled, "Stop it! Stop it!" Our other initiates seemed stunned, unable to move.

"Give up," Jacobi said. I realized she was speaking with words of power, just like the ghost Setne had done. She was using magic to paralyze my friends. "The Kanes have brought you nothing but trouble. It's time this ended."

She lifted her *netjeri* blade from Amos's throat. Quick as light, she threw it at me. As the blade flew, my mind seemed to speed up. In that millisecond, I understood that Sarah Jacobi wouldn't miss. My end would be as painful as poor Leonid's, who was bleeding to death alone in the outer tunnel. Yet I could do nothing to defend myself.

A shadow crossed in front of me. A bare hand snatched the blade out of the air. The meteoric iron turned gray and crumbled.

Jacobi's eyes widened. She hastily drew her second knife. "Who are you?" she demanded.

"Walt Stone," he said, "blood of the pharaohs. And Anubis, god of the dead."

He stepped in front of me, shielding me from my enemies. Maybe my vision was double because I'd cracked my head, but I saw the two of them with equal clarity—both handsome and powerful, both quite angry.

"We speak with one voice," Walt said. "Especially on this matter. *No one* harms Sadie Kane."

He thrust out his hand. The floor split open at Sarah Jacobi's feet, and souls of the dead sprang up like weeds— skeletal hands, glowing faces, fanged shadows, and winged *ba* with their claws extended. They swarmed Sarah Jacobi, wrapping her in ghostly linen, and dragged her screaming into the chasm. The floor closed behind her, leaving no trace that she had ever existed.

The black noose slackened around Amos's neck, and the voice of Set laughed with delight. "That's my boy!"

"Shut up, Father," Anubis said.

In the Duat, Anubis looked as he always had, with his tousled dark hair and lovely brown eyes, but I'd never seen him filled with such rage. I realized that anyone who dared to hurt me would suffer his full wrath, and Walt wasn't going to hold him back.

Jaz helped Carter to his feet. His shirt was burned, but he looked all right. I suppose a blast of lightning wasn't the worst thing that had happened to him lately.

"Magicians!" Carter managed to stand tall and confident, addressing both our initiates and the rebels. "We're wasting time. Apophis is above, about to destroy the world. A few brave gods are holding him back for *our* sakes, for the sake of Egypt and the world of mortals, but they can't do it alone. Jacobi and Kwai led you astray. Unbind the Chief Lector. We *have* to work together."

Kwai snarled. Red electricity arced between his fingers. "Never. We do not bow to gods."

I managed to rise.

"Listen to my brother," I said. "You don't trust the gods? They are already helping us. Meanwhile, Apophis wants us to fight one another. Why do you think your attack was timed for this morning, at the same moment Apophis is rising? Kwai and Jacobi have sold you out. The enemy is right in front of you!"

Even the rebel magicians now turned to stare at Kwai. The remaining ropes fell away from Amos.

Kwai sneered. "You're too late."

His voice hummed with power. His robes turned from blue to bloodred. His eyes glowed, his pupils turning to reptilian slits. "Even now, my master destroys the old gods, sweeping away the foundations of your world. He will swallow the sun. All of you will die."

Amos got to his feet. Red sand swirled around him, but I had no doubt who was in charge now. His white robes shimmered with power. The leopard-skin cape of the Chief Lector gleamed on his shoulders. He held out his staff, and multi-colored hieroglyphs filled the air.

"House of Life," he said. "To war!"

Kwai did not give up easily.

I suppose that's what happens when the Serpent of Chaos is invading your thoughts and filling you with unlimited rage and magic.

Kwai sent a chain of red lightning across the room, knocking over most of the other magicians, including his own followers. Isis must have protected me, because the electricity rippled over me with no effect. Amos didn't seem bothered in his swirling red tornado. Walt stumbled, but only briefly. Even Carter in his weakened state managed to turn aside the lightning with his pharaoh's crook.

The others weren't as lucky. Jaz collapsed. Then Julian. Then Felix and his squad of penguins. All our initiates and the rebels they'd been fighting crumpled unconscious to the floor. So much for a massive offensive.

I summoned the power of Isis. I began to cast a binding charm; but Kwai wasn't done with his tricks. He raised his hands and created his own sandstorm. Dozens of whirlwinds spun through the hall, thickening and forming into creatures of sand—sphinxes, crocodiles, wolves, and lions. They attacked in every direction, even pouncing on our defenseless friends.

"Sadie!" Amos warned. "Protect them!"

I quickly changed spells—casting hasty shields over our unconscious initiates. Amos blasted the monsters one after the other, but they just kept re-forming.

Carter summoned his avatar. He charged at Kwai, but the red magician blasted him backward with a new surge of lightning. My poor brother slammed into a stone column, which collapsed on top of him. I could only hope his avatar had taken the brunt of the impact.

Walt released a dozen magical creatures at once—his sphinx, his camels, his ibis, even Philip of Macedonia. They charged at the sand creatures, trying to keep them away from the fallen magicians.

Then Walt turned to face Kwai.

"Anubis," Kwai hissed. "You should have stayed in your funeral parlor, boy god. You are outmatched."

By way of answer, Walt spread his hands. On either side of him, the floor cracked open. Two massive jackals leaped from the crevices, their fangs bared. Walt's form shimmered. Suddenly he was dressed in Egyptian battle armor, a *was* staff twirling in his hands like a deadly fan blade.

Kwai roared. He blasted the jackals with waves of sand. He hurled lightning and words of power at Walt, but Walt deflected them with his staff, reducing Kwai's attacks to gray ashes.

The jackals harried Kwai from either side, sinking their teeth into his legs, while Walt stepped in and swung his staff like a golf club. He hit Kwai so hard, I imagined it echoed all the way through the Duat. The magician fell. His sand creatures vanished.

Walt called off his jackals. Amos lowered his staff. Carter rose from the rubble, looking dizzy but unharmed. We gathered around the fallen magician.

Kwai should have been dead. A line of blood trickled from his mouth. His eyes were glassy. But as I studied his face, he took a sharp breath and laughed weakly.

"Idiots," he rasped. *"Sahei."*

A bloodred hieroglyph burned against his chest:

His robes erupted in flames. Before our eyes, he dissolved into sand and a wave of cold—the power of Chaos—rippled through the Hall of Ages. Columns shook. Chunks of stone fell from the ceiling. A slab the size of an oven crashed into the steps of the dais, almost crushing the pharaoh's throne.

"*Bring down,*" I said, realizing what the hieroglyph meant. Even Isis seemed terrified by the invocation. "*Sahei* is *Bring down.*"

Amos swore in Ancient Egyptian—something about donkeys trampling Kwai's ghost. "He used up his life force to cast this curse. The hall is already weakened. We'll have to leave before we're buried alive."

I glanced around us at the fallen magicians. Some of our initiates were starting to stir, but there was no way we could get them all to safety in time.

"We have to stop it!" I insisted. "We have four gods present! Can't we save the hall?"

Amos furrowed his brow. "The power of Set will not help me in this. He can only destroy, not restore."

Another column toppled. It broke across the floor, barely missing one of the unconscious rebels.

Walt—who looked quite good in armor, by the way—shook his head. "This is beyond Anubis. I'm sorry."

The floor rumbled. We had only seconds to live. Then we would be just another bunch of entombed Egyptians.

"Carter?" I asked.

He regarded me helplessly. He was still weak, and I realized his battle magic wouldn't be much good in this situation.

I sighed. "So it comes down to me, as always. Fine. You three shield the others as best you can. If this doesn't work, get out quickly."

"If *what* doesn't work?" Amos said, as more chunks of ceiling rained down around us. "Sadie, what are you planning?"

"Just a word, dear uncle." I raised my staff and called on the power of Isis.

She immediately understood what I needed. Together, we tried to find calm in the Chaos. I focused on the most peaceful, well-ordered moments of my life—and there weren't many. I remembered my sixth birthday party in Los Angeles with Carter, my dad and mum—the last clear memory I had of all of us together as a family. I imagined listening to music in my room at Brooklyn House while Khufu ate Cheerios on my dresser. I imagined sitting on the terrace with my friends, having a restful breakfast as Philip of Macedonia splashed in his pool. I remembered Sunday afternoons at Gran and Gramps's flat—Muffin on my lap, Gramps's rugby game on the telly, and Gran's horrible biscuits and weak tea on the table. Good times, those were.

Most important, I faced down my own chaos. I accepted my jumbled emotions about whether I belonged in London or New York, whether I was a magician or a schoolgirl. I was Sadie Kane, and if I survived today, I could bloody well balance it all. And, yes, I accepted Walt and Anubis . . . I gave up my anger and dismay. I imagined both of them with me, and if that was peculiar, well then, it fit right in with the rest of my life. I made peace with the idea. Walt was alive. Anubis was flesh and blood. I stilled my restlessness and let go of my doubts.

"*Ma'at*," I said.

I felt as if I'd struck a tuning fork against the foundation of the earth. Deep harmony resonated outward through every level of the Duat.

The Hall of Ages stilled. Columns rose and repaired themselves. The cracks in the ceiling and floor sealed. Holographic curtains of light blazed once again along either side of the hall, and hieroglyphs once more filled the air.

I collapsed into Walt's arms. Through my fuzzy vision, I saw him smiling down at me. Anubis, too. I could see them both, and I realized I didn't have to pick.

"Sadie, you did it," he said. "You're so amazing."

"Uh-huh," I muttered. "Good night."

They tell me I was only out a few seconds, but it felt like centuries. When I came to, the other magicians were back on their feet. Amos smiled down at me. "Up you come, my girl."

He helped me to my feet. Carter hugged me quite enthusiastically, almost as if he appreciated me properly for once.

"It's not over," Carter warned. "We have to get to the surface. Are you ready?"

I nodded, though neither of us was in good shape. We'd used up too much energy in the fight for the Hall of Ages. Even with the gods' help, we were in no condition to face Apophis. But we had little choice.

"Carter," Amos said formally, gesturing to the empty throne. "You are blood of the pharaohs, Eye of Horus. You carry the crook and flail, bestowed by Ra. The kingship is yours. Will you lead us, gods and mortals, against the enemy?"

Carter stood straight. I could see the doubt and fear in

him, but possibly that was just because I knew him. I'd spoken his secret name. On the outside, he looked confident, strong, adult—even kingly.

[Yes, I said that. Don't get a big head, brother dear. You're still a huge dork.]

"I'll lead you," Carter said. "But the throne will have to wait. Right now, Ra needs us. We have to get to the surface. Can you show us the quickest way?"

Amos nodded. "And the rest of you?"

The other magicians shouted assent—even the former rebels.

"We aren't many," Walt observed. "What are your orders, Carter?"

"First we get reinforcements," he said. "It's time I summoned the gods to war."

19. Welcome to the Fun House of Evil

SADIE SAYS I LOOKED CONFIDENT?

Good one.

Actually, being offered kingship of the universe (or supreme command over gods and magicians, or whatever) pretty much had me shaking in my shoes.

I was grateful that it had happened as we headed into combat, so I didn't have time to think about it too much or freak out.

Go with it, Horus said. *Use my courage.*

For once I was glad to let him take the lead. Otherwise when we reached the surface and I saw how bad things were, I would've run back inside, screaming like a kindergartner.

(Sadie says that's not fair. Our kindergartners weren't screaming. They were more anxious for combat than I was.)

Anyway, our little band of magicians popped out of a secret tunnel halfway up Khafre's pyramid and stared down at the end of the world.

To say Apophis was huge would be like saying the *Titanic* took on a little water. Since we'd been underground, the serpent had grown. Now he coiled under the desert for miles, wrapping around the pyramids and tunneling under the outskirts of Cairo, lifting entire neighborhoods like old carpeting.

Only the serpent's head was above ground, but it rose almost as tall as the pyramids. It was formed of sandstorm and lightning, like Sadie described; and when it fanned out its cobra's crest, it displayed a blazing hieroglyph no magician would ever write: *Isfet*, the sign of Chaos:

The four gods battling Apophis looked tiny in comparison. Sobek straddled the serpent's back, chomping down again and again with his powerful crocodile jaws and smashing away with his staff. His attacks connected, but they didn't seem to bother Apophis.

Bes danced around in his Speedo, swinging a wooden club and yelling, "Boo!" so loudly, the people in Cairo were probably cowering under the beds. But the giant Chaos snake did not look terrified.

Our cat friend Bast wasn't having much luck either. She leaped onto the serpent's head and slashed wildly with her knives, then jumped away before Apophis could shake her off; but the serpent only seemed interested in one target.

Standing in desert between the Great Pyramid and the

Sphinx, Zia was surrounded in brilliant golden light. It was hard to look directly at her, but she was shooting fireballs like a Roman candle—each one exploding against the serpent's body and disrupting his form. The serpent retaliated, biting chunks out of the desert, but he couldn't seem to find Zia. Her location shifted like a mirage—always several feet away from wherever Apophis struck.

Still, she couldn't keep this up forever. Looking into the Duat, I could see the four gods' auras weakening, and Apophis kept getting larger and stronger.

"What do we do?" Jaz asked nervously.

"Wait for my signal," I said.

"Which is what?" Sadie asked.

"I don't know yet. I'll be back."

I closed my eyes and sent my *ba* into the heavens. Suddenly I stood in the throne room of the gods. Stone columns soared overhead. Braziers of magical fire stretched into the distance, their light reflecting on the polished marble floor. In the center of the room, Ra's sun boat rested on its dais. His throne of fire sat empty.

I seemed to be alone—until I called out.

"Come to me." Horus and I spoke in unison. "Fulfill your oath of loyalty."

Trails of glowing smoke drifted into the room like slow-motion comets. Lights blazed to life, swirling between the columns. All around me, the gods materialized.

A swarm of scorpions scuttled across the floor and merged to form the goddess Serqet, who glared at me distrustfully from beneath her scorpion-shaped crown. Babi the baboon god climbed down from the nearest column and bared his fangs. Nekhbet the vulture goddess perched on the prow of the sun boat. Shu the wind god blew in as a dust devil, then took the appearance of a World War II pilot, his body created entirely from dust, leaves, and scraps of paper.

There were dozens more: the moon god Khonsu in his silver suit; the sky goddess Nut, her galactic blue skin glimmering with stars; Hapi the hippie with his green fish-scale skirt and his crazy smile; and a severe-looking woman in camouflage hunting clothes, a bow at her side, grease paint on her face, and two ridiculous palm fronds sticking out of her hair—Neith, I assumed.

I'd hoped for more friendly faces, but I knew Osiris couldn't leave the Underworld. Thoth was still stuck in his pyramid. And many other gods—probably the ones most likely to help me—were also under siege from the forces of Chaos. We'd have to make do.

I faced the assembled gods and hoped my legs weren't shaking too badly. I still felt like Carter Kane, but I knew that when they looked at me, they were seeing Horus the Avenger.

I brandished the crook and flail. "These are the symbols of the pharaoh, given to me by Ra himself. He has named me your leader. Even now, he is facing Apophis. We must join the battle. Follow me and do your duty."

Serqet hissed. "We only follow the strong. Are you strong?"

I moved with lightning speed. I lashed the flail across the goddess, cutting her into a flaming pile of baked scorpions.

A few live critters scuttled out of the wreckage. They moved to a safe distance and began to re-form, until the goddess was whole again, cowering behind a brazier of blue flames.

The vulture goddess Nekhbet cackled. "He is strong."

"Then come," I said.

My *ba* returned to earth. I opened my eyes.

Above Khafre's pyramid, storm clouds gathered. With a clap of thunder they parted, and the gods charged into battle—some riding war chariots, some in floating warships, some on the backs of giant falcons. The baboon god Babi landed atop the Great Pyramid. He pounded his chest and howled.

I turned to Sadie. "How's that for a signal?"

We clambered down the pyramid to join the fight.

First tip on fighting a giant Chaos serpent: Don't.

Even with a squadron of gods and magicians at your back, it's not a battle you're likely to win. I got clued in to this as we charged closer and the world seemed to fracture. I realized Apophis wasn't just coiling in and out of the desert, wrapping himself around the pyramids. He was coiling in and out of the Duat, splintering reality into different layers. Trying to find him was like running through a fun house full of mirrors, each mirror leading to another fun house filled with more mirrors.

Our friends began to split up. All around us, gods and magicians became isolated, some sinking deeper into the Duat than others. We fought a single enemy, but we were each fighting only a fragment of his power.

At the base of the pyramid, snaky coils encircled Walt. He

tried to force his way out, blasting the serpent with gray light that turned his scales to ashes; but the serpent just regenerated, closing tighter and tighter around Walt. A few hundred feet away, Julian had summoned a full Horus avatar, a giant green hawk-headed warrior with a *khopesh* in either hand. He sliced away at the serpent's tail—or at least one version of it—while the tail lashed around and tried to impale him. Deeper in the Duat, the goddess Serqet stood in nearly the same place. She had turned herself into a giant black scorpion and was confronting another image of the serpent's tail, parrying it with her stinger in a bizarre sword fight. Even Amos had been waylaid. He faced the wrong direction (or so it looked to me) and sliced his staff through the empty air, shouting command words at nothing.

I hoped that we were weakening Apophis by forcing him to deal with so many of us at once, but I couldn't see any sign of the serpent's power decreasing.

"He's dividing us!" Sadie shouted. Even standing right next to me, she seemed to be speaking from the other side of a roaring wind tunnel.

"Grab hold!" I held out the pharaoh's crook. "We have to stay together!"

She took the other end of the crook, and we forged ahead.

The closer we got to the serpent's head, the harder it was to move. I felt like we were running through layers of clear syrup, each thicker and more resistant than the last. I looked around us and realized most of our allies had fallen away. Some I couldn't even see because of the Chaos distortion.

Ahead of us, a bright light shimmered as if through fifty feet of water.

"We have to get to Ra," I said. "Concentrate on him!"

What I was really thinking: *I have to save Zia.* But I was pretty sure Sadie knew that without my spelling it out.

I could hear Zia's voice, summoning waves of fire against her enemy. She couldn't be much farther—maybe twenty feet in mortal distance? Through the Duat it might have been a thousand miles.

"Almost there!" I said.

You're too late, little ones, the voice of Apophis hummed in my ears. *Ra will be my breakfast today.*

A snake coil as big as a subway car slammed into the sand at our feet, almost crushing us. The scales rippled with Chaos energy, making me want to double over with nausea. Without Horus shielding me, I'm pretty sure I would have been vaporized just standing so close to it. I swung my flail. Three lines of fire cut through the snake's hide, blasting it to shreds of red and gray fog.

"Okay?" I asked Sadie.

She looked pale, but nodded. We trudged on.

A few of the most powerful gods still fought around us. Babi the baboon was riding one version of the serpent's head, pounding his massive fists between Apophis's eyes, but the serpent seemed only mildly annoyed. The hunter goddess Neith hid behind a pile of stone blocks, sniping at another snakehead with her arrows. She was pretty easy to spot because of the palm fronds in her hair, and she kept yelling something about a Jelly Baby conspiracy. Farther on, another serpent's mouth sank its fangs into Nekhbet the vulture goddess, who shrieked in pain and exploded into a pile of black feathers.

"We're running out of gods!" Sadie cried.

Finally we reached the middle of the Chaos storm. Walls of red and gray smoke swirled around us, but the roar died in the center as if we'd stepped into the eye of a hurricane. Above us rose the true head of the serpent—or at least the manifestation that held most of his power.

How did I know this? His skin looked more solid, glistening with golden red scales. His mouth was a pink cavern with fangs. His eyes glowed, and his cobra's hood spread so wide, it blocked a quarter of the sky.

Before him stood Ra, a shining apparition too bright to look at directly. If I glanced from the corner of my eye, however, I could see Zia at the center of the light. She now wore the clothes of an Egyptian princess—a silky dress of white and gold, a golden necklace and armbands. Even her staff and wand were gilded. Her image danced in the hot vapor, causing the serpent to misjudge her location every time he struck.

Zia shot tracers of red flame toward Apophis—blinding his eyes and burning away patches of his skin—but the damage seemed to heal almost instantly. He was growing stronger and larger. Zia wasn't so fortunate. If I concentrated, I could sense her life force, her *ka*, growing weaker. The luminous glow at the center of her chest was becoming smaller and more concentrated, like a flame reduced to a pilot light.

Meanwhile, our feline friend Bast was doing her best to

distract her old enemy. Over and over she jumped on the serpent's back, slashing with her knives and mewling in anger, but Apophis just shook her off, throwing her back into the storm.

Sadie scanned the area with alarm. "Where's Bes?"

The dwarf god had disappeared. I was beginning to fear the worst when a small grumpy voice near the edge of the storm called, "Some help, maybe?"

I hadn't paid much attention to the ruins around us. The plains of Giza were littered with big stone blocks, trenches, and old building foundations from previous excavations. Under a nearby car-sized wedge of limestone, the dwarf god's head was sticking out.

"Bes!" Sadie cried as we ran to his side. "Are you all right?"

He glared up at us. "Do I look all right, kid? I have a ten-ton block of limestone on my chest. Snake-breath over there knocked me flat and dropped this thing on top of me. Most blatant act of dwarf cruelty ever!"

"Can you move it?" I asked.

He gave me a look almost as ugly as his *Boo!* face. "Gee, Carter, I didn't think of that. It's so comfortable under here. *Of course* I can't move it, you dolt! Blocks of stone don't scare easily. Help a dwarf out, huh?"

"Stand back," I told Sadie.

I summoned the strength of Horus. Blue light encased my hand, and I karate-chopped the stone. It cracked right down the middle, falling on either side of the dwarf god.

It would've been more impressive if I hadn't yelped like a

puppy and cradled my fingers. Apparently I needed to work on the karate trick more, because my hand felt like it was boiling in oil. I was pretty sure I'd broken some bones in there.

"All right?" Sadie asked.

"Yeah," I lied.

Bes climbed to his feet. "Thanks, kid. Now it's time for some snake-bashing."

We ran to help Zia, which turned out to be a bad idea. She glanced over and saw us—and, just for a moment, she was distracted.

"Carter, thank the gods!" She spoke in two-part harmony—partly her, partly the deep commanding voice of Ra, which was a little hard to take. Call me close-minded, but hearing my girlfriend talk like a five-thousand-year-old male god was not on my top ten list of Things I Find Attractive. Still, I was so glad to see her, I almost didn't care.

She lobbed another fireball down the throat of Apophis. "You're just in time. Our snaky friend is getting stro—"

"Look out!" Sadie screamed.

This time, Apophis wasn't fazed by the fire. He struck immediately—and he didn't miss. His mouth hit like a wrecking ball.

When Apophis rose again, Zia was gone. There was a crater in the sand where she'd been standing, and a human-sized lump illuminated the snake's gullet from the inside, glowing as it traveled down his throat.

Sadie tells me that I went a little insane. Honestly, I don't remember. The next thing I can recall, my voice was raw from screaming, and I was staggering away from Apophis, my magic almost exhausted, my broken hand throbbing, my crook and flail smoking with red-gray ooze—the blood of Chaos.

Apophis had three gashes in his neck that weren't closing. Otherwise, he looked fine. It's hard to tell if a snake has an expression, but I was pretty sure he was gloating.

"As it was foretold!" He spoke aloud, and the earth shook. Cracks spread across the desert as if it had suddenly become thin ice. The sky turned black, lit only by stars and streaks of red lightning. The temperature began to drop. "You cannot cheat destiny, Carter Kane! I have swallowed Ra. Now the end of the world is at hand!"

Sadie fell to her knees and sobbed. Despair swept over me, worse than the cold. I felt Horus's power fail, and I was just Carter Kane again. All around us, in different levels of the Duat, gods and magicians stopped battling as terror spread through their ranks.

With catlike agility, Bast landed next to me, breathing hard. Her hair was puffed out so much, it looked like a sea urchin covered with sand. Her bodysuit was ripped and torn. She had a nasty bruise on the left side of her jaw. Her knives were steaming and pitted with corrosion from the serpent's poison.

"No," she said firmly. "No, no, no. What's our plan?"

"Plan?" I tried to make sense of her question. Zia was gone. We'd failed. The ancient prophecy had come true, and I would die knowing that I was a complete and utter loser. I looked at Sadie, but she seemed just as shell-shocked.

"Wake up, kid!" Bes waddled up to me and kicked me in the kneecap, which was as high as he could reach.

"Ow!" I protested.

"You're the leader now," he growled. "So you'd *better* have a plan. I didn't come back to life to get killed again!"

Apophis hissed. The ground continued to crack, shaking the foundations of the pyramids. The air was so cold, my breath turned to mist.

"Too late, poor children." The serpent's red eyes stared down at me. "Ma'at has been dying for centuries. Your world was only a temporary speck in the Sea of Chaos. All that you built meant nothing. *I* am your past and your future! Bow to me now, Carter Kane, and perhaps I will spare you and your sister. I will enjoy having survivors to witness my triumph. Is that not preferable to death?"

My limbs felt heavy. Somewhere inside, I was a scared little boy who wanted to live. I'd lost my parents. I'd been asked to fight a war that was *way* too big for me. Why should I keep going when it was hopeless? And if I could save Sadie . . .

Then I focused on the serpent's throat. The glow of the swallowed sun god sank lower and lower into Apophis's gullet. Zia had given her life to protect us.

Never fear, she'd said. *I will hold Apophis until you come.*

Anger cleared my thoughts. Apophis was trying to sway me, the way he'd corrupted Vlad Menshikov, Kwai, Sarah Jacobi, and even Set, the god of evil himself. Apophis was the master of eroding reason and order, of destroying everything that was good and admirable. He was selfish, and he wanted me to be selfish as well.

I remembered the white obelisk rising from the Sea of Chaos. It had stood for thousands of years, against all odds. It represented courage and civilization, making the right choice instead of the easy choice. If I failed today, that obelisk would finally crumble. Everything humans had built since the first pyramids of Egypt would be for nothing.

"Sadie," I said, "you have the shadow?"

She got to her feet, her shocked expression turning to rage. "I thought you'd never ask."

From her bag she produced the granite figurine, now midnight black with the shadow of Apophis.

The serpent recoiled, hissing. I thought I detected fear in his eyes.

"Don't be foolish," Apophis snarled. "That ridiculous spell will not work—not now, when I am triumphant! Besides, you are too weak. You would never survive the attempt."

Like all effective threats, it had the ring of truth. My magic reserves were nearly tapped out. Sadie's couldn't be much better. Even if the gods helped, we would likely burn ourselves up casting an execration.

"Ready?" Sadie asked me, her tone defiant.

"Attempt it," Apophis warned, "and I will raise your souls from Chaos again and again, just so I can kill you slowly. I will do the same for your father and mother. You will know an eternity of pain."

I felt like I'd swallowed one of Ra's fireballs. My fists clenched around the crook and flail, despite the throbbing pain in my hand. The power of Horus surged back into me— and once again we were in absolute agreement. I was his Eye. I *was* the Avenger.

"Mistake," I told the serpent. "You should *never* threaten my family."

I threw the crook and flail. They smashed into Apophis's face and erupted in a column of fire like a nuclear blast.

The serpent howled in pain, engulfed in flames and smoke; but I suspected I'd only bought us a few seconds.

"Sadie," I said, "are you ready?"

She nodded and offered me the figurine. Together, we held it and prepared for what might be the last spell of our lives. There was no need to consult a scroll. We'd been practicing for this execration for months. We both knew the words by heart. The only question was whether the shadow would make the difference. Once we started, there would be no stopping. And whether we failed or succeeded, we would probably burn up.

"Bes and Bast," I said, "can you two keep Apophis away from us?"

Bast smiled and hefted her knives. "Protect my kittens? You don't even need to ask." She glanced at Bes. "And in case we die, I'm sorry about all the times I toyed with your emotions. You deserved better."

Bes snorted. "That's okay. I finally came to my senses and found the right girl. Besides, you're a cat. It's your nature to think you're the center of the universe."

She stared at him blankly. "But I *am* the center of the universe."

Bes laughed. "Good luck, kids. Time to bring on the ugly."

"DEATH!" Apophis screamed, emerging from the column of fire with his eyes blazing.

Bast and Bes—the two greatest friends and protectors we'd ever had—charged to meet Apophis.

Sadie and I began the spell.

20. I Take a Chair

LIKE I SAID, I'M NOT GOOD WITH INCANTATIONS.

Doing one right requires unbroken concentration, correct pronunciation, and perfect timing. Otherwise you're liable to destroy yourself and everyone within ten feet, or turn yourself into some form of marsupial.

Trying to cast a spell with someone else—that's doubly hard.

Sure, Sadie and I had studied the words, but it's not like we could actually *do* the execration in advance. With a spell like that, you only get one shot.

As we began, I was aware of Bast and Bes battling the serpent, and our other allies locked in combat at different levels of the Duat. The temperature kept dropping. Crevices widened in the ground. Red lightning spread across the sky like cracks in a black dome.

It was hard to keep my teeth from chattering. I concentrated on the stone figurine of Apophis. As we chanted, the statue began to smoke.

I tried not to think about the last time I'd heard this incantation. Michel Desjardins had died casting it, and he had faced only a partial manifestation of the serpent, not Apophis at his full power after triumphantly devouring Ra.

Focus, Horus told me.

Easy for him to say. The noise, cold, and explosions around us made it almost impossible—like trying to count backward from a hundred while people scream random numbers in your ears.

Bast was thrown over our heads and landed against a stone block. Bes roared in anger. He slammed his club into the snake's neck so hard, Apophis's eyes rattled in his head.

Apophis snapped at Bes, who grabbed one fang and hung on for dear life as the serpent raised his head and shook his mouth, trying to dislodge the dwarf god.

Sadie and I continued to chant. The serpent's shadow steamed as the figurine heated up. Gold and blue light swirled around us as Isis and Horus did their best to shield us. Sweat stung my eyes. Despite the frosty air, I began to feel feverish.

When we came to the most important part of the spell—the naming of the enemy—I finally began to sense the true nature of the serpent's shadow. Funny how that works: sometimes you don't really understand something until you destroy it. The *sheut* was more than just a copy or a reflection, more than a "backup disk" for the soul.

A person's shadow stood for his legacy, his impact on the

world. Some people cast hardly any shadow at all. Some cast long, deep shadows that endured for centuries. I thought about what the ghost Setne had said—how he and I had each grown up in the shadow of a famous father. I realized now that he hadn't just meant it as a figure of speech. My dad cast a powerful shadow that still affected me and the whole world.

If a person cast no shadow at all, he couldn't be alive. His existence became meaningless. Execrating Apophis by destroying his shadow would cut his connection to the mortal world completely. He'd never be able to rise again. I finally understood why he'd been so anxious to burn Setne's scrolls, and why he was afraid of this spell.

We reached the last lines. Apophis dislodged Bes from his fang, and the dwarf sailed into the side of the Great Pyramid.

The serpent turned toward us as we spoke the final words: "We exile you beyond the void. You are no more."

"NO!" Apophis roared.

The statue flared, dissolving in our hands. The shadow disappeared in a puff of vapor, and an explosive wave of darkness knocked us off our feet.

The serpent's legacy on the earth shattered—the wars, murders, turmoil, and anarchy Apophis had caused since ancient times finally lost power, no longer casting their shadow across our future. Souls of the dead were expelled from the blast—thousands of ghosts that had been trapped and crushed within the shadow of Chaos. A voice whispered in my mind: *Carter*, and I sobbed with relief. I couldn't see her, but I knew that our mother was free. Her spirit was returning to its place in the Duat.

"Shortsighted mortals!" Apophis writhed and began to shrink. "You haven't just killed me. You've exiled the gods!"

The Duat collapsed, layer upon layer, until the plains of Giza were one reality again. Our magician friends stood in a daze around us. The gods, however, were nowhere to be seen.

The serpent hissed, his scales falling away in smoking pieces. "Ma'at and Chaos are linked, you fools! You cannot push me away without pushing away the gods. As for Ra, he shall die within me, slowly digested—"

He was cut short (literally) when his head exploded. Yes, it was just as gross as it sounds. Flaming bits of reptile flew everywhere. A ball of fire rolled up from the serpent's neck. The body of Apophis crumbled into sand and steaming goo, and Zia Rashid stepped out of the wreckage.

Her dress was in tatters. Her golden staff had cracked like a wishbone, but she was alive.

I ran toward her. She stumbled and collapsed against me, completely exhausted.

Then someone else rose from the smoking ruins of Apophis.

Ra shimmered like a mirage, towering over us as a muscular old man with golden skin, kingly robes, and the pharaoh's crown. He stepped forward and daylight returned to the sky. The temperature warmed. The cracks in the ground sealed themselves.

The sun god smiled down at me. "Well done, Carter and Sadie. Now, I must withdraw as the other gods have done, but I owe you my life."

"Withdraw?" My voice didn't sound like mine. It was deeper, more gravelly—but it wasn't Horus's voice either. The war god seemed to be gone from my mind. "You mean . . . forever?"

Ra chuckled. "When you're as old as I am, you learn to be careful with that word *forever*. I thought I was leaving forever the first time I abdicated. For a while, at least, I must retreat into the sky. My old enemy Apophis was not wrong. When Chaos is pushed away, the gods of order, Ma'at, must also distance themselves. Such is the balance of the universe."

"Then . . . you should take these." Again I offered him the crook and flail.

Ra shook his head. "Keep them for me. You are the rightful pharaoh. And take care of my favored one . . ." He nodded at Zia. "She will recover, but she will need support."

Light blazed around the sun god. When it faded, he was gone. Two dozen weary magicians stood around a smoking, serpent-shaped mark in the desert as the sun rose over the pyramids of Giza.

Sadie rested her hand on my arm. "Brother, dear?"

"Yeah?"

"That was a bit too close."

For once, I had no argument with my sister.

The rest of the day was a blur. I remember helping Zia to the healing rooms of the First Nome. My own broken hand took only minutes to fix, but I stayed with Zia until Jaz told me I needed to go. She and the other healers had dozens of wounded magicians to treat—including the Russian kid Leonid, who, amazingly, was expected to pull through—and while Jaz thought I was very sweet, I was very much in the way.

I wandered through the main cavern and was shocked to see it full of people. Portals around the world had started working again. Magicians were flooding in to help with cleanup and pledge their support to the Chief Lector. Everybody loves to show up at the party once all the hard work is done.

I tried not to feel bitter about it. I knew that many of the other nomes had been fighting their own battles. Apophis had done his best to divide and conquer us. Still, it left a bad taste in my mouth. Many people stared in awe at Ra's crook and flail, which still hung from my belt. A few people congratulated me and called me a hero. I kept walking.

As I passed the staff vendor's cart, someone said, *"Psssst!"*

I glanced toward the nearest alley. The ghost Setne was leaning against the wall. I was so startled, I thought I must be hallucinating. He couldn't possibly be here, still in his horrible jacket and jewelry and jeans, his Elvis hair perfectly combed, the Book of Thoth tucked under his arm.

"You did good, pal," he called. "Not the way I would've handled it, but not bad."

Finally I unfroze. *"Tas!"*

Setne just grinned. "Yeah, we're done playing that game. But don't worry, pal. I'll see you around."

He disappeared in a puff of smoke.

I'm not sure how long I stood there before Sadie found me.

"All right?" she asked.

I told her what I'd seen. She winced, but didn't look very surprised. "I suppose we'll have to deal with that git sooner or later, but for now, you'd best come with me. Amos has called a general assembly in the Hall of Ages." She slipped her arm through mine. "And try to smile, brother dear. I know it's hard. But you're a role model now, as horrifying as I find that."

I did my best, though it was difficult to put Setne out of my mind.

We passed several of our friends helping with the restoration. Alyssa and a squad of earth elementalists were reinforcing walls and ceilings, trying to make sure the caverns didn't collapse on us.

Julian was sitting on the steps of the Scrying House, chatting up a few girls from the Scandinavian nome. "Yeah, you know," he was telling them, "Apophis saw me coming with my big combat avatar, and he pretty much knew it was over."

Sadie rolled her eyes and pulled me along.

Little Shelby and the other ankle-biters ran up to us, grinning and breathless. They'd helped themselves to some charms from one of the unmanned shopping kiosks, so they looked like they'd just come back from Egyptian Mardi Gras.

"I killed a snake!" Shelby told us. "A big snake!"

"Really?" I asked. "All by yourself?"

"Yes!" Shelby assured me. "Kill, kill, kill!" She stomped her feet, and sparks flew from her shoes. Then she ran off, chasing her friends.

"That girl has a future," Sadie said. "Reminds me of myself when I was young."

I shuddered. What a disturbing thought.

Gongs began ringing throughout the tunnels, summoning

everyone to the Hall of Ages. By the time we got there, the hall was absolutely jammed with magicians—some in robes, some in modern clothes, some in pajamas like they'd teleported straight from bed. On either side of the carpet, holographic curtains of light shimmered between the columns just as they had before.

Felix ran up to us, all smiles, with a herd of penguins behind him. (Herd? Flock? Gaggle? Oh, whatever.)

"Check it out!" he said happily. "I learned this one during the battle!"

He spoke a command word. At first I thought it was *shish kebab*, but later he told me it was: *"Se-kebeb!"*—Make cold.

Hieroglyphs appeared on the floor in frosty white:

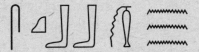

The chill spread until a twenty-foot-wide section of the floor was coated in thick white ice. The penguins waddled across it, flapping their wings. One unfortunate magician stepped back and slipped so badly, his staff went flying.

Felix pumped his fist. "Yes! I found my path. I'm supposed to follow the god of ice!"

I scratched my head. "There's a god of ice? Egypt is a desert. Who's the ice god?"

"I have no idea!" Felix beamed. He slid across the ice and went running off with his penguins.

We made our way down the hall. Magicians were trading stories, mingling, and checking in with old friends. Hieroglyphs floated through the air, brighter and thicker than I'd ever seen, like a rainbow alphabet soup.

Finally the crowd noticed Sadie and me. A hush spread through the room. All eyes turned toward us. The magicians parted, clearing the way to the throne.

Most of the magicians smiled as we walked past. A few whispered thanks and congratulations. Even the former rebel magicians seemed genuinely pleased to see us. But I did catch a few angry looks. No matter that we'd defeated Apophis; some of our fellow magicians would always doubt us. Some would never stop hating us. The Kane family still needed to watch our backs.

Sadie scanned the crowd anxiously. I realized she was looking for Walt. I'd been so focused on Zia, I hadn't thought about how worried Sadie must be. Walt had disappeared after the battle, along with the rest of the gods. He didn't seem to be here now.

"I'm sure he's fine," I told her.

"Shh." Sadie smiled at me, but her eyes said: *If you embarrass me in front of all these people, I will strangle you.*

Amos waited for us at the steps of the throne. He'd changed into a crimson suit that went surprisingly well with his leopard-skin cape. His hair was braided with garnets, and his glasses were tinted red. The color of Chaos? I got the feeling he was playing up his connection to Set—which all the other magicians had definitely heard about by now.

For the first time in history, our Chief Lector had the god of evil, strength, and Chaos on speed dial. That might make people trust him less, but magicians were like the gods—they respected strength. I doubted Amos would have much trouble enforcing his rule anymore.

He smiled as we approached. "Carter and Sadie, on behalf of the House of Life, I thank you. You have restored Ma'at! Apophis has been execrated, and Ra has once again risen into the heavens, but this time in triumph. Well done!"

The hall erupted in cheering and applause. Dozens of magicians raised their staffs and sent up miniature firework displays.

Amos embraced us. Then he stepped aside and gestured me toward the throne. I hoped that Horus might give me some words of encouragement, but I couldn't feel his presence at all.

I tried to control my breathing. That chair had been empty for thousands of years. How could I be sure it would even hold my weight? If the throne of the pharaohs broke under my royal butt, that would be a great omen.

Sadie nudged me. "Go on, then. Don't be stupid."

I climbed the steps and eased myself onto the throne. The old chair creaked, but it held me.

I gazed out over the crowd of magicians.

Horus wasn't there for me. But somehow, that was okay. I glanced over at the shimmering curtains of light—the New Age, glowing purple—and I had a feeling it was going to be an age of good things, after all.

My muscles began to relax. I felt like I'd stepped out of the war god's shadow, just as I'd stepped out of my father's. I found the words.

"I accept the throne." I held up the crook and flail. "Ra has given me authority to lead the gods and magicians in times of crisis, and I'll do my best. Apophis has been banished, but the Sea of Chaos is always there. I've seen it with my own eyes. Its forces will always try to erode Ma'at. We can't think that all our enemies are gone."

The crowd stirred nervously.

"But for now," I added, "we are at peace. We can rebuild and expand the House of Life. If war comes again, I'll be here as the Eye of Horus and as pharaoh. But as Carter Kane . . ."

I rose and placed the crook and flail on the throne. I stepped down from the dais. "As Carter Kane, I'm a kid who has a lot of catching up to do. I've got my own nome to run at Brooklyn House. And I've got to graduate from high school. So I'm going to leave day-to-day operations where they should be—in the hands of the Chief Lector, steward of the pharaoh, Amos Kane."

Amos bowed to me, which felt a little strange. The crowd applauded wildly. I wasn't sure if they approved of me, or if they were just relieved that a kid wasn't going to be giving them daily orders from the throne. Either way, I was okay with it.

Amos embraced Sadie and me again.

"I'm proud of you both," he said. "We'll speak soon, but right now, come . . ." He gestured to the side of the dais, where a door of darkness had opened in the air. "Your parents would like to see you."

Sadie looked at me nervously. "Uh-oh."

I nodded. Strange how I went instantly from the pharaoh

of the universe to a kid worried about getting grounded. As much as I wanted to see my parents, I'd broken an important promise to my father . . . I'd lost track of a dangerous prisoner.

The Hall of Judgment had turned into Party Central. Ammit the Devourer ran around the scales of justice, yapping excitedly with a birthday hat on his crocodile head. The guillotine-headed demons lounged on their pole arms, holding glasses of what looked like champagne. I didn't know how they could drink with those guillotine heads, but I didn't want to find out. Even the blue judgment god Disturber seemed to be in a good mood. His Cleopatra wig was sideways on his head. His long scroll had unraveled halfway across the room, but he was laughing and talking with the other judgment gods who had been rescued from the House of Rest. Fire-embracer and Hot Foot kept dropping cinders on his papyrus, but Disturber didn't seem to notice or care.

At the far end of the room, Dad sat on his throne, holding hands with our ghostly mom. To the left of the dais, spirits from the Underworld played in a jazz ensemble. I was pretty sure I recognized Miles Davis, John Coltrane, and a few of my dad's other favorites. Being the god of the Underworld has its perks.

Dad beckoned us forward. He didn't look mad, which was a good sign. We made our way through the crowd of happy demons and judgment gods. Ammit yapped at Sadie and purred as she scratched under his chin.

"Children." Dad held out his arms.

It felt strange being called children. I didn't feel like a child anymore. Children weren't asked to fight Chaos serpents. They didn't lead armies to stop the end of the world.

Sadie and I both hugged our dad. I couldn't hug Mom, of course, since she was a ghost, but I was happy enough to see her safe. Except for the glowing aura around her, she looked just like she did when she was alive—dressed in jeans and her *ankh* T-shirt, her blond hair gathered back in a bandana. If I didn't look directly at her, I could have almost mistaken her for Sadie.

"Mom, you survived," I said. "How—?"

"All thanks to you two." Mom's eyes sparkled. "I held on as long as I could, but the shadow was too powerful. I was consumed, along with so many other spirits. If you hadn't destroyed the *sheut* when you did and released us, I would've been . . . well, it doesn't matter now. You've done the impossible. We are so proud."

"Yes," Dad agreed, squeezing my shoulder. "Everything we've worked for, everything we've hoped for—you have accomplished. You've exceeded my highest expectations."

I hesitated. Was it possible he didn't know about Setne?

"Dad," I said, "um . . . we didn't succeed at *everything*. We lost your prisoner. I still don't understand how he escaped. He was tied up and—"

Dad raised his hand to stop me. "I heard. We may never know how Setne escaped exactly, but you can't blame yourselves."

"We can't?" Sadie asked.

"Setne has evaded capture for eons," Dad said. "He's outwitted gods, magicians, mortals, and demons. When I let you take him, I suspected he would find a way to escape. I just hoped you could control him long enough to get his help. And you did."

"He got us to the shadow," I admitted. "But he also stole the Book of Thoth."

Sadie bit her lip. "Dangerous stuff, that book. Setne may not be able to cast all the spells himself, being a ghost, but he could still cause all sorts of mischief."

"We will find him again," Dad promised. "But for now, let's celebrate your victory."

Our mom reached out and brushed her ghostly hand through Sadie's hair. "May I borrow you a moment, my dear? I have something I'd like to discuss with you."

I wasn't sure what that was about, but Sadie followed our mom toward the jazz band. I hadn't noticed before, but two of the ghostly musicians looked very familiar, and rather out of place. A big redheaded man in Western clothes sat at a steel guitar, grinning and tapping his boots as he traded solos with Miles Davis. Next to him, a pretty blond woman played the fiddle, leaning down from time to time to kiss the redheaded man on the forehead. JD Grissom and his wife, Anne, from the Dallas Museum, had finally found a party that didn't have to end. I'd never heard steel guitar and fiddle with a jazz band before, but somehow they made it work. I suppose Amos was right: music and magic both needed a little chaos within the order.

As Mom and Sadie talked, Sadie's eyes widened. Her expression turned serious. Then she smiled shyly and blushed, which wasn't like Sadie at all.

"Carter," my dad said, "you did well in the Hall of Ages. You will make a good leader. A wise leader."

I wasn't sure how he knew about my speech, but a lump formed in my throat. My dad doesn't hand out compliments lightly. Being with him again, I remembered how much easier life had been, traveling with him. He'd always known what to do. I could always count on his calming presence. Until that Christmas Eve in London when he had disappeared, I hadn't appreciated just how much I had relied on him.

"I know it's been hard," Dad said, "but you will lead the Kane family into the future. You have truly stepped out of my shadow."

"Not completely," I said. "I wouldn't want that. As dads go, you're pretty, um, shadowy."

He laughed. "I'll be here if you need me. Never doubt that. But, as Ra said, the gods will have a harder time contacting the mortal world, now that Apophis has been execrated. As Chaos retreats, so must Ma'at. Nevertheless, I don't think you'll *need* much help. You've succeeded on your own strength. Now *you* are the one casting the long shadow. The House of Life will remember you for ages to come."

He hugged me once more, and it was easy to forget that he was the god of the dead. He just seemed like my dad—warm and alive and strong.

Sadie came over, looking a little shaken.

"What?" I asked.

She giggled for no apparent reason, then got serious again. "Nothing."

Mom drifted next to her. "Off you go, you two. Brooklyn House is waiting."

Another door of darkness appeared by the throne. Sadie and I stepped through. For once I wasn't worried about what waited on the other side. I knew we were going home.

Life got back to normal with surprising speed.

I'll let Sadie tell you about the events at Brooklyn House and her own drama. I'll fast-forward to the interesting stuff.

[Ouch! I thought we agreed: no pinching!]

Two weeks after the battle with Apophis, Zia and I were sitting in the food court at the Mall of America in Bloomington, Minnesota.

Why there? I'd heard the Mall of America was the biggest in the country, and I figured we'd start big. It was an easy trip through the Duat. Freak was happy to sit on the roof and eat frozen turkeys while Zia and I explored the mall.

[That's right, Sadie. For our first real date, I picked up Zia in a boat pulled by a deranged griffin. So what? Like *your* dates aren't weird?]

Anyway, when we got to the food court, Zia's jaw dropped. "Gods of Egypt . . ."

The restaurant choices were pretty overwhelming. Since we couldn't decide, we got a little of everything: Chinese, Mexican (the Macho Nachos), pizza, and ice cream—the four basic food groups. We grabbed a table overlooking the amusement park at the center of the mall.

A lot of other kids were hanging out in the food court. Many of them stared at us. Well . . . not at *me*. They were mostly looking at Zia and no doubt wondering what a girl like her was doing with a guy like me.

She'd healed up nicely since the battle. She wore a simple sleeveless dress of beige linen and black sandals—no makeup, no jewelry except for her gold scarab necklace. She looked way more glamorous and mature than the other girls in the mall.

Her long black hair was tied back in a ponytail, except for a little strand that curled behind her right ear. She'd always had luminous amber eyes and warm coffee-and-milk skin, but since hosting Ra, she seemed to glow even more. I could feel her warmth from across the table.

She smiled at me over her bowl of chow mein. "So, this is what typical American teenagers do?"

"Well . . . sort of," I said. "Though I don't think either of us will ever pass for *typical*."

"I hope not."

I had trouble thinking straight when I looked at her. If she'd asked me to jump over the railing, I probably would've done it.

Zia twirled her fork through her noodles. "Carter, we haven't talked much about . . . you know, my being the Eye of Ra. I can guess how strange that was for you."

See? Just your typical teenage conversation in the mall.

"Hey, I understand," I said. "It wasn't strange."

She raised an eyebrow.

"Okay, it was strange," I admitted. "But Ra needed your help. You were amazing. Have you, uh, talked to him since . . . ?"

She shook her head. "He's retreated from the world, just like he said. I doubt I'll be the Eye of Ra again—unless we face another Doomsday."

"So, with our luck, not for a few more weeks, you mean."

Zia laughed. I loved her laugh. I loved that little curl of hair behind her ear.

(Sadie says I'm being ridiculous. Like she's one to talk.)

"I had a meeting with your Uncle Amos," Zia said. "He has lots of help at the First Nome now. He thought it would be good for me to spend some time away, try to live a more . . . typical life."

My heart tripped and stumbled straight into my ribs. "You mean, like, leave Egypt?"

Zia nodded. "Your sister suggested I stay at Brooklyn House, attend American school. She says . . . how did she put it? *Americans are an odd bunch, but they grow on you.*"

Zia scooted around the table and took my hand. I sensed about twenty jealous guys glaring at me from the other tables of the food court.

"Would you mind if I stayed in Brooklyn House? I could help teach the initiates. But if that would make you uncomfortable—"

"No!" I said much too loudly. "I mean, no, I don't mind. Yes, I'd like that. A lot. Quite a bit. Totally fine."

Zia smiled. The temperature in the food court seemed to go up another ten degrees. "So that's a yes?"

"Yes. I mean, unless it would make *you* uncomfortable. I wouldn't want to make things awkward or—"

"Carter?" she said gently. "Shut up."

She leaned over and kissed me.

I did as she commanded, no magic necessary. I shut up.

21. The Gods Are Sorted; My Feelings Are Not

AH, MY THREE FAVORITE WORDS: *Carter, shut up.*

Zia really has come a long way since we first met. I think there's hope for her, even if she does fancy my brother.

At any rate, Carter has wisely left the last bit of the story for me to tell.

After the battle with Apophis, I felt horrible on many levels. Physically, I was knackered. Magically, I'd used up every last bit of energy. I was afraid I might have permanently damaged myself, as I had a smoldering feeling behind my sternum that was either my exhausted magic reservoir or very bad heartburn.

Emotionally, I wasn't much better. I had watched Carter embrace Zia when she emerged from the steaming goo of the serpent, which was all very well, but it only reminded me of my own turmoil.

Where was Walt? (I'd decided to call him that, or I would

drive myself crazy figuring out his identity.) He had been standing nearby just after the battle. Now he was gone.

Had he left with the other gods? I was already worried about Bes and Bast. It wasn't like them to disappear without saying good-bye. And I wasn't keen on what Ra had said about the gods leaving the earth for a while.

You cannot push me away without pushing away the gods, Apophis had warned.

The bloody serpent might have mentioned that *before* we execrated him. I had just made my peace with the whole Walt/Anubis idea—or *mostly,* at any rate—and now Walt had vanished. If he'd been declared off-limits again, I was going to crawl into a sarcophagus and never come out.

While Carter was with Zia in the infirmary, I wandered the corridors of the First Nome, but found no sign of Walt. I tried to contact him with the *shen* amulet. No answer. I even tried to contact Isis for advice, but the goddess had gone silent. I didn't like that.

So, yes, I was quite distracted in the Hall of Ages during Carter's little acceptance speech: *I'd like to thank all the little people for making me pharaoh, et cetera, et cetera.*

I was glad to visit the Underworld and be reunited with my mum and dad. At least *they* weren't off-limits. But I was quite disappointed not to find Walt there. Even if he wasn't allowed in the mortal world, shouldn't he be in the Hall of Judgment, taking over the duties of Anubis?

That's when my mother pulled me aside. (Not literally, of course. Being a ghost, she couldn't pull me anywhere.) We stood to the left of the dais where the dead musicians played lively music. JD Grissom and his wife, Anne, smiled at me. They seemed happy, and I was glad for that, but I still had trouble seeing them without feeling guilty.

My mum tugged at her necklace—a ghostly replica of my own *tyet* amulet. "Sadie . . . we've never gotten to talk much, you and I."

Bit of an understatement, since she died when I was six. I understood what she meant, though. Even after our reunion last spring, she and I had never really chatted. Visiting her in the Duat was rather hard, and ghosts don't have e-mail or Skype or mobile phones. Even if they had had a proper Internet connection, "friending" my dead mother on Facebook would have felt rather odd.

I didn't say any of that. I just nodded.

"You've grown strong, Sadie," Mum said. "You've had to be brave for so long, it must be hard for you to let your defenses down. You're afraid to lose any more people you care about."

I felt lightheaded, as if I were turning into a ghost, too. Had I become see-through, like my mother? I wanted to argue and protest and joke. I didn't want to hear my mother's commentary, especially when it was so accurate.

At the same time, I was so mixed up inside about Walt, so worried about what had happened to him, I wanted to break down and cry on my mother's shoulder. I wanted her to hug me and tell me it was all right. Unfortunately, one can't cry on the shoulder of a ghost.

"I know," Mum said sadly, as if reading my thoughts. "I

wasn't there for you when you were small. And your father . . . well, he had to leave you with Gran and Gramps. They tried to provide you with a normal life, but you're so much *more* than normal, aren't you? And now here you are, a young woman. . . ." She sighed. "I've missed so much of your life, I don't know if you'll want my advice now. But for what it's worth: trust your feelings. I can't promise that you'll never get hurt again, but I can promise you the risk is worth it."

I studied her face, unchanged since the day she had died: her wispy blond hair, her blue eyes, the rather mischievous curve of her eyebrows. Many times, I'd been told that I looked like her. Now I could see it clearly. As I'd got older, it was quite striking how much our faces looked alike. Put some purple highlights in her hair, and Mum would've made an excellent Sadie stunt double.

"You're talking about Walt," I said at last. "This is a heart-to-heart chat about *boys*?"

Mum winced. "Yes, well . . . I'm afraid I'm rubbish at this. But I had to try. When I was a girl, Gran wasn't much of a resource for me. I never felt I could talk to her."

"I should think not." I tried to imagine talking about guys with my grandmother while Gramps yelled at the telly and called for more tea and burnt biscuits.

"I think," I ventured, "that mothers normally warn *against* following one's heart, getting involved with the wrong sort of boy, getting a bad reputation. That sort of thing."

"Ah." Mum nodded contritely. "Well, you see, I can't do that. I suppose I'm not worried about you doing the wrong thing, Sadie. I *am* worried that you might be afraid to trust someone—even the right someone. It's *your* heart, of course. Not mine. But I'd say Walt is more nervous than you are. Don't be too hard on him."

"Hard on *him?*" I almost laughed. "I don't even know where he is! And he's hosting a god who—who—"

"Whom you also like," Mum supplied. "And that's confusing, yes. But they are really one person, now. Anubis has so much in common with Walt. Neither has ever had a real life to look forward to. Now, together, they do."

"You mean . . ." The horrible burning sensation behind my sternum began to ease, ever so slightly. "You mean I *will* see him again? He's not exiled, or whatever nonsense the gods are going on about?"

"You will see him," my mother affirmed. "Because they are one, inhabiting a single mortal body, they may walk the earth, as the Ancient Egyptian god-kings did. Walt and Anubis are both good young men. They are both nervous, and quite awkward in the mortal world, and scared about how people will treat them. And they both feel the same way about you."

I was probably blushing terribly. Carter stared at me from the top of the dais, no doubt wondering what was wrong. I didn't trust myself to meet his eyes. He was a bit too good at reading my expression.

"It's so bloody *hard,*" I complained.

Mother laughed softly. "Yes, it is. But if it's any consolation . . . dealing with *any* man means dealing with multiple personalities."

I glanced up at my father, who was flickering back and forth between Dr. Julius Kane and Osiris, the Smurf-blue god of the Underworld.

"I take your point," I said. "But where *is* Anubis? I mean Walt. Ugh! There I go again."

"You will see him soon," Mum promised. "I wanted you to be prepared."

My mind said: *This is too confusing, too unfair. I can't handle a relationship like this.*

But my heart said: *Shut up! Yes, I can!*

"Thanks, Mum," I said, no doubt failing miserably to look calm and collected. "This business with the gods pulling away. Does that mean we won't see you and Dad as much?"

"Probably," she admitted. "But you know what to do. Keep teaching the path of the gods. Bring the House of Life back to its former glory. You and Carter and Amos will make Egyptian magic stronger than ever. And that's good . . . because your challenges are not over."

"Setne?" I guessed.

"Yes, him," Mum said. "But there are other challenges as well. I haven't completely lost the gift of prophecy, even in death. I see murky visions of other gods and rival magic."

That *really* didn't sound good.

"What do you mean?" I asked. "What *other gods*?"

"I don't know, Sadie. But Egypt has always faced challenges from outside—magicians from elsewhere, even gods from elsewhere. Just be vigilant."

"Lovely," I muttered. "I preferred talking about boys."

Mother laughed. "Once you return to the mortal world, there will be one more portal. Look for it tonight. Some old friends of yours would like a word."

I had a feeling I knew whom she meant.

She touched a ghostly pendant around her neck—the *tyet* symbol of Isis.

"If you need me," Mum said, "use your necklace. It will call to me, just as the *shen* necklace calls to Walt."

"That would've been handy to know sooner."

"Our connection wasn't strong enough before. Now . . . I think it is." She kissed my forehead, though it felt like only a faint cool breeze. "I'm proud of you, Sadie. You have your whole life ahead of you. Make the most of it!"

That night at Brooklyn House, a swirling sand portal opened on the terrace, just as my mother had promised.

"That's for us," I said, getting up from the dinner table. "Come on, brother, dear."

On the other side of the portal, we found ourselves at the beach by the Lake of Fire. Bast was waiting, tossing a ball of yarn from hand to hand. Her pure black bodysuit matched her hair. Her feline eyes danced in the red light of the waves.

"They're waiting for you." She pointed up the steps to the House of Rest. "We'll talk when you come back down."

I didn't need to ask why she wasn't coming. I heard the melancholy in her voice. She and Tawaret had never got along because of Bes. Obviously, Bast wanted to give the hippo goddess some space. But also, I wondered if my old friend was starting to realize that she'd let a good man get away.

I kissed her on the cheek. Then Carter and I climbed the stairs.

Inside the nursing home, the atmosphere was festive. Fresh flowers decorated the nurses' station. Heket the frog goddess walked upside down along the ceiling, hanging party streamers, while a group of elderly dog-headed gods danced and sang the hokey-pokey—a very slow version, but still impressive. *You put your walker in / you put your IV out*—and so forth. The ancient lion-headed goddess Mekhit was slow-dancing with a tall male god. She purred loudly with her head on his shoulder.

"Carter, look," I said. "Is that—?"

"Onuris!" Tawaret answered, trotting over in her nurse's outfit. "Mekhit's husband! Isn't it wonderful? We were sure he'd faded ages ago, but when Bes called the old gods to war, Onuris came tottering out of a supply closet. Many others appeared too. They were finally needed, you see! The war gave them a reason to exist."

The hippo goddess crushed us in an enthusiastic hug. "Oh, my dears! Just look how happy everyone is! You've given them new life."

"I don't see as many as before," Carter noticed.

"Some went back to the heavens," Tawaret said. "Or off to their old temples and palaces. And, of course, your dear father, Osiris, took the judgment gods back to his throne room."

Seeing the old gods so happy warmed my heart, but I still felt a twinge of worry. "Will they stay this way? I mean, they won't fade again?"

Tawaret spread her stubby hands. "I suppose that depends on you mortals. If you remember them and make them feel important, they should be fine. But come, you'll want to see Bes!"

He sat in his usual chair, staring blankly out the window at the Lake of Fire. The scene was so familiar, I feared he'd lost his *ren* again.

"Is he all right?" I cried, running up to him. "What's wrong with him?"

Bes turned, looking startled. "Besides being ugly? Nothing, kid. I was just thinking—sorry."

He rose (as much as a dwarf can rise) and hugged us both.

"Glad you kids could make it," Bes said. "You know Tawaret and I are going to build a home on the lakeside. I've gotten used to this view. She'll keep working at the House of Rest. I'll be a house dwarf for a while. Who knows? Maybe I'll get some little dwarf hippo babies to look after!"

"Oh, Bes!" Tawaret blushed fiercely and batted her hippo eyelids.

The dwarf god chuckled. "Yeah, life is good. But if you kids need me, just holler. I've always had more luck coming to the mortal world than most gods."

Carter scowled fretfully. "Do you think we'll need you a lot? I mean, of course we want to see you! I just wondered—"

Bes grunted. "Hey, I'm an ugly dwarf. I've got a sweet car, an excellent wardrobe, and amazing powers. Why *wouldn't* you need me?"

"Good point," Carter agreed.

"But, uh, don't call *too* often," Bes said. "After all, my

honeycakes and I got a few millennia of quality time to catch up on."

He took Tawaret's hand, and for once I didn't find the name of this place—Sunny Acres—quite so depressing.

"Thank you for everything, Bes," I said.

"Are you kidding?" he said. "You gave me my life back, and I don't just mean my shadow."

I got the distinct feeling the two gods wanted some time by themselves, so we said our good-byes and headed down the steps to the lake.

The white sand portal was still swirling. Bast stood next to it, engrossed in her ball of yarn. She laced it between her fingers to make a rectangle like a cat's cradle. (No, I didn't mean that as a pun, but it *did* seem appropriate.)

"Having fun?" I asked.

"Thought you'd want to see this." She held up the cat's cradle. A video image flickered across its surface like on a computer screen.

I saw the Hall of the Gods with its soaring columns and polished floors, its braziers burning with a hundred multicolored fires. On the central dais, the sun boat had been replaced with a golden throne. Horus sat there in his human form—a bald muscular teen in full battle armor. He held a crook and flail across his lap, and his eyes gleamed—one silver, one gold. At his right stood Isis, smiling proudly, her rainbow wings shimmering. On his left stood Set, the red-skinned Chaos god with his iron staff. He looked quite amused, as if he had all sorts of wicked things planned for later. The other gods knelt as

Horus addressed them. I scanned the crowd for Anubis—with or without Walt—but again, I didn't see him.

I couldn't hear the words, but I reckoned it was a similar speech to the one Carter had delivered to the House of Life.

"He's doing the same thing I did," Carter protested. "I bet he even stole my speech. That copycat!"

Bast clucked disapprovingly. "No need to call names, Carter. Cats are not copiers. We are all unique. But, yes, what you do as pharaoh in the mortal world will often be mirrored in the world of the gods. Horus and you, after all, rule the forces of Egypt."

"That," I said, "is a truly scary thought."

Carter swatted me lightly on the arm. "I just can't believe that Horus left without even a good-bye. It's as if he tossed me aside as soon as he was done using me, and then forgot about me."

"Oh, no," Bast said. "Gods wouldn't do that. He simply had to leave."

But I wondered. Gods were rather selfish creatures, even those who weren't cats. Isis hadn't given me a proper good-bye or thank-you either.

"Bast, you're coming with us, aren't you?" I pleaded. "I mean, this silly exile can't apply to you! We need our nap instructor at Brooklyn House."

Bast wadded up her ball of yarn and tossed it down the steps. Her expression was quite sad for a feline. "Oh, my kittens. If I could, I would pick you up by the scruffs of your necks and carry you forever. But you've grown. Your claws are sharp, your eyesight is keen, and cats must make their own way in the world. I must say farewell for now, though I'm sure we'll meet again."

I wanted to protest that I hadn't grown up and I didn't even have claws.

(Carter disagrees, but what does he know?)

But part of me knew Bast was right. We'd been lucky to have her with us for so long. Now we had to be adult cats—er, humans.

"Oh, Muffin . . ." I hugged her fiercely, and could feel her purring.

She ruffled my hair. Then she rubbed Carter's ears, which was quite funny.

"Go on, now," she said. "Before I start to mewl. Besides . . ." She fixed her eyes on the ball of yarn, which had rolled to the bottom of the steps. She crouched and tensed her shoulders. "I have some hunting to do."

"We'll miss you, Bast," I said, trying not to cry. "Good hunting."

"Yarn," she said absently, creeping down the steps. "Dangerous prey, yarn . . ."

Carter and I stepped through the portal. This time it deposited us onto the roof of Brooklyn House.

We had one more surprise. Standing by Freak's roost, Walt was waiting. He smiled when he saw me, and my legs felt wobbly.

"I'll, um, be inside," Carter said.

Walt walked over, and I tried to remember how to breathe.

22. The Last Waltz (for Now)

HE'D CHANGED HIS LOOK AGAIN.

His amulets were gone except for one—the *shen* that matched mine. He wore a black muscle shirt, black jeans, a black leather duster, and black combat boots—a sort of mix of Anubis's and Walt's styles, but it made him look like someone entirely different and new. Yet his eyes were quite familiar—warm, dark brown, and lovely. When he smiled, my heart fluttered as it always had.

"So," I said, "is this another good-bye? I've had quite enough good-byes today."

"Actually," Walt said, "it's more of a hello. My name's Walt Stone, from Seattle. I'd like to join the party."

He held out his hand, still smiling slyly. He was repeating exactly what he'd said the first time we met, when he arrived at Brooklyn House last spring.

Instead of taking his hand, I punched him in the chest.

"Ow," he complained. But I doubt that I'd hurt him. He had quite a solid chest.

"You think you can just merge with a god and *surprise* me like that?" I demanded. "*Oh, by the way, I'm actually two minds in one body.* I don't appreciate being taken off guard."

"I did try to tell you," he said. "Several times. Anubis did too. We kept getting interrupted. Mostly by you talking a lot."

"No excuse." I folded my arms and scowled as best I could. "My mum seems to think I should go easy on you because this is all very new to you. But I'm still cross. It's confusing enough, you know, liking someone, without their morphing into a *god* whom I also like."

"So you do like me."

"Stop trying to distract me! Are you truly asking to stay here?"

Walt nodded. He was very close now. He smelled good, like vanilla candles. I tried to remember if that was Walt's scent or Anubis's. Honestly, I couldn't recall.

"I've still got a lot to learn," he said. "I don't need to stick with charm-making anymore. I can do more intensive magic—the path of Anubis. No one's ever done that before."

"Discovering new magical ways to annoy me?"

He tilted his head. "I could do amazing tricks with mummy linen. For instance, if someone talks too much, I could summon a gag—".

"Don't you dare!"

He took my hand. I gave him a defiant scowl, but I didn't take back my hand.

"I'm still Walt," he said. "I'm still mortal. Anubis can stay in this world as long as I'm his host. I'm hoping to live a good long life. Neither of us ever thought that was possible. So I'm not going anywhere, unless you want me to leave."

My eyes probably answered for me: *No, please. Not ever.* But I couldn't very well give him the satisfaction of my saying that out loud, could I? Boys can get so full of themselves.

"Well," I grumbled, "I suppose I could tolerate it."

"I owe you a dance." Walt put his other hand on my waist—a traditional pose, very old-fashioned, as Anubis had done when we waltzed at the Brooklyn Academy. My Gran would've approved.

"May I?" he asked.

"Here?" I said. "Won't your chaperone Shu interrupt?"

"Like I said, I'm mortal now. He'll let us dance, though I'm sure he's keeping an eye on us to make sure we behave."

"To make sure *you* behave," I snipped. "I'm a proper young lady."

Walt laughed. I supposed it was funny. *Proper* wasn't the first word normally used to describe me.

I pounded his chest again, though I'll admit not very hard. I put my hand on his shoulder.

"I'll have you remember," I warned, "that my father is your employer in the Underworld. You'd best mind your manners."

"Yes, ma'am," Walt said. He leaned down and kissed me. All my anger melted into my shoes.

We started to dance. There was no music, no ghostly dancers, no floating on air—nothing magic about it. Freak watched us curiously, no doubt wondering how this activity was going to produce turkeys to feed the griffin. The old tar roof creaked under our feet. I was still quite tired from our long battle, and I hadn't cleaned up properly. No doubt I looked horrid. I wanted to melt into Walt's arms, which is basically what I did.

"So you'll let me stick around?" he asked, his breath warm on my scalp. "Let me experience a typical teenage life?"

"I suppose." I looked up at him. It took no effort at all to slip my vision into the Duat and see Anubis there, just under the surface. But it really wasn't necessary. This was a new boy in front of me, and he was everything I liked. "Not that I'm an expert myself, but there is one rule I insist on."

"Yes?"

"If anyone asks you if you're taken," I said, "the answer is *yes*."

"I think I can live with that," he promised.

"Good," I said. "Because you don't want to see me be cross."

"Too late."

"Shut up and dance, Walt."

We did—with the music of a psychotic griffin screaming behind us, and the sirens and horns of Brooklyn wailing below. It was quite romantic.

So there you have it.

We've returned to Brooklyn House. The various catastrophes plaguing the world have lessened—at least somewhat—and we are dealing with an influx of new initiates as the school year gets properly under way.

It should be obvious now why this may be our last recording. We're going to be so busy training and attending school and living our lives, I doubt we'll have time or reason to send out any more audio pleas for help.

We'll put this tape in a secure box and send it along to the chap who's been transcribing our adventures. Carter seems to think the postal service will do, but I think I'll give it to Khufu to carry through the Duat. What could possibly go wrong?

As for us, don't think our lives will be all fun and games. Amos couldn't leave a mob of teens unsupervised, and as we don't have Bast anymore, Amos has sent a few adult magicians to Brooklyn House as teachers (read: chaperones). But we all know who's really in charge—*me*. Oh, yes, and perhaps Carter a little bit.

We're not done with trouble, either. I'm still worried about that murderous ghost Setne, who's on the loose in the world with his devious mind, horrible fashion sense, and the Book of Thoth. I'm also puzzling over my mother's comments about rival magic and other gods. No idea what that means, but it doesn't sound good.

In the meantime, there are still hotspots of evil magic and demon activity all over the world that we have to take care of. We've even got reports of unexplainable magic as close as Long Island. Probably have to check that out.

But for now, I plan on enjoying my life, annoying my brother as much as possible, and making Walt into a proper boyfriend while keeping the other girls away from him—most likely with a flamethrower. My work is never done.

As for you lot out there, listening to this recording—we're never too busy for new initiates. If you have the blood of the pharaohs, what are you waiting for? Don't let your magic go to waste. Brooklyn House is open for business.

GLOSSARY

Commands used by Carter, Sadie, and others

Drowah "Boundary"

Fah "Release"

Ha-di "Destroy"

Hapi, u-ha ey pwah "Hapi, arise and attack"

Ha-tep "Be at peace"

Ha-wi "Strike"

Hi-nehm "Join together"

Isfet "Chaos"

Ma'at "Restore order"

Maw "Water"

Med-wah "Speak"

N'dah "Protect"

Sa-hei "Bring down"

Se-kebeb "Make cold"

Tas "Bind"

Other Egyptian Terms

Ankh a hieroglyphic symbol for life

Ba one of the five parts of the soul: the personality

Barque the pharaoh's boat

Canopic jar vessel used to store a mummy's organs

Criosphinx a creature with a body of a lion and head of
a ram

Duat magical realm that coexists with our world

Hieroglyphics the writing system of Ancient Egypt, which
used symbols or pictures to denote objects, concepts, or
sounds

Ib one of the five parts of the soul: the heart

Isfet the symbol for total Chaos

Ka one of the five parts of the soul: the life force

Khopesh a sword with a hook-shaped blade

Ma'at order of the universe

Netjeri blade a knife made from meteoric iron for the
opening of the mouth in a ceremony

Per Ankh the House of Life

Pharaoh a ruler of Ancient Egypt

Rekhet healer

Ren one of the five parts of the soul: the secret name;
   identity

Sarcophagus a stone coffin, often decorated with sculpture
   and inscriptions

Sau a charm maker

Scarab beetle

Shabti a magical figurine made out of clay

Shen eternal; eternity

Sheut one of the five parts of the soul: the shadow; can also
   mean statue

Sistrum bronze noisemaker

Tjesu heru a snake with two heads—one on its tail—and
   dragon legs

Tyet the symbol of Isis

Was power; staff

EGYPTIAN GODS AND
GODDESSES MENTIONED IN
THE SERPENT'S SHADOW

Anubis the god of funerals and death

Apophis the god of Chaos

Babi the baboon god

Bast the cat goddess

Bes the dwarf god

Disturber a god of judgment who works for Osiris

Geb the earth god

Gengen-Wer the goose god

Hapi the god of the Nile

Heket the frog goddess

Horus the war god, son of Isis and Osiris

Isis the goddess of magic, wife of her brother Osiris and
  mother of Horus

Khepri the scarab god, Ra's aspect in the morning

Khonsu the moon god

Mekhit minor lion goddess, married to Onuris

Neith the hunting goddess

Nekhbet the vulture goddess

Nut the sky goddess

Osiris the god of the Underworld, husband of Isis and father of Horus

Ra the sun god, the god of order. Also known as Amun-Ra.

Sekhmet the lion goddess

Serqet the scorpion goddess

Set the god of evil

Shu the air god, great-grandfather of Anubis

Sobek the crocodile god

Tawaret the hippo goddess

Thoth the god of knowledge

THE
SON OF
SOBEK

A Carter Kane/Percy Jackson Adventure

GETTING EATEN BY A GIANT CROCODILE was bad enough.

The kid with the glowing sword only made my day worse.

Maybe I should introduce myself.

I'm Carter Kane—part-time high school freshman, part-time magician, full-time worrier about all the Egyptian gods and monsters who are constantly trying to kill me.

Okay, that last part is an exaggeration. Not *all* the gods want me dead. Just a lot of them—but that kind of goes with the territory, since I'm a magician in the House of Life. We're like the police for Ancient Egyptian supernatural forces, making sure they don't cause too much havoc in the modern world.

Anyway, on this particular day I was tracking down a rogue monster on Long Island. Our scryers had been sensing magical disturbances in the area for several weeks. Then the local news started reporting that a large creature had been sighted in the ponds and marshes near the Montauk Highway—a creature that was eating the wildlife and scaring the locals. One reporter even called it the Long Island Swamp Monster. When mortals start raising the alarm, you know it's time to check things out.

Normally my sister, Sadie, or some of our other initiates from Brooklyn House would've come with me. But they were all at the First Nome, in Egypt, for a weeklong training session on controlling cheese demons (yes, they're a real thing; believe me, you don't want to know), so I was on my own.

I hitched our flying reed boat to Freak, my pet griffin, and we spent the morning buzzing around the South Shore looking for signs of trouble. If you're wondering why I didn't just ride on Freak's back, imagine two hummingbird-like wings beating faster and more powerfully than helicopter blades. Unless you want to get shredded, it's really better to ride in the boat.

Freak had a pretty good nose for magic. After a couple of hours on patrol, he shrieked, "FREEEAAAK!" and banked hard to the left, circling over a green marshy inlet between two subdivisions.

"Down there?" I asked.

Freak shivered and squawked, whipping his barbed tail nervously.

I couldn't see much below us—just a brown river glittering in the hot summer air, winding through swamp grass and clumps of gnarled trees until it emptied into Moriches Bay. The area looked a bit like the Nile Delta back in Egypt, except here the wetlands were surrounded on both sides by residential neighborhoods with row after row of gray-roofed houses. Just to the

north, a line of cars inched along the Montauk Highway—
vacationers escaping the crowds in the city to enjoy the crowds
in the Hamptons.

If there really was a carnivorous swamp monster below us,
I wondered how long it would be before it developed a taste for
humans. If that happened . . . well, it was surrounded by an all-
you-can-eat buffet.

"Okay," I told Freak. "Set me down by the riverbank."

As soon as I stepped out of the boat, Freak screeched and
zoomed into the sky, the boat trailing behind him.

"Hey!" I yelled after him, but it was too late.

Freak is easily spooked. Flesh-eating monsters tend to scare
him away. So do fireworks, clowns, and the smell of Sadie's weird
British Ribena drink. (Can't blame him on that last one. Sadie
grew up in London and developed some pretty strange tastes.)

I would have to take care of this monster problem, then
whistle for Freak to pick me up once I was done.

I opened my backpack and checked my supplies: some
enchanted rope, my curved ivory wand, a lump of wax for
making a magical *shabti* figurine, my calligraphy set, and a
healing potion my friend Jaz had brewed for me a while back.
(She knew that I got hurt a lot.)

There was just one more thing I needed.

I concentrated and reached into the Duat. Over the last
few months, I'd gotten better at storing emergency provisions in
the shadow realm—extra weapons, clean clothes, Fruit by the
Foot, and chilled six-packs of root beer—but sticking my hand

into a magical dimension still felt weird, like pushing through layers of cold, heavy curtains. I closed my fingers around the hilt of my sword and pulled it out—a heavy *khopesh* with a blade curved like a question mark. Armed with my sword and wand, I was all set for a stroll through the swamp to look for a hungry monster. Oh, joy!

I waded into the water and immediately sank to my knees. The river bottom felt like congealed stew. With every step, my shoes made such rude noises—*suck-plop, suck-plop*—that I was glad my sister Sadie wasn't with me. She never would've stopped laughing.

Even worse, making this much noise, I knew I wouldn't be able to sneak up on any monsters.

Mosquitoes swarmed me. Suddenly I felt nervous and alone.

Could be worse, I told myself. *I could be studying cheese demons.*

But I couldn't quite convince myself. In the nearby subdivision, I heard kids shouting and laughing, probably playing some kind of game. I wondered what that would be like—being a normal kid, hanging out with my friends on a summer afternoon.

The idea was so nice, I got distracted. I didn't notice the ripples in the water until fifty yards ahead of me something broke the surface—a line of leathery, blackish-green bumps. Instantly it submerged again, but I knew what I was dealing with now. I'd seen crocodiles before, and this was a freakishly big one.

I remembered El Paso, the winter before last, when my sister and I had been attacked by the crocodile god Sobek. That *wasn't* a good memory.

Sweat trickled down my neck.

"Sobek," I murmured, "if that's you, messing with me again, I swear to Ra . . ."

The croc god had promised to leave us alone now that we were tight with his boss, the sun god. Still . . . crocodiles get hungry. Then they tend to forget their promises.

No answer from the water. The ripples subsided.

When it came to sensing monsters, my magic instincts weren't very sharp; but the water in front of me seemed much darker. That meant either it was deep, or something large was lurking under the surface.

I almost hoped it *was* Sobek. At least then I stood a chance of talking to him before he killed me. Sobek loved to boast.

Unfortunately, it wasn't him.

The next microsecond, as the water erupted around me, I realized too late that I should've brought the entire Twenty-first Nome to help me. I registered glowing yellow eyes as big as my head, the glint of gold jewelry around a massive neck. Then monstrous jaws opened—ridges of crooked teeth, and an expanse of pink maw wide enough to gulp down a garbage truck.

And the creature swallowed me whole.

Imagine being shrink-wrapped upside down inside a gigantic slimy garbage bag with no air. Being in the monster's belly was like that, only hotter and smellier.

For a moment I was too stunned to do anything. I couldn't believe I was still alive. If the crocodile's mouth had been smaller, he might have snapped me in half. As it was, he had gulped me down in a single Carter-size serving, so I could look forward to being slowly digested.

Lucky, right?

The monster started thrashing around, which made it hard to think. I held my breath, knowing that it might be my last. I still had my sword and wand, but I couldn't use them with my arms pinned to my side. I couldn't reach any of the stuff in my bag.

Which left only one answer: a word of power. If I could think of the right hieroglyphic symbol and speak it aloud, I could summon some industrial strength, wrath-of-the-gods-type magic to bust my way out of this reptile.

In theory: a great solution.

In practice: I'm not so good at words of power even in the best of situations. Suffocating inside a dark, smelly reptile gullet wasn't helping me focus.

You can do this, I told myself.

After all the dangerous adventures I'd had, I couldn't die like this. Sadie would be devastated. Then, once she got over her grief, she'd track down my soul in the Egyptian afterlife and tease me mercilessly for how stupid I'd been.

My lungs burned. I was blacking out. I picked a word of power, summoned all my concentration, and prepared to speak.

Suddenly the monster lurched upward. It roared, which sounded really weird from the inside, and its throat contracted around me like I was being squeezed from a toothpaste tube. I shot out of the creature's mouth and tumbled into the marsh grass.

Somehow I got to my feet. I staggered around, half blind, gasping, and covered with crocodile goo, which smelled like a scummy fish tank.

The surface of the river churned with bubbles. The crocodile was gone, but standing in the marsh about twenty feet away was a teenage guy in jeans and a faded orange T-shirt that said CAMP something. I couldn't read the rest. He looked a little older than me—maybe seventeen—with tousled black hair and sea-green eyes. What really caught my attention was his sword—a straight double-edged blade glowing with faint bronze light.

I'm not sure which of us was more surprised.

For a second, Camper Boy just stared at me. He noted my *khopesh* and wand, and I got the feeling that he actually *saw* these things as they were. Normal mortals have trouble seeing magic. Their brains can't interpret it, so they might look at my sword, for instance, and see a baseball bat or a walking stick.

But this kid . . . he was different. I figured he must be a magician. The only problem was, I'd met most of the magicians in the North American nomes, and I'd never seen this guy before. I'd also never seen a sword like that. Everything about him seemed . . . *un-Egyptian.*

"The crocodile," I said, trying to keep my voice calm and even. "Where did it go?"

Camper Boy frowned. "You're welcome."

"What?"

"I stuck that croc in the rump." He mimicked the action with his sword. "That's why it vomited you up. So, you're welcome. What were you doing in there?"

I'll admit I wasn't in the best mood. I smelled. I hurt. And, yeah, I was a little embarrassed: the mighty Carter Kane, head of Brooklyn House, had been disgorged from a croc's mouth like a giant hairball.

"I was resting," I snapped. "What do you *think* I was doing? Now, who are you, and why are you fighting my monster?"

"*Your* monster?" The guy trudged toward me through the water. He didn't seem to have any trouble with the mud. "Look, man, I don't know who you are, but that crocodile has been terrorizing Long Island for weeks. I take that kind of personal, as this is my home turf. A few days ago, it ate one of our pegasi."

A jolt went up my spine like I'd backed into an electric fence. "Did you say *pegasi?*"

He waved the question aside. "Is it your monster or not?"

"I don't own it!" I growled. "I'm trying to stop it! Now, where—"

"The croc headed that way." He pointed his sword to the south. "I would already be chasing it, but you surprised me."

He sized me up, which was disconcerting since he was half a foot taller. I still couldn't read his T-shirt except for the word CAMP. Around his neck hung a leather strap with some colorful clay beads, like a kid's arts and crafts project. He wasn't carrying a magician's pack or a wand. Maybe he kept them in the Duat? Or maybe he was just a delusional mortal who'd accidentally found a magic sword and thought he was a super-hero. Ancient relics can really mess with your mind.

Finally he shook his head. "I give up. Son of Ares? You've got to be a half-blood, but what happened to your sword? It's all bent."

"It's a *khopesh*." My shock was rapidly turning to anger. "It's supposed to be curved."

But I wasn't thinking about the sword.

Camper Boy had just called me a *half-blood*? Maybe I hadn't heard him right. Maybe he meant something else. But my dad was African American. My mom was white. *Half-blood* wasn't a word I liked.

"Just get out of here," I said, gritting my teeth. "I've got a crocodile to catch."

"Dude, *I* have a crocodile to catch," he insisted. "Last time you tried, it ate you. Remember?"

My fingers tightened around my sword hilt. "I had everything under control. I was about to summon a fist—"

For what happened next, I take full responsibility.

I didn't mean it. Honestly. But I was angry. And as I may have mentioned, I'm not always good at channeling words of power. While I was in the crocodile's belly, I'd been preparing to summon the Fist of Horus, a giant glowing blue hand that can pulverize doors, walls, and pretty much anything else that gets in its way. My plan had been to punch my way out of the monster. Gross, yes; but hopefully effective.

I guess that spell was still in my head, ready to be triggered like a loaded gun. Facing Camper Boy, I was furious, not to mention dazed and confused; so when I meant to say the English word fist, it came out in Ancient Egyptian instead: *khefa.*

Such a simple hieroglyph:

You wouldn't think it could cause so much trouble.

As soon as I spoke the word, the symbol blazed in the air between us. A giant fist the size of a dishwasher shimmered into existence and slammed Camper Boy into the next county.

I mean I *literally* punched him out of his shoes. He rocketed from the river with a loud *suck-plop!* And the last thing I saw was his bare feet achieving escape velocity as he flew backward and disappeared from sight.

No, I didn't feel good about it. Well . . . maybe a tiny bit good. But I also felt mortified. Even if the guy was a jerk, magicians weren't supposed to go around sucker-punching kids into orbit with the Fist of Horus.

"Oh, great." I hit myself on the forehead.

I started to wade across the marsh, worried that I'd actually killed the guy. "Man, I'm sorry!" I yelled, hoping he could hear me. "Are you—?"

The wave came out of nowhere.

A twenty-foot wall of water slammed into me and pushed me back into the river. I came up spluttering, a horrible taste like fish food in my mouth. I blinked the gunk out of my eyes just in the time to see Camper Boy leaping toward me ninja-style, his sword raised.

I lifted my *khopesh* to deflect the blow. I just managed to keep my head from being cleaved in half, but Camper Boy was strong and quick. As I reeled backward, he struck again and again. Each time, I was able to parry; but I could tell I was out-matched. His blade was lighter and quicker, and—yes, I'll admit it—he was a better swordsman.

I wanted to explain that I'd made a mistake. I wasn't really his enemy. But I needed all my concentration just to keep from getting sliced down the middle.

Camper Boy, however, had no trouble talking.

"Now I get it," he said, swinging at my head. "You're some kind of monster."

CLANG! I intercepted the strike and staggered back.

"I'm not a monster," I managed.

To beat this guy, I'd have to use more than just a sword. The problem was, I didn't want to hurt him. Despite the fact that he was trying to chop me into a Kane-flavored barbecue sand-wich, I still felt bad for starting the fight.

He swung again, and I had no choice. I used my wand this time, catching his blade in the crook of ivory and channeling a burst of magic straight up his arm. The air between us flashed and crackled. Camper Boy stumbled back. Blue sparks of sorcery popped around him, as if my spell didn't know quite what to do with him. Who *was* this guy?

"You said the crocodile was *yours*." Camper Boy scowled, anger blazing in his green eyes. "You lost your pet, I suppose.

Maybe you're a spirit from the Underworld, come through the Doors of Death?"

Before I could even process that question, he thrust out his free hand. The river reversed course and swept me off my feet.

I managed to get up, but I was getting really tired of drinking swamp water. Meanwhile Camper Boy charged again, his sword raised for the kill. In desperation, I dropped my wand. I thrust my hand into my backpack, and my fingers closed around the piece of rope.

I threw it and yelled the command word *"TAS!"*—*Bind!*—just as Camper Boy's bronze blade cut into my wrist.

My whole arm erupted in agony. My vision tunneled. Yellow spots danced before my eyes. I dropped my sword and clutched my wrist, gasping for breath, everything forgotten except the excruciating pain.

In the back of my mind, I knew Camper Boy could kill me easily. For some reason he didn't. A wave of nausea made me double over.

I forced myself to look at the wound. There was a lot of blood, but I remembered something Jaz had told me once in the infirmary at Brooklyn House: cuts usually looked a lot worse than they were. I hoped that was true. I fished a piece of papyrus out of my pack and pressed it against the wound as a makeshift bandage.

The pain was still horrible, but the nausea became more manageable. My thoughts started to clear, and I wondered why I hadn't been skewered yet.

Camper Boy was sitting nearby in waist-deep water, looking

dejected. My magic rope had wrapped around his sword arm, then lashed his hand to the side of his head. Unable to let go of his sword, he looked like he had a single reindeer antler sprouting next to his ear. He tugged at the rope with his free hand, but of course he couldn't make any progress.

Finally he just sighed and glared at me. "I'm really starting to hate you."

"Hate *me*?" I protested. "I'm gushing blood here! And you started all this by calling me a half-blood!"

"Oh, please." Camper Boy rose unsteadily, his sword antenna making him top-heavy. "You can't be mortal. If you were, my sword would've passed right through you. If you're not a spirit or a monster, you've got to be a half-blood. A rogue demigod from Kronos's army, I'd guess."

Most of what this guy said, I didn't understand. But one thing sank in.

"So when you said 'half-blood'. . ."

He stared at me like I was an idiot. "I meant demigod. Yeah. What did you *think* I meant?"

I tried to process that. I'd heard the term *demigod* before, but it wasn't an Egyptian concept. Maybe this guy was sensing that I was bound to Horus, that I could channel the god's power . . . but why did he describe everything so strangely?

"What are you?" I demanded. "Part combat magician, part water elementalist? What nome are you with?"

The kid laughed bitterly. "Dude, I don't know what you're talking about. I don't hang out with gnomes. Satyrs, sometimes. Even Cyclopes. But not gnomes."

The blood loss must have been making me dizzy. His words bounced around in my head like lottery balls: *Cyclopes, satyrs, demigods, Kronos.* Earlier he'd mentioned Ares. That was a Greek god, not Egyptian.

I felt like the Duat was opening underneath me, threatening to pull me into the depths. *Greek . . . not Egyptian.*

An idea started forming in my mind. I didn't like it. In fact, it scared the holy Horus out of me.

Despite all the swamp water I'd swallowed, my throat felt dry. "Look," I said, "I'm sorry about hitting you with that fist spell. It was an accident. But the thing I don't understand . . . it should have killed you. It didn't. That doesn't make sense."

"Don't sound so disappointed," he muttered. "But while we're on the subject, you should be dead too. Not many people can fight me that well. And my sword should have vaporized your crocodile."

"For the last time, it's not *my* crocodile."

"Okay, whatever." Camper Boy looked dubious. "The point is, I stuck that crocodile pretty good, but I just made it angry. Celestial bronze should've turned it to dust."

"Celestial bronze?"

Our conversation was cut short by a scream from the nearby subdivision—the terrified voice of a kid.

My heart did a slow roll. I really was an idiot. I'd forgotten why we were here.

I locked eyes with Camper Boy. "We've got to stop the crocodile."

"Truce," he suggested.

"Yeah," I said. "We can continue killing each other after the crocodile is taken care of."

"Deal. Now, could you please untie my sword hand from my head? I feel like a freaking unicorn."

I won't say we trusted each other, but at least now we had a common cause. He summoned his shoes out of the river—I had no idea how—and put them on. Then he helped me bind my hand with a strip of linen and waited while I swigged down half of my healing potion.

After that, I felt good enough to race after him toward the sound of the screaming.

I thought I was in pretty good shape—what with combat magic practice, hauling heavy artifacts, and playing basketball with Khufu and his baboon friends (baboons don't mess around when it comes to hoops). Nevertheless, I had to struggle to keep up with Camper Boy.

Which reminded me, I was getting tired of calling him that.

"What's your name?" I asked, wheezing as I ran behind him.

He gave me a cautious glance. "I'm not sure I should tell you. Names can be dangerous."

He was right, of course. Names held power. A while back, my sister Sadie had learned my *ren*, my secret name, and it still caused me all sorts of anxiety. Even with someone's common name, a skilled magician could work all kinds of mischief.

"Fair enough," I said. "I'll go first. I'm Carter."

I guess he believed me. The lines around his eyes relaxed a bit.

"Percy," he offered.

That struck me as an unusual name—British, maybe, though the kid spoke and acted very much like an American.

We jumped a rotten log and finally made it out of the marsh. We'd started climbing a grassy slope toward the nearest houses when I realized more than one voice was screaming up there now. Not a good sign.

"Just to warn you," I told Percy, "you can't kill the monster."

"Watch me," Percy grumbled.

"No, I mean it's *immortal.*"

"I've heard that before. I've vaporized plenty of *immortals* and sent them back to Tartarus."

Tartarus? I thought.

Talking to Percy was giving me a serious headache. It reminded me of the time my dad took me to Scotland for one of his Egyptology lectures. I'd tried to talk with some of the locals and I knew they were speaking English, but every other sentence seemed to slip into an alternate language—different words, different pronunciations—and I'd wonder what the heck they were saying. Percy was like that. He and I *almost* spoke the same language—magic, monsters, et cetera. But his vocabulary was completely wrong.

"No," I tried again, halfway up the hill. "This monster is a *petsuchos*—a son of Sobek."

"Who's Sobek?" he asked.

"Lord of crocodiles. Egyptian god."

That stopped him in his tracks. He stared at me, and I could swear the air between us turned electric. A voice, very deep in my mind, said: *Shut up. Don't tell him any more.*

Percy glanced at the *khopesh* I'd retrieved from the river, then the wand in my belt. "Where are you from? Honestly."

"Originally?" I asked. "Los Angeles. Now I live in Brooklyn."

That didn't seem to make him feel any better. "So this monster, this *pet-suck-o* or whatever—"

"*Petsuchos*," I said. "It's a Greek word, but the monster is Egyptian. It was like the mascot of Sobek's temple, worshipped as a living god."

Percy grunted. "You sound like Annabeth."

"Who?"

"Nothing. Just skip the history lesson. How do we kill it?"

"I told you—"

From above came another scream, followed by a loud CRUNCH, like the sound made by a metal compactor.

We sprinted to the top of the hill, then hopped the fence of somebody's backyard and ran into a residential cul-de-sac.

Except for the giant crocodile in the middle of the street, the neighborhood could have been Anywhere, USA. Ringing the cul-de-sac were half a dozen single-story homes with well-kept front lawns, economy cars in the driveways, mailboxes at the curb, flags hanging above the front porches.

Unfortunately, the all-American scene was kind of ruined by the monster, who was busily eating a green Prius hatchback with a bumper sticker that read MY POODLE IS SMARTER THAN YOUR HONOR STUDENT. Maybe the *petsuchos* thought the Toyota was another crocodile, and he was asserting his dominance. Maybe he just didn't like poodles and/or honor students.

Whatever the case, on dry land the crocodile looked even scarier than he had in the water. He was about forty feet long, as tall as a delivery truck, with a tail so massive and powerful, it overturned cars every time it swished. His skin glistened blackish green and gushed water that pooled around his feet. I remembered Sobek once telling me that his divine sweat created the rivers of the world. Yuck. I guessed this monster had the same holy perspiration. Double yuck.

The creature's eyes glowed with a sickly yellow light. His jagged teeth gleamed white. But the weirdest thing about him was his bling. Around his neck hung an elaborate collar of gold chains and enough precious stones to buy a private island.

The necklace was how I had realized that the monster was a *petsuchos*, back at the marsh. I'd read that the sacred animal of Sobek wore something just like it back in Egypt, though what the monster was doing in a Long Island subdivision, I had no idea.

As Percy and I took in the scene, the crocodile clamped down and bit the green Prius in half, spraying glass and metal and pieces of air bag across the lawns.

As soon as he dropped the wreckage, half a dozen kids appeared from nowhere—apparently they'd been hiding behind some of the other cars—and charged the monster, screaming at the top of their lungs.

I couldn't believe it. They were just elementary-age kids, armed with nothing but water balloons and Super Soakers. I guessed that they were on summer break and had been cooling off with a water fight when the monster interrupted them.

There were no adults in sight. Maybe they were all at work. Maybe they were inside, passed out from fright.

The kids looked angry rather than scared. They ran around the crocodile, lobbing water balloons that splashed harmlessly against the monster's hide.

Useless and stupid? Yes. But I couldn't help admiring their bravery. They were trying their best to face down a monster that had invaded their neighborhood.

Maybe they saw the crocodile for what it was. Maybe their mortal brains made them think it was an escaped elephant from the zoo, or a crazed FedEx delivery driver with a death wish.

Whatever they saw, they were in danger.

My throat closed up. I thought about my initiates back at Brooklyn House, who were no older than these kids, and my protective "big brother" instincts kicked in. I charged into the street, yelling, "Get away from it! Run!"

Then I threw my wand straight at the crocodile's head. *"Sa-mir!"*

The wand hit the croc on the snout, and blue light rippled across his body. All over the monster's hide, the hieroglyph for *pain* flickered:

Everywhere it appeared, the croc's skin smoked and sparked, causing the monster to writhe and bellow in annoyance.

The kids scattered, hiding behind ruined cars and mailboxes. The *petsuchos* turned his glowing yellow eyes on me.

At my side, Percy whistled under his breath. "Well, you got his attention."

"Yeah."

"You sure we can't kill him?" he asked.

"Yeah."

The crocodile seemed to be following our conversation. His yellow eyes flicked back and forth between us, as if deciding which of us to eat first.

"Even if you *could* destroy his body," I said, "he would just reappear somewhere nearby. That necklace? It's enchanted with the power of Sobek. To beat the monster, we have to get that necklace off. Then the *petsuchos* should shrink back into a regular crocodile."

"I hate the word *should*," Percy muttered. "Fine. I'll get the necklace. You keep him occupied."

"Why do *I* get to keep him occupied?"

"Because you're more annoying," Percy said. "Just try not to get eaten again."

"ROARR!" the monster bellowed, his breath like a seafood restaurant's Dumpster.

I was about to argue that Percy was *plenty* annoying, but I didn't get the chance. The *petsuchos* charged, and my new comrade-in-arms sprinted to one side, leaving me right in the path of destruction.

* * *

First random thought: *Getting eaten twice in one day would be very embarrassing.*

Out of the corner of my eye, I saw Percy dashing toward the monster's right flank. I heard the mortal kids come out from their hiding places, yelling and throwing more water balloons like they were trying to protect me.

The *petsuchos* lumbered toward me, his jaws opening to snap me up.

And I got angry.

I'd faced the worst Egyptian gods. I'd plunged into the Duat and trekked across the Land of Demons. I'd stood at the very shores of Chaos. I was *not* going to back down to an overgrown gator.

The air crackled with power as my combat avatar formed around me—a glowing blue exoskeleton in the shape of Horus.

It lifted me off the ground until I was suspended in the middle of a twenty-foot-tall, hawk-headed warrior. I stepped forward, bracing myself, and the avatar mimicked my stance.

Percy yelled, "Holy Hera! What the—?!"

The crocodile slammed into me.

He nearly toppled me. His jaws closed around my avatar's free arm, but I slashed the hawk warrior's glowing blue sword at the crocodile's neck.

Maybe the *petsuchos* couldn't be killed. I was at least hoping to cut through the necklace that was the source of his power.

Unfortunately, my swing went wide. I hit the monster's shoulder, cleaving his hide. Instead of blood, he spilled sand, which is pretty typical for Egyptian monsters. I would have enjoyed seeing him disintegrate completely, but no such luck. As soon as I yanked my blade free, the wound started closing and the sand slowed to a trickle. The crocodile whipped his head from side to side, pulling me off my feet and shaking me by the arm like a dog with a chew toy.

When he let me go, I sailed straight into the nearest house and smashed through the roof, leaving a hawk-warrior-shaped crater in someone's living room. I really hoped I hadn't just flattened some defenseless mortal in the middle of watching *Dr. Phil*.

My vision cleared, and I saw two things that irritated me. First, the crocodile was charging me again. Second, my new friend Percy was just standing in the middle of the street, staring at me in shock. Apparently my combat avatar had startled him so much, he'd forgotten his part of the plan.

"What the creeping crud is *that*?" he demanded. "You're inside a giant glowing chicken-man!"

"Hawk!" I yelled.

I decided that if I survived this day, I would have to make sure this guy never met Sadie. They'd probably take turns insulting me for the rest of eternity. "A little help here?"

Percy unfroze and ran toward the croc. As the monster closed in on me, I kicked him in the snout, which made him sneeze and shake his head long enough for me to extricate myself from the ruined house.

Percy jumped on the creature's tail and ran up his spine. The monster thrashed around, his hide shedding water all over the place; but somehow Percy managed to keep his footing. The guy must have practiced gymnastics or something.

Meanwhile, the mortal kids had found some better ammunition—rocks, scrap metal from the wrecked cars, even a few tire irons—and were hurling the stuff at the monster. I didn't want the crocodile turning his attention toward them.

"HEY!" I swung my *khopesh* at the croc's face—a good solid strike that should've taken off his lower jaw. Instead, he somehow snapped at the blade and caught it in his mouth. We ended up wrestling for the blue glowing sword as it sizzled in his mouth, making his teeth crumble to sand. That couldn't have felt good, but the croc held on, tugging against me.

"Percy!" I shouted. "Any time now!"

Percy lunged for the necklace. He grabbed hold and started hacking at the gold links, but his bronze sword didn't make a dent.

Meanwhile, the croc was going crazy trying to yank away my sword. My combat avatar started to flicker.

Summoning an avatar is a short-term thing, like sprinting at top speed. You can't do it for very long, or you'll collapse. Already I was sweating and breathing hard. My heart raced. My reservoirs of magic were being severely depleted.

"Hurry," I told Percy.

"Can't cut it!" he said.

"A clasp," I said. "There's gotta be one."

As soon as I said that, I spotted it—at the monster's throat, a golden cartouche encircling the hieroglyphs that spelled SOBEK. "There—on the bottom!"

Percy scrambled down the necklace, climbing it like a net, but at that moment my avatar collapsed. I dropped to the ground, exhausted and dizzy. The only thing that saved my life was that the crocodile had been pulling at my avatar's sword. When the sword disappeared, the monster lurched backward and stumbled over a Honda.

The mortal kids scattered. One dove under a car, only to have the car disappear—smacked into the air by the croc's tail.

Percy reached the bottom of the necklace and hung on for dear life. His sword was gone. Probably he'd dropped it.

Meanwhile, the monster regained his footing. The good news: he didn't seem to notice Percy. The bad news: he *definitely* noticed me, and he looked mightily torqued off.

I didn't have the energy to run, much less summon magic to fight. At this point, the mortal kids with their water balloons and rocks had more of a chance of stopping the croc than I did.

In the distance, sirens wailed. Somebody had called the police, which didn't exactly cheer me up. It just meant more mortals were racing here as fast as they could to volunteer as crocodile snacks.

I backed up to the curb and tried—ridiculously—to stare down the monster. "Stay, boy."

The crocodile snorted. His hide shed water like the grossest fountain in the world, making my shoes slosh as I walked. His lamp-yellow eyes filmed over, maybe from happiness. He knew I was done for.

I thrust my hand into my backpack. The only thing I found was a clump of wax. I didn't have time to build a proper *shabti*, but I had no better idea. I dropped my pack and started working the wax furiously with both hands, trying to soften it.

"Percy?" I called.

"I can't unlock the clasp!" he yelled. I didn't dare take my eyes off the croc's, but in my peripheral vision I could see Percy pounding his fist against the base of the necklace. "Some kind of magic?"

That was the smartest thing he'd said all afternoon (not that he'd said a lot of smart things to choose from). The clasp was a hieroglyphic cartouche. It would take a magician to figure it out and open it. Whatever and whoever Percy was, he was no magician.

I was still shaping the clump of wax, trying to make it into a figurine, when the crocodile decided to stop savoring the moment and just eat me. As he lunged, I threw my *shabti*, only half formed, and barked a command word.

Instantly the world's most deformed hippopotamus sprang to life in midair. It sailed headfirst into the crocodile's left nostril and lodged there, kicking its stubby back legs.

Not exactly my finest tactical move; but having a hippo shoved up his nose must have been sufficiently distracting. The crocodile hissed and stumbled, shaking his head, as Percy dropped off and rolled away, barely avoiding the crocodile's stomping feet. He ran to join me at the curb.

I stared in horror as my wax creature, now a living (though very misshapen) hippo, either tried to wriggle free of the croc's nostril or work its way farther into the reptile's sinus cavity—I wasn't sure which.

The crocodile whipped around, and Percy grabbed me just in time, pulling me out of its trampling path.

We jogged to the opposite end of the cul-de-sac, where the mortal kids had gathered. Amazingly, none of them seemed to be hurt. The crocodile kept thrashing and wiping out homes as it tried to clear its nostril.

"You okay?" Percy asked me.

I gasped for air but nodded weakly.

One of the kids offered me his Super Soaker. I waved him off.

"You guys," Percy told the kids, "you hear those sirens? You've got to run down the road and stop the police. Tell them it's too dangerous up here. Stall them!"

For some reason, the kids listened. Maybe they were just happy to have something to do, but the way Percy spoke, I got the feeling he was used to rallying outnumbered troops. He sounded a bit like Horus—a natural commander.

After the kids raced off, I managed to say, "Good call."

Percy nodded grimly. The crocodile was still distracted by its nasal intruder, but I doubted the *shabti* would last much longer. Under that much stress, the hippo would soon melt back to wax.

"You've got some moves, Carter," Percy admitted. "Anything else in your bag of tricks?"

"Nothing," I said dismally. "I'm running on empty. But if I can get to that clasp, I think I can open it."

Percy sized up the *petsuchos*. The cul-de-sac was filling with water that poured from the monster's hide. The sirens were getting louder. We didn't have much time.

"Guess it's my turn to distract the croc," he said. "Get ready to run for that necklace."

"You don't even have your sword," I protested. "You'll die!"

Percy managed a crooked smile. "Just run in there as soon as it starts."

"As soon as *what* starts?"

Then the crocodile sneezed, launching the wax hippo across Long Island. The *petsuchos* turned toward us, roaring in anger, and Percy charged straight at him.

As it turned out, I didn't need to ask what kind of distraction Percy had in mind. Once it started, it was pretty obvious.

He stopped in front of the crocodile and raised his arms. I figured he was planning some kind of magic, but he spoke no command words. He had no staff or wand. He just stood there and looked up at the crocodile as if to say: *Here I am! I'm tasty!*

The crocodile seemed momentarily surprised. If nothing else, we would die knowing that we'd confused this monster many, many times.

Croc sweat kept pouring off his body. The brackish stuff was up to the curb now, up to our ankles. It sloughed into the storm drains but just kept spilling from the croc's skin.

Then I saw what was happening. As Percy raised his arms, the water began swirling counterclockwise. It started around the croc's feet and quickly built speed until the whirlpool encompassed the entire cul-de-sac, spinning strongly enough so that I could feel it pulling me sideways.

By the time I realized I'd better start running, the current was already too fast. I'd have to reach the necklace some other way.

One last trick, I thought.

I feared the effort might literally burn me up, but I summoned my final bit of magical energy and transformed into a falcon—the sacred animal of Horus.

Instantly, my vision was a hundred times sharper. I soared upward, above the rooftops, and the entire world switched to high-definition 3-D. I saw the police cars only a few blocks away, the kids standing in the middle of the street, waving them down. I could make out every slimy bump and pore on the crocodile's hide. I could see each hieroglyph on the clasp of the necklace. And I could see just how impressive Percy's magic trick was.

The entire cul-de-sac was engulfed in a hurricane. Percy stood at the edge, unmoved, but the water was churning so fast now that even the giant crocodile lost his footing. Wrecked cars scraped along the pavement. Mailboxes were pulled out of lawns and swept away. The water increased in volume as well as speed, rising up and turning the entire neighborhood into a liquid centrifuge.

It was my turn to be stunned. A few moments ago, I'd decided Percy was no magician. Yet I'd never seen a magician who could control so much water.

The crocodile stumbled and struggled, shuffling in a circle with the current.

"Any time now," Percy muttered through gritted teeth. Without my falcon hearing, I never would've heard him through the storm, but I realized he was talking to me.

I remembered I had a job to do. No one, magician or otherwise, could control that kind of power for long.

I folded my wings and dove for the crocodile. When I reached the necklace's clasp, I turned back to human and grabbed hold. All around me, the hurricane roared. I could barely see through the swirl of mist. The current was so strong now, it tugged at my legs, threatening to pull me into the flood.

I was *so* tired. I hadn't felt this pushed beyond my limits since I'd fought the Chaos lord, Apophis himself.

I ran my hand over the hieroglyphs on the clasp. There had to be a secret to unlocking it.

The crocodile bellowed and stomped, fighting to stay on its feet. Somewhere to my left, Percy yelled in rage and frustration, trying to keep up the storm; but the whirlpool was starting to slow.

I had a few seconds at best until the crocodile broke free and attacked. Then Percy and I would both be dead.

I felt the four symbols that made up the god's name:

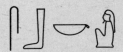

The last symbol didn't actually represent a sound, I knew. It was the hieroglyph for *god*, indicating that the letters in front of it—*SBK*—stood for a deity's name.

When in doubt, I thought, hit the god button.

I pushed on the fourth symbol, but nothing happened.

The storm was failing. The crocodile started to turn against the current, facing Percy. Out of the corner of my eye, through the haze and mist, I saw Percy drop to one knee.

My fingers passed over the third hieroglyph—the wicker basket (Sadie always called it the "teacup") that stood for the K sound. The hieroglyph felt slightly warm to the touch—or was that my imagination?

No time to think. I pressed it. Nothing happened.

The storm died. The crocodile bellowed in triumph, ready to feed.

I made a fist and slammed the basket hieroglyph with all my strength. This time the clasp made a satisfying *click* and sprang open. I dropped to the pavement, and several hundred pounds of gold and gems spilled on top of me.

The crocodile staggered, roaring like the guns of a battleship. What was left of the hurricane scattered in an explosion of wind, and I shut my eyes, ready to be smashed flat by the body of a falling monster.

Suddenly, the cul-de-sac was silent. No sirens. No crocodile roaring. The mound of gold jewelry disappeared. I was lying on my back in mucky water, staring up at the empty blue sky.

Percy's face appeared above me. He looked like he'd just run a marathon through a typhoon, but he was grinning.

"Nice work," he said. "Get the necklace."

"The necklace?" My brain still felt sluggish. Where had all that gold gone? I sat up and put my hand on the pavement. My fingers closed around the strand of jewelry, now normal-size . . . well, at least *normal* for something that could fit around the neck of an average crocodile.

"The—the monster," I stammered. "Where—?"

Percy pointed. A few feet away, looking very disgruntled, stood a baby crocodile not more than three feet long.

"You can't be serious," I said.

"Maybe somebody's abandoned pet?" Percy shrugged. "You hear about those on the news sometimes."

I couldn't think of a better explanation, but how had a baby croc gotten hold of a necklace that turned him into a giant killing machine?

Down the street, voices started yelling: "Up here! There's these two guys!"

It was the mortal kids. Apparently they'd decided the danger was over. Now they were leading the police straight toward us.

"We have to go." Percy scooped up the baby crocodile, clenching one hand around his little snout. He looked at me. "You coming?"

Together, we ran back to the swamp.

Half an hour later, we were sitting in a diner off the Montauk Highway. I'd shared the rest of my healing potion with Percy, who for some reason insisted on calling it *nectar*. Most of our wounds had healed.

We'd tied the crocodile out in the woods on a makeshift leash, just until we could figure out what to do with it. We'd cleaned up as best we could, but we still looked like we'd taken a shower in a malfunctioning car wash. Percy's hair was swept to one side and tangled with pieces of grass. His orange shirt was ripped down the front.

I'm sure I didn't look much better. I had water in my shoes, and I was still picking falcon feathers out of my shirtsleeves (hasty transformations can be messy).

We were too exhausted to talk as we watched the news on the television above the counter. Police and firefighters had responded to a freak sewer event in a local neighborhood. Apparently pressure had built up in the drainage pipes, causing a massive explosion that unleashed a flood and eroded the soil so badly, several houses on the cul-de-sac had collapsed. It was a miracle that no residents had been injured. Local kids were telling some wild stories about the Long Island Swamp Monster, claiming it had caused all the damage during a fight with two teenage boys; but of course the officials didn't believe this. The reporter admitted, however, that the damaged houses looked like "something very large had sat on them."

"A freak sewer accident," Percy said. "That's a first."

"For you, maybe," I grumbled. "I seem to cause them everywhere I go."

"Cheer up," he said. "Lunch is on me."

He dug into the pockets of his jeans and pulled out a ballpoint pen. Nothing else.

"Oh . . ." His smile faded. "Uh, actually . . . can you conjure up money?"

So, naturally, lunch was on *me*. I *could* pull money out of thin air, since I kept some stored in the Duat along with my other emergency supplies; so in no time we had cheeseburgers and fries in front of us, and life was looking up.

"Cheeseburgers," Percy said. "Food of the gods."

"Agreed," I said, but when I glanced over at him, I wondered if he was thinking the same thing I was: that we were referring to *different* gods.

Percy inhaled his burger. Seriously, this guy could eat. "So, the necklace," he said between bites. "What's the story?"

I hesitated. I still had no clue where Percy came from or what he was, and I wasn't sure I wanted to ask. Now that we'd fought together, I couldn't help but trust him. Still, I sensed we were treading on dangerous ground. Everything we said could have serious implications—not just for the two of us, but maybe for everyone we knew.

I felt sort of like I had two winters ago, when my uncle Amos explained the truth about the Kane family heritage—the House of Life, the Egyptian gods, the Duat, everything. In a single day, my world expanded tenfold and left me reeling.

Now I was standing at the edge of another moment like that. But if my world expanded tenfold *again*, I was afraid my brain might explode.

"The necklace is enchanted," I said at last. "Any reptile that wears it turns into the next *petsuchos*, the Son of Sobek. Somehow that little crocodile got it around his neck."

"Meaning someone *put* it around his neck," Percy said.

I didn't want to think about that, but I nodded reluctantly.

"So who?" he asked.

"Hard to narrow it down," I said. "I've got a lot of enemies."

Percy snorted. "I can relate to that. Any idea *why*, then?"

I took another bite of my cheeseburger. It was good, but I had trouble concentrating on it.

"Someone wanted to cause trouble," I speculated. "I think maybe . . ." I studied Percy, trying to judge how much I should say. "Maybe they wanted to cause trouble that would get our attention. *Both* of our attention."

Percy frowned. He drew something in his ketchup with a french fry—not a hieroglyph. Some kind of non-English letter. Greek, I guessed.

"The monster had a Greek name," he said. "It was eating pegasi in my . . ." He hesitated.

"In your home turf," I finished. "Some kind of camp, judging from your shirt."

He shifted on his bar stool. I still couldn't believe he was talking about pegasi as if they were real, but I remembered one time at Brooklyn House, maybe a year back, when I was certain I saw a winged horse flying over the Manhattan skyline. At the time, Sadie had told me I was hallucinating. Now, I wasn't so sure.

Finally Percy faced me. "Look, Carter. You're not nearly as annoying as I thought. And we made a good team today, but—"

"You don't want to share your secrets," I said. "Don't worry. I'm not going to ask about your camp. Or the powers you have. Or any of that."

He raised an eyebrow. "You're not curious?"

"I'm *totally* curious. But until we figure out what's going on, I think it's best we keep some distance. If someone—some*thing*—unleashed that monster here, knowing it would draw both of our attention—"

"Then maybe that someone wanted us to meet," he finished. "Hoping bad things would happen."

I nodded. I thought about the uneasy feeling I'd had in my gut earlier—the voice in my head warning me not to tell Percy anything. I'd come to respect the guy, but I still sensed that we weren't meant to be friends. We weren't meant to be anywhere *close* to each other.

A long time ago, when I was just a little kid, I'd watched my mom do a science experiment with some her college students.

Potassium and water, she'd told them. *Separate, completely harmless. But together—*

She dropped the potassium in a beaker of water, and *Ka-blam!* The students jumped back as a miniature explosion rattled all the vials in the lab.

Percy was water. I was potassium.

"But we've met now," Percy said. "You know I'm out here on Long Island. I know you live in Brooklyn. If we went searching for each other—"

"I wouldn't recommend it," I said. "Not until we know more. I need to look into some things on, uh, my side—try to figure out who was behind this crocodile incident."

"All right," Percy agreed. "I'll do the same on my side."

He pointed at the *petsuchos* necklace, which was glinting just inside my backpack. "What do we do about that?"

"I can send it somewhere safe," I promised. "It won't cause trouble again. We deal with relics like this a lot."

"*We,*" Percy said. "Meaning, there's a lot of . . . you guys?"

I didn't answer.

Percy put up his hands. "Fine. I didn't ask. I have some friends back at Ca— uh, back on my side who would love tinkering with a magic necklace like that; but I'm going to trust you here. Take it."

I didn't realize I'd been holding my breath until I exhaled. "Thanks. Good."

"And the baby crocodile?" he asked.

I managed a nervous laugh. "You want it?"

"Gods, no."

"I can take it, give it a good home." I thought about our big pool at Brooklyn House. I wondered how our giant magic crocodile, Philip of Macedonia, would feel about having a little friend. "Yeah, it'll fit right in."

Percy didn't seem to know what to think of that. "Okay, well . . ." He held out his hand. "Good working with you, Carter."

We shook. No sparks flew. No thunder boomed. But I still couldn't escape the feeling that we'd opened a door, meeting like this—a door that we might not be able to close.

"You too, Percy."

He stood to go. "One more thing," he said. "If this somebody, whoever threw us together . . . if he's an enemy to both of us— what if we *need* each other to fight him? How do I contact you?"

I considered that. Then I made a snap decision. "Can I write something on your hand?"

He frowned. "Like your phone number?"

"Uh . . . well, not exactly." I took out my stylus and a vial of magic ink. Percy held out his palm. I drew a hieroglyph there—the Eye of Horus. As soon as the symbol was complete it flared blue, then vanished.

"Just say my name," I told him, "and I'll hear you. I'll know where you are, and I'll come meet you. But it will only work once, so make it count."

Percy considered his empty palm. "So I'm trusting you that this isn't some type of magical tracking device."

"Yeah," I said. "And I'm trusting that when you call me, you won't be luring me into some sort of ambush."

He stared at me. Those stormy green eyes really were kind of scary. Then he smiled, and he looked like a regular teenager, without a care in the world.

"Fair enough," he said. "See you when I see you, C—"

"Don't say my name!"

"Just teasing." He pointed at me and winked. "Stay strange, my friend."

Then he was gone.

An hour later, I was back aboard my airborne boat with the baby crocodile and the magic necklace as Freak flew me home to Brooklyn House.

Now, looking back on it, the whole thing with Percy seems so unreal, I can hardly believe it actually happened.

I wonder how Percy summoned that whirlpool, and what the heck *Celestial bronze* is. Most of all, I keep rolling one word around in my mind: *demigod*.

I have a feeling that I could find some answers if I looked hard enough, but I'm afraid of what I might discover.

For the time being, I think I'll tell Sadie about this and no one else. At first she'll think I'm kidding. And, of course, she'll give me grief; but she also knows when I'm telling the truth. As annoying as she is, I trust her (though I would never say that to her face).

Maybe she'll have some ideas about what we should do.

Whoever brought Percy and me together, whoever orchestrated our crossing paths . . . it smacks of Chaos. I can't help thinking this was an experiment to see what kind of havoc would result. Potassium and water. Matter and antimatter.

Fortunately, things turned out okay. The *petsuchos* necklace is safely locked away. Our new baby crocodile is splashing around happily in our pool.

But next time . . . Well, I'm afraid we might not be so lucky.

Somewhere there's a kid named Percy with a secret hieroglyph on his hand. And I have a feeling that sooner or later I'll wake up in the middle of the night and hear one word, spoken urgently in my mind:

Carter.

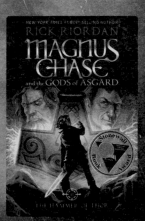